F. Scott Fitzgerald was born in 1896 and died in 1940.
He was the author of *This Side of Paradise* (1920),
The Beautiful and the Damned (1922), *The Great Gatsby* (1925),
Tender is the Night (1934) and the unfinished *The Last Tycoon* (1941),
as well as several volumes of short stories.

the last uncollected stories of

F. SCOTT FITZGERALD

THE PRICE WAS HIGH

volume 1

edited by Matthew J. Bruccoli

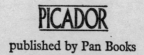

PICADOR

published by Pan Books

This collection first published in Great Britain 1979 by Quartet Books Limited
by arrangement with Harcourt Brace Jovanovich/Bruccoli Clark, New York
This two-volume Picador edition published 1981 by
Pan Books Ltd, Cavaye Place, London SW10
© Frances Scott Fitzgerald Smith 1979
Introduction and notes © Harcourt Brace Jovanovich Inc. 1979
ISBN 0 330 26286 6

Printed and bound in Great Britain by
Cox & Wyman Ltd, Reading

EDITORIAL NOTE   These stories are reprinted from their magazine appearances.
Spelling errors have been silently corrected, but acceptable variants
have been retained. Punctuation has been conservatively amended,
also silently. Since the several magazines had different house-styles, a
certain amount of regularization was necessary – for example, in the
treatment of song titles and newspapers. Some of the magazines –
notably *Woman's Home Companion* – introduced space breaks into
the stories for make-up reasons. These breaks have been removed
where they are non-structural. Deletions – identified with word
counts – have been made in two stories.

I have asked a lot of my emotions – one hundred and twenty stories. The price was high, right up with Kipling, because there was one little drop of something not blood, not a tear, not my seed, but me more intimately than these, in every story, it was the extra I had. Now it has gone and I am just like you now.

'Our April Letter,' *The Notebooks of F. Scott Fitzgerald*

COPYRIGHT
ACKNOWLEDGEMENTS

Contents

Introduction 9

The Smilers 18

Myra Meets His Family 26

Two For a Cent 49

Dice, Brassknuckles & Guitar 63

Diamond Dick and the First Law of Woman 86

The Third Casket 104

The Pusher-in-the-Face 116

One of My Oldest Friends 130

The Unspeakable Egg 144

John Jackson's Arcady 161

Not in the Guidebook 181

Presumption 197

The Adolescent Marriage 224

Your Way and Mine 241

The Love Boat 259

The Bowl 279

At Your Age 302

Indecision 316

Flight and Pursuit 332

On Your Own 348

Between Three and Four 365

A Change of Class 378

Six of One— 395

A Freeze-Out 409

$106, 585

Fitzgerald was a better just plain writer than all of us put together. Just words writing.
John O'Hara

The stories in *The Price Was High* were written for money. They brought F. Scott Fitzgerald $106,585 from the mass-circulation magazines – less agent's commissions. His stories provided most of his income before he went to Hollywood in 1937, and he expended a major part of his talent on them. In 1925 he received $11,025 for five stories, whereas *The Great Gatsby* earned $1981.85 beyond the $4264 advance. In 1934, the year *Tender Is the Night* was published, his total income from eight books was $58.35; but eight stories – even at reduced Depression prices – brought $12,475.

Fitzgerald lived off his stories. His intention was to write stories only to finance his novels. Like so many of his practical plans, it did not work out. Instead of getting financially ahead from his stories, Fitzgerald was often in debt to his literary agent, Harold Ober, for an unwritten story as he borrowed against future magazine sales.

One hundred and sixty-four of Fitzgerald's stories were published in magazines.* He collected forty-six in his four story volumes: *Flappers and Philosophers* (1920), *Tales of the Jazz Age* (1922), *All the Sad Young Men* (1926), and *Taps at Reveille* (1935). Each of these collections followed publication of a novel. Since story volumes are notoriously poor sellers, the 14,000–16,000 sales for the first three collections were more than respectable. After his death in 1940, sixty-one previously uncollected stories were included in six volumes: *The Stories of F. Scott Fitzgerald* (1951), *Afternoon of an Author* (1957), *The Pat Hobby Stories* (1962), *The Appren-*

---

*This figure includes Fitzgerald's school publications and the plays and parodies he published in his story collections. It excludes the stories by-lined 'F. Scott and Zelda Fitzgerald', which were mostly her work. See Bruccoli, *F. Scott Fitzgerald: A Descriptive Bibliography* (Pittsburgh: University of Pittsburgh Press, 1972).

tice Fiction of F. Scott Fitzgerald (1965), *The Basil and Josephine Stories* (1973), and *Bits of Paradise* (1974). Of the remaining fifty-seven published stories, forty-nine are in *The Price Was High*. Eight stories remain uncollected because Scottie Fitzgerald Smith feels that they are so far below her father's standards that they should be left in oblivion.* At least ten of Fitzgerald's unpublished stories survive. The best of these, 'On Your Own', is included in this volume.

It would be desirable to have 'The Complete Stories of F. Scott Fitzgerald' available in a uniform edition, but the present arrangement will serve. By supplementing the volumes published by Charles Scribner's Sons with *The Price Was High*, readers have access to the Fitzgerald story canon without recourse to microfilms of old magazines.

The stories in this volume are not Fitzgerald's best. They are worth collecting because he wrote them. Dorothy Parker commented that although he could write a bad story, he could not write badly. Even his weak stories are redeemed by glimpses of what can be conveniently called 'the Fitzgerald touch'– wit, sharp observations, dazzling descriptions, or the felt emotion. Even the most predictably plotted of the twenties stories have a spontaneity (which is not the same as facility) that differentiates them from other writers' work. Above all, Fitzgerald's style shines through: the colours and rhythms of his prose.

After a quarter of a century of intensive Fitzgerald criticism, the significance of the stories in his career is still not generally understood. Many critics have accepted his frequent disparagement of his stories, as when he wrote Hemingway in 1929 that 'the *Post* now pays the old whore $4000 a screw. But now it's because she's mastered the 40 positions – in her youth one was enough.' This self-abnegating remark makes the point that after a decade he had become an expert story technician. Fitzgerald bitterly resented the work that went into stories because it was work taken away from novels. Most of the stories were admittedly pot-boilers; but they required a good deal of sweat and – until 1935 – were the best work Fitzgerald was capable of for that market. They showed him as a professional writer earning his living in a highly competitive market by meeting a certain standard

---

*'Shaggy's Morning', *Esquire*, III (May 1935); 'The Count of Darkness', *Redbook*, LXV (June 1935); 'The Passionate Eskimo', *Liberty*, XII (8 June 1935); 'The Kingdom in the Dark', *Redbook*, LXV (August 1935); ' "Send Me In, Coach",' *Esquire*, VI (November 1936); 'The Honour of the Goon', *Esquire*, VII (June 1937); 'Strange Sanctuary', *Liberty*, XVI (9 December 1939); 'Gods of Darkness', *Redbook*, LXXVIII (November 1941).

of quality and satisfying commercial requirements. They were not just hack-work. In 1935 when he was finding it increasingly difficult to write commercial fiction he explained to Harold Ober: 'all my stories are conceived like novels, require a special emotion, a special experience – so that my readers, if such there be, know that each time it'll be something new, not in form but in substance. (It'd be better for me if I could do pattern stories but the pencil just goes dead on me.)'* Fitzgerald's magazine stories required structural discipline, as well as emotion and style. He commented in his *Notebooks*: 'In a short story you have only so much money to buy just one costume. Not the parts of many. One mistake in the shoes or tie, and you're gone'. Moreover, he customarily polished his stories through layers of revision. The price was high because Fitzgerald delivered what nobody else could provide. When he tried to be a hack in 1936–7, he couldn't grind out formula stories.

Fitzgerald's principal showcase was the *Saturday Evening Post*, the top story market in America. Because of its circulation and pay scale, most of the top American writers – including Faulkner and Wolfe – were glad to sell stories to the *Post*. Sixty-six Fitzgerald stories appeared in the *Post* from 1920 to 1937. Between 1929 and 1931 he received his peak *Post* price – $4000 per story, the equivalent in purchasing power of perhaps $10,000 today.

Readers for whom the old *Saturday Evening Post* is not even a memory may be surprised by the contents of the 8 October 1927 issue (2,750,000 circulation), which had 226 pages and sold for 5¢: the first part of a serial by Sir Arthur Conan Doyle, an historical article by Joseph Hergesheimer, Fitzgerald's 'The Love Boat', an article on the *Uncle Tom* plays, a story by Ben Ames Williams, a travel article by Cornelius Vanderbilt Jr, a story by Nunnally Johnson, a story by Horatio Winslow, an article on foreign policy by Henry L. Stimson, an animal story by Hal G. Evarts, a story by Thomas Beer, an article about Caruso by his daughter, a story by Octavus Roy Cohen, an article about German recovery by Isaac Marcosson, the continuation of a serial by Donn Byrne, the continuation of a serial by Frances Noyes Hart, an article on international affairs by Alonzo E. Taylor, a story by F. Britton Austin, and an article on crime by Kenneth Roberts – in addition to regular departments. Most of these names mean little now, but in their day Hergesheimer, Williams, Johnson, Beer, Cohen, and Roberts were highly successful writers. The amount of fiction is noteworthy – eight

---

As Ever, Scott Fitz –, ed. Bruccoli and Jennifer Atkinson (Philadelphia and New York: Lippincott), p. 221.

stories and three serials as against eight articles. Magazine readers had a large appetite for fiction in those days, and the mass-circulation magazines competed for story writers.

Although the *Post* was the most successful of the magazines offering a mixture of fiction and articles, others served the same readership – *Collier's*, *Liberty*, *Metropolitan*, *International*, *Scribner's*, *Red Book*, *Smart Set*, and *Woman's Home Companion*. Fitzgerald appeared in all of these. Newspapers also published a good deal of fiction – usually reprinted from magazines or books. Several of Fitzgerald's stories and two of his novels were syndicated to newspapers. Syndication brought him very little money, but it extended his exposure. In the twenties Fitzgerald may have been the most widely known living American writer of quality stories. Unfortunately, his reputation as a magazinist did not correlate with the sales of his books. There was some overlap, but in general his magazine and book audiences were discrete. Most of Fitzgerald's readers probably knew him only as a writer of magazine stories.

The magazine readers of the time expected illustrated stories. The artwork for Fitzgerald's stories contributed to their flavour and to his image as a writer – or to the image that the magazines were trying to promote.

Although Fitzgerald became typed as a writer of 'young-love stories', they were not regarded as callow or conventional in their own time. It may surprise readers born after 1940, when he died, that in the twenties he was regarded as a radical writer who announced the existence of new social values and new sexual roles. Fitzgerald's girls are not dumb dolls. At their best they are courageous and self-reliant, determined to make the best of their assets in a man's world. They are frankly sensual, though chaste – warm and promising. At an extreme there are Fitzgerald's man-eating women who dominate or destroy men, though this condition is unusual in his short stories.

It remains an open question whether Fitzgerald compromised or diluted his stories to make them acceptable to the *Post* and other popular magazines. 'May Day' and 'The Rich Boy' were declined by the *Post* because they were too 'realistic'; but the *Post* later published 'Babylon Revisited' and 'One Trip Abroad', two of his least conventional stories. While Fitzgerald had to observe *Post* strictures against profanity and adultery in stories, there is no evidence that he felt constrained by these prohibitions; he was fastidious about his material and puritanical by today's literary standards. Nonetheless, it would be foolish to claim that his awareness of the *Post's* expectations did not exert an influence on his material or that he did not to some extent tailor his stories to his best market. He was writing stories that were supposed to free him from the necessity of writing more stories; therefore he wanted the top price for his servitude. He wrote stories that he expected the *Post* or its competitors to buy; but they were stories into which he had put his own deep feelings about love, youth, ambition, and success. Fitzgerald's *Post* stories represented a marriage between the writer and the magazine. For more than a decade they needed and suited each other.

Fitzgerald's stories often served as testing-places for material and themes that were subsequently developed in his novels. There are clusters of stories connected with *The Great Gatsby* and *Tender Is the Night*. Reading these uncollected stories one frequently recognizes passages or phrases that were later incorporated into his novels. Indeed, he refused to collect some of the stories because he had a firm rule against repeating anything between book covers. A story, even a published one, that had been scrapped for a novel was classified as 'stripped and permanently buried'. Fitzgerald's *Notebooks* and story tearsheets show how carefully he conducted his salvage and banking operation.*

Fitzgerald's attitude towards publication of his uncollected stories is shown in his 1935 Preface (which he later designated as a memo for his Scribners editor, Maxwell Perkins) for a projected posthumous volume:

This collection will be published only in case of my sudden death. It contains many stories that have been chosen for anthologies but, though it is the winnowing from almost fifty stories, none I have seen fit to reprint in book form. This is in some measure because the best of these stories have been stripped of their high spots which were woven into novels – but it is also because each story contains some special fault – sentimentality, faulty construction, confusing change of pace – or else was too obviously made for the trade.

But readers of my other books will find whole passages here and there which I have used elsewhere – so I should prefer that this collection should be allowed to run what course it may have, and die with its season.

If the medieval stories are six or more they should be in a small book of their own. If less than six they should be in one section in this book. Note date above – there may be other good ones after this date.

*The story strippings are identified in *The Notebooks of F. Scott Fitzgerald*, ed. Bruccoli (New York: Harcourt Brace Jovanovich/Bruccoli Clark, 1978).

Choose from these *not more than 16*	*These are scrapped*
	1919 Myra Meets His Family The Smilers
1921 Two for a Cent	1921 The Popular Girl
	1923 Dice Brass Knuckles and Guitar
1924 One of My Oldest Friends The Pusher in the Face	1924 John Jackson's Arcady The Unspeakable Egg The Third Casket Love in the Night
1925 Presumption Adolescent Marriage	1925 Not in the Guide Book A Penny Spent
1926 The Dance	1926 Your Way and Mine
1927 Jacob's Ladder The Bowl Outside the Cabinet Makers	1927 The Love Boat Magnetism
	1928 A Night at the Fair
1929 The Rough Crossing At Your Age	1929 Forging Ahead Basil and Cleopatra The Swimmers
1930 One Trip Abroad The Hotel Child	1930 The Bridal Party A Snobbish Story
1931 A New Leaf Emotional Bankruptcy Between Three and Four A Change of Class A Freeze Out	1931 Indecision Flight and Pursuit Half a Dozen of the Others Diagnosis
	1932 What a Handsome Pair The Rubber Check On Schedule
1933 More than Just a House I Got Shoes The Family Bus	
1934 No Flowers Her Last Case	1934 New Types
1935 The Intimate Strangers And, to date, four medieval stories	1935 Shaggy's Morning

The stories in *The Price Was High* fall into two groups – dividing at 1935, when Fitzgerald largely lost his ability to produce *Post*-type stories reliably. His commercial stories became forced and padded as he struggled to simulate emotions that he no longer felt. He had anticipated this change in a 1933 essay, 'One Hundred False Starts' – which, by one of the precise ironies that abound in Fitzgerald, appeared in the *Saturday Evening Post*:

Mostly, we authors must repeat ourselves – that's the truth. We have two or three great and moving experiences in our lives – experiences so great and so moving that it doesn't seem at the time that anyone else has been so caught up and pounded and dazzled and astonished and beaten and broken and rescued and illuminated and rewarded and humbled in just that way ever before.

Then we learn our trade, well or less well, and we tell our two or three stories – each time in a new disguise – maybe ten times, maybe a hundred, as long as people will listen.

Whether it's something that happened twenty years ago or only yesterday, I must start out with an emotion – one that's close to me and that I can understand.

Even for his commercial or slick stories Fitzgerald required emotional capital to draw upon. The blows that struck commencing with his wife's breakdown in 1930 – and followed by his worsening alcoholism, illness, and loss of confidence – caused him to characterize himself as a cracked plate in 1936. It was not true, as he feared, that he was emotionally bankrupt. But the emotions of 1935–40 were not convertible into *Post* stories. In 1935 Fitzgerald found an alternate market at *Esquire*, a new magazine which paid only $250. He began selling to *Esquire* stories that had been declined by. the high-paying magazines; but after 1937 Fitzgerald was writing only for *Esquire* and developed a special short-short story format for that magazine.

When Zelda Fitzgerald suggested that he resume writing *Post* stories, Fitzgerald replied in May 1940:

It's hard to explain about the *Saturday Evening Post* matter. It isn't that I haven't tried, but the trouble with them goes back to the time of Lorimer's retirement in 1935. I wrote them three stories that year* and sent them about three others which they didn't like. The last story they

---

*The *Post* published two Fitzgerald stories in 1935: 'Zone of Accident' and 'Too Cute for Words'. Both are in this collection.

bought they published last in the issue† and my friend, Adelaide Neil [Neall] on the staff implied to me that they didn't want to pay that big price for stories unless they could use them in the beginning of the issue. Well, that was the time of my two-year sickness, TB, the shoulder, etc., and you were at a most crucial point and I was foolishly trying to take care of Scottie and for one reason or another I lost the knack of writing the particular kind of stories they wanted.

As you should know from your own attempts, high-priced commercial writing for the magazines is a very definite trick. The rather special things that I brought to it, the intelligence and the good writing and even the radicalism all appealed to old Lorimer who had been a writer himself and liked style. The man who runs the magazine now [Wesley Stout] is an up-and-coming young Republican who gives not a damn about literature and who publishes almost nothing except escape stories about the brave frontiersmen, etc., or fishing, or football captains – nothing that would even faintly shock or disturb the reactionary bourgeois. Well, I simply can't do it and, as I say, I've tried not once but twenty times.

As soon as I feel I am writing to a cheap specification my pen freezes and my talent vanishes over the hill, and I honestly don't blame them for not taking the things that I've offered to them from time to time in the past three or four years. An explanation of their new attitude is that you no longer have a chance of selling a story with an unhappy ending (in the old days many of mine *did* have unhappy endings – if you remember).‡

In the introduction to *The Portable F. Scott Fitzgerald* John O'Hara decreed that Fitzgerald was 'our best novelist, one of our best novella-ists, and one of our finest writers of short stories'. It seemed like an example of O'Haraesque eccentricity in 1945. Now it is a sound judgement, though perhaps a bit cautious. Fitzgerald was, along with O'Hara and Hemingway, one of our three best short story writers. Indeed, it is becoming fashionable to claim that Fitzgerald was better as a short story writer than as a novelist. This truly eccentric notion does not have as many adherents as the familiar dismissal of his stories as trivial pot-boilers. Most critics would still prefer

---

† ' "Trouble" ' was the third story in the 6 March 1937 issue; it is included in this collection.
‡ *The Letters of F. Scott Fitzgerald*, ed. Andrew Turnbull (New York: Scribners, 1963),

to rescue a few stories – 'May Day', 'Rich Boy', 'The Diamond as Big as the Ritz', 'Babylon Revisited' – and inter the rest.

It has been justly held that a writer deserved to be judged by his best work. Nonetheless, a writer's best work must be assessed in terms of his total work. By making an additional fifty stories available, *The Price Was High* should aid in a sounder evaluation of Fitzgerald's career. Sometimes an unsuccessful work provides a gauge for an excellent one. Moreover, these stories correct the popular assumption that Fitzgerald squandered his energy in dissipation. Much of his energy went into writing 164 commercial stories in twenty years. (Hemingway published fifty-odd stories in forty years.) Fitzgerald's name now connotes alcoholic excess; but, as he reminded Maxwell Perkins, 'even *Post* stories must be done in a state of sobriety'.

There are no masterpieces in *The Price Was High*. Certainly it would be preferable for Fitzgerald to have written another novel instead of the stories collected here. But he never really had that option. With regret and disappointment and gratitude and pleasure we take what he did write. There isn't any more now. F. Scott Fitzgerald's stories are all used up.

THE SMILERS

Smart Set, June 1920

'The Smilers' was written in St Paul in September 1919 as 'A Smile for Sylvo'. After failing at his attempt to make a fast success as an advertising writer in New York, Fitzgerald returned to St Paul to rewrite his first novel. This Side of Paradise was accepted by Scribners in September, and Fitzgerald devoted the rest of the year to writing short stories for ready money. He submitted 'The Smilers' to Scribner's Magazine, which rejected it. After Harold Ober, his literary agent, was unable to place the story in one of the magazines that paid well, Fitzgerald sold it to the Smart Set for $35: 'I want to keep in right with Menken+Nathan as they're the most powerful critics in the country.' Although the Smart Set under editors H. L. Mencken and George Jean Nathan was an influential magazine among literary people, its limited circulation did not allow for generous payment. Fitzgerald sold stories to the Smart Set when they were unplaceable in the mass-circulation magazines – including two of his masterpieces, 'The Diamond as Big as the Ritz' and 'May Day'.

Although 'The Smilers' was written soon after acceptance of This Side of Paradise, it is still very much a college literary magazine piece – self-conscious and blatantly ironic. This story shows the didactic streak that marked several of Fitzgerald's early stories, such as 'The Four Fists' and 'The Cut-Glass Bowl'. The moralizing quality in his work – especially the stories – has been obscured by Fitzgerald's image as the Boswell of the Jazz Age. Near the end of his life he noted that he sometimes wishes he had gone into musical comedy, 'but I guess I am too much a moralist at heart and really want to preach at people in some acceptable form rather than to entertain them'.

We all have that exasperated moment!

There are times when you almost tell the harmless old lady next door what you really think of her face – that it ought to be on a night-nurse in a house for the blind; when you'd like to ask the man you've been waiting ten minutes for if he isn't all overheated from racing the postman down the block; when you nearly say to the waiter that if they deducted a cent from the bill for every degree the soup was below tepid the hotel would owe you half a dollar; when – and this is the infallible earmark of true exasperation – a smile affects you as an oil-baron's undershirt affects a cow's husband.

But the moment passes. Scars may remain on your dog or your collar or your telephone receiver, but your soul has slid gently back into its place between the lower edge of your heart and the upper edge of your stomach, and all is at peace.

But the imp who turns on the shower-bath of exasperation apparently made it so hot one time in Sylvester Stockton's early youth that he never dared dash in and turn it off – in consequence no first old man in an amateur production of a Victorian comedy was ever more pricked and prodded by the daily phenomena of life than was Sylvester at thirty.

Accusing eyes behind spectacles – suggestion of a stiff neck – this will have to do for his description, since he is not the hero of this story. He is the plot. He is the factor that makes it one story instead of three stories. He makes remarks at the beginning and end.

The late afternoon sun was loitering pleasantly along Fifth Avenue when Sylvester, who had just come out of that hideous public library where he had been consulting some ghastly book, told his impossible chauffeur (it is true that I am following his movements through his own spectacles) that he wouldn't need his stupid, incompetent services any longer. Swinging his cane (which he found too short) in his left hand (which he should have cut off long ago since it was constantly offending him), he began walking slowly down the Avenue.

When Sylvester walked at night he frequently glanced behind and on both sides to see if anyone was sneaking up on him. This had become a constant mannerism. For this reason he was unable to pretend that he didn't see Betty Tearle sitting in her machine in front of Tiffany's.

Back in his early twenties he had been in love with Betty Tearle. But he had depressed her. He had misanthropically dissected every meal, motor trip and musical comedy that they attended together, and on the few occasions when she had tried to be especially nice to him – from a mother's point of view he had been rather desirable – he had suspected hidden motives and fallen into a deeper gloom than ever. Then one day she told him that she would go mad if he ever again parked his pessimism in her sun-parlour.

And ever since then she had seemed to be smiling – uselessly, insultingly, charmingly smiling.

'Hello, Sylvo,' she called.

'Why – how do, Betty.' He wished she wouldn't call him Sylvo – it sounded like a – like a darn monkey or something.

'How goes it?' she asked cheerfully. 'Not very well, I suppose.'

'Oh, yes,' he answered stiffly, 'I manage.'

'Taking in the happy crowd?'

'Heavens, yes.' He looked around him. 'Betty, why are they happy? What are they smiling at? What do they find to smile at?'

Betty flashed him a glance of radiant amusement.

'The women may smile because they have pretty teeth, Sylvo.'

'You smile,' continued Sylvester cynically, 'because you're comfortably married and have two children. You imagine you're happy, so you suppose everyone else is.'

Betty nodded.

'You may have hit it, Sylvo—' The chauffeur glanced around and she nodded at him. 'Good-bye.'

Sylvo watched with a pang of envy which turned suddenly to exasperation as he saw she had turned and smiled at him once more. Then her car was out of sight in the traffic, and with a voluminous sigh he galvanized his cane into life and continued his stroll.

At the next corner he stopped in at a cigar store and there he ran into Waldron Crosby. Back in the days when Sylvester had been a prize pigeon in the eyes of débutantes he had also been a game partridge from the point of view of promoters. Crosby, then a young bond salesman, had given him much safe and sane advice and saved him many dollars. Sylvester liked Crosby as much as he could like anyone. Most people did like Crosby.

'Hello, you old bag of nerves,' cried Crosby genially, 'come and have a big gloom-dispelling Corona.'

Sylvester regarded the cases anxiously. He knew he wasn't going to like what he bought.

'Still out at Larchmont, Waldron?' he asked.

'Right-o.'

'How's your wife?'

'Never better.'

'Well,' said Sylvester suspiciously, 'you brokers always look as if you're smiling at something up your sleeve. It must be a hilarious profession.'

Crosby considered.

'Well,' he admitted, 'it varies – like the moon and the price of soft drinks – but it has its moments.'

'Waldron,' said Sylvester earnestly, 'you're a friend of mine – please do me the favour of not smiling when I leave you. It seems like a – like a mockery.'

A broad grin suffused Crosby's countenance.

'Why, you crabbed old son-of-a-gun!'

But Sylvester with an irate grunt had turned on his heel and disappeared.

He strolled on. The sun finished its promenade and began calling in the few stray beams it had left among the westward streets. The Avenue darkened with black bees from the department stores; the traffic swelled in to an interlaced jam; the buses were packed four deep like platforms above the thick crowd; but Sylvester, to whom the daily shift and change of the city was a matter only of sordid monotony, walked on, taking only quick sideward glances through his frowning spectacles.

He reached his hotel and was elevated to his four-room suite on the twelfth floor.

'If I dine downstairs,' he thought, 'the orchestra will play either ":Smile, Smile, Smile" or "The Smiles That You Gave To Me". But then if I go to the Club I'll meet all the cheerful people I know, and if I go somewhere else where there's no music, I won't get anything fit to eat.'

He decided to have dinner in his rooms.

An hour later, after disparaging some broth, a squab and a salad, he tossed fifty cents to the room-waiter, and then held up his hand warningly.

'Just oblige me by not smiling when you say thanks?'

He was too late. The waiter had grinned.

'Now, will you please tell me,' asked Sylvester peevishly, 'what on earth you have to smile about?'

The waiter considered. Not being a reader of the magazines he was not sure what was characteristic of waiters, yet he supposed something characteristic was expected of him.

'Well, mister,' he answered, glancing at the ceiling with all the ingenuousness he could muster in his narrow, sallow countenance, 'it's just something my face does when it sees four bits comin'.'

Sylvester waved him away.

'Waiters are happy because they've never had anything better,' he thought. 'They haven't enough imagination to want anything.'

At nine o'clock from sheer boredom he sought his expressionless bed.

As Sylvester left the cigar store, Waldron Crosby followed him out, and turning off Fifth Avenue down a cross street entered a brokerage office. A plump man with nervous hands rose and hailed him.

'Hello, Waldron.'

'Hello, Potter – I just dropped in to hear the worst.'

The plump man frowned.

'We've just got the news,' he said.

'Well, what is it? Another drop?'

'Closed at seventy-eight. Sorry, old boy.'

'Whew!'

'Hit pretty hard?'

'Cleaned out!'

The plump man shook his head, indicating that life was too much for him, and turned away.

Crosby sat there for a moment without moving. Then he rose, walked into Potter's private office and picked up the phone.

'Gi'me Larchmont 838.'

In a moment he had his connection.

'Mrs Crosby there?'

A man's voice answered him.

'Yes; this you, Crosby? This is Doctor Shipman.'

'Dr Shipman?' Crosby's voice showed sudden anxiety.

'Yes – I've been trying to reach you all afternoon. The situation's changed and we expect the child tonight.'

'Tonight?'

'Yes. Everything's OK. But you'd better come right out.'

'I will. Good-bye.'

He hung up the receiver and started out the door, but paused as an idea struck him. He returned, and this time called a Manhattan number.

'Hello, Donny, this is Crosby.'

'Hello, there, old boy. You just caught me; I was going—'

'Say, Donny, I want a job right away, quick.'

'For whom?'

'For me.'

'Why, what's the—'

'Never mind. Tell you later. Got one for me?'

'Why, Waldron, there's not a blessed thing here except a clerkship. Perhaps next—'

'What salary goes with the clerkship?'

'Forty – say forty-five a week.'

'I've got you. I start tomorrow.'

'All right. But say, old man—'

'Sorry, Donny, but I've got to run.'

Crosby hurried from the brokerage office with a wave and a smile at Potter. In the street he took out a handful of small change and after surveying it critically hailed a taxi.

'Grand Central – quick!' he told the driver.

III

At six o'clock Betty Tearle signed the letter, put it into an envelope and wrote her husband's name upon it. She went into his room and after a moment's hesitation set a black cushion on the bed and laid the white letter on it so that it could not fail to attract his attention when he came in. Then with a quick glance around the room she walked into the hall and upstairs to the nursery.

'Clare,' she called softly.

'Oh, Mummy!' Clare left her doll's house and scurried to her mother.

'Where's Billy, Clare?'

Billy appeared eagerly from under the bed.

'Got anything for me?' he inquired politely.

His mother's laugh ended in a little catch and she caught both her children to her and kissed them passionately. She found that she was crying quietly and their flushed little faces seemed cool against the sudden fever racing though her blood.

'Take care of Clare – always – Billy darling—'

Billy was puzzled and rather awed.

'You're crying,' he accused gravely.

'I know – I know I am—'

Clare gave a few tentative sniffles, hesitated, and then clung to her mother in a storm of weeping.

'I d-don't feel good, Mummy – I don't feel good.'

Betty soothed her quietly.

'We won't cry any more, Clare dear – either of us.'

But as she rose to leave the room her glance at Billy bore a mute appeal, too vain, she knew, to be registered on his childish consciousness.

Half an hour later as she carried her travelling bag to a taxicab at the door she raised her hand to her face in mute admission that a veil served no longer to hide her from the world.

'But I've chosen,' she thought dully.

As the car turned the corner she wept again, resisting a temptation to give up and go back.

'Oh, my God!' she whispered. 'What am I doing? What have I done? What have I done?'

IV

When Jerry, the sallow, narrow-faced waiter, left Sylvester's rooms he reported to the head-waiter, and then checked out for the day.

He took the subway south and alighting at Williams Street walked a few blocks and entered a billiard parlour.

An hour later he emerged with a cigarette drooping from his bloodless lips, and stood on the sidewalk as if hesitating before making a decision. He set off eastward.

As he reached a certain corner his gait suddenly increased and then quite as suddenly slackened. He seemed to want to pass by, yet some magnetic attraction was apparently exerted on him, for with a sudden face-about he turned in at the door of a cheap restaurant – half cabaret, half chop-suey parlour – where a miscellaneous assortment gathered nightly.

Jerry found his way to a table situated in the darkest and most obscure corner. Seating himself with a contempt for his surroundings that betokened familiarity rather than superiority he ordered a glass of claret.

The evening had begun. A fat woman at the piano was expelling the last jauntiness from a hackneyed foxtrot, and a lean, dispirited male was assisting her with lean, dispirited notes from a violin. The attention of the patrons was directed at a dancer wearing soiled stockings and done largely in peroxide and rouge who was about to step upon a small platform, meanwhile exchanging pleasantries with a fat, eager person at the table beside her who was trying to capture her hand.

Over in the corner Jerry watched the two by the platform and, as he gazed, the ceiling seemed to fade out, the walls growing into tall buildings and the platform becoming the top of a Fifth Avenue bus on a breezy spring night three years ago. The fat, eager person disappeared, the short skirt of the dancer rolled down and the rouge faded from her cheeks – and he was beside her again in an old delirious ride, with the lights blinking kindly at them from the tall buildings beside and the voices of the street merging into a pleasant somnolent murmur around them.

'Jerry,' said the girl on top of the bus, 'I've said that when you were gettin' seventy-five I'd take a chance with you. But, Jerry, I can't wait for ever.'

Jerry watched several street numbers sail by before he answered.

'I don't know what's the matter,' he said helplessly, 'they won't raise me. If I can locate a new job—'

'You better hurry, Jerry,' said the girl; 'I'm gettin' sick of just livin' along. If I can't get married I got a couple of chances to work in a cabaret – get on the stage maybe.'

'You keep out of that,' said Jerry quickly. 'There ain't no need, if you just wait about another month or two.'

'I can't wait for ever, Jerry,' repeated the girl. 'I'm tired of stayin' poor alone.'

'It won't be so long,' said Jerry clenching his free hand, 'I can make it somewhere, if you'll just wait.'

But the bus was fading out and the ceiling was taking shape and the murmur of the April streets was fading into the rasping whine of the violin – for that was all three years before and now he was sitting here.

The girl glanced up on the platform and exchanged a metallic impersonal smile with the dispirited violinist, and Jerry shrank farther back in his corner watching her with burning intensity.

'Your hands belong to anybody that wants them now,' he cried silently and bitterly. 'I wasn't man enough to keep you out of that – not man enough, by God, by God!'

But the girl by the door still toyed with the fat man's clutching fingers as she waited for her time to dance.

V

Sylvester Stockton tossed restlessly upon his bed. The room, big as it was, smothered him, and a breeze drifting in and bearing with it a rift of moon seemed laden only with the cares of the world he would have to face next day.

'They don't understand,' he thought. 'They don't see, as I do, the underlying misery of the whole damn thing. They're hollow optimists. They smile because they think they're always going to be happy.

'Oh, well,' he mused drowsily, 'I'll run up to Rye tomorrow and endure more smiles and more heat. That's all life is – just smiles and heat, smiles and heat.'

MYRA MEETS HIS FAMILY

Saturday Evening Post, 20 March 1920

'*Myra Meets His Family*' *was rewritten in St Paul in December 1919 from an abandoned story called* '*Lilah Meets His Family.*'

When Fitzgerald submitted '*Myra*' *to Harold Ober, he admitted:* '*I'm afraid its no good and if you agree with me don't hesitate to send it back. Perhaps if you give me an idea what the matter with it is I'll be able to rewrite it.*' *Ober had no trouble selling it to the* Post *for $400; it was Fitzgerald's second* Post *appearance. In 1919–20 Fitzgerald wrote a string of excellent* Saturday Evening Post *stories, including* '*Head and Shoulders*', '*The Ice Palace*', '*The Camel's Back*', '*Bernice Bobs Her Hair*', *and* '*The Offshore Pirate*', *Fox studios bought* '*Myra*' *in 1920 for $1000 – a good price at that time – and made it into* The Husband Hunter *with Eileen Percy.*

Its popular appeal did not alter Fitzgerald's feeling about the story. In 1921 he wrote Ober about English magazine rights: '*I believe you have disposed of . . .* Myra Meets His Family *which story, however, I never have liked + do not intend ever republishing in book form.*' *The reasons for his rejection of the story are not clear. It relies on unlikely plotting, but so do a number of his other commercial stories. Perhaps he saw too great a contrast between* '*Myra*' *and* '*The Ice Palace*', *one of his finest stories, which was written during the same month.*

'*Myra Meets His Family*' *is a representative early Fitzgerald story in terms of its material and characters. It stakes out the territory of the eastern rich: and Myra is a readily recognizable Fitzgerald heroine who reappears under a dozen other names in later stories.*

Probably every boy who has attended an eastern college in the last ten years has met Myra half a dozen times, for the Myras live on the eastern colleges, as kittens live on warm milk. When Myra is young, seventeen or so, they call her a 'wonderful kid'; in her prime – say, at nineteen – she is tendered the subtle compliment of being referred to by her name alone; and after that she is a 'prom trotter' or 'the famous coast-to-coast Myra'.

You can see her practically any winter afternoon if you stroll through the Biltmore lobby. She will be standing in a group of sophomores just in from Princeton or New Haven, trying to decide whether to dance away the mellow hours at the Club de Vingt or the Plaza Red Room. Afterwards one of the sophomores will take her to the theatre and ask her down to the February prom – and then dive for a taxi to catch the last train back to college.

Invariably she has a somnolent mother sharing a suite with her on one of the floors above.

When Myra is about twenty-four she thinks over all the nice boys she might have married at one time or other, sighs a little and does the best she can. But no remarks, please! She has given her youth to you; she has blown fragrantly through many ballrooms to the tender tribute of many eyes; she has roused strange surges of romance in a hundred pagan young breasts; and who shall say she hasn't counted?

The particular Myra whom this story concerns will have to have a paragraph of history. I will get it over with as swiftly as possible.

When she was sixteen she lived in a big house in Cleveland and attended Derby School in Connecticut, and it was while she was still there that she started going to prep-school dances and college proms. She decided to spend the war at Smith College, but in January of her freshman year, falling violently in love with a young infantry officer, she failed all her midyear examinations and retired to Cleveland in disgrace. The young infantry officer arrived about a week later.

Just as she had about decided that she didn't love him after all he was ordered abroad, and in a great revival of sentiment she rushed down to the port of embarkation with her mother to bid him good-bye. She wrote him daily for two months, and then weekly for two months, and then once more. This last letter he never got, for a machine-gun bullet ripped through his head one rainy July morning. Perhaps this was just as well, for the letter informed him that it had all been a mistake, and that something told her they would never be happy together, and so on.

The 'something' wore boots and silver wings and was tall and dark. Myra was quite sure that it was the real thing at last, but as an engine went through his chest at Kelly Field in mid-August she never had a chance to find out.

Instead she came east again, a little slimmer, with a becoming pallor and new shadows under her eyes, and throughout armistice year she left the ends of cigarettes all over New York on little china trays marked 'Midnight Frolic' and 'Coconut Grove' and 'Palais Royal'. She was twenty-one now, and Cleveland people said that her mother ought to take her back home – that New York was spoiling her.

You will have to do your best with that. The story should have started long ago.

It was an afternoon in September when she broke a theatre date in order to have tea with young Mrs Arthur Elkins, once her roommate at school.

'I wish,' began Myra as they sat down exquisitely, 'that I'd been a *señorita* or a *mademoiselle* or something. Good grief! What is there to do over here once you're out, except marry and retire!'

Lilah Elkins had seen this form of ennui before.

'Nothing,' she replied coolly; 'do it.'

'I can't seem to get interested, Lilah,' said Myra, bending forward earnestly. 'I've played round so much that even while I'm kissing the man I just wonder how soon I'll get tired of him. I never get carried away like I used to.'

'How old are you, Myra?'

'Twenty-one last spring.'

'Well,' said Lilah complacently, 'take it from me, don't get married unless you're absolutely through playing round. It means giving up an awful lot, you know.'

'Through! I'm sick and tired of my whole pointless existence. Funny, Lilah, but I do feel ancient. Up at New Haven last spring men danced with me that seemed like little boys – and once I overheard a girl say in the dressing room, "There's Myra Harper! She's been coming up here for eight years." Of course she was about three years off, but it did give me the calendar blues.'

'You and I went to our first prom when we were sixteen – five years ago.'

'Heavens!' sighed Myra. 'And now some men are afraid of me. Isn't that odd? Some of the nicest boys. One man dropped me like a hotcake after coming down from Morristown for three straight weekends. Some kind friend told him I was husband hunting this year and he was afraid of getting in too deep.'

'Well, you are husband hunting, aren't you?'

'I suppose so – after a fashion.' Myra paused and looked about her rather cautiously. 'Have you ever met Knowleton Whitney? You know what a wiz he is on looks, and his father's worth a fortune, they say. Well, I noticed that the first time he met me he started when he heard my name and fought shy – and, Lilah darling, I'm not so ancient and homely as all that, am I?'

'You certainly are not!' laughed Lilah. 'And here's my advice: Pick out the best thing in sight – the man who has all the mental, physical, social and financial qualities you want, and then go after him hammer and tongs – the way we used to. After you've got him don't say to yourself, "Well, he can't sing like Billy," or "I wish he played better golf." You can't have everything. Shut your eyes and turn off your sense of humour, and then after you're married it'll be very different and you'll be mighty glad.'

'Yes,' said Myra absently; 'I've had that advice before.'

'Drifting into romance is easy when you're eighteen,' continued Lilah emphatically; 'but after five years of it your capacity for it simply burns out.'

'I've had such nice times,' sighed Myra, 'and such sweet men. To tell you the truth I have decided to go after someone.'

'Who?'

'Knowleton Whitney. Believe me, I may be a bit blasé, but I can still get any man I want.'

'You really want him?'

'Yes – as much as I'll ever want anyone. He's smart as a whip, and shy – rather sweetly shy – and they say his family have the best-looking place in Westchester County.'

Lilah sipped the last of her tea and glanced at her wrist watch.

'I've got to tear, dear.'

They rose together and, sauntering out on Park Avenue, hailed taxicabs.

'I'm awfully glad, Myra; and I know you'll be glad too.'

Myra skipped a little pool of water and, reaching her taxi, balanced on the running board like a ballet dancer.

' 'Bye, Lilah. See you soon.'

'Good-bye, Myra. Good luck!'

And knowing Myra as she did, Lilah felt that her last remark was distinctly superfluous.

II

That was essentially the reason that one Friday night six weeks later Knowleton Whitney paid a taxi bill of seven dollars and ten cents and with a mixture of emotions paused beside Myra on the Biltmore steps.

The outer surface of his mind was deliriously happy, but just below that was a slowly hardening fright at what he had done. He, protected since his freshman year at Harvard from the snares of fascinating fortune hunters, dragged away from several sweet young things by the acquiescent nape of his neck, had taken advantage of his family's absence in the West to become so enmeshed in the toils that it was hard to say which was toils and which was he.

The afternoon had been like a dream: November twilight along Fifth Avenue after the matinée, and he and Myra looking out at the swarming crowds from the romantic privacy of a hansom cab – quaint device – then tea at the Ritz and her white hand gleaming on the arm of a chair beside him; and suddenly quick broken words. After that had come the trip to the jeweller's and a mad dinner in some little Italian restaurant where he had written 'Do you?' on the back of the bill of fare and pushed it over for her to add the ever-miraculous 'You know I do!' And now at the day's end they paused on the Biltmore steps.

'Say it,' breathed Myra close to his ear.

He said it. Ah, Myra, how many ghosts must have flitted across your memory then!

'You've made me so happy, dear,' she said softly.

'No – you've made me happy. Don't you know – Myra——'

'I know.'

'For good?'

'For good. I've got this, you see.' And she raised the diamond solitaire to her lips. She knew how to do things, did Myra.

'Good night.'

'Good night. Good night.'

Like a gossamer fairy in shimmering rose she ran up the wide stairs and her cheeks were glowing wildly as she rang the elevator bell.

At the end of a fortnight she got a telegraph from him saying that his family had returned from the West and expected her up in Westchester County for a week's visit. Myra wired her train time, bought three new evening dresses and packed her trunk.

It was a cool November evening when she arrived, and stepping from the train in the late twilight she shivered slightly and looked eagerly round for Knowleton. The station platform swarmed for a moment with men returning from the city; there was a shouting medley of wives and chauffeurs, and a great snorting of automobiles as they backed and turned and slid away. Then before she realized it the platform was quite deserted and not a single one of the luxurious cars remained. Knowleton must have expected her on another train.

With an almost inaudible 'Damn!' she started towards the Elizabethan station to telephone, when suddenly she was accosted by a very dirty, dilapidated man who touched his ancient cap to her and addressed her in a cracked, querulous voice.

'You Miss Harper?'

'Yes,' she confessed, rather startled. Was this unmentionable person by any wild chance the chauffeur?

'The chauffeur's sick,' he continued in a high whine. 'I'm his son.'

Myra gasped.

'You mean Mr Whitney's chauffeur?'

'Yes; he only keeps just one since the war. Great on economizin' – regelar Hoover.' He stamped his feet nervously and smacked enormous gauntlets together. 'Well, no use waitin' here gabbin' in the cold. Le's have your grip.'

Too amazed for words and not a little dismayed, Myra followed her guide to the edge of the platform, where she looked in vain for a car. But she was not left to wonder long, for the person led her steps to a battered old flivver, wherein was deposited her grip.

'Big car's broke,' he explained. 'Have to use this or walk.'

He opened the front door for her and nodded.

'Step in.'

'I b'lieve I'll sit in the back if you don't mind.'

'Surest thing you know,' he cackled, opening the back door. 'I thought the trunk bumpin' round back there might make you nervous.'

'What trunk?'

'Yourn.'

'Oh, didn't Mr Whitney – can't you make two trips?'

He shook his head obstinately.

'Wouldn't allow it. Not since the war. Up to rich people to set 'n example; that's what Mr Whitney says. Le's have your check, please.'

As he disappeared Myra tried in vain to conjure up a picture of the chauffeur if this was his son. After a mysterious argument with the station agent he returned, gasping violently, with the trunk on his back. He deposited it in the rear seat and climbed up front beside her.

It was quite dark when they swerved out of the road and up a long dusky driveway to the Whitney place, whence lighted windows flung great blots of cheerful, yellow light over the gravel and grass and trees. Even now she could see that it was very beautiful, that its blurred outline was Georgian Colonial and that great shadowy garden parks were flung out at both sides. The car plumped to a full stop before a square stone doorway and the chauffeur's son climbed out after her and pushed open the outer door.

'Just go right in,' he cackled; and as she passed the threshold she heard him softly shut the door, closing out himself and the dark.

Myra looked round her. She was in a large sombre hall panelled in old English oak and lit by dim shaded lights clinging like luminous yellow turtles at intervals along the wall. Ahead of her was a broad staircase and on both sides there were several doors, but there was no sight or sound of life, and an intense stillness seemed to rise ceaselessly from the deep crimson carpet.

She must have waited there a full minute before she began to have that unmistakable sense of someone looking at her. She forced herself to turn casually round.

A sallow little man, bald and clean shaven, trimly dressed in a frock coat and white spats, was standing a few yards away regarding her quizzically. He must have been fifty at the least, but even before he moved she had noticed a curious alertness about him – something in his pose which promised that it had been instantaneously assumed and would be instantaneously changed in a moment. His tiny hands and feet and the odd twist to his eyebrows gave him a faintly elfish expression, and she had one of those vague transient convictions that she had seen him before, many years ago.

For a minute they stared at each other in silence and then she flushed slightly and discovered a desire to swallow.

'I suppose you're Mr Whitney.' She smiled faintly and advanced a step towards him. 'I'm Myra Harper.'

For an instant longer he remained silent and motionless, and it flashed across Myra that he might be deaf; then suddenly he jerked into spirited life exactly like a mechanical toy started by pressure of a button.

'Why, of course – why, naturally. I know – ah!' he exclaimed excitedly in a high-pitched elfin voice. Then raising himself on his toes in a sort of attenuated ecstasy of enthusiasm and smiling a wizened smile, he minced towards her across the dark carpet.

She blushed appropriately.

'That's awfully nice of—'

'Ah!' he went on. 'You must be tired; a rickety, cindery, ghastly trip, I know. Tired and hungry and thirsty, no doubt, no doubt!' He looked round him indignantly. 'The servants are frightfully inefficient in this house!'

Myra did not know what to say to this, so she made no answer. After an instant's abstraction Mr Whitney crossed over with his furious energy and pressed a button; then almost as if he were dancing he was by her side again, making thin, disparaging gestures with his hands.

'A little minute,' he assured her, 'sixty seconds, scarcely more. Here!'

He rushed suddenly to the wall and with some effort lifted a great carved Louis Fourteenth chair and set it down carefully in the geometrical centre of the carpet.

'Sit down – won't you? Sit down! I'll go get you something. Sixty seconds at the outside.'

She demurred faintly, but he kept on repeating 'Sit down!' in such an aggrieved yet hopeful tone that Myra sat down. Instantly her host disappeared.

She sat there for five minutes and a feeling of oppression fell over her. Of all the receptions she had ever received this was decidedly the oddest – for though she had read somewhere that Ludlow Whitney was considered one of the most eccentric figures in the financial world, to find a sallow, elfin little man who, when he walked, danced was rather a blow to her sense of form. Had he gone to get Knowleton! She revolved her thumbs in interminable concentric circles.

Then she started nervously at a quick cough at her elbow. It was Mr Whitney again. In one hand he held a glass of milk and in the other a blue kitchen bowl full of those hard cubical crackers used in soup.

'Hungry from your trip!' he exclaimed compassionately. 'Poor girl, poor little girl, starving!' He brought out this last word with such emphasis that some of the milk plopped gently over the side of the glass.

Myra took the refreshments submissively. She was not hungry, but it had taken him ten minutes to get them so it seemed ungracious to refuse. She sipped gingerly at the milk and ate a cracker, wondering vaguely what to say. Mr Whitney, however, solved the problem for her by disappearing again – this time by way of the wide stairs – four steps at a hop – the back of his bald head gleaming oddly for a moment in the half dark.

Minutes passed. Myra was torn between resentment and bewilderment that she should be sitting on a high comfortless chair in the middle of this big hall munching crackers. By what code was a visiting fiancée ever thus received!

Her heart gave a jump of relief as she heard a familiar whistle on the stairs. It was Knowleton at last, and when he came in sight he gasped with astonishment.

'Myra!'

She carefully placed the bowl and glass on the carpet and rose, smiling.

'Why,' he exclaimed, 'they didn't tell me you were here!'

'Your father – welcomed me.'

'Lordy! He must have gone upstairs and forgotten all about it. Did he insist on your eating this stuff? Why didn't you just tell him you didn't want any?'

'Why – I don't know.'

'You mustn't mind father, dear. He's forgetful and a little unconventional in some ways, but you'll get used to him.'

He pressed a button and a butler appeared.

'Show Miss Harper to her room and have her bag carried up – and her trunk if it isn't there already.' He turned to Myra. 'Dear, I'm awfully sorry I didn't know you were here. How long have you been waiting?'

'Oh, only a few minutes.'

It had been twenty at least, but she saw no advantage in stressing it. Nevertheless it had given her an oddly uncomfortable feeling.

Half an hour later as she was hooking the last eye on her dinner dress there was a knock on the door.

'It's Knowleton, Myra; if you're about ready we'll go in and see mother for a minute before dinner.'

She threw a final approving glance at her reflection in the mirror and turning out the light joined him in the hall. He led her down a central passage which crossed to the other wing of the house, and stopping before a closed door he pushed it open and ushered Myra into the weirdest room upon which her young eyes had ever rested.

It was a large luxurious boudoir, panelled, like the lower hall, in dark English oak and bathed by several lamps in a mellow orange glow that blurred its every outline into a misty amber. In a great armchair piled high with cushions and draped with a curiously figured cloth of silk reclined a very sturdy old lady with bright white hair, heavy features, and an air about her of having been there for many years. She lay somnolently against the cushions, her eyes half closed, her great bust rising and falling under her black négligé.

But it was something else that made the room remarkable, and Myra's eyes scarcely rested on the woman, so engrossed was she in another feature of her surroundings. On the carpet, on the chairs and sofas, on the great canopied bed and on the soft Angora rug in front of the fire sat and sprawled and slept a great army of white poodle dogs. There must have been almost two dozen of them, with curly hair twisting in front of their wistful eyes and wide yellow bows flaunting from their necks. As Myra and Knowleton entered a stir went over the dogs; they raised one-and-twenty cold black noses in the air and from one-and-twenty little throats went up a great clatter of staccato barks until the room was filled with such an uproar that Myra stepped back in alarm.

But at the din the somnolent fat lady's eyes trembled open and in a low husky voice that was in itself oddly like a bark she snapped out: 'Hush that racket!' and the clatter instantly ceased. The two or three poodles round the fire turned their silky eyes on each other reproachfully, and lying down with little sighs faded out on the white Angora rug; the tousled ball on the lady's lap dug his nose into the crook of an elbow and went back to sleep, and except for the patches of white wool scattered about the room Myra would have thought it all a dream.

'Mother,' said Knowleton after an instant's pause, 'this is Myra.'

From the lady's lips flooded one low husky word: 'Myra?'

'She's visiting us, I told you.'

Mrs Whitney raised a large arm and passed her hand across her forehead wearily.

'Child!' she said – and Myra started, for again the voice was like a low sort of growl – 'you want to marry my son Knowleton?'

Myra felt that this was putting the tonneau before the radiator, but she nodded. 'Yes, Mrs Whitney.'

'How old are you?' This very suddenly.

'I'm twenty-one, Mrs Whitney.'

'Ah – and you're from Cleveland?' This was in what was surely a series of articulate barks.

'Yes, Mrs Whitney.'

'Ah—'

Myra was not certain whether this last ejaculation was conversation or merely a groan, so she did not answer.

'You'll excuse me if I don't appear downstairs,' continued Mrs Whitney; 'but when we're in the East I seldom leave this room and my dear little doggies.'

Myra nodded and a conventional health question was trembling on her lips when she caught Knowleton's warning glance and checked it.

'Well,' said Mrs Whitney with an air of finality, 'you seem like a very nice girl. Come in again.'

'Good night, mother,' said Knowleton.

' 'Night!' barked Mrs Whitney drowsily, and her eyes sealed gradually up as her head receded back again into the cushions.

Knowleton held open the door and Myra, feeling a bit blank, left the room. As they walked down the corridor she heard a burst of furious sound behind them; the noise of the closing door had again roused the poodle dogs.

When they went downstairs they found Mr Whitney already seated at the dinner table.

'Utterly charming, completely delightful!' he exclaimed, beaming nervously. 'One big family, and you the jewel of it, my dear.'

Myra smiled, Knowleton frowned and Mr Whitney tittered.

'It's been lonely here,' he continued; 'desolate, with only us three. We expect you to bring sunlight and warmth, the peculiar radiance and efflorescence of youth. It will be quite delightful. Do you sing?'

'Why – I have. I mean, I do, some.'

He clapped his hands enthusiastically.

'Splendid! Magnificent! What do you sing? Opera? Ballads? Popular music?'

'Well, mostly popular music.'

'Good; personally I prefer popular music. By the way, there's a dance tonight.'

'Father,' demanded Knowleton sulkily, 'did you go and invite a crowd here?'

'I had Monroe call up a few people – just some of the neighbours,' he explained to Myra. 'We're all very friendly hereabouts; give informal things continually. Oh, it's quite delightful.'

Myra caught Knowleton's eye and gave him a sympathetic glance. It was obvious that he had wanted to be alone with her this first evening and was quite put out.

'I want them to meet Myra,' continued his father. 'I want them to know this delightful jewel we've added to our little household.'

'Father,' said Knowleton suddenly, 'eventually of course Myra and I will want to live here with you and mother, but for the first two or three years I think an apartment in New York would be more the thing for us.'

Crash! Mr Whitney had raked across the tablecloth with his fingers and swept his silver to a jangling heap on the floor.

'Nonsense!' he cried furiously, pointing a tiny finger at his son. 'Don't talk that utter nonsense! You'll live here, do you understand me? Here! What's a home without children?'

'But, father—'

In his excitement Mr Whitney rose and a faint unnatural colour crept into his sallow face.

'Silence!' he shrieked. 'If you expect one bit of help from me you can have it under my roof – nowhere else! Is that clear? As for you, my exquisite young lady,' he continued, turning his wavering finger on Myra, 'you'd better understand that the best thing you can do is to decide to settle down right here. This is my home, and I mean to keep it so!'

He stood then for a moment on his tiptoes, bending furiously indignant glances first on one, then on the other, and then suddenly he turned and skipped from the room.

'Well,' gasped Myra, turning to Knowleton in amazement, 'what do you know about that!'

III

Some hours later she crept into bed in a great state of restless discontent. One thing she knew – she was not going to live in this house. Knowleton would have to make his father see reason to the extent of giving them an apartment in the city. The sallow little man made her nervous; she was sure Mrs Whitney's dogs would haunt her dreams; and there was a general casualness in the chauffeur, the butler, the maids and even the guests she she had met that night, that did not in the least coincide with her ideas on the conduct of a big estate.

She had lain there an hour perhaps when she was startled from a slow reverie by a sharp cry which seemed to proceed from the adjoining room. She sat up in bed and listened, and in a minuted it was repeated. It sounded exactly like the plaint of a weary child stopped summarily by the placing of a hand over its mouth. In the dark silence her bewilderment shaded gradually off into uneasiness. She waited for the cry to recur, but straining her ears she heard only the intense crowded stillness of three o'clock. She wondered where Knowleton slept, remembered that his bedroom was over in the other wing just beyond his mother's. She was alone over here – or was she?

With a little gasp she slid down into bed again and lay listening. Not since childhood had she been afraid of the dark, but the unforseen presence of someone next door startled her and sent her imagination racing through a host of mystery stories that at one time or another had whiled away a long afternoon.

She heard the clock strike four and found she was very tired. A curtain drifted slowly down in front of her imagination, and changing her position she fell suddenly to sleep.

Next morning, walking with Knowleton under starry frosted bushes in one of the bare gardens, she grew quite light-hearted and wondered at her depression of the night before. Probably all families seemed odd when one visited them for the first time in such an intimate capacity. Yet her determination that she and Knowleton were going to live elsewhere than with the white dogs and the jumpy little man was not abated. And if the nearby Westchester County society was typified by the chilly crowd she had met at the dance—

'The family,' said Knowleton, 'must seem rather unusual. I've been brought up in an odd atmosphere, I suppose, but mother is really quite normal outside of her penchant for poodles in great quantities, and father in spite of his eccentricities seems to hold a secure position in Wall Street.'

'Knowleton,' she demanded suddenly, 'who lives in the room next door to me?'

Did he start and flush slightly – or was that her imagination?

'Because,' she went on deliberately, 'I'm almost sure I heard someone crying in there during the night. It sounded like a child, Knowleton.'

'There is no one in there,' he said decidedly. 'It was either your imagination or something you ate. Or possibly one of the maids was sick.'

Seeming to dismiss the matter without effort he changed the subject.

The day passed quickly. At lunch Mr Whitney seemed to have forgotten his temper of the previous night; he was as nervously enthusiastic as ever; and watching him Myra again had that impression that she had seen him somewhere before. She and Knowleton paid another visit to Mrs Whitney – and again the poodles stirred uneasily and set up a barking, to be summarily silenced by the harsh throaty voice. The conversation was short and of inquisitional flavour. It was terminated as before by the lady's drowsy eyelids and a paean of farewell from the dogs.

In the evening she found that Mr Whitney had insisted on organizing an informal neighbourhood vaudeville. A stage had been erected in the ballroom and Myra sat beside Knowleton in the front row and watched proceedings curiously. Two slim and haughty ladies sang, a man performed some ancient card tricks, a girl gave impersonations, and then to Myra's astonishment Mr Whitney appeared and did a rather effective buck-and-wing dance. There was something inexpressibly weird in the motion of the well-known financier flitting solemnly back and forth across the stage on his tiny feet. Yet he danced well, with an effortless grace and an unexpected suppleness, and he was rewarded with a storm of applause.

In the half dark the lady on her left suddenly spoke to her.

'Mr Whitney is passing the word along that he wants to see you behind the scenes.'

Puzzled, Myra rose and ascended the side flight of stairs that led to the raised platform. Her host was waiting for her anxiously.

'Ah,' he chuckled, 'splendid!'

He held out his hand, and wonderingly she took it. Before she realized his intention he had half led, half drawn her out on to the stage. The spotlight's glare bathed them, and the ripple of conversation washing the audience ceased. The faces before her were pallid splotches on the gloom and she felt her ears burning as she waited for Mr Whitney to speak.

'Ladies and gentlemen,' he began, 'most of you know Miss Myra Harper. You had the honour of meeting her last night. She is a delicious girl, I assure you. I am in a position to know. She intends to become the wife of my son.'

He paused and nodded and began clapping his hands. The audience immediately took up the clapping and Myra stood there in motionless horror, overcome by the most violent confusion of her life.

The piping voice went on: 'Miss Harper is not only beautiful but talented. Last night she confided to me that she sang. I asked whether she preferred the opera, the ballad or the popular song, and she confessed that her taste ran to the latter. Miss Harper will now favour us with a popular song.'

And then Myra was standing alone on the stage, rigid with embarrass-ment. She fancied that on the faces in front of her she saw critical expecta-tion, boredom, ironic disapproval. Surely this was the height of bad form – to drop a guest unprepared into such a situation.

In the first hush she considered a word or two explaining that Mr Whitney had been under a misapprehension – then anger came to her assistance. She tossed her head and those in front saw her lips close together sharply.

Advancing to the platform's edge she said succinctly to the orchestra leader: 'Have you got "Wave That Wishbone"?'

'Lemme see. Yes, we got it.'

'All right. Let's go!'

She hurriedly reviewed the words, which she had learned quite by accident at a dull house party the previous summer. It was perhaps not the song she would have chosen for her first public appearance, but it would have to do. She smiled radiantly, nodded at the orchestra leader and began the verse in a light clear alto.

As she sang a spirit of ironic humour slowly took possession of her – a desire to give them all a run for their money. And she did. She injected an East Side snarl into every word of slang; she ragged; she shimmied; she did a tickle-toe step she had learned once in an amateur musical comedy; and in a burst of inspiration finished up in an Al Jolson position, on her knees with her arms stretched out to her audience in syncopated appeal.

Then she rose, bowed and left the stage.

For an instant there was silence, the silence of a cold tomb; then perhaps half a dozen hands joined in a faint, perfunctory applause that in a second had died completely away.

'Heavens!' thought Myra. 'Was it as bad as all that? Or did I shock 'em?'

Mr Whitney, however, seemed delighted. He was waiting for her in the wings and seizing her hand shook it enthusiastically.

'Quite wonderful!' he chuckled. 'You are a delightful little actress – and you'll be a valuable addition to our little plays. Would you like to give an encore?'

'No!' said Myra shortly, and turned away.

In a shadowy corner she waited until the crowd had filed out, with an angry unwillingness to face them immediately after their rejection of her effort.

When the ballroom was quite empty she walked slowly up the stairs, and there she came upon Knowleton and Mr Whitney alone in the dark hall, evidently engaged in a heated argument.

They ceased when she appeared and looked towards her eagerly.

'Myra,' said Mr Whitney, 'Knowleton wants to talk to you.'

'Father,' said Knowleton intensely, 'I ask you—'

'Silence!' cried his father, his voice ascending testily. 'You'll do your duty – now.'

Knowleton cast one more appealing glance at him, but Mr Whitney only shook his head excitedly and turning, disappeared phantomlike up the stairs.

Knowleton stood silent a moment and finally with a look of dogged determination took her hand and led her towards a room that opened off the hall at the back. The yellow light fell through the door after them and she found herself in a dark wide chamber where she could just distinguish on the walls great square shapes which she took to be frames. Knowleton pressed a button, and immediately forty portraits sprang into life – old gallants from colonial days, ladies with floppity Gainsborough hats, fat women with ruffs and placid clasped hands.

She turned to Knowleton inquiringly, but he led her forward to a row of pictures on the side.

'Myra,' he said slowly and painfully, 'there's something I have to tell you. These' – he indicated the pictures with his hand – 'are family portraits.'

There were seven of them, three men and three women, all of them of the period just before the Civil War. The one in the middle, however. was hidden by crimson-velvet curtains.

'Ironic as it may seem,' continued Knowleton steadily, 'that frame contains a picture of my great-grandmother.'

Reaching out, he pulled a little silken cord and the curtains parted, to expose a portrait of a lady dressed as a European but with the unmistakable features of a Chinese.

'My great-grandfather, you see, was an Australian tea importer. He met his future wife in Hong Kong.'

Myra's brain was whirling. She had a sudden vision of Mr Whitney's yellowish face, peculiar eyebrows and tiny hands and feet – she remembered ghastly tales she had heard of reversions to type – of Chinese babies – and then with a final surge of horror she thought of that sudden hushed cry in the night. She gasped, her knees seemed to crumple up and she sank slowly to the floor.

In a second Knowleton's arms were round her.

'Dearest, dearest!' he cried. 'I shouldn't have told you! I shouldn't have told you!'

As he said this Myra knew definitely and unmistakably that she could never marry him, and when she realized it she cast at him a wild pitiful look, and for the first time in her life fainted dead away.

IV

When she next recovered full consciousness she was in bed. She imagined a maid had undressed her, for on turning up the reading lamp she saw that her clothes had been neatly put away. For a minute she lay there, listening idly while the hall clock struck two, and then her overwrought nerves jumped in terror as she heard again that child's cry from the room next door. The morning seemed suddenly infinitely far away. There was some shadowy secret near her – her feverish imagination pictured a Chinese child brought up there in the half dark.

In a quick panic she crept into a négligé and, throwing open the door, slipped down the corridor towards Knowleton's room. It was very dark in the other wing, but when she pushed open his door she could see by the faint hall light that his bed was empty and had not been slept in. Her terror increased. What could take him out at this hour of the night? She started for Mrs Whitney's room, but at the thought of the dogs and her bare ankles she gave a little discouraged cry and passed by the door.

Then she suddenly heard the sound of Knowleton's voice issuing from a faint crack of light far down the corridor, and with a glow of joy she fled towards it. When she was within a foot of the door she found she could see through the crack – and after one glance all thought of entering left her.

Before an open fire, his head bowed in an attitude of great dejection, stood Knowleton, and in a corner, feet perched on the table, sat Mr Whitney in his shirt sleeves, very quiet and calm, and pulling contentedly on a huge black pipe. Seated on the table was a part of Mrs Whitney – that is, Mrs Whitney without any hair. Out of the familiar great bust projected Mrs Whitney's head, but she was bald; on her cheeks was the faint stubble of a beard, and in her mouth was a large black cigar, which she was puffing with obvious enjoyment.

'A thousand,' groaned Knowleton as if in answer to a question. 'Say twenty-five hundred and you'll be nearer the truth. I got a bill from the Graham Kennels today for those poodle dogs. They're soaking me two hundred and saying that they've got to have 'em back tomorrow.'

'Well,' said Mrs Whitney in a low baritone voice, 'send 'em back. We're through with 'em.'

'That's a mere item,' continued Knowleton glumly. 'Including your salary, and Appleton's here, and that fellow who did the chauffeur, and seventy supes for two nights, and an orchestra – that's nearly twelve hundred, and then there's the rent on the costumes and that darn Chinese portrait and the bribes to the servants. Lord! There'll probably be bills for one thing or another coming in for the next month.'

'Well, then,' said Appleton, 'for pity's sake pull yourself together and carry it through to the end. Take my word for it, that girl will be out of the house by twelve noon.'

Knowleton sank into a chair and covered his face with his hands.

'Oh—'

'Brace up! It's all over. I thought for a minute there in the hall that you were going to balk at that Chinese business.'

'It was the vaudeville that knocked the spots out of me,' groaned Knowleton. 'It was about the meanest trick ever pulled on any girl, and she was so darned game about it!'

'She had to be,' said Mrs Whitney cynically.

'Oh, Kelly, if you could have seen the girl look at me tonight just before she fainted in front of that picture. Lord, I believe she loves me! Oh, if you could have seen her!'

Outside Myra flushed crimson. She leaned closer to the door, biting her lip until she could taste the faintly bitter savour of blood.

'If there was anything I could do now,' continued Knowleton – 'anything in the world that would smooth it over I believe I'd do it.'

Kelly crossed ponderously over, his bald shiny head ludicrous above his feminine négligé, and put his hand on Knowleton's shoulder.

'See here, my boy – your trouble is just nerves. Look at it this way: You undertook somep'n to get yourself out of an awful mess. It's a cinch the girl was after your money – now you've beat her at her own game an' saved yourself an unhappy marriage and your family a lot of suffering. Ain't that so, Appleton?'

'Absolutely!' said Appleton emphatically. 'Go through with it.'

'Well,' said Knowleton with a dismal attempt to be righteous, 'if she really loves me she wouldn't have let it all affect her this much. She's not marrying my family.'

Appleton laughed.

'I thought we'd tried to make it pretty obvious that she is.'

'Oh, shut up!' cried Knowleton miserably.

Myra saw Appleton wink at Kelly.

' 'At's right,' he said; 'she's shown she was after your money. Well, now then, there's no reason for not going through with it. See here. On one side, you've proved she didn't love you and you're rid of her and free as air. She'll creep away and never say a word about it – and your family never the wiser. On the other side twenty-five hundred thrown to the bow-wows, miserable marriage, girl sure to hate you as soon as she finds out, and your family all broken up and probably disownin' you for marryin' her. One big mess, I'll tell the world.'

'You're right,' admitted Knowleton gloomily. 'You're right, I suppose – but oh, the look in that girl's face! She's probably in there now lying awake, listening to the Chinese baby—'

Appleton rose and yawned.

'Well—' he began.

But Myra waited to hear no more. Pulling her silk kimono close about her she sped like lightning down the soft corridor, to dive headlong and breathless into her room.

'My heavens!' she cried, clenching her hands in the darkness. 'My heavens!'

V

Just before dawn Myra drowsed into a jumbled dream that seemed to act on through interminable hours. She awoke about seven and lay listlessly with one blue-veined arm hanging over the side of the bed. She who had danced in the dawn at many proms was very tired.

A clock outside her door struck the hour, and with her nervous start something seemed to collapse within her – she turned over and began to weep furiously into her pillow, her tangled hair spreading like a dark aura round her head. To her, Myra Harper, had been done this cheap vulgar trick by a man she had thought shy and kind.

Lacking the courage to come to her and tell her the truth he had gone into the highways and hired men to frighten her.

Between her fevered broken sobs she tried in vain to comprehend the workings of a mind which could have conceived this in all its subtlety. Her pride refused to let her think of it as a deliberate plan of Knowleton's. It was probably an idea fostered by this little actor Appleton or by the fat Kelly with his horrible poodles. But it was all unspeakable – unthinkable. It gave her an intense sense of shame.

But when she emerged from her room at eight o'clock and, disdaining breakfast, walked into the garden she was a very self-possessed young beauty, with dry cool eyes only faintly shadowed. The ground was firm and frosty with the promise of winter, and she found grey sky and dull air vaguely comforting and one with her mood. It was a day for thinking and she needed to think.

And then turning a corner suddenly she saw Knowleton seated on a stone bench, his head in his hands, in an attitude of profound dejection. He wore his clothes of the night before and it was quite evident that he had not been to bed.

He did not hear her until she was quite close to him, and then as a dry twig snapped under her heel he looked up wearily. She saw that the night had played havoc with him – his face was deathly pale and his eyes were pink and puffed and tired. He jumped up with a look that was very like dread.

'Good morning,' said Myra quietly.

'Sit down,' he began nervously. 'Sit down; I want to talk to you! I've got to talk to you.'

Myra nodded and taking a seat beside him on the bench clasped her knees with her hands and half closed her eyes.

'Myra, for heaven's sake have pity on me!'

She turned wondering eyes on him.

'What do you mean?'

He groaned.

'Myra, I've done a ghastly thing – to you, to me, to us. I haven't a word to say in favour of myself – I've been just rotten. I think it was a sort of madness that came over me.'

'You'll have to give me a clue to what you're talking about.'

'Myra – Myra' – like all large bodies his confession seemed difficult to imbue with momentum – 'Myra – Mr Whitney is not my father.'

'You mean you were adopted?'

'No; I mean – Ludlow Whitney is my father, but this man you've met isn't Ludlow Whitney.'

'I know,' said Myra coolly. 'He's Warren Appleton, the actor.'

Knowleton leaped to his feet.

'Oh,' lied Myra easily, 'I recognized him the first night. I saw him five years ago in *The Swiss Grapefruit.*'

At this Knowleton seemed to collapse utterly. He sank down limply on to the bench.

'You knew?'

'Of course! How could I help it? It simply made me wonder what it was all about.'

With a great effort he tried to pull himself together.

'I'm going to tell you the whole story, Myra.'

'I'm all ears.'

'Well, it starts with my mother – my real one, not the woman with those idiotic dogs; she's an invalid and I'm her only child. Her one idea in life has always been for me to make a fitting match, and her idea of a fitting match centres on social position in England. Her greatest disappointment was that I wasn't a girl so I could marry a title; instead she wanted to drag me to England – marry me off to the sister of an earl or the daughter of a duke. Why, before she'd let me stay up here alone this fall she made me promise I wouldn't go to see any girl more than twice. And then I met you.'

He paused for a second and continued earnestly: 'You were the first girl in my life whom I ever thought of marrying. You intoxicated me, Myra. It was just as though you were making me love you by some invisible force.'

'I was,' murmured Myra.

'Well, that first intoxication lasted a week, and then one day a letter came from mother saying she was bringing home some wonderful English girl, Lady Helena Something-or-Other. And the same day a man told me that he'd heard I'd been caught by the most famous husband hunter in New York. Well, between these two things I went half crazy. I came into town to see you and call it off – got as far as the Biltmore entrance and didn't dare. I started wandering down Fifth Avenue like a wild man, and then I met Kelly. I told him the whole story – and within an hour we'd hatched up this ghastly plan. It was his plan – all the details. His histrionic instinct got the better of him and he had me thinking it was the kindest way out.'

'Finish,' commanded Myra crisply.

'Well, it went splendidly, we thought. Everything – the station meeting, the dinner scene, the scream in the night, the vaudeville – though I thought that was a little too much—until—until— Oh, Myra, when you fainted under that picture and I held you there in my arms, helpless as a baby, I knew I loved you. I was sorry then, Myra.'

There was a long pause while she sat motionless, her hands still clasping her knees – then he burst out with a wild plea of passionate sincerity.

'Myra!' he cried. 'If by any possible chance you can bring yourself to forgive and forget I'll marry you when you say, let my family go to the devil, and love you all my life.'

For a long while she considered, and Knowleton rose and began pacing nervously up and down the aisle of bare bushes, his hands in his pockets, his tired eyes pathetic now, and full of dull appeal. And then she came to a decision.

'You're perfectly sure?' she asked calmly.

'Yes.'

'Very well, I'll marry you today.'

With her words the atmosphere cleared and his troubles seemed to fall from him like a ragged cloak. An Indian summer sun drifted out from behind the grey clouds and the dry bushes rustled gently in the breeze.

'It was a bad mistake,' she continued, 'but if you're sure you love me now, that's the main thing. We'll go to town this morning, get a licence, and

I'll call up my cousin, who's a minister in the First Presbyterian Church. We can go West tonight.'

'Myra!' he cried jubilantly. 'You're a marvel and I'm not fit to tie your shoe strings. I'm going to make up to you for this, darling girl.'

And taking her supple body in his arms he covered her face with kisses.

The next two hours passed in a whirl. Myra went to the telephone and called her cousin, and then rushed upstairs to pack. When she came down a shining roadster was waiting miraculously in the drive and by ten o'clock they were bowling happily towards the city.

They stopped for a few minutes at the City Hall and again at the jeweller's, and then they were in the house of the Reverend Walter Gregory on Sixty-ninth Street, where a sanctimonious gentleman with twinkling eyes and a slight stutter received them cordially and urged them to a breakfast of bacon and eggs before the ceremony.

On the way to the station they stopped only long enough to wire Knowleton's father, and then they were sitting in their compartment on the Broadway Limited.

'Darn!' exclaimed Myra. 'I forgot my bag. Left it at Cousin Walter's in the excitement.'

'Never mind. We can get a whole new outfit in Chicago.'

She glanced at her wrist watch.

'I've got time to telephone him to send it on.'

She rose.

'Don't be long, dear.'

She leaned down and kissed his forehead.

'You know I couldn't. Two minutes, honey.'

Outside Myra ran swiftly along the platform and up the steel stairs to the great waiting room, where a man met her – a twinkly-eyed man with a slight stutter.

'How d-did it go, M-myra?'

'Fine! Oh, Walter, you were splendid! I almost wish you'd join the ministry so you could officiate when I do get married.'

'Well – I r-rehearsed for half an hour after I g-got your telephone call.'

'Wish we'd had more time. I'd have had him lease an apartment and buy furniture.'

'H'm,' chuckled Walter. 'Wonder how far he'll go on his honeymoon.'

'Oh, he'll think I'm on the train till he gets to Elizabeth.' She shook her little fist at the great contour of the marble dome. 'Oh, he's getting off too easy – far too easy!'

'I haven't f-figured out what the f-fellow did to you, M-myra.'

'You never will, I hope.'

They had reached the side drive and he hailed her a taxicab.

'You're an angel!' beamed Myra. 'And I can't thank you enough.'

'Well, any time I can be of use t-to you— By the way, what are you going to do with all the rings?'

Myra looked laughingly at her hand.

'That's the question,' she said. 'I may send them to Lady Helena Something-or-Other – and – well, I've always had a strong penchant for souvenirs. Tell the driver "Biltmore", Walter.'

TWO FOR A CENT

Metropolitan, April 1922

'*Two For a Cent*' *was written at White Bear Lake, Minnesota, in September 1921 while the Fitzgeralds were awaiting the birth of their child. It was a measure of Fitzgerald's popularity as a magazinist that* Metropolitan (*which serialized* The Beautiful and the Damned) *had signed him to an option on his story output at $900 per story at a time when the* Saturday Evening Post *was paying him $500. Four of his stories appeared in* Metropolitan *before it went into receivership.*

Fitzgerald explained to Harold Ober in November: '*I am not very fond of* Two for a Penny. *It is a fair story with an O. Henry twist but it is neither 1st class nor popular because it has no love interest. My heart wasn't in it so I know it lacks vitality. Perhaps you'd better return it to me so I can fix it up.*' *Revision was not necessary, and it became one of his most popular stories. It was included in* The Best Stories of 1922; *it was syndicated by the Metropolitan Newspaper Service; and it brought what appears to have been Fitzgerald's first textbook appearance, in* Short Stories for Class Reading (1925).

'*Two For a Cent*' *was the first of Fitzgerald's stories in which successful men make pilgrimages to their home towns (see* '*John Jackson's Arcady*' *and* '*Diagnosis*' *in this collection), seeking their personal identities. It is noteworthy that Fitzgerald, a Midwesterner, wrote so much about the South – including* '*The Ice Palace,*' '*The Jelly Bean*', '*The Dance*', '*Family in the Wind*', *and* '*The Last of the Belles*'. *The South was associated with his own love story; nevertheless Fitzgerald was ambivalent about it – seeing it both as a place of romance and as a land in which the climate saps vitality. In 1940 he commented to his daughter:* '*It is a grotesquely pictorial country as I found out long ago, and as Mr Faulkner has since abundantly demonstrated.*'

When the rain was over the sky became yellow in the west and the air was cool. Close to the street, which was of red dirt and lined with cheap bungalows dating from 1910, a little boy was riding a big bicycle along the sidewalk. His plan afforded a monotonous fascination. He rode each time for about a hundred yards, dismounted, turned the bicycle around so that it adjoined a stone step and getting on again, not without toil or heat, retraced his course. At one end this was bounded by a coloured girl of fourteen holding an anaemic baby, and at the other by a scarred, ill-nourished kitten, squatting dismally on the kerb. These four were the only souls in sight.

The little boy had accomplished an indefinite number of trips oblivious alike to the melancholy advances of the kitten at one end and the the admiring vacuousness of the coloured girl at the other when he swerved dangerously to avoid a man who had turned the corner into the street and recovered his balance only after a moment of exaggerated panic.

But if the incident was a matter of gravity to the boy, it attracted scarcely an instant's notice from the newcomer, who turned suddenly from the sidewalk and stared with obvious and peculiar interest at the house before which he was standing. It was the oldest house in the street, built with clapboards and a shingled roof. It was a *house* – in the barest sense of the word: the sort of house that a child would draw on a blackboard. It was of a period, but of no design, and its exterior had obviously been made only as a decent cloak for what was within. It antedated the stucco bungalows by about thirty years and except for the bungalows, which were reproducing their species with prodigious avidity as though by some monstrous affiliation with the guinea-pig, it was the most common type of house in the country. For thirty years such dwellings had satisfied the canons of the middle class; they had satisfied its financial canons by being cheap, they had satisfied its aesthetic canons by being hideous. It was a house built by a race whose more energetic complement hoped either to move up or move on, and it was the more remarkable that its instability had survived so many summers and retained its pristine hideousness and discomfort so obviously unimpaired.

The man was about as old as the house, that is to say, about forty-five. But unlike the house, he was neither hideous nor cheap. His clothes were too good to have been made outside of a metropolis – moreover, they were so good that it was impossible to tell in which metropolis they were made. His name was Abercrombie and the most important event of his life had taken place in the house before which he was standing. He had been born there.

It was one of the last places in the world where he should have been born.

He had thought so within a very few years after the event and he thought so now – an ugly home in a third-rate southern town where his father had owned a partnership in a grocery store. Since then Abercrombie had played golf with the President of the United States and sat between two duchesses at dinner. He had been bored with the President, he had been bored and not a little embarrassed with the duchesses – nevertheless, the two incidents had pleased him and still sat softly upon his naive vanity. It delighted him that he had gone far.

He looked fixedly at the house for several minutes before he perceived that no one lived there. Where the shutters were not closed it was because there were no shutters to be closed and in these vacancies, blind vacuous expanses of grey window looked unseeingly down at him. The grass had grown wantonly long in the yard and faint green moustaches were sprouting facetiously in the wide cracks of the walk. But it was evident that the property had been recently occupied for upon the porch lay half a dozen newspapers rolled into cylinders for quick delivery and as yet turned only to a faint resentful yellow.

They were not nearly so yellow as the sky when Abercrombie walked up on the porch and sat down upon an immemorial bench, for the sky was every shade of yellow, the colour of tan, the colour of gold, the colour of peaches. Across the street and beyond a vacant lot rose a rampart of vivid red brick houses and it seemed to Abercrombie that the picture they rounded out was beautiful – the warm earthy brick and the sky fresh after the rain, changing and grey as a dream. All his life when he had wanted to rest his mind he had called up into it the image those two things had made for him when the air was clear just at this hour. So Abercrombie sat there thinking about his young days.

Ten minutes later another man turned the corner of the street, a different sort of man, both in the texture of his clothes and the texture of his soul. He was forty-six years old and he was a shabby drudge, married to a woman who, as a girl, had known better days. This latter fact, in the republic, may be set down in the red italics of misery.

His name was Hemmick – Henry W. or George D. or John F. – the stock that produced him had had little imagination left to waste either upon his name or his design. He was a clerk in a factory which made ice for the long southern summer. He was responsible to the man who owned the patent for canning ice, who, in his turn was responsible only to God. Never in his life had Henry W. Hemmick discovered a new way to advertise canned ice nor had it transpired that by taking a diligent correspondence course in ice canning he had secretly been preparing himself for a partnership. Never had he rushed home to his wife, crying: 'You can have that servant now, Nell, I have been made General Superintendent.' You will have to take him as you took Abercrombie, for what he is and will always be. This is a story of the dead years.

When the second man reached the house he turned in and began to mount the tipsy steps, noticed Abercrombie, the stranger, with a tired surprise, and nodded to him.

'Good evening,' he said.

Abercrombie voiced his agreement with the sentiment.

'Cool' – The newcomer covered his forefinger with his handkerchief and sent the swatched digit on a complete circuit of his collar band. 'Have you rented this?' he asked.

'No, indeed, I'm just – resting. Sorry if I've intruded – I saw the house was vacant—'

'Oh, you're not intruding!' said Hemmick hastily. 'I don't reckon anybody *could* intrude in this old barn. I got out two months ago. They're not ever goin' to rent it any more. I got a little girl about this high –' he held his hand parallel to the ground and at an indeterminate distance '– and she's mighty fond of an old doll that got left here when we moved. Began hollerin' for me to come over and look it up.'

'You used to live here?' inquired Abercrombie with interest.

'Lived here eighteen years. Came here'n I was married, raised four children in this house. Yes, *sir*. I know this old fellow.' He struck the doorpost with the flat of his hand. 'I know every leak in her roof and every loose board in her old floor.'

Abercrombie had been good to look at for so many years that he knew if he kept a certain attentive expression on his face his companion would continue to talk – indefinitely.

'You from up North?' inquired Hemmick politely, choosing with habituated precision the one spot where the anaemic wooden railing would support his weight. 'I thought so,' he resumed at Abercrombie's nod. 'Don't take long to tell a Yankee.'

'I'm from New York.'

'So?' The man shook his head with inappropriate gravity. 'Never have got up there, myself. Started to go a couple of times, before I was married, but never did get to go.'

He made a second excursion with his finger and handkerchief and then, as though having come suddenly to a cordial decision, he replaced the handkerchief in one of his bumpy pockets and extended the hand towards his companion.

'My name's Hemmick.'

'Glad to know you.' Abercrombie took the hand without rising. 'Abercrombie's mine.'

'I'm mighty glad to know you, Mr Abercrombie.'

Then for a moment they both hesitated, their two faces assumed oddly similar expressions, their eyebrows drew together, their eyes looked far away. Each was straining to force into activity some minute cell long sealed and forgotten in his brain. Each made a little noise in his throat, looked away, looked back, laughed. Abercrombie spoke first.

'We've met.'

'I know,' agreed Hemmick, 'but whereabouts? That's what's got me. You from New York you say?'

'Yes, but I was born and raised in this town. Lived in this house till I left here when I was about seventeen. As a matter of fact, I remember you – you were a couple of years older.'

'Well,' he said vaguely, 'I sort of remember, too. I *begin* to remember – I got your name all right and I guess maybe it was your daddy had this house before I rented it. But all I can recollect about you is, that there was a boy named Abercrombie and he went away.'

In a few moments they were talking easily. It amused them both to have come from the same house – amused Abercrombie especially, for he was a vain man, rather absorbed, that evening, in his own early poverty. Though he was not given to immature impulses, he found it necessary somehow to make it clear in a few sentences that five years after he had gone away from the house and the town he had been able to send for his father and mother to join him in New York.

Hemmick listened with that exaggerated attention which men who have not prospered generally render to men who have. He would have continued to listen had Abercrombie become more expansive, for he was beginning faintly to associate him with an Abercrombie who had figured in the newspapers for several years at the head of shipping boards and financial committees. But Abercrombie, after a moment, made the conversation less personal.

'I didn't realize you had so much heat here, I guess I've forgotten a lot in twenty-five years.'

'Why, this is a *cool* day,' boasted Hemmick, 'this is *cool*. I was just sort of overheated from walking when I came up.'

'It's too hot,' insisted Abercrombie with a restless movement; then he added abruptly, 'I don't like it here. It means nothing to me – nothing – I've wondered if it did, you know, that's why I came down. And I've decided.'

'You see,' he continued hesitantly, 'up to recently the North was still full of professional southerns, some real, some by sentiment, but all given to flowery monologues on the beauty of their old family plantations and all jumping up and howling when the band played "Dixie". You know what I mean' – he turned to Hemmick – 'it got to be a sort of a national joke. Oh, I was in the game, too, I suppose, I used to stand up and perspire and cheer, and I've given young men positions for no particular reason except that they claimed to come from South Carolina or Virginia—' again he broke off and became suddenly abrupt – 'but I'm through, I've been here six hours and I'm through!'

'Too hot for you?' inquired Hemmick, with mild surprise.

'Yes! I've felt the heat and I've seen the men – those two or three dozen loafers standing in front of the stores on Jackson Street – in thatched straw hats' – then he added, with a touch of humour, 'they're what my son calls "slash-pocket, belted-back boys". Do you know the ones I mean?'

'Jelly-beans,' Hemmick nodded gravely, 'we call 'em jelly-beans. No-account lot of boys all right. They got signs up in front of most of the stores asking 'em to to stand there.'

'They ought to!' asserted Abercrombie, with a touch of irascibility. 'That's my picture of the South now, you know – a skinny, dark-haired young man with a gun on his hip and a stomach full of corn liquor or Dope Dola, leaning up against a drug store waiting for the next lynching.'

Hemmick objected, though with apology in his voice.

'You got to remember, Mr Abercrombie, that we haven't had the money down here since the war—'

Abercrombie waved this impatiently aside.

'Oh, I've heard all that,' he said, 'and I'm tired of it. And I've heard the South lambasted till I'm tired of that, too. It's not taking France and Germany fifty years to get on their feet, and their war made your war look like a little fracas up an alley. And it's not your fault and it's not anybody's fault . . .'*

Hemmick nodded, thoughtfully, though without thought. He had never thought; for over twenty years he had seldom ever held opinions, save the opinions of the local press, or of some majority made articulate through

*Forty-one words have been omitted.

passion. There was a certain luxury in thinking that he had never been able to afford. When cases were set before him he either accepted them outright if they were comprehensible to him or rejected them if they required a modicum of concentration. Yet he was not a stupid man. He was poor and busy and tired and there were no ideas at large in his community, even had he been capable of grasping them. The idea that he did not think would have been equally incomprehensible to him. He was a closed book, half full of badly printed, uncorrelated trash.

Just now, his reaction to Abercrombie's assertion was exceedingly simple. Since the remarks proceeded from a man who was a southerner by birth, who was successful – moreover, who was confident and decisive and persuasive and suave – he was inclined to accept them without suspicion or resentment.

He took one of Abercrombie's cigars and pulling on it, still with a stern imitation of profundity upon his tired face, watched the colour glide out of the sky and the grey veils come down. The little boy and his bicycle, the baby, the nursemaid, the forlorn kitten, all had departed. In the stucco bungalows pianos gave out hot weary notes that inspired the crickets to competitive sound, and squeaky gramophones filled in the intervals with patches of whining ragtime until the impression was created that each living room in the street opened directly out into the darkness.

'What *I* want to find out,' Abercrombie was saying with a frown, 'is why I didn't have sense enough to *know* that this was a worthless town. It was entirely an accident that I left here, an utterly blind chance, and as it happened, the very train that took me away was full of luck for me. The man I sat beside gave me my start in life.' His tone became resentful. 'But I thought this was all right. I'd have stayed except that I'd gotten into a scrape down at the High School – I got expelled and my daddy told me he didn't want me at home any more. Why didn't I know the place wasn't any good? Why didn't I *see*?'

'Well, you'd probably never known anything better?' suggested Hemmick mildly.

'That wasn't any excuse,' insisted Abercrombie. 'If I'd been any good I'd have known. As a matter of fact – as – a – matter – of – fact,' he repeated slowly, 'I think that at heart I was the sort of boy who'd have lived and died here happily and never known there was anything better.' He turned to Hemmick with a look almost of distress. 'It worries me to think that my – that what's happened to me can be ascribed to chance. But that's the sort of boy I think I was. I didn't start off with the Dick Whittington idea – I started off by accident.'

After this confession, he stared out into the twilight with a dejected expression that Hemmick could not understand. It was impossible for the latter to share any sense of the importance of such a distinction – in fact from a man of Abercrombie's position it struck him as unnecessarily trivial. Still he felt that some manifestation of acquiescence was only polite.

'Well,' he offered, 'it's just that some boys get the bee to get up and go North and some boys don't. I happened to have the bee to go North. But I didn't. That's the difference between you and me.'

Abercrombie turned to him intently.

'You did?' he asked, with unexpected interest, 'you wanted to get out?'

'At one time.' At Abercrombie's eagerness Hemmick began to attach a new importance to the subject. 'At one time,' he repeated, as though the singleness of the occasion was a thing he had often mused upon.

'How old were you?'

'Oh – 'bout twenty.'

'What put it into your head?'

'Well let me see – ' Hemmick considered '– I don't know whether I remember sure enough but it seems to me that when I was down to the university – I was there two years – one of the professors told me that a smart boy ought to go North. He said, business wasn't going to amount to much down here for the next fifty years. And I guessed he was right. My father died about then, so I got a job as runner in the bank here, and I didn't have much interest in anything except saving up enough money to go North. I was bound to go.'

'Why didn't you? Why didn't you?' insisted Abercrombie in an aggrieved tone.

'Well, ' Hemmick hesitated. 'Well, I right near did but – things didn't work out and I didn't get to go. It was a funny sort of business. It all started about the smallest thing you can think of. It all started about a penny.'

'A penny?'

'That's what did it – one little penny. That's why I didn't go 'way from here and all, like I intended.'

'Tell me about it, man,' exclaimed his companion. He looked at his watch impatiently. 'I'd like to hear the story.'

Hemmick sat for a moment, distorting his mouth around the cigar.

'Well, to begin with,' he said at length, 'I'm going to ask you if you remember a thing that happened here about twenty-five years ago. A fellow named Hoyt, the cashier of the Cotton National Bank, disappeared one night with about thirty thousand dollars, in cash. Say, man, they didn't talk about anything else down here at the time. The whole town was shaken up about it, and I reckin you can imagine the disturbance it caused down at all the banks and especially at the Cotton National.'

'I remember.'

'Well, they caught him, and they got most of the money back, and by and by the excitement died down, except in the bank where the thing had happened. Down there it seemed as if they'd never get used to it. Mr Deems, the first vice-president, who'd always been pretty kind and decent, got to be a changed man. He was suspicious of the clerks, the tellers, the janitor, the watchman, most of the officers, and yes, by Golly, I guess he got so he kept an eye on the president himself.

'I don't mean he was just watchful – he was downright hipped on the subject. He'd come up and ask you funny questions when you were going about your business. He'd walk into the teller's cage on tiptoe and watch him without saying anything. If there was any mistake of any kind in the book-keeping, he'd not only fire a clerk or so, but he'd raise such a riot that he made you want to push him into a vault and slam the door on him.

'He was just about running the bank then, and he'd affected the other officers, and – oh, you can imagine the havoc a thing like that could work on any sort of an organization. Everybody was so nervous that they made mistakes whether they were careful or not. Clerks were staying downtown until eleven at night trying to account for a lost nickel. It was a thin year, anyhow, and everything financial was pretty rickety, so one thing worked on another until the crowd of us were as near craziness as anybody can be and carry on the banking business at all.

'I was a runner – and all through the heat of one God-forsaken summer I ran. I ran and I got mighty little money for it, and that was the time I hated that bank and this town, and all I wanted was to get out and go North. I was getting ten dollars a week, and I'd decided that when I'd saved fifty out of it I was going down to the depot and buy me a ticket to Cincinnati. I had an uncle in the banking business there, and he said he'd give me an opportunity with him. But he never offered to pay my way, and I guess he thought if I was worth having I'd manage to get up there by myself. Well, maybe I wasn't worth having because, anyhow, I never did.

'One morning on the hottest day of the hottest July I ever knew – and you know what that means down here – I left the bank to call on a man named Harlan and collect some money that'd come due on a note. Harlan had the cash waiting for me all right, and when I counted it I found it amounted to three hundred dollars and eighty-six cents, the change being in brand new coin that Harlan had drawn from another bank that morning. I put the three one-hundred-dollar bills in my wallet and the change in my vest pocket, signed a receipt and left. I was going straight back to the bank.

'Outside the heat was terrible. It was enough to make you dizzy, and I hadn't been feeling right for a couple of days, so, while I waited in the shade for a street car, I was congratulating myself that in a month or so I'd be out of this and up where it was some cooler. And then as I stood there it occurred to me all of a sudden that outside of the money which I'd just collected, which, of course, I couldn't touch, I didn't have a cent in my pocket. I'd have to walk back to the bank, and it was about fifteen blocks away. You see, on the night before, I'd found that my change came to just a dollar, and I'd traded it for a bill at the corner store and added it to the roll in the bottom of my trunk. So there was no help for it – I took off my coat and I stuck my handkerchief into my collar and struck off through the suffocating heat for the bank.

'Fifteen blocks – you can imagine what that was like, and I was sick when I started. From away up by Juniper Street – you remember where that is: the new Mieger Hospital's there now – all the way down to Jackson. After about six blocks I began to stop and rest whenever I found a patch of shade wide enough to hold me, and as I got pretty near I could just keep going by thinking of the big glass of iced tea my mother'd have waiting beside my plate at lunch. But after that I began getting too sick to even want the iced tea – I wanted to get rid of that money and then lie down and die.

'When I was still about two blocks away from the bank I put my hand into my watch pocket and pulled out that change; was sort of jingling it in my hand; making myself believe that I was so close that it was convenient to have it ready. I happened to glance into my hand, and all of a sudden I stopped up short and reached down quick into my watch pocket. The pocket was empty. There was a little hole in the bottom, and my hand held only a half dollar, a quarter and a dime. I had lost one cent.

'Well, sir, I can't tell you, I can't express to you the feeling of discouragement that this gave me. One penny, mind you – but think: just the week before a runner had lost his job because he was a little bit shy twice. It was only carelessness; but there you were! They were all in a panic that they might get fired themselves, and the best thing to do was to fire someone else – first.

'So you can see that it was up to me to appear with that penny.

'Where I got the energy to care as much about it as I did is more than I can understand. I was sick and hot and weak as a kitten, but it never occurred to me that I could do anything except find or replace that penny, and immediately I began casting about for a way to do it. I looked into a couple of stores, hoping I'd see some one I knew, but while there were a few fellows loafing in front, just as you saw them today, there wasn't one that I felt like going up to and saying: "Here! You got a penny?" I thought of a couple of offices where I could have gotten it without much trouble, but they were some distance off, and besides being pretty dizzy, I hated to go out of my route when I was carrying bank money, because it looked kind of strange.

'So what should I do but commence walking back along the street towards the Union Depot where I last remembered having the penny. It was a brand new penny, and I thought maybe I'd see it shining where it dropped. So I kept walking, looking pretty carefully at the sidewalk and thinking what I'd better do. I laughed a little, because I felt sort of silly for worrying about a penny, but I didn't enjoy laughing, and it really didn't seem silly to me at all.

'Well, by and by I got back to the Union Depot without having either seen the old penny or having thought what was the best way to get another. I hated to go all the way home, 'cause we lived a long distance out; but what else was I to do? So I found a piece of shade close to the depot, and stood there considering, thinking first one thing and then another, and not getting anywhere at all. One little penny, just *one* – something almost any man in sight would have given me; something even the nigger baggage-smashers were jingling around in their pockets . . . I must have stood there about five minutes. I remember there was a line of about a dozen men in front of an army recruiting station they'd just opened, and a couple of them began to yell" Join the Army!" at me. That woke me up and I moved on back towards the bank, getting worried now, getting mixed up and sicker and sicker and knowing a million ways to find a penny and not one that seemed convenient or right. I was exaggerating the importance of losing it, and I was exaggerating the difficulty of finding another, but you just have to believe that it seemed about as important to me just then as though it were a hundred dollars.

'Then I saw a couple of men talking in front of Moody's soda place, and recognized one of them – Mr Burling – who'd been a friend of my father's. That was a relief, I can tell you. Before I knew it I was chattering to him so quick that he couldn't follow what I was getting at.

' "Now," he said, "you know I'm a little deaf and can't understand when you talk that fast! What is it you want, Harry? Tell me from the beginning."

' "Have you got any change with you?" I asked him just as loud as I dared. "I just want—" Then I stopped short; a man a few feet away had turned around and was looking at us. It was Mr Deems, the first vice-president of the Cotton National Bank.'

Hemmick paused, and it was still light enough for Abercrombie to see that he was shaking his head to and fro in a puzzled way. When he spoke his voice held a quality of pained surprise, a quality that it might have carried over twenty years.

'I never *could* understand what it was that came over me then. I must have been sort of crazy with the heat – that's all I can decide. Instead of just saying "Howdy" to Mr Deems, in a natural way, and telling Mr Burling I wanted to borrow a nickel for tobacco, because I'd left my purse at home, I turned away quick as a flash and began walking up the street at a great rate, feeling like a criminal who had come near being caught.

'Before I'd gone a block I was sorry. I could almost hear the conversation that must've been taking place between those two men:

' "What do you reckon's the matter with that young man?" Mr Burling would say without meaning any harm. "Came up to me all excited and wanted to know if I had any money, and then he saw you and rushed away like he was crazy."

'And I could almost see Mr Deems' big eyes getting narrow with suspicion and watch him twist up his trousers and come strolling along after me. I was in a real panic now, and no mistake. Suddenly I saw a one-horse surrey going by, and recognized Bill Kennedy, a friend of mine, driving it. I yelled at him, but he didn't hear me. Then I yelled again, but he didn't pay any attention, so I started after him at a run, swaying from side to side, I guess, like I was drunk, and calling his name every few minutes. He looked around once, but he didn't see me; he kept right on going and turned out of sight at the next corner. I stopped then because I was too weak to go any further. I was just about to sit down on the curb and rest when I looked around, and the first thing I saw was Mr Deems walking after me as fast as he could come. There wasn't any of my imagination about it this time – the look in his eyes showed he wanted to know what was the matter with *me*!

'Well, that's about all I remember clearly until about twenty minutes later, when I was at home trying to unlock my trunk with fingers that were trembling like a tuning fork. Before I could get it open, Mr Deems and a policeman came in. I began talking all at once about not being a thief and trying to tell them what had happened, but I guess I was sort of hysterical, and the more I said the worse matters were. When I managed to get the story out it seemed sort of crazy, even to me – and it was true – it was true, true as I've told you – every word! – that one penny that I lost somewhere down by the station—' Hemmick broke off and began laughing grotesquely – as though the excitement that had come over him as he finished his tale was a weakness of which he was ashamed. When he resumed it was with an affectation of nonchalance.

'I'm not going into the details of what happened because nothing much did – at least not on the scale you judge events by up North. It cost me my job, and I changed a good name for a bad one. Somebody tattled and somebody lied, and the impression got around that I'd lost a lot of the bank's money and had been tryin' to cover it up.

'I had an awful time getting a job after that. Finally I got a statement out of the bank that contradicted the wildest of the stories that had started, but the people who were still interested said it was just because the bank didn't want any fuss or scandal – and the rest had forgotten: that is they'd forgotten what had happened, but they remembered that somehow I just wasn't a young fellow to be trusted—'

Hemmick paused and laughed again, still without enjoyment, but bitterly, uncomprehendingly, and with a profound helplessness.

'So, you see, that's why I didn't go to Cincinnati,' he said slowly; 'my mother was alive then, and this was a pretty bad blow to her. She had an idea – one of those old-fashioned southern ideas that stick in people's heads down here – that somehow I ought to stay here in town and prove myself honest. She had it on her mind, and she wouldn't hear of my going. She said that the day I went'd be the day she'd die. So I sort of had to stay till I'd got back my – my reputation.'

'How long did that take?' asked Abercrombie quietly.

'About – ten years.'

'Oh—'

'Ten years,' repeated Hemmick, staring out into the gathering darkness. 'This is a little town you see: I say ten years because it was about ten years when the last reference to it came to my ears. But I was married long before that; had a kid. Cincinnati was out of my mind by that time.'

'Of course,' agreed Abercrombie.

They were both silent for a moment – then Hemmick added apologetically:

'That was sort of a long story, and I don't know if it could have interested you much. But you asked me—'

'It *did* interest me,' answered Abercrombie politely. 'It interested me tremendously. It interested me much more than I thought it would.'

It occurred to Hemmick that he himself had never realized what a curious, rounded tale it was. He saw dimly now that what had seemed to him only a fragment, a grotesque interlude was really significant, complete. It was an interesting story; it was a story upon which turned the failure of his life. Abercrombie's voice broke in upon his thoughts.

'You see, it's so different from my story,' Abercrombie was saying. 'It was an accident that you stayed – and it was an accident that I went away. You deserve more actual – actual credit, if there is such a thing in the world, for your intention of getting out and getting on. You see, I'd more or less gone wrong at seventeen. I was – well, what you call a jelly-bean. All I wanted was to take it easy through life – and one day I just happened to see a sign up above my head that had on it: "Special rate to Atlanta, three dollars and forty-two cents." So I took out my change and counted it—'

Hemmick nodded. Still absorbed in his own story, he had forgotten the importance, the comparative magnificence of Abercrombie. Then suddenly he found himself listening sharply:

'I had just three dollars and forty-one cents in my pocket. But, you see, I was standing in line with a lot of other young fellows down by the Union Depot about to enlist in the army for three years. And I saw that extra penny on the walk not three feet away. I saw it because it was brand new and shining in the sun like gold.'

The Alabama night had settled over the street, and as the blue drew down upon the dust the outlines of the two men had become less distinct, so that it was not easy for anyone who passed along the walk to tell that one of these men was of the few and the other of no importance. All the detail was gone – Abercrombie's fine gold wrist watch, his collar, that he ordered by the dozen from London, the dignity that sat upon him in his chair – all faded and were engulfed with Hemmick's awkward suit and preposterous humped shoes into that pervasive depth of night that, like death, made nothing matter, nothing differentiate, nothing remain. And a little later on a passer-by saw only the two glowing discs about the size of a penny that marked the rise and fall of their cigars.

DICE, BRASSKNUCKLES AND GUITAR

Hearst's International, May 1923*

'Dice, Brassknuckles & Guitar' was written in Great Neck, Long Island, in January 1923. The Fitzgeralds had moved East from St Paul in October 1922 because they missed New York and because he wanted to be near Broadway for the production of his ill-starred comedy, The Vegetable. *'Dice' was the first story submitted under an option with the Hearst magazines for his 1923 story output.* International *paid $1500 for it – a $600 increase over what* Metropolitan *had paid Fitzgerald the year before. The story was printed with the headline 'A Typical Fitzgerald Story'.*

'Dice' is one of the Gatsby *cluster of stories written in 1922–3 in which Fitzgerald can be seen trying out material that would be developed in the novel, written in 1924. Although treated comically, the subject of 'Dice' is the familiar Fitzgerald theme of the hardness of the rich. Amanthis's comment to the outsider – 'You're better than all of them put together, Jim' – prefigures Nick Carraway's recognition that Gatsby is 'worth the whole damm bunch put together.' Another recurring Fitzgerald theme in 'Dice' is the cultural conflict between the South and the North.*

Parts of New Jersey, as you know, are under water, and other parts are under continual surveillance by the authorities. But here and there lie patches of garden country dotted with old-fashioned frame mansions, which have wide shady porches and a red swing on the lawn. And perhaps, on the widest and shadiest of the porches there is even a hammock left over from the hammock days, stirring gently in a mid-Victorian wind.

When tourists come to such last-century landmarks they stop their cars and gaze for a while and then mutter: 'Well, thank God this age is joined

*'Dice, Brassknuckles & Guitar' is the only story in this volume which has appeared in a collection. It was added to the paperback edition of *Bits of Paradise* (New York: Pocket Books, 1976).

on to *something*,' or else they say: 'Well, of course, that house is mostly halls and has a thousand rats and one bathroom, but there's an atmosphere about it—'

The tourist doesn't stay long. He drives on to his Elizabethan villa of pressed cardboard or his early Norman meat-market or his medieval Italian pigeon-coop – because this is the twentieth century and Victorian houses are as unfashionable as the works of Mrs Humphry Ward.

He can't see the hammock from the road – but sometimes there's a girl in the hammock. There was this afternoon. She was asleep in it and apparently unaware of the aesthetic horrors which surrounded her, the stone statue of Diana, for instance, which grinned idiotically under the sunlight on the lawn.

There was something enormously yellow about the whole scene – there was this sunlight, for instance, that was yellow, and the hammock was of the particularly hideous yellow peculiar to hammocks, and the girl's yellow hair was spread out upon the hammock in a sort of invidious comparison.

She slept with her lips closed and her hands clasped behind her head, as it is proper for young girls to sleep. Her breast rose and fell slightly with no more emphasis than the sway of the hammock's fringe.

Her name, Amanthis, was as old-fashioned as the house she lived in. I regret to say her mid-Victorian connections ceased abruptly at this point.

Now if this were a moving picture (as, of course, I hope it will some day be) I would take as many thousand feet of her as I was allowed – then I would move the camera up close and show the yellow down on the back of her neck where her hair stopped and the warm colour of her cheeks and arms, because I like to think of her sleeping there, as you yourself might have slept, back in your young days. Then I would hire a man named Israel Glucose to write some idiotic line of transition, and switch thereby to another scene that was taking place at no particular spot far down the road.

In a moving automobile sat a southern gentleman accompanied by his body-servant. He was on his way, after a fashion, to New York but he was somewhat hampered by the fact that the upper and lower portions of his automobile were no longer in exact juxtaposition. In fact from time to time the two riders would dismount, shove the body on to the chassis, corner to corner, and then continue onward, vibrating slightly in involuntary unison with the motor.

Except that it had no door in back the car might have been built early in the mechanical age. It was covered with the mud of eight states and adorned in front by an enormous but defunct motometer and behind by a mangy pennant bearing the legend 'Tarleton, Ga.' In the dim past someone had begun to paint the hood yellow but unfortunately had been called away when but half through the task.

As the gentleman and his body-servant were passing the house where Amanthis lay beautifully asleep in the hammock, something happened – the body fell off the car. My only apology for stating this so suddenly is that it happened very suddenly indeed. When the noise had died down and the dust had drifted away master and man arose and inspected the two halves.

'Look-a-there,' said the gentleman in disgust, 'the doggone thing got all separated that time.'

'She bust in two,' agreed the body-servant.

'Hugo,' said the gentleman, after some consideration, 'we got to get a hammer an' nails an' *tack* it on.'

They glanced up at the Victorian house. On all sides faintly irregular fields stretched away to a faintly irregular unpopulated horizon. There was no choice, so the black Hugo opened the gate and followed his master up a gravel walk, casting only the blasé glances of a confirmed traveller at the red swing and the stone statue of Diana which turned on them a storm-crazed stare.

At the exact moment when they reached the porch Amanthis awoke, sat up suddenly and looked them over.

The gentleman was young, perhaps twenty-four, and his name was Jim Powell. He was dressed in a tight and dusty ready-made suit which was evidently expected to take flight at a moment's notice, for it was secured to his body by a line of six preposterous buttons.

There were supernumerary buttons upon the coat-sleeves also and Amanthis could not resist a glance to determine whether or not more buttons ran up the side of his trouser leg. But the trouser bottoms were distinguished only by their shape, which was that of a bell. His vest was cut low, barely restraining an amazing necktie from fluttering in the wind.

He bowed formally, dusting his knees with a thatched straw hat. Simultaneously he smiled, half shutting his faded blue eyes and displaying white and beautifully symmetrical teeth.

'Good evenin',' he said in abandoned Georgian. 'My automobile has met with an accident out yonder by your gate. I wondered if it wouldn't be too much to ask you if I could have the use of a hammer and some tacks – nails, for a little while.'

Amanthis laughed. For a moment she laughed uncontrollably. Mr Jim

Powell laughed, politely and appreciatively, with her. His body-servant, deep in the throes of coloured adolescence, alone preserved a dignified gravity.

'I better introduce who I am, maybe,' said the visitor. 'My name's Powell. I'm a resident of Tarleton, Georgia. This here nigger's my boy, Hugo.'

'Your *son*!' The girl stared from one to the other in wild fascination.

'No, he's my body-servant, I guess you'd call it. We call a nigger a boy down yonder.'

At this reference to the finer customs of his native soil the boy Hugo put his hands behind his back and looked darkly and superciliously down the lawn.

'Yas'm,' he muttered, 'I'm a body-servant.'

'Where you going in your automobile,' demanded Amanthis.

'Goin' north for the summer.'

'Where to?'

The tourist waved his hand with a careless gesture as if to indicate the Adirondacks, the Thousand Islands, Newport – but he said:

'We're tryin' New York.'

'Have you ever been there before?'

'Never have. But I been to Atlanta lots of times. An' we passed through all kinds of cities this trip. Man!'

He whistled to express the enormous spectacularity of his recent travels.

'Listen,' said Amanthis intently, 'you better have something to eat. Tell your – your body-servant to go 'round in back and ask the cook to send us out some sandwiches and lemonade. Or maybe you don't drink lemonade – very few people do any more.'

Mr Powell by a circular motion of his finger sped Hugo on the designated mission. Then he seated himself gingerly in a rocking-chair and began revolving his thatched straw hat rapidly in his hands.

'You cer'nly are mighty kind,' he told her. 'An' if I wanted anything stronger than lemonade I got a bottle of good old corn out in the car. I brought it along because I thought maybe I wouldn't be able to drink the whisky they got up here.'

'Listen,' she said, 'my name's Powell too. Amanthis Powell.'

'Say, is that right?' He laughed ecstatically. 'Maybe we're kin to each other. I come from mighty good people,' he went on. 'Pore though. I got some money because my aunt she was using it to keep her in a sanitarium and she died.' He paused, presumably out of respect to his late aunt. Then he concluded with brisk nonchalance, 'I ain't touched the principal but I got a lot of the income all at once so I thought I'd come north for the summer.'

At this point Hugo reappeared on the veranda steps and became audible.

'White lady back there she asked me don't I want eat some too. What I tell her?'

'You tell her yes ma'am if she be so kind,' directed his master. And as Hugo retired he confided to Amanthis: 'That boy's got no sense at all. He don't want to do nothing without I tell him he can. I brought him up,' he added, not without pride.

When the sandwiches arrived Mr Powell stood up. He was unaccustomed to white servants and obviously expected an introduction.

'Are you a married lady?' he inquired of Amanthis, when the servant was gone.

'No,' she answered, and added from the security of eighteen, 'I'm an old maid.'

Again he laughed politely.

'You mean you're a society girl.'

She shook her head. Mr Powell noted with embarrassed enthusiasm the particular yellowness of her yellow hair.

'Does this old place look like it?' she said cheerfully. 'No, you perceive in me a daughter of the countryside. Colour – one hundred per cent spontaneous – in the daytime anyhow. Suitors – promising young barbers from the neighbouring village with somebody's late hair still clinging to their coat-sleeves.'

'Your daddy oughtn't to let you go with a country barber,' said the tourist disapprovingly. He considered – 'You ought to be a New York society girl.'

'No.' Amanthis shook her head sadly. 'I'm too good-looking. To be a New York society girl you have to have a long nose and projecting teeth and dress like the actresses did three years ago.'

Jim began to tap his foot rhythmically on the porch and in a moment Amanthis discovered that she was unconsciously doing the same thing.

'Stop!' she commanded, 'Don't make me do that.'

He looked down at his foot.

'Excuse me,' he said humbly. 'I don't know – it's just something I do.'

This intense discussion was now interrupted by Hugo who appeared on the steps bearing a hammer and a handful of nails.

Mr Powell arose unwillingly and looked at his watch.

'We got to go, daggone it,' he said, frowning heavily. 'See here. Wouldn't you *like* to be a New York society girl and go to those dances an' all, like you read about, where they throw gold pieces away ?'

She looked at him with a curious expression.

'Don't your folks know some society people ?' he went on.

'All I've got's my daddy – and, you see, he's a judge.'

'That's too bad,' he agreed.

She got herself by some means from the hammock and they went down towards the road, side by side.

'Well, I'll keep my eyes open for you and let you know,' he persisted. 'A pretty girl like you ought to go around in society. We may be kin to each other, you see, and us Powells ought to stick together.'

'What are you going to do in New York ?'

They were now almost at the gate and the tourist pointed to the two depressing sectors of his automobile.

'I'm goin' to drive a taxi. This one right here. Only it's got so it busts in two all the time.'

'You're going to drive *that* in New York ?'

Jim looked at her uncertainly. Such a pretty girl should certainly control the habit of shaking all over upon no provocation at all.

'Yes ma'am,' he said with dignity.

Amanthis watched while they placed the upper half of the car upon the lower half and nailed it severely into place. Then Mr Powell took the wheel and his body-servant climbed in beside him.

'I'm cer'nly very much obliged to you indeed for your hospitality. Convey my respects to your father.'

'I will,' she assured him. 'Come back and see me, if you don't mind barbers in the room.'

He dismissed this unpleasant thought with a gesture.

'Your company would always be charming,' He put the car into gear as though to drown out the temerity of his parting speech. 'You're the prettiest girl I've seen up North – by far.'

Then with a groan and a rattle Mr Powell of Southern Georgia with his own car and his own body-servant and his own ambitions and his own private cloud of dust continued on north for the summer.

She thought she would never see him again. She lay in her hammock, slim and beautiful, opened her left eye slightly to see June come in and then closed it and retired contentedly back into her dreams.

But one day when the midsummer vines had climbed the precarious sides of the red swing on the lawn, Mr Jim Powell of Tarleton, Georgia, came vibrating back into her life. They sat on the wide porch as before.

'I've got a great scheme,' he told her.

'Did you drive your taxi like you said?'

'Yes ma'am, but the business was right bad. I waited around in front of all those hotels and theaters an' nobody ever got in.'

'Nobody?'

'Well, one night there was some drunk fellas they got in, only just as I was gettin' started my automobile came apart. And another night it was rainin' and there wasn't no other taxis and a lady got in because she said she had to go a long ways. But before we got there she made me stop and she got out. She seemed kinda mad and she went walkin' off in the rain. Mighty proud lot of people they got up in New York.'

'And so you're going home?' asked Amanthis sympathetically.

'No *ma'am*. I got an idea.' His blue eyes grew narrow. 'Has that barber been around here – with hair on his sleeves?'

'No. He's – he's gone away.'

'Well, then, first thing is I want to leave this car of mine here with you, if that's all right. It ain't the right colour for a taxi. To pay for its keep I'd like to have you drive it as much as you want. Long as you got a hammer an' nails with you there ain't much bad that can happen—'

'I'll take care of it,' interrupted Amanthis, 'but where are *you* going?'

'Southampton. It's about the most aristocratic watering trough – watering-place there is around here, so that's where I'm going.'

She sat up in amazement.

'What are you going to do there?'

'Listen.' He leaned towards her confidentially. 'Were you serious about wanting to be a New York society girl?'

'Deadly serious.'

'That's all I wanted to know,' he said inscrutably. 'You just wait here on this porch a couple of weeks and – and sleep. And if any barbers come to see you with hair on their sleeves you tell 'em you're too sleepy to see 'em.'

'What then?'

'Then you'll hear from me. Just tell your old daddy he can do all the judging he wants but you're goin' to do some *dancin'*. Ma'am,' he continued decisively, 'you talk about society! Before one month I'm goin' to have you in more society than you ever saw.'

Further than this he would say nothing. His manner conveyed that she was going to be suspended over a perfect pool of gaiety and violently immersed, to an accompaniment of: 'Is it gay enough for you, ma'am? Shall I let in a little more excitement, ma'am?'

'Well,' answered Amanthis lazily considering, 'there are few things for which I'd forego the luxury of sleeping through July and August – but if you'll write me a letter I'll – I'll run up to Southampton'.

Jim snapped his fingers ecstatically.

'More society,' he assured her with all the confidence at his command, 'than anybody ever saw.'

Three days later a young man wearing a straw hat that might have been cut from the thatched roof of an English cottage rang the doorbell of the enormous and astounding Madison Harlan house at Southampton. He asked the butler if there were any people in the house between the ages of sixteen and twenty. He was informed that Miss Genevieve Harlan and Mr Ronald Harlan answered that description and thereupon he handed in a most peculiar card and requested in fetching Georgian that it be brought to their attention.

As a result he was closeted for almost an hour with Mr Ronald Harlan (who was a student at the Hillkiss School) and Miss Genevieve Harlan (who was not uncelebrated at Southampton dances). When he left he bore a short note in Miss Harlan's handwriting which he presented together with his peculiar card at the next large estate. It happened to be that of the Clifton Garneaus. Here, as if by magic, the same audience was granted him.

He went on – it was a hot day, and men who could not afford to do so were carrying their coats on the public highway, but Jim, a native of southernmost Georgia, was as fresh and cool at the last house as at the first. He visited ten houses that day. Anyone following him in his course might have taken him to be some curiously gifted book-agent with a much sought-after volume as his stock in trade.

There was something in his unexpected demand for the adolescent members of the family which made hardened butlers lose their critical acumen. As he left each house a close observer might have seen that fascinated eyes followed him to the door and excited voices whispered something which hinted at a future meeting.

The second day he visited twelve houses. Southampton has grown enormously – he might have kept on his round for a week and never seen the same butler twice – but it was only the palatial, the amazing houses which intrigued him.

On the third day he did a thing that many people have been told to do and few have done – he hired a hall. Perhaps the sixteen-to-twenty-year old people in the enormous houses had told him to. The hall he hired had once been 'Mr Snorkey's Private Gymnasium for Gentlemen'. It was situated over a garage on the south edge of Southampton and in the days of its prosperity had been, I regret to say, a place where gentlemen could, under Mr Snorkey's direction, work off the effects of the night before. It was now abandoned – Mr Snorkey had given up and gone away and died.

We will now skip three weeks during which time we may assume that the project which had to do with hiring a hall and visiting the two dozen largest houses in Southampton got under way.

The day to which we will skip was the July day on which Mr James Powell sent a wire to Miss Amanthis Powell saying that if she still aspired to the gaiety of the highest society she should set out for Southampton by the earliest possible train. He himself would meet her at the station.

Jim was no longer a man of leisure, so when she failed to arrive at the time her wire had promised he grew restless. He supposed she was coming on a later train, turned to go back to his – his project – and met her entering the station from the street side.

'Why, how did you—'

'Well,' said Amanthis, 'I arrived this morning instead, and I didn't want to bother you so I found a respectable, not to say dull, boarding-house on the Ocean Road.'

She was quite different from the indolent Amanthis of the porch hammock, he thought. She wore a suit of robins' egg blue and a rakish young hat with a curling feather – she was attired not unlike those young ladies between sixteen and twenty who of late were absorbing his attention. Yes, she would do very well.

He bowed her profoundly into a taxicab and got in beside her.

'Isn't it about time you told me your scheme?' she suggested.

'Well, it's about these society girls up here.' He waved his hand airily. 'I know 'em all.'

'Where are they?'

'Right now they're with Hugo. You remember – that's my body-servant.'

'With Hugo!' Her eyes widened. 'Why? What's it all about?'

'Well, I got – I got sort of a school, I guess you'd call it.'

'A school?'

'It's a sort of academy. And I'm the head of it. I invented it.'

He flipped a card from his case as though he were shaking down a thermometer.

'Look.'

She took the card. In large lettering it bore the legend

JAMES POWELL, JM

Dice, Brassknuckles and Guitar

She stared in amazement.

'Dice, Brassknuckles and Guitar?' she repeated in awe.

'Yes ma'am.'

'What does it mean? What – do you *sell* 'em?'

'No ma'am, I teach 'em. It's a profession.'

'Dice, Brassknuckles and Guitar? What's the JM?'

'That stands for Jazz Master.'

'But what *is* it? What's it about?'

'Well, you see, it's like this. One night when I was in New York I got talkin' to a young fella who was drunk. He was one of my fares. And he'd taken some society girl somewhere and lost her.'

'*Lost* her?'

'Yes ma'am. He forgot her, I guess. And he was right worried. Well, I got to thinkin' that these girls nowadays – these society girls – they lead a sort of dangerous life and my course of study offers a means of protection against these dangers.'

'You teach 'em to use brassknuckles?'

'Yes ma'am, if necessary. Look here, you take a girl and she goes into some café where she's got no business to go. Well then, her escort he gets a little too much to drink an' he goes to sleep an' then some other fella comes up and says, "Hello, sweet mamma," or whatever one of those mashers says up here. What does she do? She can't scream, on account of no real lady'll scream nowadays – no – She just reaches down in her pocket and slips her fingers into a pair of Powell's defensive brassknuckles, débutante's size, executes what I call the Society Hook, and *Wham!* that big fella's on his way to the cellar.'

'Well – what – what's the guitar for?' whispered the awed Amanthis. 'Do they have to knock somebody over with the guitar?'

'No, *ma'am!*' exclaimed Jim in horror. 'No ma'am. In my course no lady would be taught to raise a guitar against anybody. I teach 'em to play. Shucks! you ought to hear 'em. Why, when I've given 'em two lessons you'd think some of 'em was coloured.'

'And the dice?'

'Dice? I'm related to a dice. My grandfather was a dice. I teach 'em how to make those dice perform. I protect pocketbook as well as person.'

'Did you— Have you got any pupils?'

'Ma'am I got all the really nice, rich people in the place. What I told you ain't all. I teach lots of things. I teach 'em the jellyroll – and the Mississippi Sunrise. Why, there was one girl she came to me and said she wanted to learn to snap her fingers. I mean *real*ly snap 'em – like they do. She said she never could snap her fingers since she was little. I gave her two lessons and now *Wham!* Her daddy says he's goin' to leave home.'

'When do you have it?' demanded the weak and shaken Amanthis.

'Three times a week. We're goin' there right now.'

'And where do I fit in?'

'Well, you'll just be one of the pupils. I got it fixed up that you come from very high-tone people down in New Jersey. I didn't tell 'em your daddy was a judge – I told 'em he was the man that had the patent on lump sugar.'

She gasped.

'So all you got to do,' he went on, 'is to pretend you never saw no barber.'

They were now at the south end of the village and Amanthis saw a row of cars parked in front of a two-storey building. The cars were all low, long, rakish and of a brilliant hue. They were the sort of car that is manufactured to solve the millionaire's problem on his son's eighteenth birthday.

Then Amanthis was ascending a narrow stairs to the second storey. Here, painted on a door from which came the sounds of music and laughter were the words:

JAMES POWELL, JM
Dice, Brassknuckles and Guitar
Mon. – Wed. – Fri.
Hours 3–5 P.M.

'Now if you'll just step this way – ' said the Principal, pushing open the door.

Amanthis found herself in a long, bright room, populated with girls and men of about her own age. The scene presented itself to her at first as a sort of animated afternoon tea but after a moment she began to see, here and there, a motive and a pattern to the proceedings.

The students were scattered into groups, sitting, kneeling, standing, but all rapaciously intent on the subjects which engrossed them. From six young ladies gathered in a ring around some indistinguishable objects came a medley of cries and exclamations – plaintive, pleading, supplicating, exhorting, imploring and lamenting – their voices serving as tenor to an undertone of mysterious clatters.

Next to this group, four young men were surrounding an adolescent black, who proved to be none other than Mr Powell's late body-servant. The young men were roaring at Hugo apparently unrelated phrases, expressing a wide gamut of emotion. Now their voices rose to a sort of clamour, now they spoke softly and gently, with mellow implication. Every little while Hugo would answer them with words of approbation, correction or disapproval.

'What are they doing?' whispered Amanthis to Jim.

'That there's a course in southern accent. Lot of young men up here want to learn southern accent – so we teach it – Georgia, Florida, Alabama, Eastern Shore, Ole Virginian. Some of 'em even want straight nigger – for song purposes.'

They walked around among the groups. Some girls with metal knuckles were furiously insulting two punching bags on each of which was painted the leering, winking face of a 'masher'. A mixed group, led by a banjo tom-tom, were rolling harmonic syllables from their guitars. There were couples dancing flat-footed in the corner to a phonograph record made by Rastus Muldoon's Savannah Band; there were couples stalking a slow Chicago with a Memphis Side Swoop solemnly around the room.

'Are there any rules?' asked Amanthis.

Jim considered.

'Well,' he answered finally, 'they can't smoke unless they're over sixteen, and the boys have got to shoot square dice and I don't let 'em bring liquor into the Academy.'

'I see.'

'And now, Miss Powell, if you're ready I'll ask you to take off your hat and go over and join Miss Genevieve Harlan at that punching bag in the corner.' He raised his voice. 'Hugo,' he called, 'there's a new student here. Equip her with a pair of Powell's Defensive Brassknuckles – débutante size.'

I regret to say that I never saw Jim Powell's famous Jazz School in action nor followed his personally conducted tours into the mysteries of Dice, Brassknuckles and Guitar. So I can give you only such details as were later reported to me by one of his admiring pupils. During all the discussion of it afterwards no one ever denied that it was an enormous success, and no pupil ever regretted having received its degree – Bachelor of Jazz.

The parents innocently assumed that it was a sort of musical and dancing academy, but its real curriculum was transmitted from Santa Barbara to Biddeford Pool by that underground associated press which links up the so-called younger generation. Invitations to visit Southampton were at a premium – and Southampton generally is almost as dull for young people as Newport.

The Academy branched out with a small but well-groomed Jazz Orchestra.

'If I could keep it dark,' Jim confided to Amanthis, 'I'd have up Rastus Muldoon's Band from Savannah. That's the band I've always wanted to lead.'

He was making money. His charges were not exorbitant – as a rule his pupils were not particularly flush – but he moved from his boarding-house to the Casino Hotel where he took a suite and had Hugo serve him his breakfast in bed.

The establishing of Amanthis as a member of Southampton's younger set was easier than he had expected. Within a week she was known to everyone in the school by her first name. Miss Genevieve Harlan took such a fancy to her that she was invited to a sub-deb dance at the Harlan house – and evidently acquitted herself with tact, for thereafter she was invited to almost every such entertainment in Southampton.

Jim saw less of her than he would have liked. Not that her manner towards him changed – she walked with him often in the mornings, she was always willing to listen to his plans – but after she was taken up by the fashionable her evenings seemed to be monopolized. Several times Jim arrived at her boarding-house to find her out of breath, as if she had just come in at a run, presumably from some festivity in which he had no share.

So as the summer waned he found that one thing was lacking to complete the triumph of his enterprise. Despite the hospitality shown to Amanthis, the doors of Southampton were closed to him. Polite to, or rather, fascinated by him as his pupils were from three to five, after that hour they moved in another world.

His was the position of a golf professional who, though he may fraternize, and even command, on the links, loses his privileges with the sundown. He may look in the club window but he cannot dance. And, likewise, it was not given to Jim to see his teachings put into effect. He could hear the gossip of the morning after – that was all.

But while the golf professional, being English, holds himself proudly below his patrons, Jim Powell, who 'came from a right good family down there – pore though', lay awake many nights in his hotel bed and heard the music drifting into his window from the Katzby's house or the Beach Club, and turned over restlessly and wondered what was the matter. In the early days of his success he had bought himself a dress-suit, thinking that he would soon have a chance to wear it – but it still lay untouched in the box in which it had come from the tailor's.

Perhaps, he thought, there was some real gap which separated him from the rest. It worried him. One boy in particular, Martin Van Vleck, son of Van Vleck the ash-can king, made him conscious of the gap. Van Vleck was twenty-one, a tutoring-school product who still hoped to enter Yale. Several times Jim had heard him make remarks not intended for Jim's ears – once in regard to the suit with multiple buttons, again in reference to Jim's long, pointed shoes. Jim had passed these over.

He knew that Van Vleck was attending the school chiefly to monopolize the time of little Martha Katzby, who was just sixteen and too young to have attention of a boy of twenty-one – especially the attention of Van Vleck, who was so spiritually exhausted by his educational failures that he drew on the rather exhaustible innocence of sixteen.

It was late in September, two days before the Harlan dance which was to be the last and biggest of the season for this younger crowd. Jim, as usual, was not invited. He had hoped that he would be. The two young Harlans, Ronald and Genevieve, had been his first patrons when he arrived at Southampton – and it was Genevieve who had taken such a fancy to Amanthis. To have been at their dance – the most magnificent dance of all – would have crowned and justified the success of the waning summer.

His class, gathering for the afternoon, was loudly anticipating the next day's revel with no more thought of him than if he had been the family butler. Hugo, standing beside Jim, chuckled suddenly and remarked:

'Look yonder that man Van Vleck, He paralysed. He been havin' powerful lotta corn this evenin'.'

Jim turned and stared at Van Vleck, who had linked arms with little Martha Katzby and was saying something to her in a low voice. Jim saw her try to draw away.

He put his whistle to his mouth and blew it.

'All right,' he cried, ' Le's go! Group one tossin' the drumstick, high an' zigzag, group two, test your mouth organs for the Riverfront Shuffle.

Promise 'em sugar! Flatfoots this way! Orchestra – let's have the Florida Drag-Out played as a dirge.'

There was an unaccustomed sharpness in his voice and the exercises began with a mutter of facetious protest.

With his smouldering grievance directing itself towards Van Vleck, Jim was walking here and there among the groups when Hugo tapped him suddenly on the arm. He looked around. Two participants had withdrawn from the mouth organ institute – one of them was Van Vleck and he was giving a drink out of his flask to fifteen-year-old Ronald Harlan.

Jim strode across the room. Van Vleck turned defiantly as he came up.

'All right,' said Jim, trembling with anger, 'you know the rules. You get out!'

The music died slowly away and there was a sudden drifting over in the direction of the trouble. Somebody snickered. An atmosphere of anticipation formed instantly. Despite the fact that they all liked Jim their sympathies were divided – Van Vleck was one of them.

'Get out!' repeated Jim, more quietly.

'Are you talking to me?' inquired Van Vleck coldly.

'Yes.'

'Then you better say "sir".'

'I wouldn't say "sir" to anybody that'd give a little boy whisky! You get out!'

'Look here!' said Van Vleck furiously. 'You've butted in once too much. I've known Ronald since he was two years old. Ask *him* if he wants *you* to tell him what he can do!'

Ronald Harlan, his dignity offended, grew several years older and looked haughtily at Jim.

'Mind your own business!' he said defiantly, albeit a little guiltily.

'Hear that?' demanded Van Vleck. 'My God, can't you see you're just a servant? Ronald here'd no more think of asking you to his party than he would his bootlegger.'

'Youbettergetout!' cried Jim incoherently.

Van Vleck did not move. Reaching out suddenly, Jim caught his wrist and jerking it behind his back forced his arm upward until Van Vleck bent forward in agony. Jim leaned and picked the flask from the floor with his free hand. Then he signed Hugo to open the hall-door, uttered an abrupt 'You *step*!' and marched his helpless captive out into the hall where he literally *threw* him downstairs, head over heels bumping from wall to banister, and hurled his flask after him.

Then he reentered his academy, closed the door behind him and stood with his back against it.

'It – it happens to be a rule that nobody drinks while in this Academy.' He paused, looking from face to face, finding there sympathy, awe, disapproval, conflicting emotions. They stirred uneasily. He caught Amanthis's eye, fancied he saw a faint nod of encouragement and, with almost an effort, went on:

'I just *had* to throw that fella out 'an' you-all know it.' Then he concluded with a transparent affectation of dismissing an unimportant matter – 'All right, let's go! Orchestra – !'

But no one felt exactly like going on. The spontaneity of the proceedings had been violently disturbed. Someone made a run or two on the sliding guitar and several of the girls began whamming at the leer on the punching bags, but Ronald Harlan, followed by two other boys, got their hats and went silently out the door.

Jim and Hugo moved among the groups as usual until a certain measure of routine activity was restored but the enthusiasm was unrecapturable and Jim, shaken and discouraged, considered discontinuing school for the day. But he dared not. If they went home in this mood they might not come back. The whole thing depended on a mood. He must recreate it, he thought frantically – now, at once!

But try as he might, there was little response. He himself was not happy – he could communicate no gaiety to them. They watched his efforts listlessly and, he thought, a little contemptuously.

Then the tension snapped when the door burst suddenly open, precipitating a brace of middle-aged and excited women into the room. No person over twenty-one had ever entered the Academy before – but Van Vleck had gone direct to headquarters. The women were Mrs Clifton Garneau and Mrs Poindexter Katzby, two of the most fashionable and, at present, two of the most flurried women in Southampton. They were in search of their daughters as, in these days, so many women continually are.

The business was over in about three minutes.

'And as for you!' cried Mrs Clifton Garneau in an awful voice, 'your idea is to run a bar and – and *opium* den for children! You ghastly, horrible, unspeakable man! I can smell morphin fumes! Don't tell me I can't smell morphin fumes! I can smell morphin fumes!'

'And,' bellowed Mrs Poindexter Katzby, 'you have coloured men around! You have coloured girls hidden! I'm going to the police!'

Not content with herding their own daughters from the room, they insisted on the exodus of their friends' daughters. Jim was not a little touched when several of them – including even little Martha Katzby, before she was snatched fiercely away by her mother – came up and shook hands with him. But they were all going, haughtily, regretfully or with shame-faced mutters of apology.

'Good-bye,' he told them wistfully. 'In the morning I'll send you the money that's due you.'

And, after all, they were not sorry to go. Outside, the sounds of their starting motors, the triumphant *put-put* of their cut-outs cutting the warm September air, was a jubilant sound – a sound of youth and hopes high as the sun. Down to the ocean, to roll in the waves and forget – forget him and their discomfort at his humiliation.

They were gone – he was alone with Hugo in the room. He sat down suddenly with his face in his hands.

'Hugo,' he said huskily. 'They don't want us up here.'

'Don't you care,' said a voice.

He looked up to see Amanthis standing beside him.

'You better go with them,' he told her. 'You better not be seen here with me.'

'Why?'

'Because you're in society now and I'm no better to those people than a servant. You're in society – I fixed that up. You better go or they won't invite you to any of their dances.'

'They won't anyhow, Jim,' she said gently. 'They didn't invite me to the one tomorrow night.'

He looked up indignantly.

'They *did*n't?'

She shook her head.

'I'll *make* 'em!' he said wildly. 'I'll tell 'em they got to. I'll – I'll—'

She came close to him with shining eyes.

'Don't you mind, Jim,' she soothed him. 'Don't you mind. They don't matter. We'll have a party of our own tomorrow – just you and I.'

'I come from right good folks,' he said defiantly. 'Pore though.'

She laid her hand softly on his shoulder.

'I understand. You're better than all of them put together, Jim.'

He got up and went to the window and stared out mournfully into the late afternoon.

'I reckon I should have let you sleep in that hammock.'

She laughed.

'I'm awfully glad you didn't.'

He turned and faced the room, and his face was dark.

'Sweep up and lock up, Hugo,' he said, his voice trembling. 'The summer's over and we're going down home.'

Autumn had come early. Jim Powell woke next morning to find his room cool, and the phenomenon of frosted breath in September absorbed him for a moment to the exclusion of the day before. Then the lines of his face drooped with unhappiness as he remembered the humiliation which had washed the cheery glitter from the summer. There was nothing left for him except to go back where he was known, where under no provocation were such things said to white people as had been said to him here.

After breakfast a measure of his customary light-heartedness returned. He was a child of the South – brooding was alien to his nature. He could conjure up an injury only a certain number of times before it faded into the great vacancy of the past.

But when, from force of habit, he strolled over to his defunct establishment, already as obsolete as Snorkey's late sanatorium, melancholy again dwelt in his heart. Hugo was there, a spectre of despair, deep in the lugubrious blues amidst his master's broken hopes.

Usually a few words from Jim were enough to raise him to an inarticulate ecstasy, but this morning there were no words to utter. For two months Hugo had lived on a pinnacle of which he had never dreamed. He had enjoyed his work simply and passionately, arriving before school hours and lingering long after Mr Powell's pupils had gone.

The day dragged toward a not-too-promising night. Amanthis did not appear and Jim wondered forlornly if she had not changed her mind about dining with him that night. Perhaps it would be better if she were not seen with them. But then, he reflected dismally, no one would see them anyhow – everybody was going to the big dance at the Harlans' house.

When twilight threw unbearable shadows into the school hall he locked it up for the last time, took down the sign 'James Powell, JM, Dice, Brass-knuckles and Guitar', and went back to his hotel. Looking over his scrawled accounts he saw that there was another month's rent to pay on his school and some bills for windows broken and new equipment that had hardly been used. Jim had lived in state, and he realized that financially he would have nothing to show for the summer after all.

When he had finished he took his new dress-suit out of its box and inspected it, running his hand over the satin of the lapels and lining. This, at least, he owned and perhaps in Tarleton somebody would ask him to a party where he could wear it.

'Shucks!' he said scoffingly. 'It was just a no account old academy, anyhow. Some of those boys round the garage down home could of beat it all hollow.'

Whistling 'Jeanne of Jelly-bean Town' to a not-dispirited rhythm Jim encased himself in his first dress-suit and walked downtown.

'Orchids,' he said to the clerk. He surveyed his purchase with some pride. He knew that no girl at the Harlan dance would wear anything lovelier than these exotic blossoms that leaned languorously backward against green ferns.

In a taxicab, carefully selected to look like a private car, he drove to Amanthis's boarding-house. She came down wearing a rose-coloured evening dress into which the orchids melted like colours into a sunset.

'I reckon we'll go to the Casino Hotel,' he suggested, 'unless you got some other place—'

At their table, looking out over the dark ocean, his mood became a contented sadness. The windows were shut against the cool but the orchestra played 'Kalula' and 'South Sea Moon' and for a while, with her young loveliness opposite him, he felt himself to be a romantic participant in the life around him. They did not dance, and he was glad – it would have reminded him of that other brighter and more radiant dance to which they could not go.

After dinner they took a taxi and followed the sandy roads for an hour, glimpsing the now starry ocean through the casual trees.

'I want to thank you,' she said, 'for all you've done for me, Jim.'

'That's all right – we Powells ought to stick together.'

'What are you going to do?'

'I'm going to Tarleton tomorrow.'

'I'm sorry,' she said softly. 'Are you going to drive down?'

'I got to. I got to get the car south because I couldn't get what she was worth by sellin' it. You don't suppose anybody's stole my car out of your barn?' he asked in sudden alarm.

She repressed a smile.

'No.'

'I'm sorry about this – about you,' he went on huskily, 'and – and I would like to have gone to just one of their dances. You shouldn't of stayed with me yesterday. Maybe it kept 'em from asking you.'

'Jim,' she suggested eagerly, 'let's go and stand outside and listen to their old music. We don't care.'

'They'll be coming out,' he objected.

'No, it's too cold. Besides there's nothing they could do to you any more than they *have* done.'

She gave the chauffeur a direction and a few minutes later they stopped in front of the heavy Georgian beauty of the Madison Harlan house whence the windows cast their gaiety in bright patches on the lawn. There was laughter inside and the plaintive wind of fashionable horns, and now and again the slow, mysterious shuffle of dancing feet.

'Let's go up close,' whispered Amanthis in an ecstatic trance, 'I want to hear.'

They walked towards the house, keeping in the shadow of the great trees. Jim proceeded with awe – suddenly he stopped and seized Amanthis's arm.

'Man!' he cried in an excited whisper. 'Do you know what that is ?'

'A night watchman ?' Amanthis cast a startled look around.

'It's Rastus Muldoon's Band from Savannah! I heard 'em once, and I *know*. It's Rastus Muldoon's Band!'

They moved closer till they could see first pompadours, then slicked male heads and high coiffures and finally even bobbed hair pressed under black ties. They could distinguish chatter below the ceaseless laughter. Two figures appeared on the porch, gulped something quickly from flasks and returned inside. But the music had bewitched Jim Powell. His eyes were fixed and he moved his feet like a blind man.

Pressed in close behind some dark bushes they listened. The number ended. A breeze from the ocean blew over them and Jim shivered slightly. Then, in a wistful whisper:

'I've always wanted to lead that band. Just once.' His voice grew listless. 'Come on. Let's go. I reckon I don't belong around here.'

He held out his arm to her but instead of taking it she stepped suddenly out of the bushes and into a bright patch of light.

'Come on, Jim,' she said startlingly. 'Let's go inside.'

'What—?'

She seized his arm and though he drew back in a sort of stupefied horror at her boldness she urged him persistently towards the great front door.

'Watch out!' he gasped. 'Somebody's coming out of that house and see us.'

'No, Jim,' she said firmly. 'Nobody's coming out of that house – but two people are going in.'

'Why?' he demanded wildly, standing in full glare of the *porte-cochère* lamps. 'Why?'

'Why?' she mocked him. 'Why, just because this dance happens to be given for me.'

He thought she was mad.

The great doors swung open and a gentleman stepped out on the porch. In horror Jim recognized Mr Madison Harlan. He made a movement as though to break away and run. But the man walked down the steps holding out both hands to Amanthis.

'Hello at last,' he cried. 'Where on earth have you two been? Cousin Amanthis—' He kissed her, and turned cordially to Jim. 'And for you, Mr Powell,' he went on, 'to make up for being late you've got to promise that for just one number you're going to lead that band.'

New Jersey was warm, all except the part that was under water, and that mattered only to the fishes. All the tourists who rode through the long green miles stopped their cars in front of a spreading old-fashioned country house and looked at the red swing on the lawn and the wide shady porch, and sighed and drove on – swerving a little to avoid a jet-black body-servant in the road. The body-servant was applying a hammer and nails to a decayed flivver which flaunted from its rear the legend, 'Tarleton, Ga.'

A girl with yellow hair and a warm colour to her face was lying in the hammock looking as though she could fall asleep any moment. Near her sat a gentleman in an extraordinarily tight suit. They had come down together the day before from the fashionable resort at Southampton.

'When you first appeared,' she was explaining, 'I never thought I'd see you again so I made that up about the barber and all. As a matter of fact, I've been around quite a bit – with or without brassknuckles. I'm coming out this autumn.'

'I reckon I had a lot to learn,' said Jim.

'And you see,' went on Amanthis, looking at him rather anxiously, 'I'd been invited up to Southampton to visit my cousins – and when you said you were going, I wanted to see what you'd do. I always slept at the Harlans' but I kept a room at the boarding house so you wouldn't know. The reason I didn't get there on the right train was because I had to come early and warn a lot of people to pretend not to know me.'

Jim got up, nodding his head in comprehension.

'I reckon I and Hugo had better be movin' along. We got to make Baltimore by night.'

'That's a long way.'

'I want to sleep south tonight,' he said simply.

Together they walked down the path and past the idiotic statue of Diana on the lawn.

'You see,' added Amanthis gently, 'you don't have to be rich up here in order to – to go around, any more than you do in Georgia—' She broke off abruptly, 'Won't you come back next year and start another Academy?'

'No ma'am, not me. That Mr Harlan told me I could go on with the one I had but I told him no.'

'Haven't you – didn't you make money?'

'No ma'am,' he answered. 'I got enough of my own income to just get me home. I didn't have my principal long. One time I was way ahead but I was livin' high and there was my rent an' apparatus and those musicians. Besides, there at the end I had to pay what they'd advanced me for their lessons.'

'You shouldn't have done that!' cried Amanthis indignantly.

'They didn't want me to, but I told 'em they'd have to take it.'

He didn't consider is necessary to mention that Mr Harlan had tried to present him with a cheque.

They reached the automobile just as Hugo drove in his last nail. Jim opened a pocket of the door and took from it an unlabelled bottle containing a whitish-yellow liquid.

'I intended to get you a present,' he told her awkwardly, 'but my money got away before I could, so I thought I'd send you something from Georgia. This here's just a personal remembrance. It won't do for you to drink but maybe after you come out into society you might want to show some of those young fellas what good old corn tastes like.'

She took the bottle.

'Thank you, Jim.'

'That's all right.' He turned to Hugo. 'I reckon we'll go along now. Give the lady the hammer.'

'Oh, you can have the hammer,' said Amanthis tearfully. 'Oh, won't you promise to come back?'

'Someday – maybe.'

He looked for a moment at her yellow hair and her blue eyes misty with sleep and tears. Then he got into his car and as his foot found the clutch his whole manner underwent a change.

'I'll say good-bye ma'am,' he announced with impressive dignity, 'we're going South for the winter.'

The gesture of his straw hat indicated Palm Beach, St Augustine, Miami. His body-servant spun the crank, gained his seat and became part of the intense vibration into which the automobile was thrown.

'South for the winter,' repeated Jim, and then he added softly, 'You're the prettiest girl I ever knew. You go back up there and lie down in that hammock, and sleep – sle-eep—'

It was almost a lullaby, as he said it. He bowed to her, magnificently, profoundly, including the whole North in the splendour of his obeisance—

Then they were gone down the road in quite a preposterous cloud of dust. Just before they reached the first bend Amanthis saw them come to a full stop, dismount and shove the top part of the car on to the bottom part. They took their seats again without looking around. Then the bend – and they were out of sight, leaving only a faint brown mist to show that they had passed.

DIAMOND DICK AND
THE FIRST LAW OF WOMAN

Hearst's International, April 1924

'Diamond Dick and the First Law of Woman' was written in Great Neck in December 1923. International bought it for $1500.

Fitzgerald had been counting on his play, The Vegetable, *to solve his money problems. After* The Vegetable *failed at its Atlantic City tryout in November 1923, he was compelled to write himself out of debt with stories. Between November 1923 and April 1924 he wrote ten stories (of which six are included in this collection):* 'The Sensible Thing', 'Rags Martin-Jones and the Pr-nce of W-les', 'Diamond Dick and the First Law of Woman', 'Gretchen's Forty Winks', 'The Baby Party', 'The Third Casket', 'One of My Oldest Friends', 'The Pusher-in-the-Face', 'The Unspeakable Egg', *and* 'John Jackson's Arcady'. *These were competent commercial stories which paid off Fitzgerald's debts and financed the writing of* The Great Gatsby *on the Riviera in the same summer of 1924.*

When Diana Dickey came back from France in the spring of 1919, her parents considered that she had atoned for her nefarious past. She had served a year in the Red Cross and she was presumably engaged to a young American ace of position and charm. They could ask no more; of Diana's former sins only her nickname survived—

Diamond Dick! – she had selected it herself, of all the names in the world, when she was a thin, black-eyed child of ten.

'Diamond Dick,' she would insist, 'that's my name. Anybody that won't call me that's a double darn fool.'

'But that's not a nice name for a little lady,' objected her governess. 'If you want to have a boy's name why don't you call yourself George Washington?'

'Be-cause my name's Diamond Dick,' explained Diana patiently. 'Can't you understand? I got to be named that be-cause if I don't I'll have a fit and upset the family, see?'

She ended by having the fit – a fine frenzy that brought a disgusted nerve specialist out from New York – and the nickname too. And once in possession she set about modelling her facial expression on that of a butcher boy who delivered meats at Greenwich back doors. She stuck out her lower jaw and parted her lips on one side, exposing sections of her first teeth – and from this alarming aperture there issued the harsh voice of one far gone in crime.

'Miss Caruthers,' she would sneer crisply, 'what's the idea of no jam? Do you wanta whack the side of the head?'

'*Diana*! I'm going to call your mother *this minute*!'

'Look at here!' threatened Diana darkly. 'If you call her you're liable to get a bullet the side of the head.'

Miss Caruthers raised her hand uneasily to her bangs. She was somewhat awed.

'Very well,' she said uncertainly, 'if you want to act like a little ragamuffin—'

Diana did want to. The evolutions which she practised daily on the sidewalk and which were thought by the neighbours to be some new form of hopscotch were in reality the preliminary work on an Apache slouch. When it was perfected, Diana lurched forth into the streets of Greenwich, her face violently distorted and half obliterated by her father's slouch hat, her body reeling from side to side, jerked hither and yon by the shoulders, until to look at her long was to feel a faint dizziness rising to the brain.

At first it was merely absurd, but when Dianas' conversation commenced to glow with weird rococo phrases, which she imagined to be the dialect of the underworld, it became alarming. And a few years later she further complicated the problem by turning into a beauty – a dark little beauty with tragedy eyes and a rich voice stirring in her throat.

Then America entered the war and Diana on her eighteenth birthday sailed with a canteen unit to France.

The past was over; all was forgotten. Just before the armistice was signed, she was cited in orders for coolness under fire. And – this was the part that particularly pleased her mother – it was rumoured that she was engaged to be married to Mr Charley Abbot of Boston and Bar Harbor, 'a young aviator of position and charm'.

But Mrs Dickey was scarcely prepared for the changed Diana who landed in New York. Seated in the limousine bound for Greenwich, she turned to her daughter with astonishment in her eyes.

'Why, everybody's proud of you, Diana,' she cried, 'the house is simply bursting with flowers. Think of all you've seen and done, at *nineteen*!'

Diana's face, under an incomparable saffron hat, stared out into Fifth Avenue, gay with banners for the returning divisions.

'The war's over,' she said in a curious voice, as if it had just occurred to her this minute.

'Yes,' agreed her mother cheerfully, 'and we won. I knew we would all the time.'

She wondered how to best introduce the subject of Mr Abbot.

'You're quieter,' she began tentatively. 'You look as if you were more ready to settle down.'

'I want to come out this fall.'

'But I thought—' Mrs Dickey stopped and coughed – 'Rumours had led me to believe—'

'Well, go on, Mother. What did you hear?'

'It came to my ears that you were engaged to that young Charles Abbot.'

Diana did not answer and her mother licked nervously at her veil. The silence in the car became oppressive. Mrs Dickey had always stood somewhat in awe of Diana – and she began to wonder if she had gone too far.

'The Abbots are such nice people in Boston,' she ventured uneasily. 'I've met his mother several times – she told me how devoted—'

'Mother!' Diana's voice, cold as ice, broke in upon her loquacious dream. 'I don't care what you heard or where you heard it, but I'm not engaged to Charley Abbot. And please don't ever mention the subject to me again.'

In November, Diana made her début in the ballroom of the Ritz. There was a touch of irony in this 'introduction to life' – for at nineteen Diana had seen more of reality, of courage and terror and pain, than all the pompous dowagers who peopled the artificial world.

But she was young and the artificial world was redolent of orchids and pleasant, cheerful snobbery and orchestras which set the rhythm of the year, summing up the sadness and suggestiveness of life in new tunes. All night the saxophones wailed the hopeless comment of the 'Beale Street Blues', while five hundred pairs of gold and silver slippers shuffled the shining dust. At the grey tea hour there were always rooms that throbbed incessantly with this low sweet fever, while fresh faces drifted here and there like rose petals blown by the sad horns around the floor.

In the centre of this twilight universe Diana moved with the season, keeping half a dozen dates a day with half a dozen men, drowsing asleep at dawn with the beads and chiffon of an evening dress tangled among dying orchids on the floor beside her bed.

The year melted into summer. The flapper craze startled New York, and skirts went absurdly high and the sad orchestras played new tunes. For a while Diana's beauty seemed to embody this new fashion as once it had seemed to embody the higher excitement of the war; but it was noticeable that she encouraged no lovers, that for all her popularity her name never became identified with that of any one man. She had had a hundred 'chances', but when she felt that an interest was becoming an infatuation she was at pains to end it once and for all.

A second year dissolved into long dancing nights and swimming trips to the warm south. The flapper movement scattered to the winds and was forgotten; skirts tumbled precipitously to the floor and there were fresh songs from the saxophones for a new crop of girls. Most of those with whom she had come out were married now – some of them had babies. But Diana, in a changing world, danced on to newer tunes.

With a third year it was hard to look at her fresh and lovely face and realize that she had once been in the war. To the young generation it was already a shadowy event that had absorbed their older brothers in the dim past – ages ago. And Diana felt that when its last echoes had finally died away her youth, too, would be over. It was only occasionally now that anyone called her 'Diamond Dick'. When it happened, as it did sometimes, a curious puzzled expression would come into her eyes as though she could never connect the two pieces of her life that were broken sharply asunder.

Then, when five years had passed, a brokerage house failed in Boston and Charley Abbot, the war hero, came back from Paris, wrecked and broken by drink and with scarcely a penny to his name.

Diana saw him first at the Restaurant Mont Mihiel, sitting at a side table with a plump, indiscriminate blonde from the half-world. She excused herself unceremoniously to her escort and made her way towards him. He looked up as she approached and she felt a sudden faintness, for he was worn to a shadow and his eyes, large and dark like her own, were burning in red rims of fire.

'Why, Charley—'

He got drunkenly to his feet and they shook hands in a dazed way. He murmured an introduction, but the girl at the table evinced her displeasure at the meeting by glaring at Diana with cold blue eyes.

'Why, Charley—' said Diana again, 'you've come home, haven't you.'

'I'm here for good.'

'I want to see you, Charley. I – want to see you as soon as possible. Will you come out to the country tomorrow?'

'Tomorrow?' He glanced with an apologetic expression at the blonde girl. 'I've got a date. Don't know about tomorrow. Maybe later in the week—'

'Break your date.'

His companion had been drumming with her fingers on the cloth and looking restlessly around the room. At this remark she wheeled sharply back to the table.

'Charley,' she ejaculated, with a significant frown.

'Yes, I know,' he said to her cheerfully, and turned to Diana. 'I can't make it tomorrow. I've got a date.'

'It's absolutely necessary that I see you tomorrow,' went on Diana ruthlessly. 'Stop looking at me in that idiotic way and say you'll come out to Greenwich.'

'What's the idea?' cried the other girl in a slightly raised voice. 'Why don't you stay at your own table? You must be tight.'

'Now Elaine!' said Charley, turning to her reprovingly.

'I'll meet the train that gets to Greenwich at six,' Diana went on coolly. 'If you can't get rid of this – this woman—' she indicated his companion with a careless wave of her hand – 'send her to the movies.'

With an exclamation the other girl got to her feet and for a moment a a scene was imminent. But nodding to Charley, Diana turned from the table, beckoned to her escort across the room and left the café.

'I don't like her,' cried Elaine querulously when Diana was out of hearing. 'Who is she anyhow? Some old girl of yours?'

'That's right,' he answered, frowning. 'Old girl of mine. In fact, my only old girl.'

'Oh, you've known her all your life.'

'No.' He shook his head. 'When I first met her she was a canteen worker in the war.'

'*She* was!' Elaine raised her brows in surprise. 'Why she doesn't look—'

'Oh, she's not nineteen any more – she's nearly twenty-five.' He laughed.

'I saw her sitting on a box at an ammunition dump near Soissons one day with enough lieutenants around her to officer a regiment. Three weeks after that we were engaged!'

'Then what?' demanded Elaine sharply.

'Usual thing,' he answered with a touch of bitterness. 'She broke it off. Only unusual part of it was that I never knew why. Said good-bye to her one day and left for my squadron. I must have said something or done something then that started the big fuss. I'll never know. In fact I don't remember anything about it very clearly because a few hours later I had a crash and what happened just before has always been damn dim in my head. As soon as I was well enough to care about anything I saw that the situation was changed. Thought at first that there must be another man.'

'Did she break the engagement?'

'She cern'ly did. While I was getting better she used to sit by my bed for hours looking at me with the funniest expression in her eyes. Finally I asked for a mirror – I thought I must be all cut up or something. But I wasn't. Then one day she began to cry. She said she'd been thinking it over and perhaps it was a mistake and all that sort of thing. Seemed to be referring to some quarrel we'd had when we said good-bye just before I got hurt. But I was still a pretty sick man and the whole thing didn't seem to make any sense unless there was another man in it somewhere. She said that we both wanted our freedom, and then she looked at me as if she expected me to make some explanation or apology – and I couldn't think what I'd done. I remember leaning back in the bed and wishing I could die right then and there. Two months later I heard she'd sailed for home.'

Elaine leaned anxiously over the table.

'Don't go to the country with her, Charley,' she said. 'Please don't go. She wants you back – I can tell by looking at her.'

He shook his head and laughed.

'Yes she does,' insisted Elaine, 'I can tell. I hate her. She had you once and now she wants you back. I can see it in her eyes. I wish you'd stay in New York with me.'

'No,' he said stubbornly. 'Going out and look her over. Diamond Dick's an old girl of mine.'

Diana was standing on the station platform in the late afternoon, drenched with golden light. In the face of her immaculate freshness Charley Abbot felt ragged and old. He was only twenty-nine, but four wild years had left many lines around his dark, handsome eyes. Even his walk was tired – it was no longer a demonstration of fitness and physical grace. It was a way of getting somewhere, failing other forms of locomotion; that was all.

'Charley,' Diana cried, 'where's your bag?'

'I only came to dinner – I can't possibly spend the night.'

He was sober, she saw, but looked as if he needed a drink badly. She took his arm and guided him to a red-wheeled coupé parked in the street.

'Get in and and sit down,' she commanded. 'You walk as if you were about to fall down anyhow.'

'Never felt better in my life.'

She laughed scornfully.

'Why do you have to get back tonight?' she demanded.

'I promised – you see I had an engagement—'

'Oh, let her wait!' exclaimed Diana impatiently. 'She didn't look as if she had much else to do. Who is she anyhow?'

'I don't see how that could possibly interest you, Diamond Dick.'

She flushed at the familiar name.

'Everything about you interests me. Who is that girl?'

'Elaine Russel. She's in the movies – sort of.'

'She looked pulpy,' said Diana thoughtfully. 'I keep thinking of her. You look pulpy too. What are you doing with yourself – waiting for another war?'

They turned into the drive of a big rambling house on the Sound. Canvas was being stretched for dancing on the lawn.

'Look!' She was pointing at a figure in knickerbockers on a side veranda. 'That's my brother Breck. You've never met him. He's home from New Haven for the Easter holidays and he's having a dance tonight.'

A handsome boy of eighteen came down the veranda steps towards them.

'He thinks you're the greatest man in the world,' whispered Diana. 'Pretend you're wonderful.'

There was an embarrassed introduction.

'Done any flying lately?' asked Breck immediately.

'Not for some years,' admitted Charley.

'I was too young for the war myself,' said Breck regretfully, 'but I'm going to try for a pilot's licence this summer. It's the only thing, isn't it – flying, I mean.'

'Why, I suppose so,' said Charley somewhat puzzled. 'I hear you're having a dance tonight.'

Breck waved his hand carelessly.

'Oh, just a lot of people from around here. I should think anything like that'd bore you to death – after all you've seen.'

Charley turned helplessly to Diana.

'Come on,' she said, laughing, 'we'll go inside.'

Mrs Dickey met them in the hall and subjected Charley to a polite but somewhat breathless scrutiny. The whole household seemed to treat him with unusual respect, and the subject had a tendency to drift immediately to the war.

'What are you doing now?' asked Mr Dickey. 'Going into your father's business?'

'There isn't any business left,' said Charley frankly. 'I'm just about on my own.'

Mr Dickey considered for a moment.

'If you haven't made any plans why don't you come down and see me at my office some day this week. I've got a little proposition that may interest you.'

It annoyed Charley to think that Diana had probably arranged all this. He needed no charity. He had not been crippled, and the war was over five years. People did not talk like this any more.

The whole first floor had been set with tables for the supper that would follow the dance, so Charley and Diana had dinner with Mr and Mrs Dickey in the library upstairs. It was an uncomfortable meal at which Mr Dickey did the talking and Diana covered up the gaps with nervous gaiety. He was glad when it was over and he was standing with Diana on the veranda in the gathering darkness.

'Charley—' She leaned close to him and touched his arm gently. 'Don't go to New York tonight. Spend a few days down here with me. I want to talk to you and I don't feel that I can talk tonight with this party going on.'

'I'll come out again – later in the week,' he said evasively.

'Why not stay tonight?'

'I promised I'd be back at eleven.'

'At eleven?' She looked at him reproachfully. 'Do you have to account to that girl for your evenings?'

'I like her,' he said defiantly. 'I'm not a child, Diamond Dick, and I rather resent your attitude. I thought you closed out your interest in my life five years ago.'

'You won't stay?'

'No.'

'All right – then we only have an hour. Let's walk out and sit on the wall by the Sound.'

Side by side they started through the deep twilight where the air was heavy with salt and roses.

'Do you remember the last time we walked somewhere together?' she whispered.

'Why – no. I don't think I do. Where was it?'

'It doesn't matter – if you've forgotten.'

When they reached the shore she swung herself up on the low wall that skirted the water.

'It's spring, Charley.'

'Another spring.'

'No – just spring. If you say "another spring" it means you're getting old.' She hesitated. 'Charley—'

'Yes, Diamond Dick.'

'I've been waiting to talk to you like this for five years.'

Looking at him out of the corner of her eye she saw he was frowning and changed her tone.

'What kind of work are you going into, Charley?'

'I don't know. I've got a little money left and I won't have to do anything for a while. I don't seem to fit into business very well.'

'You mean like you fitted into the war.'

'Yes.' He turned to her with a spark of interest. 'I belonged to the war. It seems a funny thing to say but I think I'll always look back to those days as the happiest in my life.'

'I know what you mean,' she said slowly. 'Nothing quite so intense or so dramatic will ever happen to our generation again.'

They were silent for a moment. When he spoke again his voice was trembling a little.

'There are things lost in it – parts of me – that I can look for and never find. It was my war in a way, you see, and you can't quite hate what was your own.' He turned to her suddenly. 'Let's be frank, Diamond Dick – we loved each other once and it seems – seems rather silly to be stalling this way with you.'

She caught her breath.

'Yes,' she said faintly, 'let's be frank.'

'I know what you're up to and I know you're doing it to be kind. But life doesn't start all over again when a man talks to an old love on a spring night.'

'I'm not doing it to be kind.'

He looked at her closely.

'You lie, Diamond Dick. But – even if you loved me now it wouldn't matter. I'm not like I was five years ago – I'm a different person, can't you see? I'd rather have a drink this minute than all the moonlight in the world. I don't even think I could love a girl like you any more.'

She nodded.

'I see.'

'Why wouldn't you marry me five years ago, Diamond Dick?'

'I don't know,' she said after a minute's hesitation, 'I was wrong.'

'Wrong!' he exclaimed bitterly. 'You talk as if it had been guesswork, like betting on white or red.'

'No, it wasn't guesswork.'

There was a silence for a minute – then she turned to him with shining eyes.

'Won't you kiss me, Charley?' she asked simply.

He started.

'Would it be so hard to do?' she went on. 'I've never asked a man to kiss me before.'

With an exclamation he jumped off the wall.

'I'm going to the city,' he said.

'Am I – such bad company as all that?'

'Diana.' He came close to her and put his arms around her knees and looked into her eyes. 'You know that if I kiss you I'll have to stay. I'm afraid of you – afraid of your kindness, afraid to remember anything about you at all. And I couldn't go from a kiss of yours to – another girl.'

'Good-bye,' she said suddenly.

He hesitated for a moment then he protested helplessly.

'You put me in a terrible position.'

'Good-bye.'

'Listen Diana—'

'Please go away.'

He turned and walked quickly towards the house.

Diana sat without moving while the night breeze made cool puffs and ruffles on her chiffon dress. The moon had risen higher now and floating in the Sound was a triangle of silver scales, trembling a little to the stiff, tinny drip of the banjos on the lawn.

Alone at last – she was alone at last. There was not even a ghost left now to drift with through the years. She might stretch out her arms as far as they could reach into the night without fear that they would brush friendly cloth. The thin silver had worn off from all the stars.

She sat there for almost an hour, her eyes fixed upon the points of light on the other shore. Then the wind ran cold fingers along her silk stockings so she jumped off the wall, landing softly among the bright pebbles of the sand.

'Diana!'

Breck was coming towards her, flushed with the excitement of his party.

'Diana! I want you to meet a man in my class at New Haven. His brother took you to a prom three years ago.'

She shook her head.

'I've got a headache; I'm going upstairs.'

Coming closer Breck saw that her eyes were glittering with tears.

'Diana, what's the matter?'

'Nothing.'

'Something's the matter.'

'Nothing, Breck. But oh, take care, take care! Be careful who you love.'

'Are you in love with – Charley Abbot?'

She gave a strange, hard little laugh.

'Me? Oh, God, no, Breck! I don't love anybody. I wasn't made for anything like love, I don't even love myself any more. It was you I was talking about. That was advice, don't you understand?'

She ran suddenly toward the house, holding her skirts high out of the dew. Reaching her own room she kicked off her slippers and threw herself on the bed in the darkness.

'I should have been careful,' she whispered to herself. 'All my life I'll be punished for not being more careful. I wrapped all my love up like a box of candy and gave it away.'

Her window was open and outside on the lawn the sad, dissonant horns were telling a melancholy story. A blackamoor was two-timing the lady to whom he had pledged faith. The lady warned him, in so many words, to stop fooling 'round Sweet Jelly-Roll, even though Sweet Jelly-Roll was the colour of pale cinnamon–

The phone on the table by her bed rang imperatively. Diana took up the receiver.

'Yes.'

'One minute please, New York calling.'

It flashed through Diana's head that it was Charley – but that was impossible. He must still be on the train.

'Hello.' A woman was speaking. 'Is this the Dickey residence?'

'Yes.'

'Well, is Mr Charles Abbot there?'

Diana's heart seemed to stop beating as she recognized the voice – it was the blonde girl of the café.

'What?' she asked dazedly.

'I would like to speak to Mr Abbot at once please.'

'You – you can't speak to him. He's gone.'

There was a pause. Then the girl's voice, suspiciously:

'He isn't gone.'

Diana's hands tightened on the telephone.

'I know who's talking,' went on the voice, rising to a hysterical note, 'and I want to speak to Mr Abbot. If you're not telling the truth, and he finds out, there'll be trouble.'

'Be quiet!'

'If he's gone, where did he go?'

'I don't know.'

'If he isn't at my apartment in half an hour I'll know you're lying and I'll—'

Diana hung up the receiver and tumbled back on the bed – too weary of life to think or care. Out on the lawn the orchestra was singing and the words drifted in her window on the breeze.

Lis-sen *while I — get you tole:*
Stop foolin' 'roun' sweet – Jelly-Roll—

She listened. The Negro voices were wild and loud – life was in that key, so harsh a key. How abominably helpless she was! Her appeal was ghostly, impotent, absurd, before the barbaric urgency of this other girl's desire.

Just treat me pretty, just treat me sweet
Cause I possess a fo'ty-fo' that don't repeat.

The music sank to a weird, threatening minor. It reminded her of something – some mood in her own childhood – and a new atmosphere seemed to open up around her. It was not so much a definite memory as it was a current, a tide setting through her whole body.

Diana jumped suddenly to her feet and groped for her slippers in the darkness. The song was beating in her head and her little teeth set together in a click. She could feel the tense golf-muscles rippling and tightening along her arms.

Running into the hall she opened the door to her father's room, closed it cautiously behind her and went to the bureau. It was in the top drawer – black and shining among the pale anaemic collars. Her hand closed around the grip and she drew out the bullet clip with steady fingers. There were five shots in it.

Back in her room she called the garage.

'I want my roadster at the side entrance right away!'

Wriggling hurriedly out of her evening dress to the sound of breaking snaps she let it drop in a soft pile on the floor, replacing it with a golf sweater, a checked sport-skirt and an old blue and white blazer which she pinned at the collar with a diamond bar. Then she pulled a tam-o'-shanter over her dark hair and looked once in the mirror before turning out the light.

'Come on, Diamond Dick!' she whispered aloud.

With a short exclamation she plunged the automatic into her blazer pocket and hurried from the room.

Diamond Dick! The name had jumped out at her once from a lurid cover, symbolizing her childish revolt against the softness of life. Diamond Dick was a law unto himself, making his own judgements with his back against the wall. If justice was slow he vaulted into his saddle and was off for the foothills, for in the unvarying rightness of his instincts he was higher and harder than the law. She had seen in him a sort of deity, infinitely resourceful, infinitely just. And the commandment he laid down for himself in the cheap, ill-written pages was first and foremost to keep what was his own.

An hour and a half from the time when she had left Greenwich, Diana pulled up her roadster in front of the Restaurant Mont Mihiel. The theatres were already dumping their crowds into Broadway and half a dozen couples in evening dress looked at her curiously as she slouched through the door. A moment later she was talking to the head waiter.

'Do you know a girl named Elaine Russel?'

'Yes, Miss Dickey. She comes here quite often.'

'I wonder if you can tell me where she lives.'

The head waiter considered.

'Find out,' she said sharply, 'I'm in a hurry.'

He bowed. Diana had come there many times with many men. She had never asked him a favour before.

His eyes roved hurriedly around the room.

'Sit down,' he said.

'I'm all right. You hurry.'

He crossed the room and whispered to a man at a table – in a minute he was back with the address, an apartment on Forty-ninth Street.

In her car again she looked at her wrist watch – it was almost midnight, the appropriate hour. A feeling of romance, of desperate and dangerous adventure thrilled her, seemed to flow out of the electric signs and the rushing cabs and the high stars. Perhaps she was only one out of a hundred people bound on such an adventure tonight – for her there had been nothing like this since the war.

Skidding the corner into East Forty-ninth Street she scanned the apartments on both sides. There it was – 'The Elkson' – a wide mouth of forbidding yellow light. In the hall a Negro elevator boy asked her name.

'Tell her it's a girl with a package from the moving picture company.'

He worked a plug noisily.

'Miss Russel? There's a lady here says she's got a package from the moving picture company.'

A pause.

'That's what she says . . . All right.' He turned to Diana. 'She wasn't expecting no package but you can bring it up.' He looked at her, frowned suddenly. 'You ain't got no package.'

Without answering she walked into the elevator and he followed, shoving the gate closed with maddening languor . . .

'First door to your right.'

She waited until the elevator door had started down again. Then she knocked, her fingers tightening on the automatic in her blazer pocket.

Running footsteps, a laugh; the door swung open and Diana stepped quickly into the room.

It was a small apartment, bedroom, bath and kitchenette, furnished in pink and white and heavy with last week's smoke. Elaine Russel had opened the door herself. She was dressed to go out and a green evening cape was over her arm. Charley Abbot sipping at a highball was stretched out in the room's only easy chair.

'What is it?' cried Elaine quickly.

With a sharp movement Diana slammed the door behind her and Elaine stepped back, her mouth falling ajar.

'Good evening,' said Diana coldly, and then a line from a forgotten nickel novel flashed into her head, 'I hope I don't intrude.'

'What do you want?' demanded Elaine. 'You've got your nerve to come butting in here!'

Charley who had not said a word set down his glass heavily on the arm of the chair. The two girls looked at each other with unwavering eyes.

'Excuse me,' said Diana slowly, 'but I think you've got my man.'

'I thought you were supposed to be a lady!' cried Elaine in rising anger.

'What do you mean by forcing your way into this room?'

'I mean business. I've come for Charley Abbot.'

Elaine gasped.

'Why, you must be crazy!'

'On the contrary, I've never been so sane in my life. I came here to get something that belongs to me.'

Charley uttered an exclamation but with a simultaneous gesture the two women waved him silent.

'All right,' cried Elaine, 'we'll settle this right now.'

'I'll settle it myself,' said Diana sharply. 'There's no question or argument about it. Under other circumstances I might feel a certain pity for you – in this case you happen to be in my way. What is there between you two? Has he promised to marry you?'

'That's none of your business!'

'You'd better answer,' Diana warned her.

'I won't answer.'

Diana took a sudden step forward, drew back her arm and with all the strength in her slim hard muscles, hit Elaine a smashing blow in the cheek with her open hand.

Elaine staggered up against the wall. Charley uttered an exclamation and sprang forward to find himself looking into the muzzle of a forty-four held in a small determined hand.

'Help!' cried Elaine wildly. 'Oh, she's hurt me! She's hurt me!'

'Shut up!' Diana's voice was hard as steel. 'You're not hurt. You're just pulpy and soft. But if you start to raise a row I'll pump you full of tin as sure as you're alive. Sit down! Both of you. Sit *down*!'

Elaine sat down quickly, her face pale under her rouge. After an instant's hesitation Charley sank down again into his chair.

'Now,' went on Diana, waving the gun in a constant arc that included them both. 'I guess you know I'm in a serious mood. Understand this first of all. As far as I'm concerned neither of you have any rights whatsoever and I'd kill you both rather than leave this room without getting what I came for. I asked if he'd promised to marry you.'

'Yes,' said Elaine sullenly.

The gun moved towards Charley.

'Is that so?'

He licked his lips, nodded.

'My God!' said Diana in contempt. 'And you admit it. Oh, it's funny, it's absurd – if I didn't care so much I'd laugh.'

'Look here!' muttered Charley, 'I'm not going to stand much of this, you know.'

'Yes you are! You're soft enough to stand anything now.' She turned to the girl, who was trembling. 'Have you any letters of his?'

Elaine shook her head.

'You lie,' said Diana. 'Go and get them! I'll give you three. One—'

Elaine rose nervously and went into the other room. Diana edged along the table, keeping her constantly in sight.

'Hurry!'

Elaine returned with a small package in her hand which Diana took and slipped into her blazer pocket.

'Thanks. You had 'em all carefully preserved I see. Sit down again and we'll have a little talk.'

Elaine sat down. Charley drained off his whisky and soda and leaned back stupidly in his chair.

'Now,' said Diana, 'I'm going to tell you a little story. It's about a girl who went to a war once and met a man who she thought was the finest and bravest man she had ever known. She fell in love with him and he with her and all the other men she had ever known became like pale shadows compared with this man that she loved. But one day he was shot down out of the air, and when he woke up into the world he'd changed. He didn't know it himself but he'd forgotten things and become a different man. The girl felt sad about this – she saw that she wasn't necessary to him any more, so there was nothing to do but say good-bye.

'So she went away and every night for a while she cried herself to sleep but he never came back to her and five years went by. Finally word came to her that this same injury that had come between them was ruining his life. He didn't remember anything important any more – how proud and fine he had once been, and what dreams he had once had. And then the girl knew that she had the right to try and save what was left of his life because she was the only one who knew all the things he'd forgotten. But it was too late. She couldn't approach him any more – she wasn't coarse enough and gross enough to reach him now – he'd forgotten so much.

'So she took a revolver, very much like this one here, and she came after this man to the apartment of a poor, weak, harmless rat of a girl who had him in tow. She was going to either bring him to himself – or go back to the dust with him where nothing would matter any more.'

She paused. Elaine shifted uneasily in her chair. Charley was leaning forward with his face in his hands.

'Charley!'

The word, sharp and distinct, startled him. He dropped his hands and looked up at her.

'Charley!' she repeated in a thin clear voice. 'Do you remember Fontenay in the late fall?'

A bewildered look passed over his face.

'Listen, Charley. Pay attention. Listen to every word I say. Do you remember the poplar trees at twilight, and a long column of French infantry going through the town? You had on your blue uniform, Charley, with the little numbers on the tabs and you were going to the front in an hour. Try and remember, Charley!'

He passed his hand over his eyes and gave a funny little sigh. Elaine sat bolt upright in her chair and gazed from one to the other of them with wide eyes.

'Do you remember the poplar trees?' went on Diana. 'The sun was going down and the leaves were silver and there was a bell ringing. Do you remember, Charley? Do you remember?'

Again silence. Charley gave a curious little groan and lifted his head.

'I can't – understand,' he muttered hoarsely. 'There's something funny here.'

'Can't you remember?' cried Diana. The tears were streaming from her eyes. 'Oh God! Can't you remember? The brown road and the poplar trees and the yellow sky.' She sprang suddenly to her feet. 'Can't you remember?' she cried wildly. 'Think, think – there's time. The bells are ringing – the bells are ringing, Charley! And there's just one hour!'

Then he too was on his feet, reeling and swaying.

'Oh-h-h-h!' he cried.

'Charley,' sobbed Diana, 'remember, remember, remember!'

'I see!' he said wildly. 'I can see now – I remember, oh I remember!'

With a choking sob his whole body seemed to wilt under him and he pitched back senseless into his chair.

In a minute the two girls were beside him.

'He's fainted!' Diana cried. 'Get some water quick.'

'You devil!' screamed Elaine, her face distorted. 'Look what's happened! What right have you to do this? What right? What right?'

'What right?' Diana turned to her with black, shining eyes. 'Every right in the world. I've been married to Charley Abbot for five years.'

Charley and Diana were married again in Greenwich early in June. After the wedding her oldest friends stopped calling her Diamond Dick – it had been a most inappropriate name for some years, they said, and it was thought that the effect on her children might be unsettling, if not distinctly pernicious.

Yet perhaps if the occasion should arise Diamond Dick would come to life again from the coloured cover and, with spurs shining and buckskin fringes fluttering in the breeze, ride into the lawless hills to protect her own. For under all her softness Diamond Dick was always hard as steel – so hard that the years knew it and stood still for her and the clouds rolled apart and a sick man, hearing those untiring hoofbeats in the night, rose up and shook off the dark burden of the war.

THE THIRD CASKET

Saturday Evening Post, 31 May 1924

'The Third Casket' was written in Great Neck in March 1924. The Post *paid $1750 for it. After the expiration of the story options with* Metropolitan *and* International, *Fitzgerald became virtually a* Post *author for the next decade. All of his best stories were offered there first, and the* Post *steadily raised his story price to a peak of $4000 in 1929. The* Post *obviously regarded Fitzgerald as a star author. His name regularly appeared on the cover, and his stories were prominently positioned. 'Casket' was the lead story in the issue, following a serial.*

Like most of the stories Fitzgerald wrote in 1924, 'The Third Casket' depends on plot rather than character. Here he adapted an episode from The Merchant of Venice – *which Shakespeare had borrowed from somebody else. 'The Third Casket' was tailored to the business values of the* Post. *The simple message is that work is more rewarding than leisure.*

When you come into Cyrus Girard's office suite on the thirty-second floor you think at first that there has been a mistake, that the elevator instead of bringing you upstairs has brought you uptown, and that you are walking into an apartment on Fifth Avenue where you have no business at all. What you take to be the sound of a stock ticker is only a businesslike canary swinging in a silver cage overhead, and while the languid débutante at the mahogany table gets ready to ask you your name you can feast your eyes on etchings, tapestries, carved panels and fresh flowers.

Cyrus Girard does not, however, run an interior-decorating establishment, though he has, on occasion, run almost everything else. The lounging aspect of his ante-room is merely an elaborate camouflage for the wild clamour of affairs that goes on ceaselessly within. It is merely the padded glove over the mailed fist, the smile on the face of the prize fighter.

No one was more intensely aware of this than the three young men who were waiting there one April morning to see Mr Girard. Whenever the door marked Private trembled with the pressure of enormous affairs they started nervously in unconscious unison. All three of them were on the hopeful side of thirty, each of them had just got off the train, and they had never seen one another before. They had been waiting side by side on a Circassian leather lounge for the best part of an hour.

Once the young man with the pitch-black eyes and hair had pulled out a package of cigarettes and offered it hesitantly to the two others. But the others had refused in such a politely alarmed way that the dark young man, after a quick look around, had returned the package unsampled to his pocket. Following this disrespectful incident a long silence had fallen, broken only by the clatter of the canary as it ticked off the bond market in bird land.

When the Louis XIII clock stood at noon the door marked Private swung open in a tense, embarrassed way, and a frantic secretary demanded that the three callers step inside. They stood up as one man.

'Do you mean – all together?' asked the tallest one in some embarrassment.

'All together.'

Falling unwillingly into a sort of lock step and glancing neither to left or right, they passed through a series of embattled rooms and marched into the private office of Cyrus Girard, who filled the position of Telamonian Ajax among the Homeric characters of Wall Street.

He was a thin, quiet-mannered man of sixty, with a fine, restless face and the clear, fresh, trusting eyes of a child. When the procession of young men walked in he stood up behind his desk with an expectant smile.

'Parrish?' he said eagerly.

The tall young man said, 'Yes, sir,' and was shaken by the hand.

'Jones?'

This was the young man with the black eyes and hair. He smiled back at Cyrus Girard and announced in a slightly southern accent that he was mighty glad to meet him.

'And so you must be Van Buren,' said Girard, turning to the third. Van Buren acknowledged as much. He was obviously from a large city – unflustered and very spick-and-span.

'Sit down,' said Girard, looking eagerly from one to the other. 'I can't tell you the pleasure of this minute.'

They all smiled nervously and sat down.

'Yes, sir,' went on the older man, 'if I'd had any boys of my own I don't know but what I'd have wanted them to look just like you three.' He saw that they were all growing pink, and he broke off with a laugh. 'All right, I won't embarrass you any more. Tell me about the health of your respective fathers and we'll get down to business.'

Their fathers, it seemed, were very well; they had all sent congratulatory messages by their sons for Mr Girard's sixtieth birthday.

'Thanks. Thanks. Now that's over.' He leaned back suddenly in his chair. 'Well, boys, here's what I have to say. I'm retiring from business next year. I've always intended to retire at sixty, and my wife's always counted on it, and the time's come. I can't put it off any longer. I haven't any sons and I haven't any nephews and I haven't any cousins and I have a brother who's fifty years old and in the same boat I am. He'll perhaps hang on for ten years more down here; after that it looks as if the house, Cyrus Girard Incorporated, would change its name.

'A month ago I wrote to the three best friends I had in college, the three best friends I ever had in my life, and asked them if they had any sons between twenty-five and thirty years old. I told them I had room for just one young man here in my business, but he had to be about the best in the market. And as all three of you arrived here this morning I guess your fathers think you are. There's nothing complicated about my proposition. It'll take me three months to find out what I want to know, and at the end of that time two of you'll be disappointed; the other one can have about everything they used to give away in the fairy tales, half my kingdom and, if she wants him, my daughter's hand.' He raised his head slightly. 'Correct me, Lola, if I've said anything wrong.'

At these words the three young men started violently, looked behind them, and then jumped precipitately to their feet. Reclining lazily in an armchair not two yards away sat a gold-and-ivory little beauty with dark eyes and a moving, childish smile that was like all the lost youth in the world. When she saw the startled expressions on their faces she gave vent to a suppressed chuckle in which the victims after a moment joined.

'This is my daughter,' said Cyrus Girard, smiling innocently. 'Don't be so alarmed. She has many suitors come from near and far – and all that sort of thing. Stop making these young men feel silly, Lola, and ask them if they'll come to dinner with us tonight.'

Lola got to her feet gravely and her grey eyes fell on them one after another.

'I only know part of your names,' she said.

'Easily arranged,' said Van Buren. 'Mine's George.'

The tall young man bowed.

'I respond to John Hardwick Parrish,' he confessed, 'or anything of that general sound.'

She turned to the dark-haired southerner, who had volunteered no information. 'How about Mr Jones?'

'Oh, just – Jones,' he answered uneasily.

She looked at him in surprise.

'Why, how partial!' she exclaimed, laughing. 'How – I might even say how fragmentary.'

Mr Jones looked around him in a frightened way.

'Well, I tell you,' he said finally, 'I don't guess my first name is much suited to this sort of thing.'

'What is it?'

'It's Rip.'

'Rip!'

Eight eyes turned reproachfully upon him.

'Young man,' exclaimed Girard, 'you don't mean that my old friend in his senses named his son that!'

Jones shifted defiantly on his feet.

'No, he didn't,' he admitted. 'He named me Oswald.'

There was a ripple of sympathetic laughter.

'Now you four go along,' said Girard, sitting down at his desk. 'To-morrow at nine o'clock sharp you report to my general manager, Mr Galt, and the tournament begins. Meanwhile if Lola has her coupé-sport-limousine-roadster-landaulet, or whatever she drives now, she'll probably take you to your respective hotels.'

After they had gone Girard's face grew restless again and he stared at nothing for a long time before he pressed the button that started the long-delayed stream of traffic through his mind.

'One of them's sure to be all right,' he muttered, 'but suppose it turned out to be the dark one. Rip Jones Incorporated!'

II

As the three months drew to an end it began to appear that not one, but all of the young men were going to turn out all right. They were all indus-trious, they were all possessed of that mysterious ease known as personality and, moreover, they all had brains. If Parrish, the tall young man from the West, was a little quicker in sizing up the market; if Jones, the southerner, was a bit the most impressive in his relations with customers, then Van

Buren made up for it by spending his nights in the study of investment securities. Cyrus Girard's mind was no sooner drawn to one of them by some exhibition of shrewdness or resourcefulness than a parallel talent appeared in one of the others. Instead of having to enforce upon himself a strict neutrality he found himself trying to concentrate upon the individual merits of first one and then another – but so far without success.

Every weekend they all came out to the Girard place at Tuxedo Park, where they fraternized a little self-consciously with the young and lovely Lola, and on Sunday mornings tactlessly defeated her father at golf. On the last tense weekend before the decision was to be made Cyrus Girard asked them to meet him in his study after dinner. On their respective merits as future partners in Cyrus Girard Inc. he had been unable to decide, but his despair had evoked another plan, on which he intended to base his decision.

'Gentlemen,' he said, when they had convoked in his study at the appointed hour, 'I have brought you here to tell you that you're all fired.'

Immediately the three young men were on their feet, with shocked, reproachful expressions in their eyes.

'Temporarily,' he added, smiling good-humouredly. 'So spare a decrepit old man your violence and sit down.'

They sat down, with short relieved smiles.

'I like you all,' he went on, 'and I don't know which one I like better than the others. In fact – this thing hasn't come out right at all. So I'm going to extend the competition for two more weeks – but in an entirely different way.'

They all sat forward eagerly in their chairs.

'Now my generation,' he went on, 'have made a failure of our leisure hours. We grew up in the most hard-boiled commercial age any country ever knew, and when we retire we never know what to do with the rest of our lives. Here I am, getting out at sixty, and miserable about it. I haven't any resources – I've never been much of a reader, I can't stand golf except once a week, and I haven't got a hobby in the world. Now some day you're going to be sixty too. You'll see other men taking it easy and having a good time, and you'll want to do the same. I want to find out which one of you will be the best sort of man after his business days are over.'

He looked from one to the other of them eagerly. Parrish and Van Buren nodded at him comprehendingly. Jones after a puzzled half-moment nodded too.

'I want you each to take two weeks and spend them as you think you'll spend your time when you're too old to work. I want you to solve my problem for me. And whichever one I think has got the most out of his leisure – he'll be the man to carry on my business. I'll know it won't swamp him like it's swamped me.'

'You mean you want us to enjoy ourselves ?' inquired Rip Jones politely. 'Just go out and have a big time ?'

Cyrus Girard nodded.

'Anything you want to do.'

'I take it Mr Girard doesn't include dissipation,' remarked Van Buren.

'Anything you want to do,' repeated the older man, 'I don't bar anything. When it's all done I'm going to judge of its merits.'

'Two weeks of travel for me,' said Parrish dreamily. 'That's what I've always wanted to do. I'll—'

'Travel!' interrupted Van Buren contemptuously. 'When there's so much to do here at home ? Travel, perhaps, if you have a year; but for two weeks —I'm going to try and see how the retired businessman can be of some use in the world.'

'I said travel,' repeated Parrish sharply. 'I believe we're all to employ our leisure in the best—'

'Wait a minute,' interrupted Cyrus Girard. 'Don't fight this out in talk. Meet me in the office at 10.30 on the morning of August first – that's two weeks from tomorrow – and then let's see what you've done.' He turned to Rip Jones. 'I suppose you've got a plan too.'

'No, sir,' admitted Rip Jones with a puzzled look; 'I'll have to think this over.'

But though he thought it over for the rest of the evening Rip Jones went to bed still uninspired. At midnight he got up, found a pencil and wrote out a list of all the good times he had ever had. But all his holidays now seemed unprofitable and stale, and when he fell asleep at five his mind still threshed disconsolately on the prospect of hollow useless hours.

Next morning as Lola Girard was backing her car out of the garage she saw him hurrying towards her over the lawn.

'Ride in town, Rip ?' she asked cheerfully.

'I reckon so.'

'Why do you only reckon so ? Father and the others left on the nine-o'clock train.'

He explained to her briefly that they had all temporarily lost their jobs and there was no necessity of getting to the office today.

'I'm kind of worried about it,' he said gravely. 'I sure hate to leave my work. I'm going to run in this afternoon and see if they'll let me finish up a few things I had started.'

'But you better be thinking how you're going to amuse yourself.'

He looked at her helplessly.

'All I can think of doing is maybe take to drink,' he confessed. 'I come from a little town, and when they say leisure they mean hanging round the corner store.' He shook his head. 'I don't want any leisure. This is the first chance I ever had, and I want to make good.'

'Listen, Rip,' said Lola on a sudden impulse. 'After you finish up at the office this afternoon you meet me and we'll fix up something together.'

He met her, as she suggested, at five o'clock, but the melancholy had deepened in his dark eyes.

'They wouldn't let me in,' he said. 'I met your father in there, and he told me I had to find some way to amuse myself or I'd be just a bored old man like him.'

'Never mind. We'll go to a show,' she said consolingly; 'and after that we'll run up on some roof and dance.'

It was the first of a week of evenings they spent together. Sometimes they went to the theatre, sometimes to a cabaret; once they spent most of an afternoon strolling in Central Park. But she saw that from having been the most light-hearted and gay of the three young men, he was now the most moody and depressed. Everything whispered to him of the work he was missing.

Even when they danced at teatime, the click of bracelets on a hundred women's arms only reminded him of the busy office sound on Monday morning. He seemed incapable of inaction.

'This is mighty sweet of you,' he said to her one afternoon, 'and if it was after business hours I can't tell you how I'd enjoy it. But my mind is on all the things I ought to be doing. I'm – I'm right sad.'

He saw than that he had hurt her, that by his frankness he had rejected all she was trying to do for him. But he was incapable of feeling differently.

'Lola, I'm mighty sorry,' he said softly, 'and maybe some day it'll be after hours again, and I can come to you—'

'I won't be interested,' she said coldly. 'And I see I was foolish ever to be interested at all.'

He was standing beside her car when this conversation took place, and before he could reply she had thrown it into gear and started away.

He stood there looking after her sadly, thinking that perhaps he would never see her any more and that she would remember him always as ungrateful and unkind. But there was nothing he could have said. Something dynamic in him was incapable of any except a well-earned rest.

'If it was only after hours,' he muttered to himself as he walked slowly away. 'If it was only after hours.'

III

At ten o'clock on the morning of August first a tall, bronzed young man presented himself at the office of Cyrus Girard Inc., and sent in his card to the president. Less than five minutes later another young man arrived, less blatantly healthy, perhaps, but with the light of triumphant achievement blazing in his eyes. Word came out through the palpitating inner door that they were both to wait.

'Well, Parrish,' said Van Buren condescendingly, 'how did you like Niagara Falls?'

'I couldn't tell you,' answered Parrish haughtily. 'You can determine that on your honeymoon.'

'My honeymoon!' Van Buren started. 'How – what made you think I was contemplating a honeymoon?'

'I merely meant that when you do contemplate it you will probably choose Niagara Falls.'

They sat for a few minutes in stony silence.

'I suppose,' remarked Parrish coolly, 'that you've een making a serious study of the deserving poor.'

'On the contrary, I have done nothing of the ki .' Van Buren looked at his watch. 'I'm afraid that our competitor with the rakish name is going to be late. The time set was 10.30; it now lacks three minutes of the half hour.'

The private door opened, and at a command from the frantic secretary they both arose eagerly and went inside. Cyrus Girard was standing behind his desk waiting for them, watch in hand.

'Hello!' he exclaimed in surprise. 'Where's Jones?'

Parrish and Van Buren exchanged a smile. If Jones were snagged somewhere so much the better.

'I beg your pardon, sir,' spoke up the secretary, who had been lingering near the door; 'Mr Jones is in Chicago.'

'What's he doing there?' demanded Cyrus Girard in astonishment.

'He went out to handle the matter of those silver shipments. There wasn't anyone else who knew much about it, and Mr Galt thought—'

'Never mind what Mr Galt thought,' broke in Girard impatiently. 'Mr Jones is no longer employed by this concern. When he gets back from

Chicago pay him off and let him go.' He nodded curtly. 'That's all.'

The secretary bowed and went out. Girard turned to Parrish and Van Buren with an angry light in his eyes.

'Well, that finishes him,' he said determinedly. 'Any young man who won't attempt to obey my orders doesn't deserve a good chance.' He sat down and began drumming with his fingers on the arm of his chair.

'All right, Parrish, let's hear what you've been doing with your leisure hours.'

Parrish smiled ingratiatingly.

'Mr Girard,' he began, 'I've had a bully time. I've been travelling.'

'Travelling where? The Adirondacks? Canada?'

'No sir. I've been to Europe.'

Cyrus Girard sat up.

'I spent five days going over and five days coming back. That left me two days in London and a run over to Paris by aeroplane to spend the night. I saw Westminster Abbey, the Tower of London and the Louvre, and spent an afternoon at Versailles. On the boat I kept in wonderful condition – swam, played deck tennis, walked five miles every day, met some interesting people and found time to read. I came back after the greatest two weeks of my life, feeling fine and knowing more about my own country since I had something to compare it with. That, sir, is how I spent my leisure time and that's how I intend to spend my leisure time after I'm retired.'

Girard leaned back thoughtfully in his chair.

'Well, Parrish, that isn't half bad,' he said. 'I don't know but what the idea appeals to me – take a run over there for the sea voyage and a glimpse of the London Stock Ex— I mean the Tower of London. Yes, sir, you've put an idea in my head.' He turned to the other young man, who during this recital had been shifting uneasily in his chair. 'Now, Van Buren, let's hear how you took your ease.'

'I thought over the travel idea,' burst out Van Buren excitedly, 'and I decided against it. A man of sixty doesn't want to spend his time running back and forth between the capitals of Europe. It might fill up a year or so, but that's all. No, sir, the main thing is to have some strong interest – and especially one that'll be for the public good, because when a man gets along in years he wants to feel that he's leaving the world better for having lived in it. So I worked out a plan – it's for a historical and archaeological endowment centre, a thing that'd change the whole face of public education, a thing that any man would be interested in giving his time and money to.

I've spent my whole two weeks working out the plan in detail, and let me tell you it'd be nothing but play work – just suited to the last years of an active man's life. It's been fascinating, Mr Girard. I've learned more from doing it than I ever knew before – and I don't think I ever had a happier two weeks in my life.'

When he had finished, Cyrus Girard nodded his head up and down many times in an approving and yet somehow dissatisfied way.

'Found an institute, eh?' he muttered aloud. 'Well, I've always thought that maybe I'd do that some day – but I never figured on running it myself. My talents aren't much in that line. Still, it's certainly worth thinking over.'

He got restlessly to his feet and began walking up and down the carpet, the dissatisfied expression deepening on his face. Several times he took out his watch and looked at it as if hoping that perhaps Jones had not gone to Chicago after all, but would appear in a few moments with a plan nearer his heart.

'What's the matter with me?' he said to himself unhappily. 'When I say a thing I'm used to going through with it. I must be getting old.'

Try as he might, however, he found himself unable to decide. Several times he stopped in his walk and fixed his glance first on one and then on the other of the two young men, trying to pick out some attractive characteristic to which he could cling and make his choice. But after several of these glances their faces seemed to blur together and he couldn't tell one from the other. They were twins who had told him the same story – of carrying the stock exchange by aeroplane to London and making it into a moving-picture show.

'I'm sorry, boys,' he said haltingly. 'I promised I'd decide this morning, and I will, but it means a whole lot to me and you'll have to give me a little time.'

They both nodded, fixing their glances on the carpet to avoid encountering his distraught eyes.

Suddenly he stopped by the table and picking up the telephone called the general manager's office.

'Say, Galt,' he shouted into the mouthpiece, 'you sure you sent Jones to Chicago?'

'Positive,' said a voice on the other end. 'He came in here couple of days ago and said he was half crazy for something to do. I told him it was against orders, but he said he was out of the competition anyhow and we needed somebody who was competent to handle that silver. So I—'

'Well you shouldn't have done it, see? I wanted to talk to him about something, and you shouldn't have done it.'

Clack! He hung up the receiver and resumed his endless pacing up and down the floor. Confound Jones, he thought. Most ungrateful thing he ever heard of after he'd gone to all this trouble for his father's sake. Outrageous! His mine went off on a tangent and he began to wonder whether Jones would handle that business out in Chicago. It was a complicated situation – but then, Jones was a trustworthy fellow. They were all trustworthy fellows. That was the whole trouble.

Again he picked up the telephone. He would call Lola; he felt vaguely that if she wanted to she could help him. The personal element had eluded him here; her opinion would be better than his own.

'I have to ask your pardon, boys,' he said unhappily; 'I didn't mean there to be all this fuss and delay. But it almost breaks my heart when I think of handing this shop over to anybody at all, and when I try to decide, it all gets dark in my mind.' He hesitated. 'Have either one of you asked my daughter to marry him?'

'I did,' said Parrish; 'three weeks ago.'

'So did I,' confessed Van Buren; 'and I still have hopes that she'll change her mind.'

Girard wondered if Jones had asked her also. Probably not; he never did anything he was expected to do. He even had the wrong name.

The phone in his hand rang shrilly and with an automatic gesture he picked up the receiver.

'Chicago calling, Mr Girard.'

'I don't want to talk to anybody.'

'It's personal. It's Mr Jones.'

'All right,' he said, his eyes narrowing. 'Put him on.'

A series of clicks – then Jones' faintly southern voice over the wire.

'Mr Girard?'

'Yeah.'

'I've been trying to get you since ten o'clock in order to apologize.'

'I should think you would!' exploded Girard. 'Maybe you know you're fired.'

'I knew I would be,' said Jones gloomily. 'I guess I must be pretty dumb, Mr Girard, but I'll tell you the truth – I can't have a good time when I quit work.'

'Of course you can't!' snapped Girard. 'Nobody can—' He corrected himself. 'What I mean is, it isn't an easy matter.'

There was a pause at the other end of the line.

'That's exactly the way I feel,' came Jones' voice regretfully. 'I guess we understand each other, and there's no use my saying any more.'

'What do you mean – we understand each other?' shouted Girard. 'That's an impertinent remark, young man. We don't understand each other at all.'

'That's what I meant,' amended Jones; 'I don't understand you and you don't understand me. I don't want to quit working and you – you do.'

'Me quit work!' cried Girard, his face reddening. 'Say, what are you talking about? Did you say I wanted to quit work?' He shook the telephone up and down violently. 'Don't talk back to me, young man! Don't tell me I want to quit! Why – why, I'm not going to quit work at all! Do you hear that? I'm not going to quit work at all!'

The transmitter slipped from his grasp and bounced from the table to the floor. In a minute he was on his knees, groping for it wildly.

'Hello!' he cried. 'Hello – hello! Say get Chicago back! I wasn't through!'

The two young men were on their feet. He hung up the receiver and turned to them, his voice husky with emotion.

'I've been an idiot,' he said brokenly. 'Quit work at sixty! Why – I must have been an idiot! I'm still a young man – I've got twenty good years in front of me! I'd like to see anybody send me home to die!'

The phone rang again and he took up the receiver with fire blazing in his eyes.

'Is this Jones? No, I want Mr Jones; Rip Jones. He's – he's my partner.' There was a pause. 'No, Chicago, that must be another party. I don't know any Mrs Jones – I want Mr—'

He broke off and the expression on his face changed slowly. When he spoke again his husky voice had grown suddenly quiet.

'Why – why, Lola—'

THE PUSHER-IN-THE-FACE

Woman's Home Companion, February 1925

'The Pusher-in-the-Face' was written in Great Neck in March 1924. It was bought for $1750 by Woman's Home Companion, *which featured fiction as well as household articles. Although this story is an extended gag and does not display the qualities of Fitzgerald's best magazine fiction, it was very popular. 'Pusher' was syndicated by the Metro Newspaper Service; it was included in* The Cream of the Jug, *a 1927 humour anthology; and it was made into a movie in 1929.*

Though many – perhaps most – of Fitzgerald's stories rely on wit, he was not a comic writer. His infrequent attempts at straight comedy – as in 'Pusher' – rely heavily on slapstick. This story reads like a movie scenario, and maybe it was intended as one.

The last prisoner was a man – his masculinity was not much in evidence, it is true; he would perhaps better be described as a 'person', but he undoubtedly came under that general heading and was so classified in the court record. He was a small, somewhat shrivelled, somewhat wrinkled American who had been living along for probably thirty-five years.

His body looked as if it had been left by accident in his suit the last time it went to the tailor's and pressed out with hot, heavy irons to its present sharpness. His face was merely a face. It was the kind of face that makes up crowds, grey in colour with ears that shrank back against the head as if fearing the clamour of the city, and with the tired, tired eyes of one whose forebears have been underdogs for five thousand years.

Brought into the dock between two towering Celts in executive blue he seemed like the representative of a long extinct race, a very fagged-out and shrivelled elf who had been caught poaching on a buttercup in Central Park.

'What's your name?'

'Stuart.'

'Stuart what?'

'Charles David Stuart.'

The clerk recorded it without comment in the book of little crimes and great mistakes.

'Age?'

'Thirty.'

'Occupation?'

'Night cashier.'

The clerk paused and looked at the judge. The judge yawned.

'Wha's charge?' he asked.

'The charge is' – the clerk looked down at the notation in his hand – 'the charge is that he pushed a lady in the face.'

'Pleads guilty?'

'Yes.'

The preliminaries were now disposed of. Charles David Stuart, looking very harmless and uneasy, was on trial for assault and battery.

The evidence disclosed, rather to the judge's surprise, that the lady whose face had been pushed was not the defendant's wife.

On the contrary the victim was an absolute stranger – the prisoner had never seen her before in his life. His reasons for the assault had been two: first, that she talked during a theatrical performance; and second, that she kept joggling the back of his chair with her knees. When this had gone on for some time he had turned around and without any warning pushed her severely in the face.

'Call the plaintiff,' said the judge, sitting up a little in his chair. 'Let's hear what she has to say.'

The courtroom, sparsely crowded and unusually languid in the hot afternoon, had become suddenly alert. Several men in the back of the room moved into benches near the desk and a young reporter leaned over the clerk's shoulder and copied the defendant's name on the back of an envelope.

The plaintiff arose. She was a woman just this side of fifty with a determined, rather overbearing face under yellowish white hair. Her dress was a dignified black and she gave the impression of wearing glasses; indeed the young reporter, who believed in observation, had so described her in his mind before he realized that no such adornment sat upon her thin, beaked nose.

It developed that she was Mrs George D. Robinson of 1219 Riverside

Drive. She had always been fond of the theatre and sometimes she went to the matinée. There had been two ladies with her yesterday, her cousin, who lived with her, and a Miss Ingles – both ladies were in court.

This is what had occurred:

As the curtain went up for the first act a woman sitting behind had asked her to remove her hat. Mrs Robinson had been about to do so anyhow, and so she was a little annoyed at the request and had remarked as much to Miss Ingles and her cousin. At this point she had first noticed the defendant who was sitting directly in front, for he had turned around and looked at her quickly in a most insolent way. Then she had forgotten his existence until just before the end of the act when she made some remark to Miss Ingles – when suddenly he had stood up, turned around and pushed her in the face.

'Was it a hard blow?' asked the judge at this point.

'A hard blow!' said Mrs Robinson indignantly. 'I should say it was. I had hot and cold applications on my nose all night.'

'– on her nose all night.'

This echo came from the witness bench where two faded ladies were leaning forward eagerly and nodding their heads in corroboration.

'Were the lights on?' asked the judge.

No, but everyone around had seen the incident and some people had taken hold of the man right then and there.

This concluded the case for the plaintiff. Her two companions gave similar evidence and in the minds of everyone in the courtroom the incident defined itself as one of unprovoked and inexcusable brutality.

The one element which did not fit in with this interpretation was the physiognomy of the prisoner himself. Of any one of a number of minor offences he might have appeared guilty – pickpockets were notoriously mild-mannered, for example – but of this particular assault in a crowded theatre he seemed physically incapable. He did not have the kind of voice or the kind of clothes or the kind of moustache that went with such an attack.

'Charles David Stuart,' said the judge, 'you've heard the evidence against you?'

'Yes.'

'And you plead guilty?'

'Yes.'

'Have you anything to say before I sentence you?'

'No.' The prisoner shook his head hopelessly. His small hands were trembling.

'Not one word in extenuation of this unwarranted assault?'

The prisoner appeared to hesitate.

'Go on,' said the judge. 'Speak up – it's your last chance.'

'Well,' said Stuart with an effort, 'she began talking about the plumber's stomach.'

There was a stir in the courtroom. The judge leaned forward.

'What do you mean?'

'Why, at first she was only talking about her own stomach to – to those two ladies there' – he indicated the cousin and Miss Ingles – 'and that wasn't so bad. But when she began talking about the plumber's stomach it got different.'

'How do you mean – different?'

Charles Stuart looked around helplessly.

'I can't explain,' he said, his moustache wavering a little, 'but when she began talking about the plumber's stomach you – you had to listen.'

A snicker ran about the courtroom. Mrs Robinson and her attendant ladies on the bench were visibly horrified. The guard took a step nearer as if at a nod from the judge he would whisk off this criminal to the dingiest dungeon in Manhattan.

But much to his surprise the judge settled himself comfortably in his chair.

'Tell us about it, Stuart,' he said not unkindly. 'Tell us the whole story from the beginning.'

This request was a shock to the prisoner and for a moment he looked as though he would have preferred the order of condemnation. Then after one nervous look around the room he put his hands on the edge of the desk, like the paws of a fox-terrier just being trained to sit up, and began to speak in a quavering voice.

'Well, I'm a night cashier, your honour, in T. Cushmael's restaurant on Third Avenue. I'm not married' – he smiled a little, as if he knew they had all guessed *that* – 'and so on Wednesday and Saturday afternoons I usually go to the matinee. It helps to pass the time till dinner. There's a drug store, maybe you know, where you can get tickets for a dollar sixty-five to some of the shows and I usually go there and pick out something. They got awful prices at the box office now.' He gave out a long silent whistle and looked feelingly at the judge. 'Four or five dollars for one seat—'

The judge nodded his head.

'Well,' continued Charles Stuart, 'when I pay even a dollar sixty-five I expect to see my money's worth. About two weeks ago I went to one of these here mystery plays where they have one fella that did the crime and nobody knows who it was. Well, the fun at a thing like that is to guess who did it. And there was a lady behind me that'd been there before and she gave it all away to the fella with her. Gee' – his face fell and he shook his head from side to side – 'I like to died right there. When I got home to my room I was so mad that they had to come and ask me to stop walking up and down. Dollar sixty-five of my money gone for nothing.

'Well, Wednesday came around again, and this show was one show I wanted to see. I'd been wanting to see it for months, and every time I went into the drug store I asked them if they had any tickets. But they never did.' He hesitated. 'So Tuesday I took a chance and went over to the box office and got a seat. Two seventy-five it cost me.' He nodded impressively. 'Two seventy-five. Like throwing money away. But I wanted to see that show.'

Mrs Robinson in the front row rose suddenly to her feet.

'I don't see what all this story has to do with it,' she broke out a little shrilly. 'I'm sure I don't care—'

The judge brought his gavel sharply down on the desk.

'Sit down, please,' he said.

'This is a court of law, not a matinee.'

Mrs Robinson sat down, drawing herself up into a thin line and sniffing a little as if to say she'd see about this after a while. The judge pulled out his watch.

'Go on,' he said to Stuart. 'Take all the time you want.'

'I got there first,' continued Stuart in a flustered voice. 'There wasn't anybody in there but me and the fella that was cleaning up. After a while the audience came in, and it got dark and the play started, but just as I was all settled in my seat and ready to have a good time I heard an awful row directly behind me. Somebody had asked this lady' – he pointed directly to Mrs Robinson – 'to remove her hat like she should of done anyhow and she was sore about it. She kept telling the two ladies that was with her how she'd been at the theatre before and knew enough to take off her hat. She kept that up for a long time, five minutes maybe, and then every once in a while she'd think of something new and say it in a loud voice. So finally I turned around and looked at her because I wanted to see what a lady looked like that could be so inconsiderate as that. Soon as I turned back she began on me. She said I was insolent and then she said *Tchk ! Tchk ! Tchk !* a lot with her tongue and the two ladies that was with her said *Tchk ! Tchk !*

Tchk! until you could hardly hear yourself think, much less listen to the play. You'd have thought I'd done something terrible.

'By and by, after they calmed down and I began to catch up with what was doing on the stage, I felt my seat sort of creak forward and then creak back again and I knew the lady had her feet on it and I was in for a good rock. Gosh!' He wiped his pale, narrow brow on which the sweat had gathered thinly. 'It was awful. I hope to tell you I wished I'd never come at all. Once I got excited at a show and rocked a man's chair without knowing it and I was glad when he asked me to stop. But I knew this lady wouldn't be glad if I asked her. She'd of just rocked harder than ever.'

Some time before, the population of the courtroom had begun stealing glances at the middle-aged lady with yellowish-white hair. She was of a deep, lifelike lobster colour with rage.

'It got to be near the end of the act,' went on the little pale man, 'and I was enjoying it as well as I could, seeing that sometimes she'd push me towards the stage and sometimes she'd let go, and the seat and me would fall back into place. Then all of a sudden she began to talk. She said she had an operation or something – I remember she said she told the doctor that she guessed she knew more about her own stomach than he did. The play was getting good just then – the people next to me had their handkerchiefs out and was weeping – and I was feeling sort of that way myself. And all of a sudden this lady began to tell her friends what she told the plumber about his indigestion. Gosh!' Again he shook his head from side to side; his pale eyes fell involuntarily on Mrs Robinson – then looked quickly away. 'You couldn't help but hear some and I begun missing things and then missing more things and then everybody began laughing and I didn't know what they were laughing at and, as soon as they'd leave off, her voice would begin again. Then there was a great big laugh that lasted for a long time and everybody bent over double and kept laughing and laughing, and I hadn't heard a word. First thing I knew the curtain came down and then I don't know what happened. I must have been a little crazy or something because I got up and closed my seat, and reached back and pushed the lady in the face.'

As he concluded there was a long sigh in the courtroom as though everyone had been holding his breath waiting for the climax. Even the judge gasped a little and the three ladies on the witness bench burst into a shrill chatter and grew louder and louder and shriller and shriller until the judge's gavel rang out again upon his desk.

'Charles Stuart,' said the judge in a slightly raised voice, 'is this the only extenuation you can make for raising your hand against a woman of the plaintiff's age?'

Charles Stuart's head sank a little between his shoulders, seeming to withdraw as far as it was able into the poor shelter of his body.

'Yes, sir,' he said faintly.

Mrs Robinson sprang to her feet.

'Yes, judge,' she cried shrilly, 'and there's more than that. He's a liar too, a dirty little liar. He's just proclaimed himself a dirty little—'

'Silence!' cried the judge in a terrible voice. 'I'm running this court, and I'm capable of making my own decisions!' He paused. 'I will now pronounce sentence upon Charles Stuart,' he referred to the register, 'upon Charles David Stuart of 212½ West Twenty-second Street.'

The courtroom was silent. The reporter drew nearer – he hoped the sentence would be light – just a few days on the Island in lieu of a fine.

The judge leaned back in his chair and hid his thumbs somewhere under his black robe.

'Assault justified,' he said. 'Case dismissed.'

The little man, Charles Stuart, came blinking out into the sunshine, pausing for a moment at the door of the court and looking furtively behind him as if he half expected that it was a judicial error. Then sniffling once or twice, not because he had a cold but for those dim psychological reasons that make people sniff, he moved slowly south with an eye out for a subway station.

He stopped at a news-stand to buy a morning paper; then entering the subway was borne south to Eighteenth Street where he disembarked and walked east to Third Avenue. Here he was employed in an all-night restaurant built of glass and plaster white tile. Here he sat at a desk from curfew until dawn, taking in money and balancing the books of T. Cushmael, the proprietor. And here, through the interminable nights, his eyes, by turning a little to right or left, could rest upon the starched linen uniform of Miss Edna Shaeffer.

Miss Edna Shaeffer was twenty-three, with a sweet mild face and hair that was a living example of how henna should not be applied. She was unaware of this latter fact, because all the girls she knew used henna just this way, so perhaps the odd vermilion tint of her coiffure did not matter.

Charles Stuart had forgotten about the colour of her hair long ago – if he had ever noticed its strangeness at all. He was much more interested in her eyes, and in her white hands which, as they moved deftly among piles of plates and cups, always looked as if they should be playing the piano. He had almost asked her to go to a matinee with him once, but when she had faced him her lips half-parted in a weary, cheerful smile, she had seemed so beautiful that he had lost courage and mumbled something else instead.

It was not to see Edna Schaeffer, however, that he had come to the restaurant so early in the afternoon. It was to consult with T. Cushmael, his employer, and discover if he had lost his job during his night in jail. T. Cushmael was standing in the front of the restaurant looking gloomily out the plate-glass window, and Charles Stuart approached him with ominous forebodings.

'Where've you been?' demanded T. Cushmael.

'Nowhere,' answered Charles Stuart discreetly.

'Well, you're fired.'

Stuart winced.

'Right now?'

Cushmael waved his hands apathetically.

'Stay two or three days if you want to, till I find somebody. Then' – he made a gesture of expulsion – 'outside for you.'

Charles Stuart assented with a weary little nod. He assented to everything. At nine o'clock, after a depressed interval during which he brooded upon the penalty of spending a night among the police, he reported for work.

'Hello, Mr Stuart,' said Edna Schaeffer, sauntering curiously toward him as he took his place behind the desk. 'What became of you last night? Get pinched?'

She laughed, cheerfully, huskily, charmingly he thought, at her joke.

'Yes,' he answered on a sudden impulse, 'I was in the Thirty-fifth Street jail.'

'Yes, you were,' she scoffed.

'That's the truth,' he insisted, 'I was arrested.'

Her face grew serious at once.

'Go on. What did you do?'

He hesitated.

'I pushed somebody in the face.'

Suddenly she began to laugh, at first with amusement and then immoderately.

'It's a fact,' mumbled Stuart. 'I almost got sent to prison account of it.'

Setting her hand firmly over her mouth Edna turned away from him and retired to the refuge of the kitchen. A little later, when he was pretending to be busy at the accounts, he saw her retailing the story to the two other girls.

The night wore on. The little man in the greyish suit with the greyish face attracted no more attention from the customers than the whirring electric fan over his head. They gave him their money and his hand slid their change into a little hollow in the marble counter. But to Charles Stuart the hours of this night, this last night, began to assume a quality of romance. The slow routine of a hundred other nights unrolled with a new enchantment before his eyes. Midnight was always a sort of a dividing point – after that the intimate part of the evening began. Fewer people came in, and the ones that did seemed depressed and tired: a casual ragged man for coffee, the beggar from the street corner who ate a heavy meal of cakes and a beefsteak, a few nightbound street-women and a watchman with a red face who exchanged warning phrases with him about his health.

Midnight seemed to come early tonight and business was brisk until after one. When Edna began to fold napkins at a nearby table he was tempted to ask her if she too had not found the night unusually short. Vainly he wished that he might impress himself on her in some way, make some remark to her, some sign of his devotion that she would remember for ever.

She finished folding the vast pile of napkins, loaded it on to the stand and bore it away, humming to herself. A few minutes later the door opened and two customers came in. He recognized them immediately, and as he did so a flush of jealousy went over him. One of them, a young man in a handsome brown suit, cut away rakishly from his abdomen, had been a frequent visitor for the last ten days. He came in always at about this hour, sat down at one of Edna's tables, and drank two cups of coffee with lingering ease. On his last two visits he had been accompanied by his present companion, a swarthy Greek with sour eyes who ordered in a loud voice and gave vent to noisy sarcasm when anything was not to his taste.

It was chiefly the young man, though, who annoyed Charles Stuart. The young man's eyes followed Edna wherever she went and on his last two visits he had made unnecessary requests in order to bring her more often to his table.

'Good evening, girlie,' Stuart heard him say tonight. 'How's tricks?'

'OK,' answered Edna formally. 'What'll it be?'

'What have you?' smiled the young man. 'Everything, eh? Well, what'd you recommend?'

124

Edna did not answer. Her eyes were staring straight over his head into some invisible distance.

He ordered finally at the urging of his companion. Edna withdrew and Stuart saw the young man turn and whisper to his friend, indicating Edna with his head.

Stuart shifted uncomfortably in his seat. He hated that young man and wished passionately that he would go away. It seemed as if his last night here, his last chance to watch Edna, and perhaps even in some blessed moment to talk to her a little, was marred by every moment this man stayed.

Half a dozen more people had drifted into the restaurant – two or three workmen, the newsdealer from over the way – and Edna was too busy for a few minutes to be bothered with attentions. Suddenly Charles Stuart became aware that the sour-eyed Greek had raised his hand and was beckoning him. Somewhat puzzled he left his desk and approached the table.

'Say, fella,' said the Greek, 'what time does the boss come in?'

'Why – two o'clock. Just a few minutes now.'

'All right. That's all. I just wanted to speak to him about something.'

Stuart realized that Edna was standing beside the table; both men turned towards her.

'Say, girlie,' said the young man, 'I want to talk to you. Sit down.'

'I can't.'

'Sure you can. The boss don't mind.' He turned menacingly to Stuart. 'She can sit down, can't she?'

Stuart did not answer.

'I say she can sit down, can't she?' said the young man more intently, and added, 'Speak up, you little dummy.'

Still Stuart did not answer. Strange blood currents were flowing all over his body. He was frightened; anything said determinedly had a way of frightening him. But he could not move.

'Sh!' said the Greek to his companion.

But the younger man was angered.

'Say,' he broke out, 'some time somebody's going to take a paste at you when you don't answer what they say. Go on back to your desk!'

Still Stuart did not move.

'Go on away!' repeated the young man in a dangerous voice. 'Hurry up! *Run!*'

Then Stuart ran. He ran as hard as he was able. But instead of running away from the young man he ran *towards* him, stretching out his hands as he came near in a sort of straight arm that brought his two palms, with all the force of his hundred and thirty pounds, against his victim's face. With a crash of china the young man went over backward in his chair and, his head striking the edge of the next table, lay motionless on the floor.

The restaurant was in a small uproar. There was a terrified scream from Edna, an indignant protest from the Greek, and the customers arose with exclamations from their tables. Just at this moment the door opened and Mr Cushmael came in.

'Why you little fool!' cried Edna wrathfully. 'What are you trying to do? Lose me my job?'

'What's this?' demanded Mr Cushmael, hurrying over. 'What's the idea?'

'Mr Stuart pushed a customer in the face!' cried a waitress, taking Edna's cue. 'For no reason at all!'

The population of the restaurant had now gathered around the prostrate victim. He was doused thoroughly with water and a folded tablecloth was placed under his head.

'Oh, he did, did he?' shouted Mr Cushmael in a terrible voice, seizing Stuart by the lapels of his coat.

'He's raving crazy!' sobbed Edna. 'He was in jail last night for pushing a lady in the face. He told me so himself!'

A large labourer reached over and grasped Stuart's small trembling arm. Stuart gazed around dumbly. His mouth was quivering.

'Look what you done!' shouted Mr Cushmael. 'You like to kill a man.'

Stuart shivered violently. His mouth opened and he fought the air for a moment. Then he uttered a half-articulate sentence:

'Only meant to push him in the face.'

'Push him in the face?' ejaculated Cushmael in a frenzy. 'So you got to be a pusher-in-the-face, eh? Well, we'll push your face right into jail!'

'I – I couldn't help it,' gasped Stuart. 'Sometimes I can't help it.' His voice rose unevenly. 'I guess I'm a dangerous man and you better take me and lock me up!' He turned wildly to Cushmael, 'I'd push you in the face if he'd let go of my arm. Yes, I would! I'd push you – right-in-the-*face*!'

For a moment an astonished silence fell, broken by the voice of one of the waitresses who had been groping under the table.

'Some stuff dropped out of this fella's back pocket when he tipped over,' she explained, getting to her feet. 'It's – why, it's a revolver and—'

She had been about to say handkerchief, but as she looked at what she was holding her mouth fell open and she dropped the thing quickly on the table. It was a small black mask about the size of her hand.

Simultaneously the Greek, who had been shifting uneasily upon his feet ever since the accident, seemed to remember an important engagement that had slipped his mind. He dashed suddenly around the table and made for the front door, but it opened just at that moment to admit several customers who, at the cry of 'Stop him!' obligingly spread out their arms. Barred in that direction, he jumped an overturned chair, vaulted over the delicatessen counter, and set out for the kitchen, collapsing precipitately in the firm grasp of the chef in the doorway.

'Hold him! Hold him!' screamed Mr Cushmael, realizing the turn of the situation. 'They're after my cash drawer!'

Willing hands assisted the Greek over the counter, where he stood panting and gasping under two dozen excited eyes.

'After my money, hey?' shouted the proprietor, shaking his fist under the captive's nose.

The stout man nodded, panting.

'We'd of got it too!' he gasped, 'if it hadn't been for that little pusher-in-the-face.'

Two dozen eyes looked around eagerly. The little pusher-in-the-face had disappeared.

The beggar on the corner had just decided to tip the policeman and shut up shop for the night when he suddenly felt a small, somewhat excited hand fall on his shoulder.

'Help a poor man to get a place to sleep—' he was beginning automatically when he recognized the little cashier from the restaurant. 'Hello, brother,' he added, leering up at him and changing his tone.

'You know what?' cried the little cashier in a strangely ominous tone. 'I'm going to push you in the face!'

'What do you mean?' snarled the beggar. 'Why, you Ga—'

He got no farther. The little man seemed to run at him suddenly, holding out his hands, and there was a sharp, smacking sound as the beggar came in contact with the sidewalk.

'You're a faker!' shouted Charles Stuart wildly. 'I gave you a dollar when I first came here, before I found out you had ten times as much as I had. And you never gave it back!'

A stout, faintly intoxicated gentleman who was strutting expansively along the other sidewalk had seen the incident and came running benevolently across the street.

'What does this mean!' he exclaimed in a hearty, shocked voice. 'Why poor fellow—' He turned indignant eyes on Charles Stuart and knelt unsteadily to raise the beggar.

The beggar stopped cursing and assumed a piteous whine.

'I'm a poor man, Cap'n—'

'This is – this is *horrible!*' cried the Samaritan, with tears in his eyes. 'It's a disgrace! Police! *Pol—!*'

He got no farther. His hands, which he was raising for a megaphone, never reached his face – other hands reached his face, however, hands held stiffly out from a one-hundred-and-thirty-pound body! He sank down suddenly upon the beggar's abdomen, forcing out a sharp curse which faded into a groan.

'This beggar'll take you home in his car!' shouted the little man who stood over him. 'He's got it parked around the corner.'

Turning his face towards the hot strip of sky which lowered over the city the little man began to laugh, with amusement at first, then loudly and triumphantly until his high laughter ran out in the quiet street with a weird, elfish sound, echoing up the sides of the tall buildings, growing shriller and shriller until people blocks away heard its eerie cadence on the air and stopped to listen.

Still laughing the little man divested himself of his coat and then of his vest and hurriedly freed his neck of tie and collar. Then he spat upon his hands and with a wild, shrill, exultant cry began to run down the dark street.

He was going to clean up New York, and his first objective was the disagreeable policeman on the corner!

They caught him at two o'clock, and the crowd which had joined in the chase were flabbergasted when they found that the ruffian was only a weeping little man in his shirt sleeves. Someone at the station house was wise enough to give him an opiate instead of a padded cell, and in the morning he felt much better.

Mr Cushmael, accompanied by an anxious young lady with crimson hair, called at the jail before noon.

'I'll get you out,' cried Mr Cushmael, shaking hands excitedly through the bars. 'One policeman, he'll explain it all to the other.'

'And there's a surprise for you too,' added Edna softly, taking his other hand. 'Mr Cushmael's got a big heart and he's going to make you his day man now.'

'All right,' agreed Charles Stuart calmly. 'But I can't start till tomorrow.'

'Why not?'

'Because this afternoon I got to go to a matinée – with a friend.'

He relinquished his employer's hand but kept Edna's white fingers twined firmly in his.

'One more thing,' he went on in a strong, confident voice that was new to him, 'if you want to get me off don't have the case come up in the Thirty-fifth Street court.'

'Why not?'

'Because,' he answered with a touch of swagger in his voice, 'that's the judge I had when I was arrested last time.'

'Charles,' whispered Edna suddenly, 'what would you do if I refused to go with you this afternoon?'

He bristled. Colour came into his cheeks and he rose defiantly from his bench.

'Why, I'd – I'd—'

'Never mind,' she said, flushing slightly. 'You'd do nothing of the kind.'

ONE OF MY OLDEST FRIENDS

Woman's Home Companion, September 1925

*'One of My Oldest Friends' was written in Great Neck in March 1924.
When Fitzgerald sent it to Ober he noted, 'Here's the revised story. I don't
know what to think of it but I'd rather not offer it to the* Post. *The ending
is effective but a little sensational.'* Woman's Home Companion *paid
$1750 for it and used it as a lead piece.*

*Fitzgerald's reservations about the story were well-founded. The use of a
crucifix at the end represents one of his rare excursions into forced religious
symbolism. Nonetheless, 'One of My Oldest Friends' was a popular story.
It was included in* The World's Best Short Stories of 1926 *and was
probably syndicated in newspapers, as short stories often were at that time.*

All afternoon Marion had been happy. She wandered from room to room
of their little apartment, strolling into the nursery to help the nurse-girl feed
the children from dripping spoons, and then reading for a while on their
new sofa, the most extravagant thing they had bought in their five years of
marriage.

When she heard Michael's step in the hall she turned her head and
listened; she liked to hear him walk, carefully always as if there were
children sleeping close by.

'Michael.'

'Oh – hello.' He came into the room, a tall, broad, thin man of thirty
with a high forehead and kind black eyes.

'I've got some news for you,' he said immediately. 'Charley Hart's
getting married.'

'No!'

He nodded.

'Who's he marrying?'

'One of the little Lawrence girls from home.' He hesitated. 'She's arriving in New York tomorrow and I think we ought to do something for them while she's here. Charley's about my oldest friend.'

'Let's have them up for dinner—'

'I'd like to do something more than that,' he interrupted. 'Maybe a theatre party. You see—' Again he hesitated. 'It'd be a nice courtesy to Charley.'

'All right,' agreed Marion, 'but we mustn't spend much – and I don't think we're under any obligation.'

He looked at her in surprise.

'I mean,' went on Marion, 'we – we hardly see Charley any more.We hardly ever see him at all.'

'Well, you know how it is in New York,' explained Michael apologetically. 'He's just as busy as I am. He has made a big name for himself and I suppose he's pretty much in demand all the time.'

They always spoke of Charley Hart as their oldest friend. Five years before, when Michael and Marion were first married, the three of them had come to New York from the same western city. For over a year they had seen Charley nearly every day and no domestic adventure, no uprush of their hopes and dreams, was too insignificant for his ear. His arrival in times of difficulty never failed to give a pleasant, humorous cast to the situation.

Of course Marion's babies had made a difference, and it was several years now since they had called up Charley at midnight to say that the pipes had broken or the ceiling was falling in on their heads; but so gradually had they drifted apart that Michael still spoke of Charley rather proudly as if he saw him every day. For a while Charley dined with them once a month and all three found a great deal to say; but the meetings never broke up any more with 'I'll give you a ring tomorrow.' Instead it was 'You'll have to come to dinner more often,' or even, after three or four years, 'We'll see you soon.'

'Oh, I'm perfectly willing to give a little party,' said Marion now, looking speculatively about her. 'Did you suggest a definite date?'

'Week from Saturday.' His dark eyes roamed the floor vaguely. 'We can take up the rugs or something.'

'No.' She shook her head. 'We'll have a dinner, eight people, very formal and everything, and afterwards we'll play cards.'

She was already speculating on whom to invite. Charley of course, being an artist, probably saw interesting people every day.

'We could have the Willoughbys,' she suggested doubtfully. 'She's on the stage or something – and he writes movies.'

'No – that's not it,' objected Michael. 'He probably meets that crowd at lunch and dinner every day until he's sick of them. Besides, except for the Willoughbys, who else like that do we know ? I've got a better idea. Let's collect a few people who've drifted down here from home. They've all followed Charley's career and they'd probably enjoy seeing him again. I'd like them to find out how natural and unspoiled he is after all.'

After some discussion they agreed on this plan and within an hour Marion had her first guest on the telephone:

'It's to meet Charley Hart's fiancée,' she explained. 'Charley Hart, the artist. You see, he's one of our oldest friends.'

As she began her preparations her enthusiasm grew. She rented a serving-maid to assure an impeccable service and persuaded the neighbourhood florist to come in person and arrange the flowers. All the 'people from home' had accepted eagerly and the number of guests had swollen to ten.

'What'll we talk about, Michael ?' she demanded nervously on the eve of the party. 'Suppose everything goes wrong and everybody gets mad and goes home ?'

He laughed.

'Nothing will. You see, these people all know each other—'

The phone on the table asserted itself and Michael picked up the receiver.

"Hello . . . why, hello, Charley.'

Marion sat up alertly in her chair.

'Is that so ? Well, I'm very sorry. I'm very, very sorry . . . I hope it's nothing serious.'

'Can't he come ?' broke out Marion.

'Sh!' Then into the phone, 'Well, it certainly is too bad, Charley. No, it's no trouble for us at all. We're just sorry you're ill.'

With a dismal gesture Michael replaced the receiver.

'The Lawrence girl had to go home last night and Charley's sick in bed with grip.'

'Do you mean he can't come ?'

'He can't come.'

Marion's face contracted suddenly and her eyes filled with tears.

'He says he's had the doctor all day,' explained Michael dejectedly. 'He's got fever and they didn't even want him to go to the telephone.'

'I don't care,' sobbed Marion. 'I think it's terrible. After we've invited all these people to meet him.'

'People can't help being sick.'

'Yes they *can*,' she wailed illogically, 'they can help it some way. And if the Lawrence girl was going to leave last night why didn't he let us know *then*?'

'He said she left unexpectedly. Up to yesterday afternoon they both intended to come.'

'I don't think he c-cares a bit. I'll bet he's glad he's sick. If he'd cared he'd have brought her to see us long ago.'

She stood up suddenly.

'I'll tell you one thing,' she assured him vehemently, 'I'm just going to telephone everybody and call the whole thing off.'

'Why, Marion—'

But in spite of his half-hearted protests she picked up the phone book and began looking for the first number.

They bought theatre tickets next day hoping to fill the hollowness which would invest the evening. Marion had wept when the unintercepted florist arrived at five with boxes of flowers and she felt that she must get out of the house to avoid the ghosts who would presently people it. In silence they ate an elaborate dinner composed of all the things that she had bought for the party.

'It's only eight,' said Michael afterwards. 'I think it'd be sort of nice if we dropped in on Charley for a minute, don't you?'

'Why, no,' Marion answered, startled, 'I wouldn't think of it.'

'Why not? If he's seriously sick I'd like to see how well he's being taken care of.'

She saw that he had made up his mind, so she fought down her instinct against the idea and they taxied to a tall pile of studio apartments on Madison Avenue.

'You go on in,' urged Marion nervously, 'I'd rather wait out here.'

'Please come in.'

'Why? He'll be in bed and he doesn't want any women around.'

'But he'd like to see you – it'd cheer him up. And he'd know that we understood about tonight. He sounded awfully depressed over the phone.'

He urged her from the cab.

'Let's only stay a minute,' she whispered tensely as they went up in the elevator. 'The show starts at half past eight.'

'Apartment on the right,' said the elevator man.

They rang the bell and waited. The door opened and they walked directly into Charley Hart's great studio room.

It was crowded with people; from end to end ran a long lamp-lit dinner table strewn with ferns and young roses, from which a gay murmur of laughter and conversation arose into the faintly smoky air. Twenty women in evening dress sat on one side in a row chatting across the flowers at twenty men, with an elation born of the sparkling Burgundy which dripped from many bottles into thin chilled glass. Up on the high narrow balcony which encircled the room a string quartet was playing something by Stravinsky in a key that was pitched just below the women's voices and filled the air like an audible wine.

The door had been opened by one of the waiters, who stepped back deferentially from what he thought were two belated guests – and immediately a handsome man at the head of the table started to his feet, napkin in hand, and stood motionless, staring towards the newcomers. The conversation faded into half silence and all eyes followed Charley Hart's to the couple at the door. Then, as if the spell was broken, conversation resumed, gathering momentum word by word – the moment was over.

'Let's get out!' Marion's low, terrified whisper came to Michael out of a void and for a minute he thought he was possessed by an illusion, that there was no one but Charley in the room after all. Then his eyes cleared and he saw that there were many people here – he had never seen so many! The music swelled suddenly into the tumult of a great brass band and a wind from the loud horns seemed to blow against them; without turning he and Marion each made one blind step backward into the hall, pulling the door to after them.

'Marion—!'

She had run towards the elevator, stood with one finger pressed hard against the bell which rang through the hall like a last high note from the music inside. The door of the apartment opened suddenly and Charley Hart came out into the hall.

'Michael!' he cried, 'Michael and Marion, I want to explain! Come inside. I want to *explain*, I tell you.'

He talked excitedly – his face was flushed and his mouth formed a word or two that did not materialize into sound.

'Hurry up, Michael,' came Marion's voice tensely from the elevator.

'Let me explain,' cried Charley frantically. 'I want—'

Michael moved away from him – the elevator came and the gate clanged open.

'You act as if I committed some crime,' Charley was following Michael along the hall. 'Can't you understand that this is all an accidental situation?'

'It's all right,' Michael muttered, 'I understand.'

'No, you don't.' Charley's voice rose with exasperation. He was working up anger against them so as to justify his own intolerable position. 'You're going away mad and I asked you to come in and join the party. Why did you come up here if you won't come in? Did you—?'

Michael walked into the elevator.

'Down, please!' cried Marion. 'Oh, I want to go down, *please*!'

The gates clanged shut.

They told the taxi-man to take them directly home – neither of them could have endured the theatre. Driving uptown to their apartment, Michael buried his face in his hands and tried to realize that the friendship which had meant so much to him was over. He saw now that it had been over for some time, that not once during the past year had Charley sought their company and the shock of the discovery far outweighed the affront he had received.

When they reached home, Marion, who had not said a word in the taxi, led the way into the living-room and motioned for her husband to sit down.

'I'm going to tell you something that you ought to know,' she said. 'If it hadn't been for what happened tonight I'd probably never have told you – but now I think you ought to hear the whole story.'

She hesitated. 'In the first place, Charley Hart wasn't a friend of yours at all.'

'What?' He looked up at her dully.

'He wasn't your friend,' she repeated. 'He hasn't been for years. He was a friend of mine.'

'Why, Charley Hart was—'

'I know what you're going to say – that Charley was a friend to both of us. But it isn't true. I don't know how he considered you at first but he stopped being your friend three or four years ago.'

'Why—' Michael's eyes glowed with astonishment. 'If that's true, why was he with us all the time?'

'On account of me,' said Marion steadily. 'He was in love with me.'

'What?' Michael laughed incredulously. 'You're imagining things. I know how he used to pretend in a kidding way—'

'It wasn't kidding,' she interrupted, 'not underneath. It began that way – and it ended by his asking me to run away with him.'

Michael frowned.

'Go on,' he said quietly, 'I suppose this is true or you wouldn't be telling me about it – but it simply doesn't seem real. Did he just suddenly begin to – to—'

He closed his mouth suddenly, unable to say the words.

'It began one night when we three were out dancing.' Marion hesitated. 'And at first I thoroughly enjoyed it. He had a faculty for noticing things – noticing dresses and hats and the new ways I'd do my hair. He was good company. He could always make me feel important, somehow, and attractive. Don't get the idea that I preferred his company to yours – I didn't. I knew how completely selfish he was, and what a will-o'-the-wisp. But I encouraged him, I suppose – I thought it was fine. It was a new angle on Charley, and he was amusing at it just as he was at everything he did.'

'Yes – ' agreed Michael with an effort, 'I suppose it was – hilariously amusing.'

'At first he liked you just the same. It didn't occur to him that he was doing anything treacherous to you. He was just following a natural impulse – that was all. But after a few weeks he began to find you in the way. He wanted to take me to dinner without you along – and it couldn't be done. Well, that sort of thing went on for over a year.'

'What happened then?'

'Nothing happened. That's why he stopped coming to see us any more.'

Michael rose slowly to his feet.

'Do you mean—'

'Wait a minute. If you'll think a little you'll see it was bound to turn out that way. When he saw that I was trying to let him down easily so that he'd be simply one of our oldest friends again, he broke away. He didn't want to be one of our oldest friends – that time was over.'

'I see.'

'Well—' Marion stood up and began biting nervously at her lip, 'that's all. I thought this thing tonight would hurt you less if you understood the whole affair.'

'Yes,' Michael answered in a dull voice, 'I suppose that's true.'

Michael's business took a prosperous turn, and when summer came they went to the country, renting a little old farmhouse where the children played all day on a tangled half-acre of grass and trees. The subject of Charley was never mentioned between them and as the months passed he receded to a shadowy background in their minds. Sometimes, just before dropping off to sleep, Michael found himself thinking of the happy times the three of them had had together five years before – then the reality would intrude upon the illusion and he would be repelled from the subject with almost physical distaste.

One warm evening in July he lay dozing on the porch in the twilight. He had had a hard day at his office and it was welcome to rest here while the summer light faded from the land.

At the sound of an automobile he raised his head lazily. At the end of the path a local taxicab had stopped and a young man was getting out. With an exclamation Michael sat up. Even in the dusk he recognized those shoulders, that impatient walk—

'Well, I'm damned,' he said softly.

As Charley Hart came up the gravel path Michael noticed in a glance that he was unusually dishevelled. His handsome face was drawn and tired, his clothes were out of press and he had the unmistakable look of needing a good night's sleep.

He came up on the porch, saw Michael and smiled in a wan, embarrassed way.

'Hello, Michael.'

Neither of them made any move to shake hands but after a moment Charley collapsed abruptly into a chair.

'I'd like a glass of water,' he said huskily, 'it's hot as hell.'

'Without a word Michael went into the house – returned with a glass of water which Charley drank in great noisy gulps.

'Thanks,' he said, gasping, 'I thought I was going to pass away.'

He looked about him with eyes that only pretended to take in his surroundings.

'Nice little place you've got here,' he remarked; his eyes returned to Michael. 'Do you want me to get out?'

'Why – no. Sit and rest if you want to. You look all in.'

'I am. Do you want to hear about it?'

'Not in the least.'

'Well, I'm going to tell you anyhow,' said Charley defiantly. 'That's what I came out here for. I'm in trouble, Michael, and I haven't got anybody to go to except you.'

'Have you tried your friends?' asked Michael coolly.

'I've tried about everybody – everybody I've had time to go to. God!' He wiped his forehead with his hand. 'I never realized how hard it was to raise a simple two thousand dollars.'

'Have you come to me for two thousand dollars?'

'Wait a minute, Michael. Wait till you hear. It just shows you what a mess a man can get into without meaning any harm. You see, I'm the treasurer of a society called the Independent Artists' Benefit – a thing to help struggling students. There was a fund, thirty-five hundred dollars, and it's been lying in my bank for over a year. Well, as you know, I live pretty high – make a lot and spend a lot – and about a month ago I began speculating a little through a friend of mine—'

'I don't know why you're telling me all this,' interrupted Michael impatiently, 'I—'

'Wait a minute, won't you – I'm almost through.' He looked at Michael with frightened eyes. 'I used that money sometimes without even realizing that it wasn't mine. I've always had plenty of my own, you see. Till this week.' He hesitated. 'This week there was a meeting of this society and they asked me to turn over the money. Well, I went to a couple of men to try and borrow it and as soon as my back was turned one of them blabbed. There was a terrible blow-up last night. They told me unless I handed over the two thousand this morning they'd send me to jail—' His voice rose and he looked around wildly. 'There's a warrant out for me now – and if I can't get the money I'll kill myself, Michael; I swear to God I will; I won't go to prison. I'm an artist – not a businessman. I—'

He made an effort to control his voice.

'Michael,' he whispered, 'you're my oldest friend. I haven't got anyone in the world but you to turn to.'

'You're a little late,' said Michael uncomfortably, 'you didn't think of me four years ago when you asked my wife to run away with you.'

A look of sincere surprise passed over Charley's face.

'Are you mad at me about that?' he asked in a puzzled way. 'I thought you were mad because I didn't come to your party.'

Michael did not answer.

'I supposed she'd told you about that long ago,' went on Charley. 'I couldn't help it about Marion, I was lonesome and you two had each other. Every time I went to your house you'd tell me what a wonderful girl Marion was and finally I – I began to agree with you. How could I help falling in love with her, when for a year and a half she was the only decent girl I knew?' He looked defiantly at Michael. 'Well, you've got her, haven't you. I didn't take her away. I never so much as kissed her – do you have to rub it in?'

'Look here,' said Michael sharply, 'just why should I lend you this money?'

'Well—' Charley hesitated, laughed uneasily. 'I don't know any exact reason. I just thought you would.'

'Why should I?'

'No reason at all, I suppose, from your way of looking at it.'

'That's the trouble. If I gave it to you it would just be because I was slushy and soft. I'd be doing something that I don't want to do.'

'All right,' Charley smiled unpleasantly, 'that's logical. Now that I think, there's no reason why you should lend it to me. Well—' He shoved his hands into his coat pocket and throwing his head back slightly seemed to shake the subject off like a cap. 'I won't go to prison – and maybe you'll feel differently about it tomorrow.'

'Don't count on that.'

'Oh, I don't mean I'll ask you again. I mean something – quite different.'

He nodded his head, turned quickly and walking down the gravel path was swallowed up in the darkness. Where the path met the road Michael heard his footsteps cease as if he were hesitating. Then they turned down the road toward the station a mile away.

Michael sank into his chair, burying his face in his hands. He heard Marion come out the door.

'I listened,' she whispered, 'I couldn't help it. I'm glad you didn't lend him anything.'

She came close to him and would have sat down in his lap but an almost physical repulsion came over him and he got up quickly from his chair.

'I was afraid he'd work on your sentiment and make a fool of you,' went on Marion. She hesitated. 'He hated you, you know. He used to wish you'd die. I told him that if he ever said so to me again I'd never see him any more.'

Michael looked up at her darkly.

'In fact, you were very noble.'

'Why, Michael—'

'You let him say things like that to you – and then when he comes here, down and out, without a friend in the world to turn to, you say you're glad I sent him away.'

'It's because I love you, dear—'

'No, it isn't!' He interrupted savagely. 'It's because hate's cheap in this world. Everybody's got it for sale. My God! What do you suppose I think of myself now?'

'He's not worth feeling that way about.'

'Please go away!' cried Michael passionately. 'I want to be alone.'

Obediently she left him and he sat down again in the darkness of the porch, a sort of terror creeping over him. Several times he made a motion to get up but each time he frowned and remained motionless. Then after another long while he jumped suddenly to his feet, cold sweat starting from his forehead. The last hour, the months just passed, were washed away and he was swept years back in time. Why, they were after Charley Hart, his old friend. Charley Hart who had come to him because he had no other place to go. Michael began to run hastily about the porch in a daze, hunting for his hat and coat.

'Why Charley!' he cried aloud.

He found his coat finally and, struggling into it, ran wildly down the steps. It seemed to him that Charley had gone only a few minutes before. 'Charley!' he called when he reached the road. 'Charley, come back here. There's been a mistake!'

He paused, listening. There was no answer. Panting a little he began to run doggedly along the road through the hot night.

It was only half past eight o'clock but the country was very quiet and the frogs were loud in the strip of wet marsh that ran along beside the road. The sky was salted thinly with stars and after a while there would be a moon, but the road ran among dark trees and Michael could scarcely see ten feet in front of him. After a while he slowed down to a walk, glancing at the phosphorous dial of his wrist watch – the New York train was not due for an hour. There was plenty of time.

In spite of this he broke into an uneasy run and covered the mile between his house and the station in fifteen minutes. It was a little station, crouched humbly beside the shining rails in the darkness. Beside it Michael saw the lights of a single taxi waiting for the next train.

The platform was deserted and Michael opened the door and peered into the dim waiting-room. It was empty.

'That's funny,' he muttered.

Rousing a sleepy taxi driver, he asked if there had been anyone waiting for the train. The taxi driver considered – yes, there had been a young man waiting, about twenty minutes ago. He had walked up and down for a while, smoking a cigarette, and then gone away into the darkness.

'That's funny,' repeated Michael. He made a megaphone of his hands and facing towards the wood across the track shouted aloud.

'Charley!'

There was no answer. He tried again. Then he turned back to the driver. 'Have you any idea what direction he went?'

The man pointed vaguely down the New York road which ran along beside the railroad track.

'Down there somewhere.'

With increasing uneasiness Michael thanked him and started swiftly along the road which was white now under the risen moon. He knew now as surely as he knew anything that Charley had gone off by himself to die. He remembered the expression on his face as he had turned away and the hand tucked down close in his coat pocket as if it clutched some menacing thing.

'Charley!' he called in a terrible voice.

The dark trees gave back no sound. He walked on past a dozen fields bright as silver under the moon, pausing every few minutes to shout and then waiting tensely for an answer.

It occurred to him that it was foolish to continue in this direction – Charley was probably back by the station in the woods somewhere. Perhaps it was all imagination, perhaps even now Charley was pacing the station platform waiting for the train from the city. But some impulse beyond logic made him continue. More than that – several times he had the sense that someone was in front of him, someone who just eluded him at every turning, out of sight and earshot, yet leaving always behind him a dim, tragic aura of having passed that way. Once he thought he heard steps among the leaves on the side of the road but it was only a piece of vagrant newspaper blown by the faint hot wind.

It was a stifling night – the moon seemed to be beating hot rays down upon the sweltering earth. Michael took off his coat and threw it over his arm as he walked. A little way ahead of him now was a stone bridge over the tracks and beyond that an interminable line of telephone poles which stretched in diminishing perspective towards an endless horizon. Well, he would walk to the bridge and then give up. He would have given up before except for this sense he had that someone was walking very lightly and swiftly just ahead.

Reaching the stone bridge he sat down on a rock, his heart beating in loud exhausted thumps under his dripping shirt. Well, it was hopeless – Charley was gone, perhaps out of range of his help for ever. Far away beyond the station he heard the approaching siren of the nine-thirty train.

Michael found himself wondering suddenly why he was here. He despised himself for being here. On what weak chord in his nature had Charley played in those few minutes, forcing him into this senseless, frightened run through the night? They had discussed it all and Charley had been unable to give a reason why he should be helped.

He got to his feet with the idea of retracing his steps but before turning he stood for a minute in the moonlight looking down the road. Across the track stretched the line of telephone poles and, as his eyes followed them as far as he could see, he heard again, louder now and not far away, the siren of the New York train which rose and fell with musical sharpness on the still night. Suddenly his eyes, which had been travelling down the tracks, stopped and were focussed suddenly upon one spot in the line of poles, perhaps a quarter of a mile away. It was a pole just like the others and yet it was different – there was something about it that was indescribably different.

And watching it as one might concentrate on some figure in the pattern of a carpet, something curious happened in his mind and instantly he saw everything in a completely different light. Something had come to him in a whisper of the breeze, something that changed the whole complexion of the situation. It was this: He remembered having read somewhere that at some point back in the dark ages a man named Gerbert had all by himself summed up the whole of European civilization. It became suddenly plain to Michael that he himself had just now been in a position like that. For one minute, one spot in time, all the mercy in the world had been vested in him.

He realized all this in the space of a second with a sense of shock and instantly he understood the reason why he should have helped Charley Hart. It was because it would be intolerable to exist in a world where there was no help – where any human being could be as alone as Charley had been alone this afternoon.

Why, that was it, of course – he had been trusted with that chance. Someone had come to him who had no other place to go – and he had failed.

All this time, this moment, he had been standing utterly motionless staring at the telephone pole down the track, the one that his eye had picked out as being different from the others. The moon was so bright now that near the top he could see a white bar set crosswise on the pole and as he looked the pole and the bar seemed to have become isolated as if the other poles had shrunk back and away.

Suddenly a mile down the track he heard the click and clamour of the electric train when it left the station, and as if the sound had startled him into life he gave a short cry and set off at a swaying run down the road, in the direction of the pole with the crossed bar.

The train whistled again. *Click – click – click –* it was nearer now, six hundred, five hundred yards away and as it came under the bridge he was running in the bright beam of its searchlight. There was no emotion in his mind but terror – he knew only that he must reach that pole before the train and it was fifty yards away, struck out sharp as a star against the sky.

There was no path on the other side of the tracks under the poles but the train was so close now that he dared wait no longer or he would be unable to cross at all. He darted from the road, cleared the tracks in two strides and with the sound of the engine at his heels raced along the rough earth. Twenty feet, thirty feet – as the sound of the electric train swelled to a roar in his ears he reached the pole and threw himself bodily on a man who stood close to the tracks, carrying him heavily to the ground with the impact of his body.

There was the thunder of steel in his ear, the heavy clump of the wheels on the rails, a swift roaring of air, and the nine-thirty train had gone past.

'Charley,' he gasped incoherently, 'Charley.'

A white face looked up at him in a daze. Michael rolled over on his back and lay panting. The hot night was quiet now – there was no sound but the far-away murmur of the receding train.

'Oh, God!'

Michael opened his eyes to see that Charley was sitting up, his face in his hands.

'S'all right,' gasped Michael, 's'all right, Charley. You can have the money. I don't know what I was thinking about. Why – why, you're one of my oldest friends.'

Charley shook his head.

'I don't understand,' he said brokenly. 'Where did you come from – how did you get here?'

'I've been following you. I was just behind.'

'I've been here for half an hour.'

'Well, it's good you chose this pole to – to wait under. I've been looking at it from down by the bridge. I picked it out on account of the crossbar.'

Charley had risen unsteadily to his feet and now he walked a few steps and looked up the pole in the full moonlight.

'What did you say?' he asked after a minute, in a puzzled voice. 'Did you say this pole had a crossbar?'

'Why, yes. I was looking at it a long time. That's how—'

Charley looked up again and hesitated curiously before he spoke.

'There isn't any crossbar,' he said.

THE UNSPEAKABLE EGG

Saturday Evening Post, 12 July 1924

'The Unspeakable Egg' was written in Great Neck in April 1924. The Post
paid $1750 for it.

*Most of the 1924 stories depend on trick plots; and 'Egg' employs the
concealed identity gimmick that Fitzgerald had used effectively before. It
seems probable that some of these stories were written with the hope of a
movie sale, since three of his stories had been made into movies. There were
no takers for 'Egg'.*

Fitzgerald has been critized for the facility of his Post *stories – which was
what he was being paid for. He was writing entertainment for the 2,750,000
customers who bought the magazine in the twenties. But what seemed like
facility was not the result of easy writing. His stories had a finish or polish
that was achieved with painstaking care. Even the commercial stories were
distinctive because of the deft touches that made them recognizable as
Fitzgerald stories. One such passage in 'Egg' is the description of the
newspaper report of a society wedding.*

When Fifi visited her Long Island aunts the first time she was only ten
years old, but after she went back to New York the man who worked
around the place said that the sand dunes would never be the same again.
She had spoiled them. When she left, everything on Montauk Point seemed
sad and futile and broken and old. Even the gulls wheeled about less
enthusiastically, as if they missed the brown, hardy little girl with big eyes
who played barefoot in the sand.

The years bleached out Fifi's tan and turned her a pale-pink colour, but
she still managed to spoil many places and plans for many hopeful men. So
when at last it was announced in the best newspapers that she had con-
centrated on a gentleman named Van Tyne everyone was rather glad that
all the sadness and longing that followed in her wake should become the

responsibility of one self-sacrificing individual; not better for the individual, but for Fifi's little world very much better indeed.

The engagement was not announced on the sporting page, nor even in the help-wanted column, because Fifi's family belonged to the Society for the Preservation of Large Fortunes; and Mr Van Tyne was descended from the man who accidentally founded that society, back before the Civil War. It appeared on the page of great names and was illustrated by a picture of a cross-eyed young lady holding the hand of a savage gentleman with four rows of teeth. That was how their pictures came out, anyhow, and the public was pleased to know that they were ugly monsters for all their money, and everyone was satisfied all around. The society editor set up a column telling how Mrs Van Tyne started off in the *Aquitania* wearing a blue travelling dress of starched felt with a round square hat to match; and so far as human events can be prophesied, Fifi was as good as married; or, as not a few young men considered, as bad as married.

'An exceptionally brilliant match,' remarked Aunt Cal on the eve of the wedding, as she sat in her house on Montauk Point and clipped the notice for the cousins in Scotland, and then she added abstractedly, 'All is forgiven.'

'Why, Cal!' cried Aunt Josephine. 'What do you mean when you say all is forgiven? Fifi has never injured you in any way.'

'In the past nine years she has not seen fit to visit us here at Montauk Point, though we have invited her over and over again.'

'But I don't blame her,' said Aunt Josephine, who was only thirty-one herself. 'What would a young pretty girl do down here with all this sand?'

'We like the sand, Jo.'

'But we're old maids, Cal, with no vices except cigarettes and double-dummy mah-jong. Now Fifi, being young, naturally likes exciting, vicious things – late hours, dice playing, all the diversions we read about in these books.'

She waved her hand vaguely.

'I don't blame her for not coming down here. If I were in her place—'

What unnatural ambitions lurked in Aunt Jo's head were never disclosed, for the sentence remained unfinished. The front door of the house opened in an abrupt, startled way, and a young lady walked into the room in a dress marked 'Paris, France'.

'Good evening, dear ladies,' she cried, smiling radiantly from one to the other. 'I've come down here for an indefinite time in order to play in the sand.'

'Fifi!'

'Fifi!'

'Aunts!'

'But, my dear child,' cried Aunt Jo, 'I thought this was the night of the bridal dinner.'

'It is,' admitted Fifi cheerfully. 'But I didn't go. I'm not going to the wedding either. I sent in my regrets today.'

It was all very vague; but it seemed, as far as her aunts could gather, that young Van Tyne was too perfect – whatever that meant. After much urging Fifi finally explained that he reminded her of an advertisement for a new car.

'A new car?' inquired Aunt Cal, wide eyed. 'What new car?'

'Any new car.'

'Do you mean—'

Aunt Cal blushed.

'I don't understand this new slang, but isn't there some part of a car that's called – the clutch?'

'Oh, I like him physically,' remarked Fifi coolly. Her aunts started in unison. 'But he was just— Oh, too perfect, too new; as if they'd fooled over him at the factory for a long time and put special curtains on him—'

Aunt Jo had visions of a black-leather sheikh.

'—and balloon tyres and a permanent shave. He was too civilized for me, Aunt Cal.' She sighed. 'I must be one of the rougher girls, after all.'

She was as immaculate and dainty sitting there as though she were the portrait of a young lady and about to be hung on the wall. But underneath her cheerfulness her aunts saw that she was in a state of hysterical excitement, and they persisted in suspecting that something more definite and shameful was the matter.

'But it isn't,' insisted Fifi. 'Our engagement was announced three months ago, and not a single chorus girl has sued George for breach of promise. Not one! He doesn't use alcohol in any form except as hair tonic. Why, we've never even quarrelled until today!'

'You've made a serious mistake,' said Aunt Cal.

Fifi nodded.

'I'm afraid I've broken the heart of the nicest man I ever met in my life, but it can't be helped. Immaculate! Why, what's the use of being immaculate, when, no matter how hard you try, you can't be half so immaculate as your husband? And tactful? George could introduce Mr Trotsky to Mr Rockefeller and there wouldn't be a single blow. But after a certain point, I want to have all the tact in my family, and I told him so. I've never left a man practically at the church door before, so I'm going to stay here until everyone has had a chance to forget.'

And stay she did – rather to the surprise of her aunts, who expected that next morning she would rush wildly and remorsefully back to New York. She appeared at breakfast very calm and fresh and cool, and as though she had slept soundly all night, and spent the day reclining under a red parasol beside the sunny dunes, watching the Atlantic roll in from the east. Her aunts intercepted the evening paper and burnt it unseen in the open fire, under the impression that Fifi's flight would be recorded in red headlines across the front page. They accepted the fact that Fifi was here, and except that Aunt Jo was inclined to go mah-jong without a pair when she speculated on the too perfect man, their lives went along very much the same. But not quite the same.

'What's the matter with that niece of yourn?' demanded the yardman gloomily of Aunt Josephine. 'What's a young pretty girl want to come and hide herself down here for?'

'My niece is resting,' declared Aunt Josephine stiffly.

'Them dunes ain't good for wore-out people,' objected the yardman, soothing his head with his fingers. 'There's a monotoness about them. I seen her yesterday take her parasol and like to beat one down, she got so mad at it. Some day she's going to notice how many of them there are, and all of a sudden go loony.' He sniffed. 'And then what kind of a proposition we going to have on our hands?'

'That will do, Percy,' snapped Aunt Jo. 'Go about your business. I want ten pounds of broken-up shells rolled into the front walk.'

'What'll I do with that parasol?' he demanded. 'I picked up the pieces.'

'It's not my parasol,' said Aunt Jo tartly. 'You can take the pieces and roll them into the front walk too.'

And so the June of Fifi's abandoned honeymoon drifted away, and every morning her rubber shoes left wet footprints along a desolate shore at the end of nowhere. For a while she seemed to thrive on the isolation, and the sea wind blew her cheeks scarlet with health; but after a week had passed, her aunts saw that she was noticeably restless and less cheerful even than when she came.

'I'm afraid it's getting on your nerves, my dear,' said Aunt Cal one particularly wild and windy afternoon. 'We love to have you here, but we hate to see you looking so sad. Why don't you ask your mother to take you to Europe for the summer?'

'Europe's too dressed up,' objected Fifi wearily. 'I like it here where everything's rugged and harsh and rude, like the end of the world. If you don't mind, I'd like to stay longer.'

She stayed longer, and seemed to grow more and more melancholy as the days slipped by to the raucous calls of the gulls and the flashing tumult of the waves along the shore. Then one afternoon she returned at twilight from the longest of her long walks with a strange derelict of a man. And after one look at him her aunts thought that the gardener's prophecy had come true and that solitude had driven Fifi mad at last.

II

He was a very ragged wreck of a man as he stood in the doorway on that summer evening, blinking into Aunt Cal's eyes; rather like a beachcomber who had wandered accidentally out of a movie of the South Seas. In his hands he carried a knotted stick of a brutal, treacherous shape. It was a murderous-looking stick, and the sight of it caused Aunt Cal to shrink back a little into the room.

Fifi shut the door behind them and turned to her aunts as if this were the most natural occasion in the world.

'This is Mr Hopkins,' she announced, and then turned to her companion for corroboration. 'Or is it Hopwood?'

'Hopkins,' said the man hoarsely. 'Hopkins.'

Fifi nodded cheerfully.

'I've asked Mr Hopkins to dinner,' she said.

There was some dignity which Aunt Cal and Aunt Josephine had acquired, living here beside the proud sea, that would not let them show surprise. The man was a guest now; that was enough. But in their hearts all was turmoil and confusion. They would have been no more surprised had Fifi brought in a many-headed monster out of the Atlantic.

'Won't you – won't you sit down, Mr Hopkins?' said Aunt Cal nervously.

Mr Hopkins looked at her blankly for a moment, and then made a loud clicking sound in the back of his mouth. He took a step towards a chair and sank down on its gilt frailty as though he meant to annihilate it immediately. Aunt Cal and Aunt Josephine collapsed rather weakly on the sofa.

'Mr Hopkins and I struck up an acquaintance on the beach,' explained Fifi. 'He's been spending the summer down here for his health.'

Mr Hopkins fixed his eyes glassily on the two aunts.

'I come down for my health,' he said.

Aunt Cal made some small sound; but recovering herself quickly, joined Aunt Jo in nodding eagerly at the visitor, as if they deeply sympathized.

'Yeah,' he repeated cheerfully.

'He thought the sea air would make him well and strong again,' said Fifi eagerly. 'That's why he came down here. Isn't that it, Mr Hopkins?'

'You said it, sister,' agreed Mr Hopkins, nodding.

'So you see, Aunt Cal,' smiled Fifi, 'you and Aunt Jo aren't the only two people who believe in the medicinal quality of this location.'

'No,' agreed Aunt Cal faintly. 'There are – there are three of us now.'

Dinner was announced.

'Would you – would you' – Aunt Cal braced herself and looked Mr Hopkins in the eye – 'would you like to wash your hands before dinner?'

'Don't mention it.' Mr Hopkins waved his fingers at her carelessly.

They went in to dinner, and after some furtive backing and bumping due to the two aunts trying to keep as far as possible from Mr Hopkins, sat down at table.

'Mr Hopkins lives in the woods,' said Fifi. 'He has a little house all by himself, where he cooks his own meals and does his own washing week in and week out.'

'How fascinating!' said Aunt Jo, looking searchingly at their guest for some signs of the scholarly recluse. 'Have you been living near here for some time?'

'Not so long,' he answered with a leer. 'But I'm stuck on it, see? I'll maybe stay here till I rot.'

'Are you – do you live far away?' Aunt Cal was wondering what price she could get for the house at a forced sale, and how she and her sister could ever bear to move.

'Just a mile down the line . . . This is a pretty gal you got here,' he added, indicating their niece with his spoon.

'Why – yes.' The two ladies glanced uneasily at Fifi.

'Some day I'm going to pick her up and run away with her,' he added pleasantly.

Aunt Cal, with a heroic effort, switched the subject away from their niece. They discussed Mr Hopkins' shack in the woods. Mr Hopkins liked it well enough, he confessed, except for the presence of minute animal life, a small fault in an otherwise excellent habitat.

After dinner Fifi and Mr Hopkins went out to the porch, while her aunts sat side by side on the sofa turning over the pages of magazines and from time to time glancing at each other with stricken eyes. That a savage had a few minutes since been sitting at their dinner table, that he was now alone with their niece on the dark veranda – no such terrible adventure had ever been allotted to their prim, quiet lives before.

Aunt Cal determined that at nine, whatever the consequences, she would call Fifi inside; but she was |saved this necessity, for after half an hour the young lady strolled in calmly and announced that Mr Hopkins had gone home. They looked at her, speechless.

'Fifi!' groaned Aunt Cal, 'My poor child! Sorrow and loneliness have driven you insane!'

'We understand, my dear,' said Aunt Jo, touching her handkerchief to her eyes. 'It's our fault for letting you stay. A few weeks in one of those rest-cure places, or perhaps even a good cabaret, will—'

'What do you mean?' Fifi looked from one to the other in surprise. 'Do you mean you object to my bringing Mr Hopkins here?'

Aunt Cal flushed a dull red and her lips shut tight together.

' "Object" is not the word. You find some horrible, brutal roustabout along the beach—'

She broke off and gave a little cry. The door had swung open suddenly and a hairy face was peering into the room.

'I left my stick.'

Mr Hopkins discovered the unpleasant weapon leaning in the corner and withdrew as unceremoniously as he had come, banging the door shut behind him. Fifi's aunt sat motionless until his footsteps left the porch. Then Aunt Cal went swiftly to the door and pulled down the latch.

'I don't suppose he'll try to rob us tonight,' she said grimly, 'because he must know we'll be prepared. But I'll warn Percy to go around the yard several times during the night.'

'Rob you!' cried Fifi incredulously.

'Don't excite yourself, Fifi,' commanded Aunt Cal. 'Just rest quietly in that chair while I call up your mother.'

'I don't want you to call up my mother.'

'Sit calmly and close your eyes and try to – try to count sheep jumping over a fence.'

'Am I never to see another man unless he has a cutaway coat on?' exclaimed Fifi with flashing eyes. 'Is this the Dark Ages, or the century of – of illumination? Mr Hopkins is one of the most attractive eggs I've ever met in my life.'

'Mr Hopkins is a savage!' said Aunt Cal succinctly.

'Mr Hopkins is a very attractive egg.'

'A very attractive what?'

'A very attractive egg.'

'Mr Hopkins is a – a – an unspeakable egg,' proclaimed Aunt Cal, adopting Fifi's locution.

'Just because he's natural,' cried Fifi impatiently. 'All right, I don't care; he's good enough for me.'

The situation, it seemed, was even worse than they thought. This was no temporary aberration; evidently Fifi, in the reaction from her recent fiancé, was interested in this outrageous man. She had met him several days ago, she confessed, and she intended to see him tomorrow. They had a date to go walking.

The worst of it was that after Fifi had gone scornfully to bed, Aunt Cal called up her mother – and found that her mother was not at home; her mother had gone to White Sulphur Springs and wouldn't be home for a week. It left the situation definitely in the hands of Aunt Cal and Aunt Jo, and the situation came to a head the next afternoon at teatime, when Percy rushed in upon them excitedly through the kitchen door.

'Miss Marsden,' he exclaimed in a shocked, offended voice, 'I want to give up my position!'

'Why, Percy!'

'I can't help it. I lived here on the Point for more'n forty-five years, and I never seen such a sight as I seen just now.'

'What's the matter?' cried the two ladies, springing up in wild alarm.

'Go to the window and look for yourself. Miss Fifi is kissing a tramp in broad daylight, down on the beach!'

III

Five minutes later two maiden ladies were making their way across the sand towards a couple who stood close together on the shore, sharply outlined against the bright afternoon sky. As they came closer Fifi and Mr Hopkins, absorbed in the contemplation of each other, perceived them and drew lingeringly apart. Aunt Cal began to speak when they were still thirty yards away.

'Go into the house, Fifi!' she cried.

Fifi looked at Mr Hopkins, who touched her hand reassuringly and nodded. As if under the influence of a charm, Fifi turned away from him, and with her head lowered walked with slender grace towards the house.

'Now, my man,' said Aunt Cal, folding her arms, 'what are your intentions?'

Mr Hopkins returned her glare rudely. Then he gave a low hoarse laugh.

'What's that to you?' he demanded.

'It's everything to us. Miss Marsden is our niece, and your attentions are unwelcome – not to say obnoxious.'

Mr Hopkins turned half away.

'Aw, go on and blab your mouth out!' he advised her.

Aunt Cal tried a new approach.

'What if I were to tell you that Miss Marsden were mentally deranged?'

'What's that?'

'She's – she's a little crazy.'

He smiled contemptuously.

'What's the idea? Crazy 'cause she likes me?'

'That merely indicates it,' answered Aunt Cal bravely. 'She's had an unfortunate love affair and it's affected her mind. Look here!' She opened the purse that swung at her waist. 'If I give you fifty – a hundred dollars right now in cash, will you promise to move yourself ten miles up the beach?'

'Ah-h-h-h!' he exclaimed, so venomously that the two ladies swayed together.

'Two hundred!' cried Aunt Cal, with a catch in her voice.

He shook his finger at them.

'You can't buy me!' he growled. 'I'm as good as anybody. There's chauffeurs and such that marry millionaires' daughters every day in the week. This is Umerica, a free country, see?'

'You won't give her up?' Aunt Cal swallowed hard on the words. 'You won't stop bothering her and go away?'

He bent over suddenly and scooped up a large double handful of sand, which he threw in a high parabola so that it scattered down upon the horrified ladies, enveloping them for a moment in a thick mist. Then laughing once again in his hoarse, boorish way, he turned and set off at a loping run along the sand.

In a daze the two women brushed the casual sand from their shoulders and walked stiffly towards the house.

'I'm younger than you are,' said Aunt Jo firmly when they reached the living-room. 'I want a chance now to see what I can do.'

She went to the telephone and called a New York number.

'Doctor Roswell Gallup's office? Is Doctor Gallup there?' Aunt Cal sat down on the sofa and gazed tragically at the ceiling. 'Doctor Gallup? This is Miss Josephine Marsden, of Montauk Point . . . Doctor Gallup, a very curious state of affairs has arisen concerning my niece. She has become entangled with a – a – an unspeakable egg.' She gasped as she said this, and went on to explain in a few words the uncanny nature of the situation.

'And I think that perhaps psychoanalysis might clear up what my sister and I have been unable to handle.'

Doctor Gallup was interested. It appeared to be exactly his sort of a case.

'There's a train in half an hour that will get you here at nine o'clock,' said Aunt Jo. 'We can give you dinner and accommodate you overnight.'

She hung up the receiver.

'There! Except for our change from bridge to mah-jong, this will be the first really modern step we've ever taken on our lives.'

The hours passed slowly. At seven Fifi came down to dinner, as unperturbed as though nothing had happened; and her aunts played up bravely to her calmness, determined to say nothing until the doctor had actually arrived. After dinner Aunt Jo suggested mah-jong, but Fifi declared that she would rather read, and settled on the sofa with a volume of the encyclopedia. Looking over her shoulder, Aunt Cal noted with alarm that she had turned to the article on the Australian bush.

It was very quiet in the room. Several times Fifi raised her head as if listening, and once she got up and went to the door and stared out for a long time into the night. Her aunts were both poised in their chairs to rush after her if she showed signs of bolting, but after a moment she closed the door with a sigh and returned to her chair. It was with relief that a little after nine they heard the sound of automobile wheels on the shell drive and knew that Doctor Gallup had arrived at last.

He was a short, stoutish man, with alert black eyes and an intense manner. He came in, glancing eagerly about him, and his eye brightened as it fell on Fifi like the eye of a hungry man when he sees prospective food. Fifi returned his gaze curiously, evidently unaware that his arrival had anything to do with herself.

'Is this the lady?' he cried, dismissing her aunts with a perfunctory handshake and approaching Fifi at a lively hop.

'This gentleman is Doctor Gallup, dear,' beamed Aunt Jo, expectant and reassured. 'He's an old friend of mine who's going to help you.'

'Of course I am!' insisted Doctor Gallup, jumping around her cordially. 'I'm going to fix her up just fine.'

'He understands everything about the human mind,' said Aunt Jo.

'Not everything,' admitted Doctor Gallup, smiling modestly. 'But we often make the regular doctors wonder.' He turned roguishly to Fifi. 'Yes, young lady, we often make the regular doctors wonder.'

Clapping his hands together decisively, he drew up a chair in front of Fifi.

'Come,' he cried, 'let us see what can be the matter. We'll start by having you tell me the whole story in your own way. Begin.'

'The story,' remarked Fifi, with a slight yawn, 'happens to be none of your business.'

'None of my business!' he exclaimed incredulously. 'Why, my girl, I'm trying to help you! Come now, tell old Doctor Gallup the whole story.'

'Let my aunts tell you,' said Fifi coldly. 'They seem to know more about it than I do.'

Doctor Gallup frowned.

'They've already outlined the situation. Perhaps I'd better begin by asking you questions.'

'You'll answer the doctor's questions, won't you, dear?' coaxed Aunt Jo. 'Doctor Gallup is one of the most modern doctors in New York.'

'I'm an old-fashioned girl,' objected Fifi maliciously. 'And I think it's immoral to pry into people's affairs. But go ahead and I'll try to think up a comeback for everything you say.'

Doctor Gallup overlooked the unnecessary rudeness of this remark and mustered a professional smile.

'Now, Miss Marsden, I understand that about a month ago you came out here for a rest.'

Fifi shook her head.

'No, I came out to hide my face.'

'You were ashamed because you had broken your engagement?'

'Terribly. If you desert a man at the altar you brand him for the rest of his life.'

'Why?' he demanded sharply.

'Why not?'

'You're not asking me. I'm asking you . . . However, let that pass. Now, when you arrived here, how did you pass your time?'

'I walked mostly – walked along the beach.'

'It was on one of these walks that you met the – ah – person your aunt told me of over the telephone?'

Fifi pinkened slightly.

'Yes.'

'What was he doing when you first saw him?'

'He was looking down at me out of a tree.'

There was a general exclamation from her aunts, in which the word 'monkey' figured.

'Did he attract you immediately?' demanded Doctor Gallup.

'Why, not especially. At first I only laughed.'

'I see. Now, as I understand, this man was very – ah – very originally clad.'

'Yes,' agreed Fifi.

'He was unshaven?'

'Yes.'

'Ah!' Doctor Gallup seemed to go through a sort of convolution like a medium coming out of a trance. 'Miss Fifi,' he cried out triumphantly, 'did you ever read *The Sheikh*?'

'Never heard of it.'

'Did you ever read any book in which a girl was wooed by a so-called sheikh or cave man?'

'Not that I remember.'

'What, then, was your favourite book when you were a girl?'

'*Little Lord Fauntleroy*.'

Doctor Gallup was considerably disappointed. He decided to approach the case from a new angle.

'Miss Fifi, won't you admit that there's nothing behind this but some fancy in your head?'

'On the contrary,' said Fifi startlingly, 'there's a great deal more behind it than any of you suspect. He's changed my entire attitude on life.'

'What do you mean?'

She seemed on the point of making some declaration, but after a moment her lovely eyes narrowed obstinately and she remained silent.

'Miss Fifi' – Doctor Gallup raised his voice sharply – 'the daughter of C. T. J. Calhoun, the biscuit man, ran away with a taxi driver. Do you know what she's doing now?'

'No.'

'She's working in a laundry on the East Side, trying to keep her child's body and soul together.'

He looked at her keenly; there were signs of agitation in her face.

'Estelle Holliday ran away in 1920 with her father's second man!' he cried. 'Shall I tell you where I heard of her last? She stumbled into a charity hospital, bruised from head to foot, because her drunken husband had beaten her to within an inch of her life!'

Fifi was breathing hard. Her aunts leaned forward. Doctor Gallup sprang suddenly to his feet.

'But they were playing safe compared to you!' he shouted. 'They didn't woo an ex-convict with blood on his hands.'

And now Fifi was on her feet, too, her eyes flashing fire.

'Be careful!' she cried. 'Don't go too far!'

'I can't go too far!' He reached in his pocket, plucked out a folded evening paper and slapped it down on the table.

'Read that, Miss Fifi!' he shouted. 'It'll tell you how four man-killers entered a bank in West Crampton three weeks ago. It'll tell you how they shot down the cashier in cold blood, and how one of them, the most brutal, the most ferocious, the most inhuman, got away. And it will tell you that that human gorilla is now supposed to be hiding in the neighbourhood of Montauk Point!'

There was a short stifled sound as Aunt Jo and Aunt Cal, who had always done everything in complete unison, fainted away together. At the same moment there was loud, violent knocking, like the knocking of a heavy club, upon the barred front door.

IV

'Who's there?' cried Doctor Gallup, starting. 'Who's there – or I'll shoot!'

His eyes roved quickly about the room, looking for a possible weapon.

'Who are you?' shouted a voice from the porch. 'You better open up or I'll blow a hole through the door.'

'What'll we do?' exclaimed Doctor Gallup, perspiring freely.

Fifi, who had been sprinkling water impartially upon her aunts, turned around with a scornful smile.

'It's just Percy, the yardman,' she explained. 'He probably thinks that you're a burglar.'

She went to the door and lifted the latch. Percy, gun in hand, peered cautiously into the room.

'It's all right, Percy. This is just an insane specialist from New York.'

'Everything's a little insane tonight,' announced Percy in a frightened voice. 'For the last hour I've been hearing the sound of oars.'

The eyes of Aunt Jo and Aunt Cal fluttered open simultaneously.

'There's a fog all over the Point,' went on Percy dazedly, 'and it's got voices in it. I couldn't see a foot before my face, but I could swear there was boats offshore, and I heard a dozen people talkin' and callin' to each other, just as if a lot of ghosts was havin' a picnic supper on the beach.'

'What was that noise?' cried Aunt Jo, sitting upright.

'The door was locked,' explained Percy, 'so I knocked on it with my gun.'

'No, I mean now!'

They listened. Through the open door came a low, groaning sound, issuing out of the dark mist which covered shore and sea alike.

'We'll go right down and find out!' cried Doctor Gallup, who had recovered his shattered equilibrium; and, as the moaning sound drifted in again, like the last agony of some monster from the deep, he added, 'I think you needed more than a psychoanalyst here tonight. Is there another gun in the house?'

Aunt Cal got up and took a small pearl-mounted revolver from the desk drawer.

'You can't leave us in this house alone,' she declared emphatically. 'Wherever you go we're going too!'

Keeping close together, the four of them, for Fifi had suddenly disappeared, made their way outdoors and down the porch steps, where they hesitated a moment, peering into the impenetrable haze, more mysterious than darkness upon their eyes.

'It's out there,' whispered Percy, facing the sea.

'Forward we go!' muttered Doctor Dallup tensely. 'I'm inclined to think this is all a question of nerves.'

They moved slowly and silently along the sand, until suddenly Percy caught hold of the doctor's arm.

'Listen!' he whispered sharply.

They all became motionless. Out of the neighbouring darkness a dim, indistinguishable figure had materialized, walking with unnatural rigidity along the shore. Pressed against his body he carried some long, dark drape that hung almost to the sand. Immediately he disappeared into the mist, to be succeeded by another phantom walking at the same military gait, this one with something white and faintly terrible dangling from his arm. A moment later, not ten yards away from them, in the direction in which the figure had gone, a faint dull glow sprang to life, proceeding apparently from behind the largest of the dunes.

Huddled together, they advanced towards the dune, hesitated, and then, following Doctor Gallup's example, dropped to their knees and began to crawl cautiously up its shoreward side. The glow became stronger as they reached the top, and at the same moment their heads popped up over the crest. This is what they saw:

In the light of four strong pocket flash lights, borne by four sailors in spotless white, a gentleman was shaving himself, standing clad only in athletic underwear upon the sand. Before his eyes an irreproachable valet held a silver mirror which gave back the soapy reflection of his face. To right and left stood two additional men-servants, one with a dinner coat and trousers hanging from his arm and the other bearing a white stiff shirt whose studs glistened in the glow of the electric lamps. There was not a sound except the dull scrape of the razor along its wielder's face and the intermittent groaning sound that blew in out of the sea.

But it was not the bizarre nature of the ceremony, with its dim, weird surroundings under the unsteady light, that drew from the two women a short involuntary sigh. It was the fact that the face in the mirror, the unshaven half of it, was terribly familiar, and in a moment they knew to whom that half face belonged – it was the countenance of their niece's savage wooer who had lately prowled half naked along the beach.

Even as they looked he completed one side of his face, whereupon a valet stepped forward and with a scissors sheared off the exterior growth more on the other, disclosing, in its entirety now, the symmetrical visage of a young, somewhat haggard but not unhandsome man. He lathered the bearded side, pulled the razor quickly over it and then applied a lotion to the whole surface, and inspected himself with considerable interest in the mirror. The sight seemed to please him, for he smiled. At a word one of the valets held forth the trousers in which he now incased his likely legs. Diving into his open shirt, he procured the collar, flipped a proper black bow with a practiced hand and slipped into the waiting dinner coat. After a transformation which had taken place before their very eyes, Aunt Cal and Aunt Jo found themselves gazing upon as immaculate and impeccable a young man as they had ever seen.

'Walters!' he said suddenly, in a clear, cultured voice.

One of the white-clad sailors stepped forward and saluted.

'You can take the boats back to the yacht. You ought to be able to find it all right by the foghorn.'

'Yes, sir.'

'When the fog lifts you'd better stand out to sea. Meanwhile, wireless New York to send down my car. It's to call for me at the Marsden house on Montauk Point.'

As the sailor turned away, his torch flashed upward accidentally wavering upon the four amazed faces which were peering down at the curious scene.

'Look there, sir!' he exclaimed.

The four torches picked out the eavesdropping party at the top of the hill.

'Hands up, there!' cried Percy, pointing his rifle down into the glare of light.

'Miss Marsden!' called the young man eagerly. 'I was just coming to call.'

'Don't move!' shouted Percy; and then to the doctor, 'Had I better fire?'

'Certainly not!' cried Doctor Gallup. 'Young man, does your name happen to be what I think it is?'

The young man bowed politely.

'My name is George Van Tyne.'

A few minutes later the immaculate young man and two completely bewildered ladies were shaking hands. 'I owe you more apologies than I can ever make,' he confessed, 'for having sacrificed you to the strange whim of a young girl.'

'What whim?' demanded Aunt Cal.

'Why' – he hesitated – 'you see, all my life I have devoted much attention to the so-called niceties of conduct; niceties of dress, of manner, of behaviour—'

He broke off apologetically.

'Go on,' commanded Aunt Cal.

'And your niece has too. She always considered herself rather a model of – of civilized behaviour' – he flushed – 'until she met me.'

'I see,' Doctor Gallup nodded. 'She couldn't bear to marry anyone who was more of a – shall we say, a dandy? – than herself.'

'Exactly,' said George Van Tyne, with a perfect eighteenth-century bow. 'It was necessary to show her what a – what an—'

'—unspeakable egg,' supplied Aunt Josephine.

'—what an unspeakable egg I could be. It was difficult, but not impossible. If you know what's correct, you must necessarily know what's incorrect; and my aim was to be as ferociously incorrect as possible. My one hope is that some day you'll be able to forgive me for throwing the sand – I'm afraid that my impersonation ran away with me.'

A moment later they were all walking toward the house.

'But I still can't believe that a gentleman could be so – so unspeakable,' gasped Aunt Jo. 'And what will Fifi say?'

'Nothing,' answered Van Tyne cheerfully. 'You see, Fifi knew about it all along. She even recognized me in the tree that first day. She begged me to – to desist until this afternoon; but I refused until she had kissed me tenderly, beard and all.'

Aunt Cal stopped suddenly.

'This is all very well, young man,' she said sternly; 'but since you have so many sides to you, how do we know that in one of your off moments you aren't the murderer who's hiding out on the Point?'

'The murderer?' asked Van Tyne blankly. 'What murderer?'

'Ah, I can explain that, Miss Marsden,' Doctor Gallup smiled apologetically. 'As a matter of fact, there wasn't any murderer.'

'No murderer?' Aunt Cal looked at him sharply.

'No, I invented the bank robbery and the escaped murderer and all. I was merely applying a form of strong medicine to your niece.'

Aunt Cal looked at him scornfully and turned to her sister. 'All your modern ideas are not so successful as mah-jong,' she remarked significantly.

The fog had blown back to sea, and as they came in sight of the house the lamps were glowing out into the darkness. On the porch waited an immaculate girl in a gleaming white dress, strung with beads which glistened in the new moonlight.

'The perfect man,' murmured Aunt Jo, flushing, 'is, of course, he who will make any sacrifice.'

Van Tyne did not answer; he was engaged in removing some imperceptible flaw, less visible than a hair, from his elbow, and when he had finished he smiled. There was now not the faintest imperfection anywhere about him, except where the strong beating of his heart disturbed faintly the satin facing of his coat.

JOHN JACKSON'S ARCADY

Saturday Evening Post, 26 July 1924

*'John Jackson's Arcady' was written in April 1924 – the last story
Fitzgerald wrote in Great Neck before moving to the Riviera. The* Post
*paid $1750 for it. The departure for France was motivated by Fitzgerald's
wish to escape the interruptions of metropolitan life, which had delayed work
on* The Great Gatsby, *as well as by a desire to economize. Fitzgerald
treated his financial problems humorously in two 1924* Post *articles –
'How to Live on $36,000 a Year' and 'How to Live on Practically
Nothing a Year'.*

*Although this story is marred by its patently sentimental ending, it is
interesting as a treatment of Fitzgerald's roots-pilgrimage theme –
reflecting his increasing sense of deracination and estrangement from his
Midwestern values.*

*In 1928 'John Jackson's Arcady' was republished as a pamphlet for
public reading contests.*

The first letter, crumpled into an emotional ball, lay at his elbow, and it
did not matter faintly now what this second letter contained. For a long
time after he had stripped off the envelope, he still gazed up at the oil painting of slain grouse over the sideboard, just as though he had not faced it
every morning at breakfast for the past twelve years. Finally he lowered his
eyes and began to read:

Dear Mr Jackson: This is just a reminder that you have consented to
speak at our annual meeting Thursday. We don't want to dictate your
choice of a topic, but it has occurred to me that it would be interesting
to hear from you on What Have I Got Out of Life. Coming from you
this should be an inspiration to everyone.

We are delighted to have you anyhow, and we appreciate the honour that you confer on us by coming at all.

Most cordially yours,

ANTHONY ROREBACK,

Sec. Civic Welfare League.

'What have I got out of life?' repeated John Jackson aloud, raising up his head.

He wanted no more breakfast, so he picked up both letters and went out on his wide front porch to smoke a cigar and lie about for a lazy half hour before he went downtown. He had done this each morning for ten years – ever since his wife ran off one windy night and gave him back the custody of his leisure hours. He loved to rest on this porch in the fresh warm mornings and through a porthole in the green vines watch the automobiles pass along the street, the widest, shadiest, pleasantest street in town.

'What have I got out of life?' he said again, sitting down on a creaking wicker chair; and then, after a long pause, he whispered, 'Nothing.'

The word frightened him. In all his forty-five years he had never said such a thing before. His greatest tragedies had not embittered him, only made him sad. But here beside the warm friendly rain that tumbled from his eaves onto the familiar lawn, he knew at last that life had stripped him clean of all happiness and all illusion.

He knew this because of the crumpled ball which closed out his hope in his only son. It told him what a hundred hints and indication had told him before; that his son was weak and vicious, and the language in which it was conveyed was no less emphatic for being polite. The letter was from the dean of the college in New Haven, a gentleman who said exactly what he meant in every word:

Dear Mr Jackson: It is with much regret that I write to tell you that your son, Ellery Hamil Jackson, has been requested to withdraw from the university. Last year largely, I am afraid, out of personal feeling towards you, I yielded to your request that he be allowed another chance. I see now that this was a mistake, and I should be failing in my duty if I did not tell you that he is not the sort of boy we want here. His conduct at the sophomore dance was such that several undergraduates took it upon themselves to administer violent correction.

It grieves me to write you this, but I see no advantage in presenting the case otherwise than as it is. I have requested that he leave New Haven by the day after tomorrow. I am, sir,

Yours very sincerely,

AUSTIN SCHEMMERHORN,
Dean of the College.

What particularly disgraceful thing his son had done John Jackson did not care to imagine. He knew without any question that what the dean said was true. Why, there were houses already in this town where his son, John Jackson's son, was no longer welcome! For a while Ellery had been forgiven because of his father, and he had been more than forgiven at home, because John Jackson was one of those rare men who can forgive even their own families. But he would never be forgiven any more. Sitting on his porch this morning beside the gentle April rain, something had happened in his father's heart.

'What have I had out of life?' John Jackson shook his head from side to side with quiet, tired despair. 'Nothing!'

He picked up the second letter, the civic-welfare letter, and read it over; and then helpless, dazed laughter shook him physically until he trembled in his chair. On Wednesday, at the hour when his deliquent boy would arrive at the motherless home, John Jackson would be standing on a platform downtown, delivering one hundred resounding platitudes of inspiration and cheer. 'Members of the association' – their faces, eager, optimistic, optimistic, impressed, would look up at him like hollow moons – 'I have been requested to try to tell you in a few words what I have had from life—'

Many people would be there to hear, for the clever young secretary had hit upon a topic with the personal note – what John Jackson, successful, able and popular, had found for himself in the tumultuous grab bag. They would listen with wistful attention, hoping that he would disclose some secret formula that would make their lives as popular and successful and happy as his own. They believed in rules; all the young men in the city believed in hard-and-fast rules, and many of them clipped coupons and sent away for little booklets that promised them the riches and good fortune they desired.

'Members of the association, to begin with, let me say that there is so much in life that if we don't find it, it is not the fault of life, but of ourselves.'

The ring of the stale, dull words mingled with the patter of the rain went on and on endlessly, but John Jackson knew that he would never make that speech, or any speeches ever again. He had dreamed his last dream too long, but he was awake at last.

'I shall not go on flattering a world that I have found unkind,' he whispered to the rain. 'Instead, I shall go out of this house and out of this town and somewhere find again the happiness that I possessed when I was young.'

Nodding his head, he tore both letters into small fragments and dropped them on the table beside him. For half an hour longer he sat there, rocking a little and smoking his cigar slowly and blowing the blue smoke out into the rain.

II

Down at his office, his chief clerk, Mr Fowler, approached him with his morning smile.

'Looking fine, Mr Jackson. Nice day if it hadn't rained.'

'Yeah,' agreed John Jackson cheerfully. 'Clear up in an hour. Anybody outside?'

'A lady named Mrs Ralston.'

Mr Fowler raised his grizzled eyebrows in facetious mournfulness.

'Tell her I can't see her,' said John Jackson, rather to his clerk's surprise. 'And let me have a pencil memorandum of the money I've given away through her these twenty years.'

'Why – yes, sir.'

Mr Fowler had always urged John Jackson to look more closely into his promiscuous charities; but now, after these two decades, it rather alarmed him.

When the list arrived – its preparation took an hour of burrowing through old ledgers and cheque stubs – John Jackson studied it for a long time in silence.

'That woman's got more money than you have,' grumbled Fowler at his elbow. 'Every time she comes in she's wearing a new hat. I bet she never hands out a cent herself – just goes around asking other people.'

John Jackson did not answer. He was thinking that Mrs Ralston had been one of the first women in town to bar Ellery Jackson from her house. She did quite right, of course; and yet perhaps back there when Ellery was sixteen, if he had cared for some nice girl—

'Thomas J. MacDowell's outside. Do you want to see him? I said I didn't think you were in, because on second thoughts, Mr Jackson, you look tired this morning—'

'I'll see him,' interrupted John Jackson.

He watched Fowler's retreating figure with an unfamiliar expression in his eyes. All that cordial diffuseness of Fowler's – he wondered what it covered in the man's heart. Several times, without Fowler's knowledge, Jackson had seen him giving imitations of the boss for the benefit of the other employees; imitations with a touch of malice in them that John Jackson had smiled at then, but that now crept insinuatingly into his mind.

'Doubtless he considers me a good deal of a fool,' murmured John Jackson thoughtfully, 'because I've kept him long after his usefulness was over. It's a way men have, I suppose, to despise anyone they can impose on.'

Thomas J. MacDowell, a big barn door of a man with huge white hands, came boisterously into the office. If John Jackson had gone in for enemies he must have started with Tom MacDowell. For twenty years they had fought over every question of municipal affairs, and back in 1908 they had once stood facing each other with clenched hands on a public platform, because Jackson had said in print what everyone knew – that MacDowell was the worst political influence that the town had ever known. That was forgotten now; all that was remembered of it went into a peculiar flash of the eye that passed between them when they met.

'Hello, Mr Jackson,' said MacDowell with full, elaborate cordiality. 'We need your help and we need your money.'

'How so?'

'Tomorrow morning, in the *Eagle*, you'll see the plan for the new Union Station. The only thing that'll stand in the way is the question of location. We want your land.'

'My land?'

'The railroad wants to build on the twenty acres just this side of the river, where your warehouse stands. If you'll let them have it cheap we get our station; if not, we can just whistle into the air.'

Jackson nodded.

'I see.'

'What price?' asked MacDowell mildly.

'No price.'

His visitor's mouth dropped open in surprise.

'That from you?' he demanded.

John Jackson got to his feet.

'I've decided not to be the local goat any more,' he announced steadily. 'You threw out the only fair, decent plan because it interfered with some private reservations of your own. And now that there's a snag, you'd like the punishment to fall on me. I tear down my warehouse and hand over some of the best property in the city for a song because you made a little "mistake" last year!'

'But last year's over now,' protested MacDowell. 'Whatever happened then doesn't change the situation now. The city needs the station, and so' – there was a faint touch of irony in his voice – 'and so naturally I come to its leading citizen, counting on his well-known public spirit.'

'Go out of my office, MacDowell,' said John Jackson suddenly. 'I'm tired.'

MacDowell scrutinized him severely.

'What's come over you today?'

Jackson closed his eyes.

'I don't want to argue,' he said after a while.

MacDowell slapped his fat upper leg and got to his feet.

'This is a funny attitude from you,' he remarked. 'You better think it over.'

'Good-bye.'

Perceiving, to his astonishment, that John Jackson meant what he said, MacDowell took his monstrous body to the door.

'Well, well,' he said, turning and shaking his finger at Jackson as if he were a bad boy, 'who'd have thought it from you after all?'

When he had gone Jackson rang again for his clerk.

'I'm going away,' he remarked casually. 'I may be gone for some time – perhaps a week, perhaps longer. I want you to cancel every engagement I have and pay off my servants at home and close up my house.'

Mr Fowler could hardly believe his ears.

'Close up your house?'

Jackson nodded.

'But why – why is it?' demanded Fowler in amazement.

Jackson looked out the high window upon the grey little city drenched now by slanting, slapping rain – his city, he had felt sometimes, in those rare moments when life had lent him time to be happy. That flash of green trees running up the main boulevard – he had made that possible, and Children's Park, and the white dripping buildings around Courthouse Square over the way.

'I don't know,' he answered, 'but I think I ought to get a breath of spring.'

When Fowler had gone he put on his hat and raincoat and, to avoid anyone who might be waiting, went through an unused filing room that gave access to the elevator. The filing room was actively inhabited this morning, however; and, rather to his surprise, by a young boy about nine years old, who was laboriously writing his initials in chalk on the steel files.

'Hello!' exclaimed John Jackson.

He was accustomed to speak to children in a tone of interested equality. 'I didn't know this office was occupied this morning.'

The little boy looked at him steadily.

'My name's John Jackson Fowler,' he announced.

'What?'

'My name's John Jackson Fowler.'

'Oh, I see. You're – you're Mr Fowler's son?'

'Yeah, he's my father.'

'I see.' John Jackson's eyes narrowed a little. 'Well, I bid you good morning.'

He passed on out the door, wondering cynically what particular axe Fowler hoped to grind by this unwarranted compliment. John Jackson Fowler! It was one of his few sources of relief that his own son did not bear his name.

A few minutes later he was writing on a yellow blank in the telegraph office below:

ELLERY JACKSON, CHAPEL STREET, NEW HAVEN, CONNECTICUT.
THERE IS NOT THE SLIGHTEST REASON FOR COMING HOME, BECAUSE YOU
HAVE NO HOME TO COME TO ANY MORE. THE MAMMOTH TRUST COMPANY
OF NEW YORK WILL PAY YOU FIFTY DOLLARS A MONTH FOR THE REST OF
YOUR LIFE, OR FOR AS LONG AS YOU CAN KEEP YOURSELF OUT OF JAIL.
JOHN JACKSON.

'That's – that's a long message, sir,' gasped the dispatcher, startled.' Do you want it to go straight?'

'Straight,' said John Jackson, nodding.

167

He rode seventy miles that afternoon, while the rain dried up into rills of dust on the windows of the train and the country became green with vivid spring. When the sun was growing definitely crimson in the west he disembarked at a little lost town named Florence, just over the border of the next state. John Jackson had been born in this town; he had not been back here for twenty years.

The taxi driver, whom he recognized, silently, as a certain George Stirling, playmate of his youth, drove him to a battered hotel, where, to the surprise of the delighted landlord, he engaged a room. Leaving his raincoat on the sagging bed, he strolled out through a deserted lobby into the street.

It was a bright, warm afternoon, and the silver sliver of a moon riding already in the east promised a clear, brilliant night. John Jackson walked along a somnolent Main Street, where every shop and hitching post and horse fountain made some strange thing happen inside him, because he had known these things for more than inanimate objects as a little boy. At one shop, catching a glimpse of a familiar face through the glass, he hesitated; but changing his mind, continued along the street, turning off at a wide road at the corner. The road was lined sparsely by a row of battered houses, some of them repainted a pale unhealthy blue and all of them set far back in large plots of shaggy and unkempt land.

He walked along the road for a sunny half-mile – a half-mile shrunk up now into a short green aisle crowded with memories. Here, for example, a careless mule had stamped permanently on his thigh the mark of an iron shoe. In that cottage had lived two gentle old maids, who gave brown raisin cakes every Thursday to John Jackson and his little brother – the brother who had died as a child.

As he neared the end of his pilgrimage his breath came faster and the house where he was born seemed to run up to him on living feet. It was a collapsed house, a retired house, set far back from the road and sunned and washed to the dull colour of old wood.

One glance told him it was no longer a dwelling. The shutters that remained were closed tight, and from the tangled vines arose, as a single chord, a rich shrill sound of a hundred birds. John Jackson left the road and stalked across the yard knee-deep in abandoned grass. When he came near, something choked up his throat. He paused and sat down on a stone in a patch of welcome shade.

This was his own house, as no other house would ever be; within these plain walls he had been incomparably happy. Here he had known and learned that kindness which he had carried into life. Here he had found the secret of those few simple decencies, so often invoked, so inimitable and so rare, which in the turmoil of competitive industry had made him to coarser men a source of half-scoffing, half-admiring surprise. This was his house, because his honour had been born and nourished here; he had known every hardship of the country poor, but no preventable regret.

And yet another memory, a memory more haunting than any other, and grown strong at this crisis in his life, had really drawn him back. In this yard, on this battered porch, in the very tree over his head, he seemed still to catch the glint of yellow hair and the glow of bright childish eyes that had belonged to his first love, the girl who had lived in the long-vanished house across the way. It was her ghost who was most alive here, after all.

He got up suddenly, stumbling through the shrubbery, and followed an almost obliterated path to the house, starting at the whirring sound of a blackbird which rose out of the grass close by. The front porch sagged dangerously at his step as he pushed open the door. There was no sound inside, except the steady slow throb of silence; but as he stepped in a word came to him, involuntary as his breath, and he uttered it aloud, as if he were calling to someone in the empty house.

'Alice,' he cried; and then louder, 'Alice!'

From a room at the left came a short, small frightened cry. Startled, John Jackson paused in the door, convinced that his own imagination had evoked the reality of the cry.

'Alice!' he called doubtfully.

'Who's there?'

There was no mistake this time. The voice, frightened, strange, and yet familiar, came from what had once been the parlour, and as he listened John Jackson was aware of a nervous step within. Trembling a little, he pushed open the parlour door.

A woman with alarmed bright eyes and reddish gold hair was standing in the centre of the bare room. She was of that age that trembles between the enduring youth of a fine, unworried life and the imperative call of forty years, and there was that indefinable loveliness in her face that youth gives sometimes just before it leaves a dwelling it has possessed for long. Her figure, just outside of slenderness, leaned with dignified grace against the old mantel on which her white hand rested, and through a rift in the shutter a shaft of late sunshine fell through upon her gleaming hair.

When John Jackson came in the doorway her large grey eyes closed and then opened again, and she gave another little cry. Then a curious thing happened; they stared at each other for a moment without a word, her hand dropped from the mantel and she took a swaying step towards him. And, as it it were the most natural thing in the world, John Jackson came forward, too, and took her into his arms and kissed her as if she were a little child.

'Alice!' he said huskily.

She drew a long breath and pushed herself away from him.

'I've come back here,' he muttered unsteadily, 'and find you waiting in this room where we used to sit, just as if I'd never been away.'

'I only dropped in for a minute,' she said, as if that was the most important thing in the world. 'And now, naturally, I'm going to cry.'

'Don't cry.'

'I've got to cry. You don't think' – she smiled through wet eyes – 'you don't think that things like this hap – happen to a person every day.'

John Jackson walked in wild excitement to the window and threw it open to the afternoon.

'What were you doing here?' he cried, turning around. 'Did you just come by accident today?'

'I come every week. I bring the children sometimes, but usually I come alone.'

'The children!' he exclaimed. 'Have you got children?'

She nodded.

'I've been married for years and years.'

They stood there looking at each other for a moment; then they both laughed and glanced away.

'I kissed you,' she said.

'Are you sorry?'

She shook her head.

'And the last time I kissed you was down by that gate ten thousand years ago.'

He took her hand, and they went out and sat side by side on the broken stoop. The sun was painting the west with sweeping bands of peach bloom and pigeon blood and golden yellow.

'You're married,' she said. 'I saw in the paper – years ago.'

He nodded.

'Yes, I've been married,' he answered gravely. 'My wife went away with someone she cared for many years ago.'

'Ah, I'm sorry.' And after another long silence – 'It's a gorgeous evening, John Jackson.'

'It's a long time since I've been so happy.'

There was so much to say and to tell that neither of them tried to talk, but only sat there holding hands, like two children who had wandered for a long time through a wood and now came upon each other with unimaginable happiness in an accidental glade. Her husband was poor, she said; he knew that from the worn, unfashionable dress which she wore with such an air. He was George Harland – he kept a garage in the village.

'George Harland – a red-headed boy?' he asked wonderingly.

She nodded.

'We were engaged for years. Sometimes I thought we'd never marry. Twice I postponed it, but it was getting late to be just a girl – I was twenty-five, and so finally we did. After that I was in love with him for over a year.'

When the sunset fell together in a jumbled heap of colour in the bottom of the sky, they strolled back along the quiet road, still hand in hand.

'Will you come to dinner? I want you to see the children. My oldest boy is just fifteen.'

She lived in a plain frame house two doors from the garage, where two little girls were playing around a battered and ancient but occupied baby carriage in the yard.

'Mother! Oh, mother!' they cried.

Small brown arms swirled around her neck as she knelt beside them on the walk.

'Sister says Anna didn't come, so we can't have any dinner.'

'Mother'll cook dinner. What's the matter with Anna?'

'Anna's father's sick. She couldn't come.'

A tall, tired man of fifty, who was reading a paper on the porch, rose and slipped a coat over his suspenders as they mounted the steps.

'Anna didn't come,' he said in a noncommittal voice.

'I know. I'm going to cook dinner. Who do you suppose this is here?'

The two men shook hands in a friendly way, and with a certain deference to John Jackson's clothes and his prosperous manner, Harland went inside for another chair.

'We've heard about you a great deal, Mr Jackson,' he said as Alice disappeared into the kitchen. 'We heard about a lot of ways you made them sit up and take notice over yonder.'

John nodded politely, but at the mention of the city he had just left a wave of distaste went over him.

'I'm sorry I ever left here,' he answered frankly. 'And I'm not just saying that either. Tell me what the years have done for you, Harland, I hear you've got a garage.'

'Yeah – down the road a ways. I'm doing right well, matter of fact. Nothing you'd call well in the city,' he added in hasty depreciation.

'You know, Harland,' said John Jackson, after a moment, 'I'm very much in love with your wife.'

'Yeah?' Harland laughed. 'Well, she's a pretty nice lady, I find.'

'I think I always have been in love with her, all these years.'

'Yeah?' Harland laughed again. That someone should be in love with his wife seemed the most casual pleasantry. 'You better tell her about it. She don't get so many nice compliments as she used to in her young days.'

Six of them sat down at table, including an awkward boy of fifteen, who looked like his father, and two little girls whose faces shone from a hasty toilet. Many things had happened in the town, John discovered; the factitious prosperity which had promised to descend upon it in the late nineties had vanished when two factories had closed up and moved away, and the population was smaller now by a few hundred than it had been a quarter of a century ago.

After a plentiful plain dinner they all went to the porch, where the children silhouetted themselves in silent balance on the railing and unrecognizable people called greetings as they passed along the dark, dusty street. After a while the younger children went to bed, and the boy and his father arose and put on their coats.

'I guess I'll run up to the garage,' said Harland. 'I always go up about this time every night. You two just sit here and talk about old times.'

As father and son moved out of sight along the dim street John Jackson turned to Alice and slipped his arm about her shoulder and looked into her eyes.

'I love you, Alice.'

'I love you.'

Never since his marriage had he said that to any woman excep this wife. But this was a new world tonight, with spring all about him in the air, and he felt as if he were holding his own lost youth in his arms.

'I've always loved you,' she murmured. 'Just before I go to sleep every night, I've always been able to see your face. Why didn't you come back?'

Tenderly he smoothed her hair. He had never known such happiness before. He felt that he had established dominance over time itself, so that it rolled away for him, yielding up one vanished springtime after another to the mastery of his overwhelming emotion.

'We're still young, we two people,' he said exultantly. 'We made a silly mistake a long, long time ago, but we found out in time.'

'Tell me about it,' she whispered.

'This morning, in the rain, I heard your voice.'

'What did my voice say?'

'It said, "Come home."'

'And here you are, my dear.'

'Here I am.'

Suddenly he got to his feet.

'You and I are going away,' he said. 'Do you understand that?'

'I always knew that when you came for me I'd go.'

Later, when the moon had risen, she walked with him to the gate.

'Tomorrow!' he whispered.

'Tomorrow!'

His heart was going like mad, and he stood carefully away from her to let footsteps across the way approach, pass and fade out down the dim street. With a sort of wild innocence he kissed her once more and held her close to his heart under the April moon.

IV

When he awoke it was eleven o'clock, and he drew himself a cool bath, splashing around in it with much of the exultation of the night before.

'I have thought too much these twenty years,' he said to himself. 'It's thinking that makes people old.'

It was hotter than it had been the day before, and as he looked out the window the dust in the street seemed more tangible than on the night before. He breakfasted alone downstairs, wondering with the incessant wonder of the city man why fresh cream is almost unobtainable in the country. Word had spread already that he was home, and several men rose to greet him as he came into the lobby. Asked if he had a wife and children, he said no, in a careless way, and after he had said it he had a vague feeling of discomfort.

'I'm all alone,' he went on, with forced jocularity. 'I wanted to come back and see the old town again.'

'Stay long?' They looked at him curiously.

'Just a day or so.'

He wondered what they would think tomorrow. There would be excited little groups of them here and there along the street with the startling and audacious news.

'See here,' he wanted to say, 'you think I've had a wonderful life over there in the city, but I haven't. I came down here because life had beaten me, and if there's any brightness in my eyes this morning it's because last night I found a part of my lost youth tucked away in this little town.'

At noon, as he walked towards Alice's house, the heat increased and several times he stopped to wipe the sweat from his forehead. When he turned in at the gate he saw her waiting on the porch, wearing what was apparently a Sunday dress and moving herself gently back and forth in a rocking-chair in a way that he remembered her doing as a girl.

'Alice!' he exclaimed happily.

Her finger rose swiftly and touched her lips.

'Look out!' she said in a low voice.

He sat down beside her and took her hand, but she replaced it on the arm of her chair and resumed her gentle rocking.

'Be careful. The children are inside.'

'But I can't be careful. Now that life's begun all over again, I've forgotten all the caution that I learned in the other life, the one that's past!'

'Sh-h-h!'

Somewhat irritated, he glanced at her closely. Her face, unmoved and unresponsive, seemed vaguely older than it had yesterday; she was white and tired. But he dismissed the impression with a low, exultant laugh.

'Alice, I haven't slept as I slept last night since I was a little boy, except that several times I woke up just for the joy of seeing the same moon we once we knew together. I'd got it back.'

'I didn't sleep at all.'

'I'm sorry.'

'I realized about two o'clock or three o'clock that I could never go away from my children – even with you.'

He was struck dumb. He looked at her blankly for a moment, and then he laughed – a short, incredulous laugh.

'Never, never!' she went on, shaking her head passionately. 'Never, never, never! When I thought of it I began to tremble all over, right in my bed.' She hesitated. 'I don't know what came over me yesterday evening, John. When I'm with you, you can always make me do or feel or think exactly what you like. But this is too late, I guess. It doesn't seem real at all; it just seems sort of crazy to me, as if I'd dreamed it, that's all.'

John Jackson laughed again, not incredulously this time, but on a menacing note.

'What do you mean?' he demanded.

She began to cry and hid her eyes behind her hand because some people were passing along the road.

'You've got to tell me more than that,' cried John Jackson, his voice rising a little. 'I can't just take that and go away.'

'Please don't talk so loud,' she implored him. 'It's so hot and I'm so confused. I guess I'm just a small-town woman, after all. It seems somehow awful to be talking here with you, when my husband's working all day in the dust and heat.'

'Awful to be talking here?' he repeated.

'Don't look that way!' she cried miserably. 'I can't bear to hurt you so. You have children, too, to think of – you said you had a son.'

'A son.' The fact seemed so far away that he looked at her, startled. 'Oh, yes, I have a son.'

A sort of craziness, a wild illogic in the situation had communicated itself to him; and yet he fought blindly against it as he felt his own mood of ecstasy slipping away. For twenty hours he had recaptured the power of seeing things through a mist of hope – hope in some vague, happy destiny that lay just over the hill – and now with every word she uttered the mist was passing, the hope, the town, the memory, the very face of this woman before his eyes.

'Never again in this world,' he cried with a last despairing effort, 'will you and I have a chance at happiness!'

But he knew, even as he said this, that it had never been a chance; simply a wild, desperate sortie from two long-beleaguered fortresses by night.

He looked up to see that George Harland had turned in at the gate.

'Lunch is ready,' called Alice, raising her head with an expression of relief. 'John's going to be with us too.'

'I can't,' said John Jackson quickly. 'You're both very kind.'

'Better stay.' Harland, in oily overalls, sank wearily on the steps and with a large handkerchief polished the hot space beneath his thin grey hair. 'We can give you some iced tea.' He looked up at John. 'I don't know whether these hot days make you feel your age like I feel mine.'

'I guess – it affects all of us alike,' said John Jackson with an effort. 'The awful part of it is that I've got to go back to the city this afternoon.'

'Really?' Harland nodded with polite regret.

'Why, yes. The fact is I promised to make a speech.'

'Is that so ? Speak on some city problem, I suppose.'

'No; the fact is' – the words, forming in his mind to a senseless rhythm pushed themselves out – 'I'm going to speak on What Have I Got Out of Life.'

Then he became conscious of the heat indeed; and still wearing that smile he knew so well how to muster, he felt himself sway dizzily against the porch rail. After a minute they were walking with him toward the gate.

'I'm sorry you're leaving,' said Alice, with frightened eyes. 'Come back and visit your old town again.'

'I will.'

Blind with unhappiness, he set off up the street at what he felt must be a stumble; but some dim necessity made him turn after he had gone a little way and smile back at them and wave his hand. They were still standing there, and they waved at him and he saw them turn and walk together into their house.

'I must go back and make my speech,' he said to himself as he walked on, swaying slightly, down the street. 'I shall get up and ask aloud "What have I got out of life ?" And there before them all I shall answer, "Nothing." I shall tell them the truth; that life has beaten me at every turning and used me for its own obscure purposes over and over; that everything I have loved has turned to ashes, and that every time I have stooped to pat a dog I have felt his teeth in my hand. And so at last they will learn the truth about one man's heart.'

V

The meeting was at four, but it was nearly five when he dismounted from the sweltering train and walked towards the Civic Club hall. Numerous cars were parked along the surrounding streets, promising an unusually large crowd. He was surprised to find that even the rear of the hall was thronged with standing people, and that there were recurrent outbursts of applause at some speech which was being delivered upon the platform.

'Can you find me a seat near the rear ?' he whispered to an attendant. 'I'm going to speak later, but I don't – don't want to go upon the platform just now.'

'Certainly, Mr Jackson.'

The only vacant chair was half behind a pillar in a far corner of the hall but he welcomed its privacy with relief; and settling himself, looked curiously around him. Yes, the gathering was large, and apparently enthusiastic. Catching a glimpse of a face here and there, he saw that he knew most of them, even by name; faces of men he had lived beside and worked with for over twenty years. All the better. These were the ones he must reach now, as soon as that figure on the platform there ceased mouthing his hollow cheer.

His eyes swung back to the platform, and as there was another ripple of applause he leaned his face around the corner to see. Then he uttered a low exclamation – the speaker was Thomas MacDowell. They had not been asked to speak together in several years.

'I've had many enemies in my life,' boomed the loud voice over the hall, 'and don't think I've had a change of heart, now that I'm fifty and a little grey. I'll go on making enemies to the end. This is just a little lull when I want to take off my armour and pay tribute to an enemy – because that enemy happens to be the finest man I ever knew.'

John Jackson wondered what candidate or protégé of MacDowell's was in question. It was typical of the man to seize any opportunity to make his own hay.

'Perhaps I wouldn't have said what I've said,' went on the booming voice, 'were he here today. But if all the young men in this city came up to me and asked me, "What is being honourable?" I'd answer them, "Go up to that man and look into his eyes." They're not happy eyes. I've often sat and looked at him and wondered what went on back of them that made those eyes so sad. Perhaps the fine, simple hearts that spend their hours smoothing other people's troubles never find time for happiness of their own. It's like the man at the soda fountain who never makes an ice-cream soda for himself.'

There was a faint ripple of laughter here, but John Jackson saw wonderingly that a woman he knew just across the aisle was dabbing with a handkerchief at her eyes.

His curiosity increased.

'He's gone away now,' said the man on the platform, bending his head and staring down for a minute at the floor: 'gone away suddenly, I understand. He seemed a little strange when I saw him yesterday; perhaps he gave in at last under the strain of trying to do many things for many men. Perhaps this meeting we're holding here comes a little too late now. But we'll all feel better for having said our say about him.

'I'm almost through. A lot of you will think it's funny that I feel this way about a man who, in fairness to him, I must call an enemy. But I'm going to say one thing more' – his voice rose defiantly – 'and it's a stranger thing still. Here, at fifty, there's one honour I'd like to have more than any honour this city ever gave me, or ever had in its power to give. I'd like to be able to stand up here before you and call John Jackson my friend.'

He turned away and a storm of applause rose like thunder through the hall. John Jackson half rose to his feet, and then sank back again in a stupefied way, shrinking behind the pillar. The applause continued until a young man arose on the platform and waved them silent.

'Mrs Ralston,' he called, and sat down.

A woman rose from the line of chairs and came forward to the edge of the stage and began to speak in a quiet voice. She told a story about a man whom – so it seemed to John Jackson – he had known once, but whose actions, repeated here, seemed utterly unreal, like something that had happened in a dream. It appeared that every year many hundreds of babies in the city owed their lives to something this man had done five years before; he had put a mortgage upon his own house to assure the children's hospital on the edge of town. It told how this had been kept secret at the man's own request, because he wanted the city to take pride in the hospital as a community affair, when but for the man's effort, made after the community attempt had failed, the hospital would never have existed at all.

Then Mrs Ralston began to talk about the parks; how the town had baked for many years under the midland heat; and how this man, not a very rich man, had given up land and time and money for many months that a green line of shade might skirt the boulevards, and that the poor children could leave the streets and play in fresh grass in the centre of town.

That was only the beginning, she said; and she went on to tell how, when any such plan tottered, or the public interest lagged, word was brought to John Jackson, and somehow he made it go and seemed to give it life out of his own body, until there was scarcely anything in this city that didn't have a little of John Jackson's heart in it, just as there were few people in this city that didn't have a little of their hearts for John Jackson.

Mrs Ralston's speech stopped abruptly at this point. She had been crying a little for several moments, but there must have been many people there in the audience who understood what she meant – a mother or a child here and there who had been the recipients of some of that kindness – because the applause seemed to fill the whole room like an ocean, and echoed back and forth from wall to wall.

Only a few people recognized the short grizzled man who now got up from his chair in the rear of the platform, but when he began to speak silence settled gradually over the house.

'You didn't hear my name,' he said in a voice which trembled a little, 'and when they first planned this surprise meeting I wasn't expected to speak at all. I'm John Jackson's head clerk. Fowler's my name, and when they decided they were going to hold the meeting, anyhow, even though John Jackson had gone away, I thought perhaps I'd like to say a few words' – those who were closest saw his hands clench tighter – 'say a few words that I couldn't say if John Jackson was here.

'I've been with him twenty years. That's a long time. Neither of us had grey hair when I walked into his office one day just fired from somewhere and asked him for a job. Since then I can't tell you, gentlemen, I can't tell you what his – his presence on this earth has meant to me. When he told me yesterday, suddenly, that he was going away, I thought to myself that if he never came back I didn't – I didn't want to go on living. That man makes everything in the world seem all right. If you knew how we felt around the office—' He paused and shook his head wordlessly. 'Why, there's three of us there – the janitor and one of the other clerks and me – that have sons named after John Jackson. Yes, sir. Because none of us could think of anything better than for a boy to have that name or that example before him through life. But would we tell him? Not a chance. He wouldn't even know what it was all about. Why' – he sank his voice to a hushed whisper – 'he'd just look at you in a puzzled way and say, "What did you wish that on the poor kid for?" '

He broke off, for there was a sudden and growing interruption. An epidemic of head turning had broken out and was spreading rapidly from one corner of the hall until it affected the whole assemblage. Someone had discovered John Jackson behind the post in the corner, and first an exclamation and then a growing mumble that mounted to a cheer swept over the auditorium.

Suddenly two men had taken him by the arms and set him on his feet, and then he was pushed and pulled and carried towards the platform, arriving somehow in a standing position after having been lifted over many heads.

They were all standing now, arms waving wildly, voices filling the hall with tumultous clamour. Some in the back of the hall began to sing 'For he's a jolly good fellow', and five hundred voices took up the air and sang it with such feeling, with such swelling emotion, that all eyes were wet and the song assumed a significance far beyond the spoken words.

This was John Jackson's chance now to say to these people that he had got so little out of life. He stretched out his arms in a sudden gesture and they were quiet, listening, every man and woman and child.

'I have been asked—' His voice faltered. 'My dear friends, I have been asked to – to tell you what I have got out of life—'

Five hundred faces, touched and smiling, every one of them full of encouragement and love and faith, turned up to him.

'What have I got out of life?'

He stretched out his arms wide, as if to include them all, as if to take to his breast all the men and women and children of this city. His voice rang in the hushed silence.

'Everything!'

At six o'clock, when he walked up his street alone, the air was already cool with evening. Approaching his house, he raised his head and saw that someone was sitting on the outer doorstep, resting his face in his hands. When John Jackson came up the walk, the caller – he was a young man with dark, frightened eyes – saw him and sprang to his feet.

'Father,' he said quickly, 'I got your telegram, but I – I came home.'

John Jackson looked at him and nodded.

'The house was locked,' said the young man in an uneasy way.

'I've got the key.'

John Jackson unlocked the front door and preceded his son inside.

'Father,' cried Ellery Jackson quickly, 'I haven't any excuse to make – anything to say. I'll tell you all about it if you're still interested – if you can stand to hear—'

John Jackson rested his hand on the young man's shoulder.

'Don't feel too badly,' he said in his kind voice. 'I guess I can always stand anything my son does.'

This was an understatement. For John Jackson could stand anything now for ever – anything that came, anything at all.

NOT IN THE GUIDEBOOK

Woman's Home Companion, November 1925

*'Not in the Guidebook' was written in Rome's Hotel des Princes in December
1924, just after* The Great Gatsby *had been sent to Scribners. The
Fitzgeralds had gone to Rome from the Riviera, planning to spend the
winter of 1924-5 there, but were unhappy and moved on to Capri in
February. When Fitzgerald reread this story, he decided to rewrite it,
which he did at the Hotel Tiberio in Capri. Although he doubted whether it
would be saleable,* Woman's Home Companion *paid $1750.*
*'Not in the Guidebook' was the second story Fitzgerald wrote with a
European setting. Whereas the first, 'Love in the Night', is distinguished by
rich descriptions of the Riviera, 'Not in the Guidebook' depends on a
predictable plot trick. Part of the problem may have been that at this time
Fitzgerald did not know Paris well – having spent only a few days there.*

*Fitzgerald was ashamed of his 1924 story output and wrote John Peale
Bishop: 'I've done about 10 pieces of horrible junk in the last year tho
that I can never republish or bear to look at – cheap and without the
spontaneity of my first work.'*

This story began three days before it got into the papers. Like many other
news-hungry Americans in Paris this spring, I opened the *Franco-
American Star* one morning, and having skimmed the hackneyed headlines
(largely devoted to reporting the sempiternal 'Layfayette-love-Washington'
bombast of French and American orators) I came upon something of
genuine interest.

'Look at that!' I exclaimed, passing it over to the twin bed. But the
occupant of the twin bed immediately found an article about Leonora
Hughes, the dancer, in another column, and began to read it. So of course
I demanded the paper back.

'You don't realize—' I began.

'I wonder,' interrupted the occupant of the twin bed, 'if she's a real blonde.'

However, when I issued from the domestic suite a little later I found other men in various cafés saying, 'Look at that!' as they pointed to the Item of Interest. And about noon I found another writer (whom I have since bribed with champagne to hold his peace) and together we went down into Franco-American officialdom to see.

It began on a boat, and with a young woman who, though she wasn't even faintly uneasy, was leaning over the rail. She was watching the parallels of longitude as they swam beneath the keel, and trying to read the numbers on them, but of course the SS *Olympic* travels too fast for that, and all that the young woman could see was the agate-green, foliage-like spray, changing and complaining around the stern. Though there was little to look at except the spray and a dismal Scandinavian tramp in the distance and the admiring millionaire who was trying to catch her eye from the first-class deck above, Milly Cooley was perfectly happy. For she was beginning life over.

Hope is a usual cargo between Naples and Ellis Island, but on ships bound east for Cherbourg it is noticeably rare. The first-class passengers specialize in sophistication and the steerage passengers go in for disillusion (which is much the same thing) but the young woman by the rail was going in for hope raised to the ultimate power. It was not her own life she was beginning over, but someone else's, and this is a much more dangerous thing to do.

Milly was a frail, dark, appealing girl with the spiritual, haunted eyes that so frequently accompany South European beauty. By birth her mother and father had been respectively Czech and Romanian, but Milly had missed the overshort upper lip and the pendulous, pointed nose that disfigure the type; her features were regular and her skin was young and olive-white and clear.

The good-looking, pimply young man with eyes of a bright marbly blue who was asleep on a dunnage bag a few feet away was her husband – it was his life that Milly was beginning over. Through the six months of their marriage he had shown himself to be shiftless and dissipated, but now they were getting off to a new start. Jim Cooley deserved a new start, for he had been a hero in the war. There was a thing called 'shell shock' which justified anything unpleasant in a war hero's behaviour – Jim Cooley had explained that to her on the second day of their honeymoon when he had got abominably drunk and knocked her down with his open hand.

'I get crazy,' he said emphatically next morning, and his marbly eyes rolled back and forth realistically in his head. 'I get started thinkin' I'm fightin' the war, an' I take a poke at whatever's in front of me, see?'

He was a Brooklyn boy, and he had joined the marines. And on a June twilight he had crawled fifty yards out of his lines to search the body of a Bavarian captain that lay out in plain sight. He found a copy of German regimental orders, and in consequence his own brigade attacked much sooner than would otherwise have been possible, and perhaps the war was shortened by so much as a quarter of an hour. The fact was appreciated by the French and American races in the form of engraved slugs of precious metal which Jim showed around for four years before it occurred to him how nice it would be to have a permanent audience. Milly's mother was impressed with his martial achievement, and a marriage was arranged. Milly didn't realize her mistake until twenty-four hours after it was too late.

At the end of several months Milly's mother died and left her daughter two hundred and fifty dollars. The event had a marked effect on Jim. He sobered up and one night came home from work with a plan for turning over a new leaf, for beginning life over. By the aid of his war record he had obtained a job with a bureau that took care of American soldier graves in France. The pay was small but then, as everyone knew, living was dirt cheap over there. Hadn't the forty a month that he drew in the war looked good to the girls and the winesellers of Paris? Especially when you figured it in French money.

Milly listened to his tales of the land where grapes were full of champagne and then thought it all over carefully. Perhaps the best use for her money would be in giving Jim his chance, the chance that he had never had since the war. In a little cottage in the outskirts of Paris they could forget this last six months and find peace and happiness and perhaps even love as well.

'Are you going to try?' she asked simply.

'Of course I'm going to try, Milly.'

'You're going to make me think I didn't make a mistake?'

'Sure I am, Milly; it'll make a different person out of me. Don't you believe it?'

She looked at him. His eyes were bright with enthusiasm, with determination. A warm glow had spread over him at the prospect – he had never really had his chance before.

'All right,' she said finally. 'We'll go.'

They were there. The Cherbourg breakwater, a white stone snake, glittered along the sea at dawn: behind it red roofs and steeples and then small neat hills traced with a warm, orderly pattern of toy farms. 'Do you like this French arrangement?' it seemed to say. 'It's considered very charming, but if you don't agree just shift it about – set this road here, this steeple there. It's been done before, and it always comes out lovely in the end!'

It was Sunday morning, and Cherbourg was in flaring collars and high lace hats. Donkey carts and diminutive automobiles moved to the sound of incessant bells. Jim and Milly went ashore on a tugboat and were inspected by customs officials and immigration authorities. Then they were free with an hour before the Paris train, and they moved out into the bright thrilling world of French blue. At a point of vantage, a pleasant square that continually throbbed with soldiers and innumerable dogs and the clack of wooden shoes, they sat down at a café.

'Du vaah,' said Jim to the waiter. He was a little disappointed when the answer came in English. After the man went for the wine he took out his two war medals and pinned them to his coat. The waiter returned with the wine, seemed not to notice the medals, made no remark. Milly wished Jim hadn't put them on – she felt vaguely ashamed.

After another glass of wine it was time for the train. They got into the strange little third-class carriage, an engine that was out of some boy's playroom began to puff and, in a pleasant, informal way, jogged them leisurely south through the friendly lived-over land.

'What are we going to do first when we get there?' asked Milly.

'First?' Jim looked at her abstractly and frowned. 'Why, first I got to see about the job, see?' The exhilaration of the wine had passed and left him surly. 'What do you want to ask so many questions for? Buy yourself a guidebook, why don't you?'

Milly felt a slight sinking of the heart; he hadn't grumbled at her like this since the trip was first proposed.

'It didn't cost as much as we thought, anyhow,' she said cheerfully. 'We must have over a hundred dollars left anyway.'

He grunted. Outside the window Milly's eyes were caught by the sight of a dog drawing a legless man.

'Look!' she exclaimed. 'How funny!'

'Aw, dry up. I've seen it all before.'

An encouraging idea occurred to her: it was in France that Jim's nerves had gone to pieces, it was natural that he should be cross and uneasy for a few hours.

Westward through Caen, Lisieux and the rich green plains of Calvados. When they reached the third stop Jim got up and stretched himself.

'Going out on the platform,' he said gloomily. 'I need to get a breath of air; hot in here.'

It was hot, but Milly didn't mind. Her eyes were excited with all she saw – a pair of little boys in black smocks began to stare at her curiously through the windows of the carriage.

'American?' cried one of them suddenly.

'Hello,' said Milly, 'what place is this?'

'Pardon?'

They came closer.

Suddenly the two boys poked each other in the stomach and went off into roars of laughter. Milly didn't see that she had said anything funny.

There was an abrupt jerk as the train started. Milly jumped up in alarm and put her head out the carriage window.

'Jim!' she called.

She looked up and down the platform. He wasn't there. The boys, seeing her distraught face, ran along beside the train as it moved from the station. He must have jumped for one of the rear cars. But—

'Jim!' she cried wildly. The station slid past. 'Jim!'

Trying desperately to control her fright, she sank back into her seat and tried to think. Her first supposition was that he had gone to a café for a drink and missed the train – in that case she should have got off too while there was still time, for otherwise there was no telling what would happen to him. If this were one of his spells he might just go on drinking, until he had spent every cent of their money. It was unbelievably awful to imagine – but it was possible.

She waited, gave him ten, fifteen minutes to work his way up to this car – then she admitted to herself that he wasn't on the train. A dull panic began. The sudden change in her relations to the world was so startling that she thought neither of his delinquency nor of what must be done, but only of the immediate fact that she was alone. Erratic as his protection had been, it was something. Now – why, she might sit in this strange train until it carried her to China and there was no one to care!

After a long while it occurred to her that he might have left part of the money in one of the suitcases. She took them down from the rack and went feverishly through all the clothes. In the bottom of an old pair of pants that Jim had worn on the boat she found two bright American dimes. The sight of them was somehow comforting and she clasped them tight in her hand. The bags yielded up nothing more.

An hour later, when it was dark outside, the train slid in under the yellow misty glow of the Gare du Nord. Strange, incomprehensible station cries fell on her ears, and her heart was beating loudly as she wrenched at the handle of the door. She took her own bag with one hand and picked up Jim's suitcase in the other, but it was heavy and she couldn't get out the door with both, so in a rush of anger she left the suitcase in the carriage.

On the platform she looked left and right with the forlorn hope that he might appear, but she saw no one except a Swedish brother and sister from the boat whose tall bodies, straight and strong under the huge bundles they both carried, were hurrying out of sight. She took a quick step after them and then stopped, unable to tell them of the shameful thing that had happened to her. They had worries of their own.

With the two dimes in one hand and her suitcase in the other, Milly walked slowly aong the platform. People hurried by her, baggage-smashers under forests of golf sticks, excited American girls full of the irrepressible thrill of arriving in Paris, obsequious porters from the big hotels. They were all walking and talking very fast, but Milly walked slowly because ahead of her she saw only the yellow arc of the waiting-room and the door that led out of it and after that she did not know where she would go.

By 10 p.m. Mr Bill Driscoll was usually weary, for by that time he had a full twelve-hour day behind him. After that he only went out with the most celebrated people. If someone had tipped off a multimillionaire or a moving-picture director – at that time American directors were swarming over Europe looking for new locations – about Bill Driscoll, he would fortify himself with two cups of coffee, adorn his person with his new dinner-coat and show them the most dangerous dives of Montmartre in the very safest way.

Bill Driscoll looked well in his new dinner-coat, with his reddish brown hair soaked in water and slicked back from his attractive forehead. Often he regarded himself admiringly in the mirror, for it was the first dinner-coat he had ever owned. He had earned it himself, with his wits, as he had earned the swelling packet of American bonds which awaited him in a New York bank. If you had been in Paris during the past two years you must have seen his large white autobus with the provoking legend on the side:

WILLIAM DRISCOLL
HE SHOWS YOU THINGS NOT IN THE GUIDEBOOK

When he found Milly Cooley it was after three o'clock and he had just left Director and Mrs Claude Peebles at their hotel after escorting them to those celebrated apache dens, Zelli's and Le Rat Mort (which are about as dangerous, all things considered, as the Biltmore Hotel at noon), and he was walking homeward toward his *pension* on the left bank. His eye was caught by two disreputable-looking parties under the lamp-post who were giving aid to what was apparently a drunken girl. Bill Driscoll decided to cross the street – he was aware of the tender affection which the French police bore towards embattled Americans, and he made a point of keeping out of trouble. Just at that moment Milly's subconscious self came to her aid and she called out 'Let me go!' in an agonized moan.

The moan had a Brooklyn accent. It was a Brooklyn moan.

Driscoll altered his course uneasily and, approaching the group, asked politely what was the matter; whereat one of the disreputable parties desisted in his attempt to open Milly's tightly clasped left hand.

The man answered quickly that she had fainted. He and his friend were assisting her to the gendarmery. They loosened their hold on her and she collapsed gently to the ground.

Bill came closer and bent over her, being careful to choose a position where neither man was behind him. He saw a young, frightened face that was drained now of the colour it possed by day.

'Where did you find her?' he inquired in French.

'Here. Just now. She looked to be so tired—'

Billy put his hand in his pocket and when he spoke he tried very hard to suggest by his voice that he had a revolver there.

'She is American,' he said. 'You leave her to me.'

The man made a gesture of acquiescence and took a step backward, his hand going with a natural movement to his coat as if he intended buttoning it. He was watching Bill's right hand, the one in his coat pocket, and Bill happened to be left-handed. There is nothing much faster than an un-telegraphed left-hand blow – this one travelled less than eighteen inches and the recipient staggered back against a lamp-post, embraced it transiently and regretfully and settled to the ground. Nevertheless Bill Driscoll's successful career might have ended there, ended with the strong shout of '*Voleurs!*' which he raised into the Paris night, had the other man had a gun. The other man indicated that he had no gun by retreating ten yards down the street. His prostrate companion moved slightly on the sidewalk and, taking a step towards him, Billy drew back his foot and kicked him full in the head as a football player kicks a goal from placement. It was not a pretty gesture, but he had remembered that he was wearing his new dinner-coat and he didn't want to wrestle on the ground for the piece of poisonous hardware.

In a moment two gendarmes in a great hurry came running down the moonlit street.

Two days after this it came out in the papers – 'War hero deserts wife en route to Paris', I think, or 'American bride arrives penniless, husband-less at Gare du Nord'. The police were informed, of course, and word was sent out to the provincial departments to seek an American named James Cooley who was without *carte d'identité*. The newspapers learned the story at the American Aid Society, and made a neat, pathetic job of it because Milly was young and pretty and curiously loyal to her husband. Almost her first words were to explain that it was all because his nerves had been shattered in the war.

Young Driscoll was somewhat disappointed to find that she was married. Not that he had fallen in love at first sight – on the contrary, he was unus-ally level-headed – but after the moonlight rescue, which rather pleased him, it didn't seem appropriate that she should have a heroic husband wandering over France. He had carried her to his own *pension* that night and his landlady, an American widow named Mrs Horton, had taken a fancy to Milly and wanted to look after her, but before eleven o'clock on the day the paper appeared, the office of the American Aid Society was literally jammed with Samaritans. They were mostly rich old ladies from America who were tired of the Louvre and the Tuileries, and anxious for something to do. Several eager but sheepish Frenchmen, inspired by a mysterious and unfathomable gallantry, hung about outside the door.

The most insistent of the ladies was a Mrs Coots, who considered that Providence had sent her Milly as a companion. If she had heard Milly's story in the street she wouldn't have listened to a word, but print makes things respectable. After it got into the *Franco-American Star*, Mrs Coots was sure Milly wouldn't make off with her jewels.

'I'll pay you well, my dear,' she insisted shrilly. 'Twenty-five a week. How's that?'

Milly cast an anxious glance at Mrs Horton's faded, pleasant face.

'I don't know—' she said hesitantly.

'I can't pay you anything.' Mrs Horton was confused by Mrs Coots' affluent, positive manner. 'You do as you like. I'd love to have you.'

'You've certainly been kind,' said Milly, 'but I don't want to impose—'

Driscoll, who had been walking up and down with his hands in his pockets, stopped and turned towards her quickly.

'I'll take care of that,' he said quickly. 'You don't have to worry about that.'

Mrs Coots' eyes flashed at him indignantly.

'She's better with me,' she insisted. 'Much better.' She turned to the secretary and remarked in a pained, disapproving stage whisper, 'Who is this forward young man?'

Again Milly looked appealingly at Mrs Horton.

'If it's not too much trouble I'd rather stay with you,' she said. 'I'll help you all I can—'

It took another half an hour to get rid of Mrs Coots, but finally it was arranged that Milly was to stay at Mrs Horton's *pension*, until some trace of her husband was found. Later the same day they ascertained that the American Bureau of Military Graves had never heard of Jim Cooley – he had no job promised him in France.

However distressing her situation, Milly was young and she was in Paris in mid-June. She decided to enjoy herself. At Mr Bill Driscoll's invitation she went on an excursion to Versailles next day in his rubberneck wagon. She had never been on such a trip before. She sat among garment buyers from Sioux City and schoolteachers from California and honeymoon couples from Japan, and was whirled through fifteen centuries of Paris, while their guide stood up in front with the megaphone pressed to his voluble and original mouth.

'Building on your left is the Louvre, ladies and gentlemen. Excursion number twenty-three leaving tomorrow at ten sharp takes you inside. Sufficient to remark now that it contains fifteen thousand works of art of every description. The oil used in its oil paintings would lubricate all the cars in the state of Oregon over a period of two years. The frames alone if placed end to end—'

Milly watching him, believed every word. It was hard to remember that he had come to her rescue that night. Heroes weren't like that – she knew; she had lived with one. They brooded constantly on their achievements and retailed them to strangers at least once a day. When she thanked this young man he told her gravely that Mr Carnegie had been trying to get him on the ouija board all that day.

After a dramatic stop before the house in which Landru, the Bluebeard of France, had murdered his fourteen wives, the expedition proceeded to Versailles. There, in the great hall of mirrors, Bill Driscoll delved into the forgotten scandal of the eighteenth century as he described the meeting between 'Louie's girl and Louie's wife'.

'Du Barry skipped in, wearing a creation of mauve georgette, held out by bronze hoops over a *tablier* of champagne lace. The gown had a ruched collarette of Swedish fox, lined with yellow satin *fulgurante* which matched the hansom that brought her to the party. She was nervous, ladies. She didn't know how the queen was going to take it. After a while the queen walked in, wearing an oxidized silver gown with collar, cuffs and flounces of Russian ermine and strappings of dentist's gold. The bodice was cut with a very long waistline and the skirt arranged full in front and falling in picot-edged points tipped with the crown jewels. When Du Barry saw her she leaned over to King Louie and whispered: "Royal Honey-boy, who's that lady with all the laundry on that just came in the door?"

' "That isn't a lady," said Louie, "that's my wife." '

That was the first of many trips that Milly took in the rubberneck wagon – to Malmaison, to Passy, to St Cloud. The weeks passed, three of them, and still there was no word from Jim Cooley, who seemed to have stepped off the face of the earth when he vanished from the train.

In spite of a sort of dull worry that possessed her when she thought of her situation, Milly was happier than she had ever been. It was a relief to be rid of the incessant depression of living with a morbid and broken man. Moreover, it was thrilling to be in Paris when it seemed that all the world was there, when each arriving boat dumped a new thousand into the pleasure ground, when the streets were so clogged with sightseers that Billy Driscoll's buses were reserved for days ahead. And it was pleasantest of all to stroll down to the corner and watch the blood-red sun sink like a slow penny into the Seine while she sipped coffee with Bill Driscoll at a café.

'How would you like to go to Château-Thierry with me tomorrow?' he asked her one evening.

The name struck a chord in Milly. It was at Château-Thierry that Jim Cooley, at the risk of his life, had made his daring expedition between the lines.

'My husband was there,' she said proudly.

'So was I,' he remarked. 'And I didn't have any fun at all.'

He thought for a moment.

'How old are you?' he asked suddenly.

'Eighteen.'

'Why don't you get a divorce?'

The suggestion shocked Milly.

'I think you'd better,' he continued, looking down. 'It's easier here than anywhere else. Then you'd be free.'

'I couldn't,' she said, frightened. 'It wouldn't be fair. You see he doesn't—'

'I know,' he interrupted. 'But I'm beginning to think that you're spoiling your life with this man. Is there anything except his war record to his credit?'

'Isn't that enough?' answered Milly gravely.

'Milly—' He raised his eyes. 'Won't you think it over carefully?'

She got up uneasily. He looked very honest and safe and cool sitting there, and for a moment she was tempted to do what he said, to put the whole thing in his hands. But looking at him she saw now what she hadn't seen before, that the advice was not disinterested – there was more than an impersonal care for her future in his eyes. She turned away with a mixture of emotions.

Side by side and in silence they walked back towards the *pension*. From a high window the plaintive wail of a violin drifted down into the street, mingling with practice chords from an invisible piano and a shrill incomprehensible quarrel of French children over the way. The twilight was fast dissolving into a starry blue Parisian evening, but it was still light enough for them to make out the figure of Mrs Horton standing in front of the pension. She came towards them swiftly, talking as she came.

'I've got some news for you,' she said. 'The secretary of the American Aid Society just telephoned. They've located your husband, and he'll be in Paris the day after tomorrow.'

When Jim Cooley, the war hero, left the train at the small town of Evreux, he walked very fast until he was several hundred yards from the station. Then, standing behind a tree, he watched until the train pulled out and the last puff of smoke burst up behind a little hill. He stood for several minutes, laughing and looking after the train, until abruptly his face resumed his normal injured expression and he turned to examine the place in which he had chosen to be free.

It was a sleepy provincial village with two high lines of silver sycamores along its principal street, at the end of which a fine fountain purred crystal water from a cat's mouth of cold stone. Around the fountain was a square and on the sidewalks of the square several groups of small iron tables indicated open-air cafés. A farm wagon drawn by a single white ox was toiling towards the fountain and several cheap French cars, together with an ancient American one, were parked along the street.

'It's a hick town,' he said to himself with some disgust. 'Reg'lar hick town.'

But it was peaceful and green, and he caught sight of two stockingless ladies entering the door of a shop; and the little tables by the fountain were inviting. He walked up the street and at the first café sat down and ordered a lager beer.

'I'm free,' he said to himself. 'Free, by God!'

His decision to desert Milly had been taken suddenly – in Cherbourg, as they got on the train. Just at that moment he had seen a little French girl who was the real thing and he realized that he didn't want Milly 'hanging on him' any more. Even on the boat he had played with the idea, but until Cherbourg he had never quite made up his mind. He was rather sorry now that he hadn't thought to leave Milly a little money, enough for one night – but then somebody would be sure to help her when she got to Paris. Besides, what he didn't know didn't worry him, and he wasn't going ever to hear about her again.

'Cognac this time,' he said to the waiter.

He needed something strong. He wanted to forget. Not to forget Milly, that was easy, she was already behind him; but to forget himself. He felt that he had been abused. He felt that it was Milly who had deserted him, or at least that her cold mistrust was responsible for driving him away. What good would it have done if he had gone on to Paris anyways ? There wasn't enough money left to keep two people for very long, and he had invented the job on the strength of a vague rumour that the American Bureau of Military Graves gave jobs to veterans who were broke in France. He shouldn't have brought Milly, wouldn't have if he had had the money to get over. But, though he was not aware of it, there was another reason why he had brought Milly. Jim Cooley hated to be alone.

'Cognac,' he said to the waiter. 'A big one. *Très grand.*'

He put his hand in his pocket and fingered the blue notes that had been given him in Cherbourg in exchange for his American money. He took them out and counted them. Crazy-looking kale. It was funny you could buy things with it just like you could do with the real mazuma.

He beckoned to the waiter.

'Hey!' he remarked conversationally. 'This is funny money you got here, ain't it?'

But the waiter spoke no English, and was unable to satisfy Jim Cooley's craving for companionship. Never mind. His nerves were at rest now – body was glowing triumphantly from top to toe.

'This is the life,' he muttered to himself. 'Only live once. Might as well enjoy it.' And then aloud to the waiter, ' 'Nother one of those big cognacs. Two of them. I'm set to go.'

He went – for several hours. He awoke at dawn in a bedroom of a small inn, with red streaks in his eyes and fever pounding his head. He was afraid to look in his pockets until he had ordered and swallowed another cognac, and then he found that his worst fears were justified. Of the ninety-odd dollars with which he had got off the train only six were left.

'I must have been crazy,' he whispered.

There remained his watch. His watch was large and methodical, and on the outer case two hearts were picked out in diamonds from the dark solid gold. It had been part of the booty of Jim Cooley's heroism, for when he had located the paper in the German officer's pocket he had found it clasped tight in the dead hand. One of the diamond hearts probably stood for some human grief back in Friedland or Berlin, but when Jim married he told Milly that the diamond hearts stood for their hearts and would be a token of their everlasting love. Before Milly fully appreciated this sentimental suggestion their enduring love had been tarnished beyound repair and the watch went back into Jim's pocket where it confined itself to marking time instead of emotion.

But Jim Cooley had loved to show the watch, and he found that parting with it would be much more painful than parting with Milly – so painful, in fact, that he got drunk in anticipation of the sorrow. Late that afternoon, already a reeling figure at which the town boys jeered along the streets, he found his way into the shop of a *bijoutier*, and when he issued forth into the street he was in possession of a ticket of redemption and a note for two thousand francs which, he figured dimly, was about one hundred and twenty dollars. Muttering to himself, he stumbled back to the square.

'One American can lick three Frenchmen!' he remarked to three small stout bourgeois drinking their beer at a table.

They paid no attention. He repeated his jeer.

'One American –' tapping his chest, 'can beat up three dirty frogs, see?'

Still they didn't move. It infuriated him. Lurching forward, he seized the back of an unoccupied chair and pulled at it. In what seemed less than a minute there was a small crowd around him and the three Frenchmen were all talking at once in excited voices.

'Aw, go on, I meant what I said!' he cried savagely. 'One American can wipe up the ground with three Frenchmen!'

And now there were two men in uniform before him – two men with revolver holsters on their hips, dressed in red and blue.

'You heard what I said,' he shouted, 'I'm a hero – I'm not afraid of the whole damn French army!'

A hand fell on his arm, but with blind passion he wrenched it free and struck at the black-moustached face before him. Then there was a rushing, crashing noise in his ears as fists and then feet struck at him, and the world seemed to close like water over his head.

When they located him and, after a personal expedition by one of the American vice-consuls, got him out of jail Milly realized how much these weeks had meant to her. The holiday was over. But even though Jim would be in Paris tomorrow, even though the dreary round of her life with him was due to recommence, Milly decided to take the trip to Château-Thierry just the same. She wanted a last few hours of happiness that she could always remember. She supposed they would return to New York – what chance Jim might have had of obtaining a position had vanished now that he was marked by a fortnight in a French prison.

The bus, as usual, was crowded. As they approached the little village of Château-Thierry, Bill Driscoll stood up in front with his megaphone and began to tell his clients how it had looked to him when his division went up to the line five years before.

'It was nine o'clock at night,' he said, 'and we came out of a wood and there was the western front. I'd read about it for three years back in America, and here it was at last – it looked like the line of a forest fire at night except that fireworks were blazing up instead of grass. We relieved a French regiment in new trenches that weren't three feet deep. At that, most of us were too excited to be scared until the top sergeant was blown to pieces with shrapnel about two o'clock in the morning. That made us think. Two days later we went over and the only reason I didn't get hit was that I was shaking so much they couldn't aim at me.'

The listeners laughed and Milly felt a faint thrill of pride. Jim hadn't been scared – she'd heard him say so, many times. All he'd thought about was doing a little more than his duty. When others were in the comparative safety of the trenches he had gone into no-man's-land alone.

After lunch in the village the party walked over the battlefield, changed now into a peaceful undulating valley of graves. Milly was glad she had come – the sense of rest after a struggle soothed her. Perhaps after the bleak future her life might be quiet as this peaceful land. Perhaps Jim would change some day. If he had risen once to such a height of courage there must be something deep inside him that was worth while, that would make him try once more.

Just before it was time to start home Driscoll, who had hardly spoken to her all day, suddenly beckoned her aside.

'I want to talk to you for the last time,' he said.

The last time! Milly felt a flutter of unexpected pain. Was tomorrow so near?

'I'm going to say what's in my mind,' he said, 'and please don't be angry. I love you, and you know it; but what I'm going to say isn't because of that – it's because I want you to be happy.'

Milly nodded. She was afraid she was going to cry.

'I don't think your husband's any good,' he said.

She looked up.

'You don't know him,' she exclaimed quickly. 'You can't judge.'

'I can judge from what he did to you. I think this shell-shock business is all a plain lie. And what does it matter what he did five years ago?'

'It matters to me,' cried Milly. She felt herself growing a little angry. 'You can't take that away from him. He acted brave.'

Driscoll nodded.

'That's true. But other men were brave.'

'You weren't,' she said scornfully; 'you just said you were scared to death – and when you said it all the people laughed. Well, nobody laughed at Jim – they gave him a medal because he wasn't afraid.'

When Milly had said this she was sorry, but it was too late now. At his next words she leaned forward in surprise.

'That was a lie too,' said Bill Driscoll slowly. 'I told it because I wanted them to laugh. I wasn't even in the attack.'

He stared silently down the hill.

'Well, then,' said Milly contemptuously, 'how can you sit here and say things about my husband when – when you didn't even—'

'It was only a professional lie,' he said impatiently. 'I happened to be wounded the night before.'

He stood up suddenly.

'There's no use,' he said. 'I seem to have made you hate me, and that's the end. There's no use saying any more.'

He stared down the hill with haunted eyes.

'I shouldn't have talked to you here,' he cried. 'There's no luck here for me. Once before I lost something I wanted, not a hundred yards from this hill. And now I've lost you.'

'What was it you lost?' demanded Milly bitterly. 'Another girl?'

'There's never been any other girl but you.'

'What was it then?'

He hesitated.

'I told you I was wounded,' he said. 'I was. For two months I didn't know I was alive. But the worst of it was that some dirty sneak thief had been through my pockets, and I guess he got the credit for a copy of German orders that I'd just brought in. He took a gold watch too. I'd pinched them both off the body of a German officer out between the lines.'

Mr and Mrs William Driscoll were married the following spring and started off on their honeymoon in a car that was much larger than the king of England's. There were two dozen vacant places in it, so they gave many rides to tired pedestrians along the white poplar-lined roads of France. The wayfarers, however, always sat in the back seat as the conversation in front was not for profane ears. The tour progressed through Lyons, Avignon, Bordeaux, and smaller places not in the guidebook.

PRESUMPTION

Saturday Evening Post, 9 January 1926

'Presumption' was written in Paris in November 1925. The Post *paid*
$2500 – a raise of $500 – and printed it as a lead piece.
The Great Gatsby *had been published in April 1925, but its disappointing*
sale (23,000 copies) compelled Fitzgerald to resume writing stories instead of
concentrating on a new novel. This story has obvious connections with
Gatsby *in its treatment of the poor boy who falls in love with a rich girl*
and sets out to win her by becoming financially worthy of her. Because
'Presumption' was written for the Post *it has a happy ending through one*
of the reversals of fortune that frequently occur in Fitzgerald's commercial
fiction. 'Rich girls can't live on air.' Neither Fitzgerald nor their suitors
expected them to.

Sitting by the window and staring out into the early autumn dusk, San
Juan Chandler remembered only that Noel was coming tomorrow; but
when, with a romantic sound that was half gasp, half sigh, he turned from
the window, snapped on the light and looked at himself in the mirror, his
expression became more materially complicated. He leaned closer. Delicacy
balked at the abominable word 'pimple', but some such blemish had un-
doutedly appeared on his cheek within the last hour, and now formed, with
a pair from last week, a distressing constellation of three. Going into the
bathroom adjoining his room – Juan had never possessed a bathroom to
himself before – he opened a medicine closet, and, after peering about,
carefully extracted a promising-looking jar of black ointment and covered
each slight protuberance with a black gluey mound. Then, strangely dotted,
he returned to the bedroom, put out the light and resumed his vigil over
the shadowy garden.

He waited. That roof among the trees on the hill belonged to Noel
Garneau's house. She was coming back to it tomorrow; he would see her

there . . . A loud clock on the staircase inside struck seven. Juan went to the glass and removed the ointment with a handkerchief. To his chagrin, the spots were still there, even slightly irritated from the chemical sting of the remedy. That settled it – no more chocolate malted milks or eating between meals during his visit to Culpepper Bay. Taking the lid from the jar of talcum he had observed on the dressing table, he touched the laden puff to his cheek. Immediately his brows and lashes bloomed with snow and he coughed chokingly, observing that the triangle of humiliation was still observable upon his otherwise handsome face.

'Disgusting,' he muttered to himself. 'I never saw anything so disgusting.' At twenty, such childish phenomena should be behind him.

Downstairs three gongs, melodious and metallic, hummed and sang. He listened for a moment, fascinated. Then he wiped the powder from his face, ran a comb through his yellow hair and went down to dinner.

Dinner at Cousin Cora's he had found embarrassing. She was so stiff and formal about things like that, and so familiar about Juan's private affairs. The first night of his visit he had tried politely to pull out her chair and bumped into the maid; the second night he remembered the experience – but so did the maid, and Cousin Cora seated herself unassisted. At home Juan was accustomed to behave as he liked; like all children of deferent and indulgent mothers, he lacked both confidence and good manners.

Tonight there were guests.

'This is San Juan Chandler, my cousin's son – Mrs Holyoke – and Mr Holyoke.'

The phrase 'my cousin's son' seemed to explain him away, seemed to account for his being in Miss Chandler's house: 'You understand – we must have our poor relations with us occasionally.' But a tone which implied that would be rude – and certainly Cousin Cora, with all her social position, couldn't be rude.

Mr and Mrs Holyoke acknowledged the introduction politely and coolly, and dinner was served. The conversation, dictated by Cousin Cora, bored Juan. It was about the garden and about her father, for whom she lived and who was dying slowly and unwillingly upstairs. Towards the salad Juan was wedged into the conversation by a question from Mr Holyoke and a quick look from his cousin.

'I'm just staying for a week,' he answered politely; 'then I've got to go home because college opens pretty soon.'

'Where are you at college?'

Juan named his college, adding almost apologetically, 'You see, my father went there.'

He wished that he could have answered that he was at Yale or Princeton, where he wanted to go. He was prominent at Henderson and belonged to a good fraternity, but it annoyed him when people occasionally failed to recognize his alma mater's name.

'I suppose you've met all the young people here,' supposed Mrs Holyoke '– my daughter?'

'Oh, yes' – her daughter was the dumpy, ugly girl with the thick spectacles – 'oh, yes.' And he added, 'I knew some people who lived here before I came.'

'The litte Garneau girl,' explained Cousin Cora.

'Oh, yes. Noel Garneau,' agreed Mrs Holyoke. 'Her mother's a great beauty. How old is Noel now? She must be—'

'Seventeen,' supplied Juan; 'but she's old for her age.'

'Juan met her on a ranch last summer. They were on a ranch together. What is it that they call those ranches, Juan?'

'Dude ranches.'

'Dude ranches. Juan and another boy worked for their board.' Juan saw no reason why Cousin Cora should have supplied this information; she continued on an even more annoying note: 'Noel's mother sent her out there to keep her out of mischief, but Juan says the ranch was pretty gay itself.'

Mr Holyoke supplied a welcome change of subject.

'Your name is—' he inquired, smiling and curious.

'San Juan Chandler. My father was wounded in the battle of San Juan Hill and so they called me after it – like Kenesaw Mountain Landis.'

He had explained this so many times that the sentences rolled off automatically – in school he had been called Santy, in college he was Don.

'You must come to dinner while you're here,' said Mrs Holyoke vaguely.

The conversation slipped away from him as he realized freshly, strongly, that Noel would arrive tomorrow. And she was coming because he was here. She had cut short a visit in the Adirondacks on receipt of his letter. Would she like him now – in this place that was so different from Montana? There was a spaciousness, an air of money and pleasure about Culpepper Bay for which San Juan Chandler – a shy, handsome, spoiled, brilliant, penniless boy from a small Ohio city – was unprepared. At home, where his father was a retired clergyman, Juan went with the nice people. He didn't realize until this visit to a fashionable New England resort that where there are enough rich families to form a self-sufficient and exclusive group, such a group is invariably formed. On the dude ranch they had all dressed alike; here his ready-made Prince of Wales suit seemed exaggerated in style, his hat correct only in theory – an imitation hat – his very ties only projections of the ineffable Platonic ties which were worn here at Culpepper Bay. Yet all the differences were so small that he was unable quite to discern them.

But from the morning three days ago when he had stepped off the train into a group of young people who were waiting at the station for some friend of their own, he had been uneasy; and Cousin Cora's introductions, which seemed to foist him horribly upon whomever he was introduced to, did not lessen his discomfort. He thought mechanically that she was being kind, and considered himself lucky that her invitation had coincided with his wild desire to see Noel Garneau again. He did not realize that in three days he had come to hate Cousin Cora's cold and snobbish patronage.

Noel's fresh, adventurous voice on the telephone next morning made his own voice quiver with nervous happiness. She would call for him at two and they would spend the afternoon together. All morning he lay in the garden, trying unsuccessfully to renew his summer tan in the mild lemon light of the September sun, sitting up quickly whenever he heard the sound of Cousin Cora's garden shears at the end of a neighbouring border. He was back in his room, still meddling desperately with the white powder puff, when Noel's roadster stopped outside and she came up the front walk.

Noel's eyes were dark blue, almost violet, and her lips, Juan had often thought, were like very small, very soft, red cushions – only cushions sounded all wrong, for they were really the most delicate lips in the world. When she talked they parted to the shape of 'Oo!' and her eyes opened wide as though she was torn between tears and laughter at the poignancy of what she was saying. Already, at seventeen, she knew that men hung on her words in a way that frightened her. To Juan her most indifferent remarks assumed a highly ponderable significance and begot an intensity in him – a fact which Noel had several times found somewhat of a strain.

He ran downstairs, down the gravel path towards her.

'Noel, my dear,' he wanted so much to say, 'you are the loveliest thing – the loveliest thing. My heart turns over when I see your beautiful face and smell that sweet fresh smell you have around you.' That would have been the precious, the irreplaceable truth. Instead he faltered, 'Why, hello, Noel! How are you? . . . Well, I certainly am glad. Well, is this your car? What kind is it? Well, you certainly look fine.'

And he couldn't look at her, because when he did his face seemed to him to be working idiotically – like someone else's face. He got in, they drove off and he made a mighty effort to compose himself; but as her hand left the steering wheel to fall lightly on his, a perverse instinct made him jerk his hand away. Noel perceived the embarrassment and was puzzled and sorry.

They went to the tennis tournament at the Culpepper Club. He was so little aware of anything except Noel that later he told Cousin Cora they hadn't seen the tennis, and believed it himself.

Afterwards they loitered about the grounds, stopped by innumerable people who welcomed Noel home. Two men made him uneasy – one a small handsome youth of his own age with shining brown eyes that were bright as the glass eyes of a stuffed owl; the other a tall, languid dandy of twenty-five who was introduced to her, Juan rightly deduced, at his own request.

When they were in a group of girls he was more comfortable. He was able to talk, because being with Noel gave him confidence before these others, and his confidence before the others made him more confident with Noel. The situation improved.

There was one girl, a sharp, pretty blonde named Holly Morgan, with whom he had spent some facetiously sentimental hours the day before, and in order to show Noel that he had been able to take care of himself before her return he made a point of talking aside to Holly Morgan. Holly was not responsive. Juan was Noel's property, and though Holly liked him, she did not like him nearly well enough to annoy Noel.

'What time do you want me for dinner, Noel? she asked.

'Eight o'clock,' said Noel. 'Billy Harper'll call for you.'

Juan felt a twinge of disappointment. He had thought that he and Noel were to be alone for dinner; that afterwards they would have a long talk on the dark veranda and he would kiss her lips as he had upon that never-to-be-forgotten Montana night, and give her his DKE pin to wear. Perhaps the others would leave early – he had told Holly Morgan of his love for Noel; she should have sense enough to know.

At twilight Noel dropped him at Miss Chandler's gate, lingered for a moment with the engine cut off. The promise of the evening – the first lights in the houses along the bay, the sound of a remote piano, the little coolness in the wind – swung them both up suddenly into that paradise which Juan, drunk with ecstasy and terror, had been unable to evoke.

'Are you glad to see me?' she whispered.

'Am I glad?' The words trembled on his tongue. Miserably he struggled to bend his emotion into a phrase, a look, a gesture, but his mind chilled at the thought that nothing, nothing, nothing could express what he felt in his heart.

'You embarrass me,' he said wretchedly. 'I don't know what to say.'

Noel waited, attuned to what she expected, sympathetic, but too young quite to see that behind the mask of egotism, of moody childishness, which the intensity of Juan's devotion compelled him to wear, there was a tremendous emotion.

'Don't be embarrassed,' Noel said. She was listening to the music now, a tune they had danced to in the Adirondacks. The wings of a trance folded about her and the inscrutable someone who waited always in the middle distance loomed down over her with passionate words and dark romantic eyes. Almost mechanically, she started the engine and slipped the gear into first.

'At eight o'clock,' she said, almost abstractedly. 'Good-bye, Juan.'

The car moved off down the road. At the corner she turned and waved her hand and Juan waved back, happier than he had ever been in his life, his soul dissolved to a sweet gas that buoyed up his body like a balloon. Then the roadster was out of sight and, all unaware, he had lost her.

II

Cousin Cora's chauffeur took him to Noel's door. The other male guest, Billy Harper, was, he discovered, the young man with the bright brown eyes whom he had met that afternoon. Juan was afraid of him; he was on such familiar, facetious terms with the two girls – towards Noel his attitude seemed almost irreverent – that Juan was slighted during the conversation at dinner. They talked of the Adirondacks and they all seemed to know the group who had been there. Noel and Holly spoke of boys at Cambridge and New Haven and of how wonderful it was that they were going to school in New York this winter. Juan meant to invite Noel to the autumn dance at his college, but he thought that he had better wait and do it in a letter, later on. He was glad when dinner was over.

The girls went upstairs. Juan and Billy Harper smoked.

'She certainly is attractive,' broke out Juan suddenly, his repression bursting into words.

'Who? Noel?'

'Yes.'

'She's a nice girl,' agreed Harper gravely.

Juan fingered the DKE pin in his pocket.

'She's wonderful,' he said. 'I like Holly Morgan pretty well – I was handing her a sort of line yesterday afternoon – but Noel's really the most attractive girl I ever knew.'

Harper looked at him curiously, but Juan, released from the enforced and artificial smile of dinner, continued enthusiastically: 'Of course it's silly to fool with two girls. I mean, you've got to be careful not to get in too deep.'

Billy Harper didn't answer. Noel and Holly came downstairs. Holly suggested bridge, but Juan didn't play bridge, so they sat talking by the fire. In some fashion Noel and Billy Harper became involved in a conversation about dates and friends, and Juan began boasting to Holly Morgan, who sat beside him on the sofa.

'You must come to a prom at college,' he said suddenly. 'Why don't you ? It's a small college, but we have the best bunch in our house and the proms are fun.'

'I'd love it.'

'You'd only have to meet the people in our house.'

'What's that ?'

'DKE.' He drew the pin from his pocket. 'See ?'

Holly examined it, laughed and handed it back.

'I wanted to go to Yale,' he went on, 'but my family always go to the same place.'

'I love Yale,' said Holly.

'Yes,' he agreed vaguely, half hearing her, his mind moving between himself and Noel. 'You must come up. I'll write you about it.'

Time passed. Holly played the piano. Noel took a ukulele from the top of the piano, strummed it and hummed. Billy Harper turned the pages of the music. Juan listened, restless, unamused. Then they sauntered out into the dark garden, and finding himself beside Noel at last, Juan walked her quickly ahead until they were alone.

'Noel,' he whispered, 'here's my Deke pin. I want you to have it.'

She looked at him expressionlessly.

'I saw you offering it to Holly Morgan,' she said.

'Noel,' he cried in alarm, 'I wasn't offering it to her. I just showed it to her. Why, Noel, do you think—'

'You invited her to the prom.'

'I didn't. I was just being nice to her.'

The others were close behind. She took the Deke pin quickly and put her finger to his lips in a facile gesture of caress.

He did not realize that she had not been really angry about the pin or the prom, and that his unfortunate egotism was forfeiting her interest.

At eleven o'clock Holly said she must go, and Billy Harper drove his car to the front door.

'I'm going to stay a few minutes if you don't mind,' said Juan, standing in the door with Noel. 'I can walk home.'

Holly and Billy Harper drove away. Noel and Juan strolled back into the drawing-room, where she avoided the couch and sat down in a chair.

'Let's go out on the veranda,' suggested Juan uncertainly.

'Why?'

'Please, Noel.'

Unwillingly she obeyed. They sat side by side on a canvas settee and he put his arm around her.

'Kiss me,' he whispered. She had never seemed so desirable to him before.

'No.'

'Why not?'

'I don't want to. I don't kiss people any more.'

'But – me?' he demanded incredulously.

'I've kissed too many people. I'll have nothing left if I keep on kissing people.'

'But you'll kiss me, Noel?'

'Why?'

He could not even say, 'Because I love you.' But he could say it, he knew that he could say it, when she was in his arms.

'If I kiss you once, will you go home?'

'Why, do you want me to go home?'

'I'm tired. I was travelling last night and I can never sleep on a train. Can you? I can never—'

Her tendency to leave the subject willingly made him frantic.

'Then kiss me once,' he insisted.

'You promise?'

'You kiss me first.'

'No, Juan, you promise first.'

'Don't you want to kiss me?'

'Oh-h-h!' she groaned.

With gathering anxiety Juan promised and took her in his arms. For one moment at the touch of her lips, the feeling of her, of Noel, close to him, he forgot the evening, forgot himself – rather became the inspired, romantic self that she had known. But it was too late. Her hands were on his shoulders, pushing him away.

'You promised.'

'Noel—'

She got up. Confused and unsatisfied, he followed her to the door.

'Noel—'

'Good night, Juan.'

As they stood on the doorstep her eyes rose over the line of dark trees towards the ripe harvest moon. Some glowing thing would happen to her soon, she thought, her mind far away. Something that would dominate her, snatch her up out of life, helpless, ecstatic, exalted.

'Good night, Noel. Noel, please—'

'Good night, Juan. Remember we're going swimming tomorrow. It's wonderful to see you again. Good night.'

She closed the door.

III

Towards morning he awoke from a broken sleep, wondering if she had not kissed him because of the three spots on his cheek. He turned on the light and looked at them. Two were almost invisible. He went into the bathroom, doused all three with the black ointment and crept back into bed.

Cousin Cora greeted him stiffly at breakfast next morning.

'You kept your great-uncle awake last night,' she said. 'He heard you moving around in your room.'

'I only moved twice,' he said unhappily. 'I'm terribly sorry.'

'He has to have his sleep, you know. We all have to be more considerate when there's someone sick. Young people don't always think of that. And he was so unusually well when you came.'

It was Sunday, and they were to go swimming at Holly Morgan's house, where a crowd always collected on the bright easy beach. Noel called for him, but they arrived before any of his half-humble remarks about the night before had managed to attract her attention. He spoke to those he knew and was introduced to others, made ill at ease again by their cheerful familiarity with one another, by the correct informality of their clothes. He was sure they noticed that he had worn only one suit during his visit to Culpepper Bay, varying it with white flannel trousers. Both pairs of trousers were out of press now, and after keeping his great-uncle awake, he had not felt like bothering Cousin Cora about it at breakfast.

Again he tried to talk to Holly, with the vague idea of making Noel jealous, but Holly was busy and she eluded him. It was ten minutes before he extricated himself from a conversation with the obnoxious Miss Holyoke. At the moment he managed this he perceived to his horror that Noel was gone.

When he last saw her she had been engaged in a light but somehow intent conversation with the tall well-dressed stranger she had met yesterday. Now she wasn't in sight. Miserable and horribly alone, he strolled up and down the beach, trying to look as if he were having a good time, seeming to watch the bathers, but keeping a sharp eye out for Noel. He felt that his self-conscious perambulations were attracting unbearable attention, and sat down unhappily on a sand dune beside Billy Harper. But Billy Harper was neither cordial nor communicative, and after a minute hailed a man across the beach and went to talk to him.

Juan was desperate. When, suddenly, he spied Noel coming down from the house with the tall man, he stood up with a jerk, convinced that his features were working wildly.

She waved at him.

'A buckle came off my shoe,' she called. 'I went to have it put on. I thought you'd gone in swimming.'

He stood perfectly still, not trusting his voice to answer. He understood that she was through with him; there was someone else. Immediately he wanted above all things to be away. As they came nearer, the tall man glanced at him negligently and resumed his vivacious, intimate conversation with Noel. A group suddenly closed around them.

Keeping the group in the corner of his eye, Juan began to move carefully and steadily towards the gate that led to the road. He started when the casual voice of a man behind him said, 'Going?' and he answered, 'Got to' with what purported to be a reluctant nod. Once behind the shelter of the parked cars, he began to run, slowed down as several chauffeurs looked at him curiously. It was a mile and a half to the Chandler house and the day was broiling, but he walked fast lest Noel, leaving the party – 'With that man,' he thought bitterly – should overtake him trudging along the road. That would be more than he could bear.

There was the sound of a car behind him. Immediately Juan left the road and sought concealment behind a convenient hedge. It was no one from the party, but thereafter he kept an eye out for available cover, walking fast, or even running, over unpromising open spaces.

He was within sight of his cousin's house when it happened. Hot and dishevelled, he had scarcely flattened himself against the back of a tree when Noel's roadster, with the tall man at the wheel, flashed by down the road. Juan stepped out and looked after them. Then, blind with sweat and misery, he continued on towards home.

IV

At luncheon, Cousin Cora looked at him closely.

'What's the trouble?' she inquired. 'Did something go wrong at the beach this morning?'

'Why, no,' he exclaimed in simulated astonishment. 'What made you think that?'

'You have such a funny look. I thought perhaps you'd had some trouble with the little Garneau girl.'

He hated her.

'No, not at all.'

'You don't want to get any idea in your head about her,' said Cousin Cora.

'What do you mean?' He knew with a start what she meant.

'Any ideas about Noel Garneau. You've got your own way to make.' Juan's face burned. He was unable to answer. 'I say that in all kindness. You're not in any position to think anything serious about Noel Garneau.'

Her implications cut deeper than her words. Oh, he had seen well enough that he was not essentially of Noel's sort, that being nice in Akron wasn't enough at Culpepper Bay. He had that realization that comes to all boys in his position that for every advantage – that was what his mother called this visit to Cousin Cora's – he paid a harrowing price in self-esteem. But a world so hard as to admit such an intolerable state of affairs was beyond his comprehension. His mind rejected it all completely, as it had rejected the dictionary name for the three spots on his face. He wanted to let go, to vanish, to be home. He determined to go home tomorrow, but after this heart-rending conversation he decided to put off the announcement until tonight.

That afternoon he took a detective story from the library and retired upstairs to read on his bed. He finished the book by four o'clock and came down to change it for another. Cousin Cora was on the veranda arranging three tables for tea.

'I thought you were at the club,' she exclaimed in surprise. 'I thought you'd gone up to the club.'

'I'm tired,' he said. 'I thought I'd read.'

'Tired!' she exclaimed. 'A boy your age! You ought to be out in the open air playing golf – that's why you have that spot on your cheek' – Juan winced; his experiments with the black salve had irritated it to a sharp redness – 'instead of lying around reading on a day like this.'

'I haven't any clubs,' said Juan hurriedly.

'Mr Holyoke told you you could use his brother's clubs. He spoke to the caddie master. Run on now. You'll find lots of young people up there who want to play. I'll begin to think you're not having a good time.'

In agony Juan saw himself dubbing about the course alone – seeing Noel coming under his eye. He never wanted to see Noel again except out in Montana – some bright day, when she would come saying, 'Juan, I never knew – never understood what your love was.'

Suddenly he remembered that Noel had gone into Boston for the afternoon. She would not be there. The horror of playing alone suddenly vanished.

The caddie master looked at him disapprovingly as he displayed his guest card, and Juan nervously bought a half-dozen balls at a dollar each in an effort to neutralize the imagined hostility. On the first tee he glanced around. It was after four and there was no one in sight except two old men practising drives from the top of a little hill. As he addressed his ball he heard someone come up on the tee behind him and he breathed easier at the sharp crack that sent his ball a hundred and fifty yards down the fairway.

'Playing alone?'

He looked around. A stout man of fifty, with a huge face, high forehead, long wide upper lip and great undershot jaw, was taking a driver from a bulging bag.

'Why – yes.'

'Mind if I go round with you?'

'Not at all.'

Juan greeted the suggestion with a certain gloomy relief. They were evenly matched, the older man's steady short shots keeping pace with Juan's occasional brilliancy. Not until the seventh hole did the conversation rise above the fragmentary boasting and formalized praise which forms the small talk of golf.

'Haven't seen you around before.'

'I'm just visiting here,' Juan explained, 'staying with my cousin, Miss Chandler.'

'Oh yes – know Miss Chandler very well. Nice old snob.'

'What?' inquired Juan.

'Nice old snob, I said. No offence . . . Your honour, I think.'

Not for several holes did Juan venture to comment on his partner's remark.

'What do you mean when you say she's a nice old snob?' he inquired with interest.

'Oh, it's an old quarrel between Miss Chandler and me,' answered the older man brusquely. 'She's an old friend of my wife's. When we were married and came out to Culpepper Bay for the summer, she tried to freeze us out. Said my wife had no business marrying me. I was an outsider.'

'What did you do?'

'We just let her alone. She came round, but naturally I never had much love for her. She even tried to put her oar in before we were married.' He laughed. 'Cora Chandler of Boston – how she used to boss the girls around in those days! At twenty-five she had the sharpest tongue in Back Bay. They were old people there, you know – Emerson and Whittier to dinner and all that. My wife belonged to that crowd too. I was from the Middle West . . . Oh, too bad. I should have stopped talking. That makes me two up again.'

Suddenly Juan wanted to present his case to this man – not quite as it was, but adorned with a dignity and significance it did not so far possess. It began to round out in his mind as the sempiternal struggle of the poor young man against a snobbish, purse-proud world. This new aspect was comforting, and he put out of his mind the less pleasant realization that, superficially at least, money hadn't entered into it. He knew in his heart that it was his unfortunate egotism that had repelled Noel, his embarrassment, his absurd attempt to make her jealous with Holly. Only indirectly was his poverty concerned; under different circumstances it might have given a touch of romance.

'I know exactly how you must have felt,' he broke out suddenly as they walked toward the tenth tee. 'I haven't any money and I'm in love with a girl who has – and it seems as if every busybody in the world is determined to keep us apart.'

For a moment Juan believed this. His companion looked at him sharply. 'Does the girl care about you?' he inquired.

'Yes.'

'Well, go after her, young man. All the money in this world hasn't been made by a long shot.'

'I'm still in college,' said Juan, suddenly taken aback.

'Won't she wait for you?'

'I don't know. You see, the pressure's pretty strong. Her family want her to marry a rich man' – his mind visualized the tall well-dressed stranger of this morning and invention soared – 'an easterner that's visiting here, and I'm afraid they'll all sweep her off her feet. If it's not this man, it's the next.'

His friend considered.

'You can't have everything, you know,' he said presently. 'I'm the last man to advise a young man to leave college, especially when I don't know anything about him or his abilities; but if it's going to break you up not to get her, you better think about getting to work.'

'I've been considering that,' said Juan frowning. The idea was ten seconds old in his mind.

'All girls are crazy now, anyhow,' broke out the older man. 'They begin to think of men at fifteen, and by the time they're seventeen they run off with the chauffeur next door.'

'That's true,' agreed Juan absently. He was absorbed in the previous suggestion. 'The trouble is that I don't live in Boston. If I left college I'd want to be near her, because it might be a few months before I'd be able to support her. And I don't know how I'd go about getting a position in Boston.'

'If you're Cora Chandler's cousin, that oughtn't to be difficult. She knows everybody in town. And the girl's family will probably help you out, once you've got her – some of them are fools enough for anything in these crazy days.'

'I wouldn't like that.'

'Rich girls can't live on air,' said the older man grimly.

They played for a while in silence. Suddenly, as they approached a green, Juan's companion turned to him frowning.

'Look here, young man,' he said, 'I don't know whether you are really thinking of leaving college or whether I've just put the idea in your head. If I have, forget it. Go home and talk it over with your family. Do what they tell you to.'

'My father's dead.'

'Well, then ask your mother. She's got your best interest at heart.'

His attitude had noticeably stiffened, as if he were sorry he had become even faintly involved in Juan's problem. He guessed that there was something solid in the boy, but he suspected his readiness to confide in strangers and his helplessness about getting a job. Something was lacking – not confidence, exactly – 'It might be a few months before I was able to support her' – but something stronger, fiercer, more external. When they walked together into the caddie house he shook hands with him and was about to turn away, when impulse impelled him to add one word more.

'If you decide to try Boston come and see me,' he said. He pressed a card into Juan's hand. 'Good-bye. Good luck. Remember, a woman's like a street car—'

He walked into the locker room. After paying his caddie, Juan glanced down at the card which he still held in his hand.

'Harold Garneau,' it read, '23–7 State Street.'

A moment later Juan was walking nervously and hurriedly from the grounds of the Culpepper Club, casting no glance behind.

V

One month later San Juan Chandler arrived in Boston and took an inexpensive room in a small downtown hotel. In his pocket was two hundred dollars in cash and an envelope full of liberty bonds aggregating fifteen hundred dollars more – the whole being a fund which had been started by his father when he was born, to give him his chance in life. Not without argument had he come into possession of this – not without tears had his decision to abandon his last year at college been approved by his mother. He had not told her everything; simply that he had an advantageous offer of a position in Boston; the rest she guessed and was tactfully silent. As a matter of fact, he had neither a position nor a plan, but he was twenty-one now, with the blemishes of youth departed for ever. One thing Juan knew – he was going to marry Noel Garneau. The sting and hurt and shame of that Sunday morning ran through his dreams, stronger than any doubts he might have felt, stronger even than the romantic boyish love for her that had blossomed one dry, still Montana night. That was still there, but locked apart; what had happened later overlay it, muffled it. It was necessary now to his pride, his self-respect, his very existence, that he have her, in order to wipe out his memory of the day on which he had grown three years.

He hadn't seen her since. The following morning he had left Culpepper Bay and gone home.

Yes, he had a wonderful time. Yes, Cousin Cora had been very nice.

Nor had he written, though a week later a surprised but somehow flippant and terrible note had come from her, saying how pleasant it was to have seen him again and how bad it was to leave without saying good-bye.

'Holly Morgan sends her best,' it concluded, with kind, simulated reproach. 'Perhaps she ought to be writing instead of me. I always thought you were fickle, and now I know it.'

The poor effort which she had made to hide her indifference made him shiver. He did not add the letter to a certain cherished package tied with blue ribbon, but burned it up in an ash tray – a tragic gesture which almost set his mother's house on fire.

So he began his life in Boston, and the story of his first year there is a fairy tale too immoral to be told. It is the story of one of those mad, illogical successes upon whose substantial foundations ninety-nine failures are later reared. Though he worked hard, he deserved no special credit for it – no credit, that is, commensurate with the reward he received. He ran into a man who had a scheme, a preposterous scheme, for the cold storage of sea food which he had been trying to finance for several years. Juan's inexperience allowed him to be responsive and he invested twelve hundred dollars. In his first year this appalling indiscretion paid him 400 per cent. His partner attempted to buy him out, but they reached a compromise and Juan kept his shares.

The inner sense of his own destiny which had never deserted him whispered that he was going to be a rich man. But at the end of that year an event took place which made him think that it didn't matter after all.

He had seen Noel Garneau twice – once entering a theatre and once riding through a Boston street in the back of her limousine, looking, he thought afterwards, bored and pale and tired. At the time he had thought nothing; an overwhelming emotion had seized his heart, held it helpless, suspended, as though it were in the grasp of material fingers. He had shrunk back hastily under the awning of a shop and waited trembling, horrified, ecstatic, until she went by. She did not know he was in Boston – he did not want her to know until he was ready. He followed her every move in the society columns of the papers. She was at school, at home for Christmas, at Hot Springs for Easter, coming out in the fall. Then she was a débutante, and every day he read of her at dinners and dances and assemblies and balls and charity functions and theatricals of the Junior

League. A dozen blurred newspaper unlikenesses of her filled a drawer of his desk. And still he waited. Let Noel have her fling.

When he had been sixteen months in Boston, and when Noel's first season was dying away in the hum of the massed departure for Florida, Juan decided to wait no longer. So on a raw, damp February day, when children in rubber boots were building dams in the snow-filled gutters, a blond, handsome, well-dressed young man walked up the steps of the Garneau's Boston house and handed his card to the maid. With his heart beating loud, he went into a drawing-room and sat down.

A sound of a dress on the stairs, light feet in the hall, an exclamation – Noel!

'Why, Juan,' she exclaimed, surprised, pleased, polite, 'I didn't know you were in Boston. It's so good to see you. I thought you'd thrown me over for ever.'

In a moment he found voice – it was easier now than it had been. Whether or not she was aware of the change, he was a nobody no longer. There was something solid behind him that would prevent him ever again from behaving like a self-centred child.

He explained that he might settle in Boston, and allowed her to guess that he had done extremely well; and, though it cost him a twinge of pain, he spoke humourously of their last meeting, implying that he had left the swimming party on an impulse of anger at her. He could not confess that the impulse had been one of shame. She laughed. Suddenly he grew curiously happy.

Half an hour passed. The fire glowed in the hearth. The day darkened outside and the room moved into that shadowy twilight, that weather of indoors, which is like a breathless starshine. He had been standing; now he sat down beside her on the couch.

'Noel—'

Footsteps sounded lightly through the hall as the maid went through to the front door. Noel reached up quickly and turned up the electric lamp on the table behind her head.

'I didn't realize how dark it was growing,' she said rather quickly, he thought. Then the maid stood in the doorway.

'Mr Templeton,' she announced.

'Oh, yes,' agreed Noel.

Mr Templeton, with a Harvard-Oxford drawl, mature, very much at home, looked at him with just a flicker of surprise, nodded, mumbled a bare politeness and took an easy position in front of the fire. He exchanged several remarks with Noel which indicated a certain familiarity with her movements. Then a short silence fell. Juan rose.

'I want to see you soon,' he said. 'I'll phone, shall I, and you tell me when I can call?'

She walked with him to the door.

'So good to talk to you again,' she told him cordially. 'Remember, I want to see a lot of you, Juan.'

When he left he was happier than he had been for two years. He ate dinner alone at a restaurant, almost singing to himself; and then, wild with elation, walked along the waterfront till midnight. He awoke thinking of her, wanting to tell people that what had been lost was found again. There had been more between them than the mere words said – Noel's sitting with him in the half-darkness, her slight but perceptible nervousness as she came with him to the door.

Two days later he opened the *Transcript* to the society page and read down to the third item. There his eyes stopped, became like china eyes:

Mr and Mrs Harold Garneau announce the engagement of their daughter Noel to Mr Brooks Fish Templeton. Mr Templeton graduated from Harvard in the class of 1912 and is a partner in—

VI

At three o'clock that afternoon Juan rang the Garneaus' doorbell and was shown into the hall. From somewhere upstairs he heard girls' voices, and another murmur came from the drawing-room on the right, where he had talked to Noel only the week before.

'Can you show me into some room that isn't being used?' he demanded tensely of the maid. 'I'm an old friend – it's very important – I've got to see Miss Noel alone.'

He waited in a small den at the back of the hall. Ten minutes passed – ten minutes more; he began to be afraid she wasn't coming. At the end of half an hour the door bounced open and Noel came hurriedly in.

'Juan!' she cried happily. 'This is wonderful! I might have known you'd be the first to come.' Her expression changed as she saw his face, and she hesitated. 'But why were you shown in here?' she went on quickly. 'You must come and meet everyone. I'm rushing around today like a chicken without a head.'

'Noel!' he said thickly.

'What?'

Her hand was on the door knob. She turned, startled.

'Noel, I haven't come to congratulate you,' Juan said, his face white and firm, his voice harsh with his effort at self-control. 'I've come to tell you you're making an awful mistake.'

'Why – Juan!'

'And you know it,' he went on. 'You know no one loves you as I love you, Noel. I want you to marry me.'

She laughed nervously.

'Why, Juan, that's silly! I don't understand your talking like this. I'm engaged to another man.'

'Noel, will you come here and sit down?'

'I can't, Juan – there're a dozen people outside. I've got to see them. It wouldn't be polite. Another time, Juan. If you come another time I'd love to talk to you.'

'Now!' The word was stark, unyielding, almost savage. She hesitated. 'Ten minutes,' he said.

'I've really got to go, Juan.'

She sat down uncertainly, glancing at the door. Sitting beside her, Juan told her simply and directly everything that had happened to him since they had met, a year and a half before. He told her of his family, his Cousin Cora, of his inner humiliation at Culpepper Bay. Then he told her of his coming to Boston and of his success, and how at last, having something to bring her, he had come only to find he was too late. He kept back nothing. In his voice, as in his mind, there was no pretence now, no self-consciousness, but only a sincere and overmastering emotion. He had no defence for what he was doing, he said, save this – that he had somehow gained the right to present his case, to have her know how much his devotion had inspired him, to have her look once, if only in passing, upon the fact that for two years he had loved her faithfully and well.

When Juan finished, Noel was crying. It was terrible, she said, to tell her all this – just when she had decided about her life. It hadn't been easy, yet it was done now, and she was really going to marry this other man. But she had never heard anything like this before – it upset her. She was – oh, so terribly sorry, but there was no use. If he had cared so much he might have let her know before.

But how could he let her know? He had had nothing to offer her except the fact that one summer night out West they had been overwhelmingly drawn together.

'And you love me now,' he said in a low voice. 'You wouldn't cry, Noel, if you didn't love me. You wouldn't care.'

'I'm – I'm sorry for you.'

'It's more than that. You loved me the other day. You wanted me to sit beside you in the dark. Didn't I feel it – didn't I know? There's something between us, Noel – a sort of pull. Something you always do to me and I to you – except that one sad time. Oh, Noel, don't you know how it breaks my heart to see you sitting there two feet away from me, to want to put my arms around you and know you've made a senseless promise to another man?'

There was a knock outside the door.

'Noel!'

She raised her head, putting a handkerchief quickly to her eyes.

'Yes?'

'It's Brooks. May I come in?' Without waiting for an answer, Templeton opened the door and stood looking at them curiously. 'Excuse me,' he said. He nodded brusquely at Juan. 'Noel, there are lots of people here—'

'In a minute,' she said lifelessly.

'Aren't you well?'

Yes.'

He came into the room, frowning.

'What's been upsetting you, dear?' He glanced quickly at Juan, who stood up, his eyes blurred with tears. A menacing note crept into Templeton's voice. 'I hope no one's been upsetting you.'

For answer, Noel flopped down over a hill of pillows and sobbed aloud.

'Noel' – Templeton sat beside her, and put his arm on her shoulder – 'Noel.' He turned again to Juan, 'I think it would be best if you left us alone, Mr—' the name escaped his memory. 'Noel's a little tired.'

'I won't go,' said Juan.

'Please wait outside then. We'll see you later.'

'I won't wait outside. I want to speak to Noel. It was you who interrupted.'

'And I have a perfect right to interrupt.' His face reddened angrily. 'Just who the devil are you, anyhow?'

'My name is Chandler.'

'Well, Mr Chandler, you're in the way here – is that plain? Your presence here is an intrusion and a presumption.'

'We look at it in different ways.'

216

They glared at each other angrily. After a moment Templeton raised Noel to a sitting posture.

'I'm going to take you upstairs, dear,' he said. 'This has been a strain today. If you lie down till dinnertime—'

He helped her to her feet. Not looking at Juan, and still dabbing her face with her handkerchief, Noel suffered herself to be persuaded into the hall. Templeton turned in the doorway.

'The maid will give you your hat and coat, Mr Chandler.'

'I'll wait right here,' said Juan.

VII

He was still there at half past six, when, following a quick knock, a large broad bulk which Juan recognized as Mr Harold Garneau came into the room.

'Good evening, sir,' said Mr Garneau, annoyed and peremptory. 'Just what can I do for you?'

He came closer and a flicker of recognition passed over his face.

'Oh!' he muttered.

'Good evening, sir,' said Juan.

'It's you, is it?' Mr Garneau appeared to hesitate. 'Brooks Templeton said that you were – that you insisted on seeing Noel' – he coughed – 'that you refused to go home.'

'I want to see Noel, if you don't mind.'

'What for?'

'That's between Noel and me, Mr Garneau.'

'Mr Templeton and I are quite entitled to represent Noel in this case,' said Mr Garneau patiently. 'She has just made the statement before her mother and me that she doesn't want to see you again. Isn't that plain enough?'

'I don't believe it,' said Juan stubbornly.

'I'm not in the habit of lying.'

'I beg your pardon. I meant—'

'I don't want to discuss this unfortunate business with you,' broke out Garneau contemptuously. 'I just want you to leave right now – and not come back.'

'Why do you call it an unfortunate business?' inquired Juan coolly.

'Good night, Mr Chandler.'

'You call it an unfortunate business because Noel's broken her engagement.'

'You are presumptuous, sir!' cried the older man. 'Unbearably presumptuous.'

'Mr Garneau, you yourself were once kind enough to tell me—'

'I don't give a damn what I told you!' cried Garneau. 'You get out of here now!'

'Very well, I have no choice. I wish you to be good enough to tell Noel that I'll be back tomorrow afternoon.'

Juan nodded, went into the hall and took his hat and coat from a chair. Upstairs, he heard running footsteps and a door opened and closed – not before he had caught the sound of impassioned voices and a short broken sob. He hesitated. Then he continued on along the hall towards the front door. Through a *portière* of the dining-room he caught sight of a man-servant laying the service for dinner.

He rang the bell the next afternoon at the same hour. This time the butler, evidently instructed, answered the door.

Miss Noel was not at home. Could he leave a note? It was no use; Miss Noel was not in the city. Incredulous but anxious, Juan took a taxicab to Harold Garneau's office.

'Mr Garneau can't see you. If you like, he will speak to you for a moment on the phone.'

Juan nodded. The clerk touched a button on the waiting-room switchboard and handed an instrument to Juan.

'This is San Juan Chandler speaking. They told me at your residence that Noel had gone away. Is that true?'

'Yes.' The monosyllable was short and cold. 'She's gone away for a rest. Won't be back for several months. Anything else?'

'Did she leave any word for me?'

'No! She hates the sight of you.'

'What's her address?'

'That doesn't happen to be your affair. Good morning.'

Juan went back to his apartment and mused over the situation. Noel had been spirited out of town – that was the only expression he knew for it. And undoubtedly her engagement to Templeton was at least temporarily broken. He had toppled it over within an hour. He must see her again – that was the immediate necessity. But where? She was certainly with friends, and probably with relatives. That latter was the first clue to follow – he must find out the names of the relatives she had most frequently visited before.

He phoned Holly Morgan. She was in the south and not expected back in Boston till May.

Then he called the society editor of the *Boston Transcript*. After a short wait, a polite, attentive, feminine voice conversed with him on the wire.

'This is Mr San Juan Chandler,' he said, trying to intimate by his voice that he was a distinguished leader of cotillions in the Back Bay. 'I want to get some information, if you please, about the family of Mr Harold Garneau.'

'Why don't you apply directly to Mr Garneau?' advised the society editor, not without suspicion.

'I'm not on speaking terms with Mr Garneau.'

A pause; then – 'Well, really, we can't be responsible for giving out information in such a peculiar way.'

'But there can't be any secret about who Mr and Mrs Garneau's relations are!' protested Juan in exasperation.

'But how can we be sure that you—'

He hung up the receiver. Two other papers gave no better results, a third was willing, but ignorant. It seemed absurd, almost like a conspiracy, that in a city where the Garneaus were so well known he could not obtain the desired names. It was as if everything had tightened up against his arrival on the scene. After a day of fruitless and embarrassing inquiries in stores, where his questions were looked upon with the suspicion that he might be compiling a sucker list, and of poring through back numbers of the *Social Register*, he saw that there was but one resource – that was Cousin Cora. Next morning he took the three-hour ride to Culpepper Bay.

It was the first time he had seen her for a year and a half, since the disastrous termination of his summer visit. She was offended – that he knew – especially since she had heard from his mother of the unexpected success. She greeted him coldly and reproachfully; but she told him what he wanted to know, because Juan asked his questions while she was still startled and surprised by his visit. He left Culpepper Bay with the information that Mrs Garneau had one sister, the famous Mrs Morton Poindexter, with whom Noel was on terms of great intimacy. Juan took the midnight train for New York.

The Morton Poindexters' telephone number was not in the New York phone book, and Information refused to divulge it; but Juan procured it by another reference to the *Social Register*. He called the house from his hotel.

'Miss Noel Garneau – is she in the city?' he inquired, according to his plan. If the name was not immediately familiar, the servant would reply that he had the wrong number.

'Who wants to speak to her, please?'

That was a relief; his heart sank comfortably back into place.

'Oh – a friend.'

'No name?'

'No name.'

'I'll see.'

The servant returned in a moment.

No, Miss Garneau was not there, was not in the city, was not expected. The phone clicked off suddenly.

Late that afternoon a taxi dropped him in front of the Morton Poindexters' house. It was the most elaborate house that he had ever seen, rising to five storeys on a corner of Fifth Avenue and adorned even with that ghost of a garden which, however minute, is the proudest gesture of money in New York.

He handed no card to the butler, but it occurred to him that he must be expected, for he was shown immediately into the drawing-room. When, after a short wait, Mrs Poindexter entered he experienced for the first time in five days a touch of uncertainty.

Mrs Poindexter was perhaps thirty-five, and of that immaculate fashion which the French describe as *bien soignée*. The inexpressible loveliness of her face was salted with another quality which for want of a better word might be called dignity. But it was more than dignity, for it wore no rigidity, but instead a softness so adaptable, so elastic, that it would withdraw from any attack which life might bring against it, only to spring back at the proper moment, taut, victorious and complete. San Juan saw that even though his guess was correct as to Noel's being in the house, he was up against a force with which he had no contact before. This woman seemed to be not entirely of America, to possess resources which the American woman lacked or handled ineptly.

She received him with a graciousness which, though it was largely external, seemed to conceal no perturbation underneath. Indeed, her attitude appeared to be perfectly passive, just short of encouraging. It was with an effort that he resisted the inclination to lay his cards on the table.

'Good evening.' She sat down on a stiff chair in the centre of the room and asked him to take an easy-chair near by. She sat looking at him silently until he spoke.

'Mrs Poindexter, I am very anxious to see Miss Garneau. I telephoned your house this morning and was told that she was not here.' Mrs Poindexter nodded. 'However, I know she is here,' he continued evenly. 'And I'm determined to see her. The idea that her father and mother can prevent me from seeing her, as though I had disgraced myself in some way – or that you, Mrs Poindexter, can prevent me from seeing her' – his voice rose a little – 'is preposterous. This is not the year 1500 – nor even the year 1910.'

He paused. Mrs Poindexter waited for a moment to see if he had finished. Then she said, quietly and unequivocally, 'I quite agree with you.'

Save for Noel, Juan thought he had never seen anyone so beautiful before.

'Mrs Poindexter,' he began again, in a more friendly tone, 'I'm sorry to seem rude. I've been called presumptuous in this matter, and perhaps to some extent I am. Perhaps all poor boys who are in love with wealthy girls are presumptuous. But it happens that I am no longer a poor boy, and I have good reason to believe that Noel cares for me.'

'I see,' said Mrs Poindexter attentively. 'But of course I knew nothing about all that.'

Juan hesitated, again disarmed by her complaisance. Then a surge of determination went over him.

'Will you let me see her?' he demanded. 'Or will you insist on keeping up this farce a little longer?'

Mrs Poindexter looked at him as though considering.

'Why should I let you see her?'

'Simply because I ask you. Just as, when someone says "Excuse me" you step aside for him in a doorway.'

Mrs Poindexter frowned.

'But Noel is concerned in this matter as much as you. And I'm not like person in a crowd. I'm more like a bodyguard, with instructions to let no one pass, even if they say "Excuse me" in a most appealing voice.'

'You have instructions only from her father and mother,' said Juan, with rising impatience. 'She's the person concerned.'

'I'm glad you begin to admit that.'

'Of course I admit it,' he broke out. 'I want you to admit it.'

'I do.'

'Then what's the point of all this absurd discussion?' he demanded heatedly.

She stood up suddenly.

'I bid you good evening, sir.'

Taken aback, Juan stood up too.

'Why, what's the matter?'

'I will not be spoken to like that,' said Mrs Poindexter, still in a low cool voice. 'Either you can conduct yourself quietly or you can leave this house at once.'

Juan realized that he had taken the wrong tone. The words stung at him and for a moment he had nothing to say – as though he were a scolded boy at school.

'This is beside the question,' he stammered finally. 'I want to talk to Noel.'

'Noel doesn't want to talk to you.'

Suddenly Mrs Poindexter held out a sheet of note paper to him. He opened it. It said:

Aunt Jo: As to what we talked about this afternoon: If that intolerable bore calls, as he will probably do, and begins his presumptuous whining, please speak to him frankly. Tell him I never loved him, that I never at any time claimed to love him and that his persistence is revolting to me. Say that I am old enough to know my own mind and that my greatest wish is never to see him again in this world.

Juan stood there aghast. His universe was suddenly about him. Noel did not care, she had never cared. It was all a preposterous joke on him, played by those to whom the business of life had been such jokes from the beginning. He realized now that fundamentally they were all akin – Cousin Cora, Noel, her father, this cold, lovely woman here – affirming the prerogative of the rich to marry always within their caste, to erect artificial barriers and standards against those who could presume upon a summer's philandering. The scales fell from his eyes and he saw his year and a half of struggle and effort not as progress towards a goal but only as a little race he had run by himself, outside, with no one to beat except himself – no one who cared.

Blindly he looked about for his hat, scarcely realizing it was in the hall. Blindly he stepped back when Mrs Poindexter's hand moved towards him half a foot through the mist and Mrs Poindexter's voice said softly, 'I'm sorry.' Then he was in the hall, the note still clutched in the hand that struggled through the sleeve of his overcoat, the words which he felt he must somehow say choking through his lips.

'I didn't understand. I regret very much that I've bothered you. It wasn't clear to me how matters stood – between Noel and me—'

His hand was on the door knob.

'I'm sorry, too,' said Mrs Poindexter. 'I didn't realize from what Noel said that what I had to do would be so hard – Mr Templeton.'

'Chandler,' he corrected her dully. 'My name's Chandler.'

She stood dead still; suddenly her face went white.

'What ?'

'My name – it's Chandler.'

Like a flash she threw herself against the half-open door and it bumped shut. Then in a flash she was at the foot of the staircase.

'Noel!' she cried in a high, clear call. 'Noel! Noel! Come down, Noel!' Her lovely voice floated up like a bell through the long high central hall. 'Noel! Come down! It's Mr Chandler! It's Chandler!'

THE ADOLESCENT MARRIAGE

Saturday Evening Post, 6 March 1926

'The Adolescent Marriage' was written in Paris in December 1925 and was almost lost. Fitzgerald entrusted the typescript to someone who was returning to America but who failed to deliver it to Harold Ober; then the carbon was ruined. However, the typist had kept the manuscript, and Fitzgerald rewrote the story from that. The Post *bought it for $2500 but annoyed Fitzgerald by cutting it. He wrote Ober: 'They have a right to be silly at ($)2500 a story but when two very clever paragraphs disappear of which I have no duplicate or record it makes me angry . . . Could you get me the ms. or an uncut proof of it so I can clip the uncut pps for my files? Especially the one about a church with car-cards in the pews or something.'**

Chauncey Garnett, the architect, once had a miniature city constructed, composed of all the buildings he had ever designed. It proved to be an expensive and somewhat depressing experiment; for the toy did not result in a harmonious whole. Garnett found it depressing to be reminded that he himself had often gone in for monstrosities, and even more depressing to realize that his architectural activities had extended over half a century. In disgust, he distributed the tiny houses to his friends and they ended up as the residences of undiscriminating dolls.

Garnett had never – at least not yet – been called a nice old man; yet he was both old and nice. He gave six hours a day to his offices in Philadelphia or to his branch in New York, and during the remaining time demanded only a proper peace in which to brood quietly over his crowded and colourful past. In several years no one had demanded a favour that could not be granted with pen and cheque book, and it seemed that he had reached an age safe from the intrusion of other people's affairs. This calm,

---

*This material has not been found.

however, was premature, and it was violently shattered one afternoon in the summer of 1925 by the shrill clamour of a telephone bell.

George Wharton was speaking. Could Chauncey come to his house at once on a matter of the greatest importance?

On the way to Chestnut Hill, Garnett dozed against the grey duvetyn cushions of his limousine, his sixty-eight-year-old body warmed by the June sunshine, his sixty-eight-year-old mind blank save for some vivid, unsubstantial memory of a green branch overhanging green water. Reaching his friend's house, he awoke placidly and without a start. George Wharton, he thought, was probably troubled by some unexpected surplus of money. He would want Garnett to plan one of these modern churches, perhaps. He was of a younger generation than Garnett – a modern man.

Wharton and his wife were waiting in the gilt-and-morocco intimacy of the library.

'I couldn't come to your office,' said Wharton immediately. 'In a minute you'll understand why.'

Garnett noticed that his friend's hands were slightly trembling.

'It's about Lucy,' Wharton added.

It was a moment before Garnett placed Lucy as their daughter.

'What's happened to Lucy?'

'Lucy's married. She ran up to Connecticut about a month ago and got married.' A moment's silence. 'Lucy's only sixteen,' continued Wharton. 'The boy's twenty.'

'That's very young,' said Garnett considerately; 'but then my grandmother married at sixteen and no one thought much about it. Some girls develop much quicker than others.'

'We know all that, Chauncey.' Wharton waved it aside impatiently. 'The point is, these young marriages don't work nowadays. They're not normal. They end in a mess.'

Again Garnett hesitated.

'Aren't you a little premature in looking ahead for trouble? Why don't you give Lucy a chance? Why not wait and see if it's going to turn out a mess?'

'It's a mess already,' cried Wharton passionately. 'And Lucy's life's a mess. The one thing her mother and I cared about – her happiness – that's a mess, and we don't know what to do – what to do.'

His voice trembled and he turned away to the window – came back again impulsively.

'Look at us, Chauncey. Do we look like the kind of parents who would drive a child into a thing like this? She and her mother have been like sisters – just like sisters. She and I used to go on parties together – football games and all that sort of thing – ever since she was a little kid. She's all we've got, and we always said we'd try to steer a middle course with her – give her enough liberty for her self-respect and yet keep an eye on where she went and who she went with, at least till she was eighteen. Why Chauncey, if you'd told me six weeks ago that this thing could happen—' He shook his head helplessly. Then he continued in a quieter voice. 'When she came and told us what she'd done it just about broke our hearts, but we tried to make the best of it. Do you know how long the marriage – if you can call it that – lasted? Three weeks. It lasted three weeks. She came home with a big bruise on her shoulder where he'd hit her.'

'Oh, dear!' said Mrs Wharton in a low tone. 'Please—'

'We talked it over,' continued her husband grimly, 'and she decided to go back to this – this young—' again he bowed his head before the insufficiency of expletives – 'and try to make a go of it. But last night she came home again, and now she says it's definitely over.'

Garnett nodded. 'Who's the man?' he inquired.

'Man!' cried Wharton. 'It's a boy. His name's Llewellyn Clark.'

'What's that?' exclaimed Garnett in surprise. 'Llewellyn Clark? Jesse Clark's son? The young fellow in my office?'

'Yes.'

'Why, he's a nice young fellow,' Garnett declared. 'I can't believe he'd—'

'Neither could I,' interrupted Wharton quietly. 'I thought he was a nice young fellow too. And what's more, I rather suspected that my daughter was a pretty decent young girl.'

Garnett was astonished and annoyed. He had seen Llewellyn Clark not an hour before in the small drafting room he occupied in the Garnett & Linquist offices. He understood now why Clark wasn't going back to Boston Tech this fall. And in the light of this revelation he remembered that there had been a change in the boy during the past month – absences, late arrivals, a certain listlessness in his work.

Mrs Wharton's voice broke in upon the ordering of his mind.

'Please do something, Chauncey,' she said. 'Talk to him. Talk to them both. She's only sixteen and we can't bear to see her life ruined by a divorce. It isn't that we care what people will say; it's only Lucy we care about, Chauncey.'

'Why don't you send her abroad for a year?'

Wharton shook his head.

'That doesn't solve the problem. If they have an ounce of character between them they'll make an attempt to live together.'

'But if you think so badly of him—'

'Lucy's made her choice. He's got some money – enough. And there doesn't seem to be anything vicious in his record so far.'

'What's his side of it?'

Wharton waved his hands helplessly.

'I'm damned if I know. Something about a hat. Some bunch of rubbish. Elsie and I have no idea why they ran away, and now we can't get a clear idea why they won't stick together. Unfortunately, his father and mother are dead.' He paused. 'Chauncey, if you could see your way clear—'

An unpleasant prospect began to take shape before Garnett's eyes. He was an old man with one foot, at least, in the chimney corner. From where he stood, this youngest generation was like something infinitely distant, and perceived through the large end of a telescope.

'Oh, of course,' he heard himself saying vaguely. So hard to think back to that young time. Since his youth such a myriad of prejudices and conventions had passed through the fashion show and died away with clamour and acrimony and commotion. It would be difficult even to communicate with these children. How hollowly and fatuously his platitudes would echo on their ears. And how bored he would be with their selfishness and with their shallow confidence in opinions manufactured day before yesterday.

He sat up suddenly. Wharton and his wife were gone, and a slender, dark-haired girl whose body hovered delicately on the last edge of childhood had come quietly into the room. She regarded him for a moment with a shadow of alarm in her intent brown eyes; then sat down on a stiff chair near him.

'I'm Lucy,' she said. 'They told me you wanted to talk to me.'

She waited. It occurred to Garnett that he must say something, but the form his speech should take eluded him.

'I haven't seen you since you were ten years old,' he began uneasily.

'Yes,' she agreed, with a small, polite smile.

There was another silence. He must say something to the point before her young attention slipped utterly away.

'I'm sorry you and Llewellyn have quarrelled,' he broke out. 'It's silly to quarrel like that. I'm very fond of Llewellyn, you know.'

'Did he send you here?'

Garnett shook his head. 'Are you – in love with him?' he inquired.

'Not any more.'

'Is he in love with you?'

'He says so, but I don't think he is – any more.'

'You're sorry you married him?'

'I'm never sorry for anything that's done.'

'I see.'

Again she waited.

'Your father tells me this is a permanent separation.'

'Yes.'

'May I ask why?'

'We just couldn't get along,' she answered simply. 'I thought he was terribly selfish and he thought the same about me. We fought all the time, from almost the first day.'

'He hit you?'

'Oh, that!' She dismissed that as unimportant.

'How do you mean – selfish?'

'Just selfish,' she answered childishly. 'The most selfish thing I ever saw in my life. I never saw anything so selfish in my life.'

'What did he do that was selfish?' persisted Garnett.

'Everything. He was so stingy – gosh!' Her eyes were serious and sad. 'I can't stand anybody to be so stingy – about money,' she explained contemptuously. 'Then he'd lose his temper and swear at me and say he was going to leave me if I didn't do what he wanted me to.' And she added, still very gravely, 'Gosh!'

'How did he happen to hit you?'

'Oh, he didn't mean to hit me. I was trying to hit him on account of something he did, and he was trying to hold me and so I bumped into a still.'

'A still!' exclaimed Garnett, startled.

'The woman had a still in our room because she had no other place to keep it – down on Beckton Street, where we lived.'

'Why did Llewellyn take you to such a place?'

'Oh, it was a perfectly good place except that the woman had this still. We looked around two or three days and it was the only apartment we could afford.' She paused reminiscently and then added, 'It was very nice and quiet.'

'H'm – you never really got along at all ?'

'No.' She hesitated. 'He spoiled it all. He was always worrying about whether we'd done the right thing. He'd get out of bed at night and walk up and down worrying about it. I wasn't complaining. I was perfectly willing to be poor if we could get along and be happy. I wanted to go to cooking school, for instance, and he wouldn't let me. He wanted me to sit in the room all day and wait for him.'

'Why ?'

'He was afraid that I wanted to go home. For three weeks it was one long quarrel from morning till night. I couldn't stand it.'

'It seems to me that a lot of this quarrelling was over nothing,' ventured Garnett.

'I haven't explained it very well, I guess,' she said with sudden weariness.

'I knew a lot of it was silly and so did Llewellyn. Sometimes we'd apologize to each other, and be in love like we were before we were married. That's why I went back to him. But it wasn't any use.' She stood up. 'What's the good of talking about it any more ? You wouldn't understand.'

Garnett wondered if he could get back to his office before Llewellyn Clark went home. He could talk to Clark, while the girl only confused him as she teetered disconcertingly between adolescence and disillusion. But when Clark reported to him just as the five-o'clock bell rang, the same sensation of impotence stole over Garnett, and he stared at his apprentice blankly for a moment, as if he had never seen him before.

Llewellyn Clark looked older than his twenty years – a tall, almost thin, young man with dark-red hair of a fine, shiny texture, and auburn eyes. He was of a somewhat nervous type, talented and impatient, but Garnett could find little of the egotist in his reserved, attentive face.

'I hear you've been getting married,' Garnet began abruptly.

Clark's cheeks deepened to the colour of his hair.

'Who told you that ?' he demanded.

'Lucy Wharton. She told me the whole story.'

'Then you know it, sir,' said Clark almost rudely. 'You know all there is to know.'

'What do you intend to do ?'

'I don't know.' Clark stood up, breathing quickly. 'I can't talk about it. It's my affair, you see. I—'

'Sit down, Llewellyn.'

The young man sat down, his face working. Suddenly it crinkled uncontrollably and two great tears, stained faintly with the dust of the day's toil, gushed from his eyes.

'Oh, hell!' he said brokenly, wiping his eyes with the back of his hand.

'I've been wondering why you two can't make a go of it, after all.' Garnett looked down at his desk. 'I like you, Llewellyn, and I like Lucy. Why not fool everybody and—'

Llewelly shook his head emphatically.

'Not me,' he said. 'I don't care a snap of my finger about her. She can go jump in the lake for all I care.'

'Why did you take her away?'

'I don't know. We'd been in love for almost a year and marriage seemed a long way off. It came over us all of a sudden.'

'Why couldn't you get along?'

'Didn't she tell you?'

'I want your version.'

'Well, it started one afternoon when she took all our money and threw it away.'

'Threw it away?'

'She took it and bought a new hat. It was only thirty-five dollars, but it was all we had. If I hadn't found forty-five cents in an old suit we wouldn't have had any dinner.'

'I see,' said Garnett drily.

'Then – oh, one thing happened after another. She didn't trust me, she didn't think I could take care of her, she kept saying she was going home to her mother. And finally we began to hate each other. It was a great mistake, that's all, and I'll probably spend a good part of my life paying for it. Wait till it leaks out!' He laughed bitterly.

'Aren't you thinking about yourself a little too much?' suggested Garnett coldly.

Llewellyn looked at him in unfeigned surprise.

'About myself?' he repeated. 'Mr Garnett, I'll give you my word of honour, this is the first time I've ever thought about that side of it. Right now I'd do anything in the world to save Lucy any pain – except live with her. She's got great things in her, Mr Garnett.' His eyes filled again with tears. 'She's just as brave and honest, and sweet sometimes. I'll never marry anybody else, you can bet your life on that, but – we were just poison to each other. I never want to see her any more.'

After all, thought Garnett, it was only the old human attempt to get something for nothing – neither of them had brought to the marriage any trace of tolerance or moral experience. However trivial the reasons for their incompatibility, it was firmly established now in both their hearts, and perhaps they were wise in realizing that the wretched voyage, too hastily embarked upon, was over.

That night, Garnett had a long and somewhat painful talk with George Wharton, and on the following morning he went to New York, where he spent several days. When he returned to Philadelphia, it was with the information that the marriage of Lucy and Llewellyn Clark had been annulled by the state of Connecticut on the grounds of their minority. They were free.

II

Almost everyone who knew Lucy Wharton liked her, and her friends rose rather valiantly to the occasion. There was a certain element, of course, who looked at her with averted eyes; there were slights, there were stares of the curious; but since it was wisely given out, upon Chauncey Garnett's recommendation, that the Whartons themselves had insisted upon the annulment, the burden of the affair fell less heavily upon Lucy than upon Llewellyn. He became not exactly a pariah – cities live too quickly to linger long over any single scandal – but he was cut off entirely from the crowd in which he had grown up, and much bitter and unpleasant comment reached his ears.

He was a boy who felt things deeply, and in the first moment of depression he contemplated leaving Philadelphia. But gradually a mood of defiant indifference took possession of him; try as he might, he wasn't able to feel in his heart that he had done anything morally wrong. He hadn't thought of Lucy as being sixteen, but only as the girl whom he loved beyond understanding. What did age matter? Hadn't people married as children, almost one hundred – two hundred years ago? The day of his elopement with Lucy had been like an ecstatic dream; he the young knight, scorned by her father, the baron, as a mere youth, bearing her away, and all willing, on his charger, in the dead of the night.

And then the realization, almost before his eyes had opened from their romantic vision, that marriage meant the complicated adjustment of two lives to each other, and that love is a small part only of the long, long marriage day. Lucy was a devoted child whom he had contracted to amuse – an adorable and somewhat frightened child, that was all.

As suddenly as it had begun, it was over. Doggedly Llewellyn went his way, along with his mistake. And so quickly had his romance bloomed and turned to dust that after a month a merciful unreality began to clothe it as if it were something vaguely sad that had happened long ago.

One day in July he was summoned to Chauncey Garnett's private office. Few words had passed between them since their conversation the month before, but Llewellyn saw that there was no hostility in the older man's attitude.

He was glad of that, for now that he felt himself utterly alone, cut off from the world in which he had grown up, his work had come to be the most important thing in his life.

'What are you doing, Llewellyn?' asked Garnett, picking up a yellow pamphlet from the litter of his desk.

'Helping Mr Carson with the Municipal Country Club.'

'Take a look at this.' He handed the pamphlet to Llewellyn. 'There isn't a gold mine in it, but there's a good deal of this gilt-edge hot air they call publicity. It's a syndicate of twenty papers, you see. The best plans for – what is it? – a neighbourhood store – you know, a small drug store or grocery store that could fit into a nice street without being an eyesore. Or else for a surburban cottage – that'll be the regular thing. Or thirdly for a small factory recreation house.'

Llewellyn read over the specifications.

'The last two aren't so interesting,' he said. 'Suburban cottage – that'll be the usual thing, as you say – recreation house, no. But I'd like to have a shot at the first, sir – the store.'

Garnett nodded. 'The best part is that the plan which wins each competition materializes as a building right away, and therein lies the prize. The building is yours. You design it, it's put up for you, then you sell it and the money goes into your pocket. Matter of six or seven thousand dollars – and there won't be more than six or seven hundred other young architects trying.'

Llewellyn read it over again carefully.

'I like it,' he said. 'I'd like to try the store.'

'Well, you've got one month. I wouldn't mind it a bit, Llewellyn, if that prize came into this office.'

'I can't promise you that.' Again Llewellyn ran his eyes over the conditions, while Garnett watched him with quiet interest.

'By the way,' he asked suddenly, 'what do you do with yourself all the time, Llewellyn?'

'How do you mean, sir?'

'At night – over the weekends. Do you ever go out?'

Llewellyn hesitated.

'Well, not so much – now.'

'You mustn't let yourself brood over this business, you know.'

'I'm not brooding.'

Mr Garnett put his glasses carefully away in their case.

'Lucy isn't brooding,' he said suddenly. 'Her father told me that she's trying to live just as normal a life as possible.'

Silence for a moment.

'I'm glad,' said Llewellyn in an expressionless voice.

'You must remember that you're free as air now,' said Garnett. 'You don't want to let yourself dry up and get bitter. Lucy's father and mother are encouraging her to have callers and go to dances – behave just as she did before.'

'Before Rudolf Rassendyll* came along,' said Llewellyn grimly. He held up the pamphlet. 'May I keep this, Mr Garnett?'

'Oh, yes.' His employer's hand gave him permission to retire. 'Tell Mr Carson that I've taken you off the country club for the present.'

'I can finish that too,' said Llewellyn promptly. 'In fact —'

His lips shut. He had been about to remark that he was doing practically the whole thing himself anyhow.

'Well?'

'Nothing, sir. Thank you very much.'

Llewellyn withdrew, excited by his opportunity and relieved by the news of Lucy. She was herself again, so Mr Garnett had implied; perhaps her life wasn't so irrevocably wrecked after all. If there were men to come and see her, to take her out to dances, then there were men to care for her. He found himself vaguely pitying them – if they knew what a handful she was, the absolute impossibility of dealing with her, even of talking to her. At the thought of those desolate weeks he shivered, as though recalling a nightmare.

Back in his room that night, he experimented with a few tentative sketches. He worked late, his imagination warming to the set task, but next day the result seemed 'arty' and pretentious – like a design for a tea shop. He scrawled 'Ye Olde-Fashioned Butcher Shoppe – Veree Unsanitaree', across the face of it and tore it into pieces, which he tossed into the wastebasket.

*The hero of *The Prisoner of Zenda* – ed.

During the first weeks in August he continued his work on the plans for the country club, trusting that for the more personal venture some burst of inspiration would come to him toward the end of the allotted time. And then one day occurred an incident which he had long dreaded in the secret corners of his mind – walking home along Chestnut Street he ran unexpectedly into Lucy.

It was about five o'clock, when the crowds were thickest. Suddenly they found themselves in an eddy facing each other, and then borne along side by side as if fate had pressed into service all these swarming hundreds to throw them together.

'Why, Lucy!' he exclaimed, raising his hat automatically. She stared at him with startled eyes. A woman laden with bundles collided with her and a purse slipped from Lucy's hand.

'Thank you very much,' she said as he retrieved it. Her voice was tense, breathless. 'That's all right. Give it to me. I have a car right here.'

Their eyes joined for a moment, cool, impersonal, and he had a vivid memory of their last meeting – of how they had stood, like this, hating each other with a cold fury.

'Are you sure I can't help you?'

'Quite sure. Our car's at the kerb.'

She nodded quickly. Llewellyn caught a glimpse of an unfamiliar limousine and a short smiling man of forty who helped her inside.

He walked home – for the first time in weeks he was angry, excited, confused. He must get away tomorrow. It was all too recent for any such casual encounter as this; the wounds she had left on him were raw and they opened easily.

'The little fool!' he said to himself bitterly. 'The selfish little fool! She thought I wanted to walk along the street with her as if nothing had ever happened. She dares to imagine that I'm made of the same flimsy stuff as herself!'

He wanted passionately to spank her, to punish her in some way like an insolent child. Until dinnertime he paced up and down in his room, going over in his mind the forlorn and useless arguments, reproaches, imprecations, furies, that had made up their short married life. He rehearsed every quarrel from its trivial genesis down to the time when a merciful exhaustion intervened and brought them, almost hysterical, into each other's arms. A brief moment of peace – then again the senseless, miserable human battle.

'Lucy,' he heard himself saying, 'listen to me. It isn't that I want you to sit here waiting for me. It's your hands, Lucy. Suppose you went to cooking school and burned your pretty hands. I don't want your hands coarsened and roughened, and if you'll just have patience till next week when my money comes in— I won't stand it! Do you hear? I'm not going to have my wife doing that! No use of being stubborn.'

Wearily, just as he had been made weary by those arguments in reality, he dropped into a chair and reached listlessly for his drawing materials. Laying them out, he began to sketch, crumpling each one into a ball before a dozen lines marred the paper. It was her fault, he whispered to himself, it was all her fault. 'If I'd been fifty years old I couldn't have changed her.'

Yet he could not rid himself of her dark young face set sharp and cool against the August gloaming, against the hot hurrying crowds of that afternoon.

'Quite sure. Our car's at the kerb.'

Llewellyn nodded to himself and tried to smile grimly.

'Well, I've got one thing to be thankful for,' he told himself. 'My responsibility will be over before long.'

He had been sitting for a long while, looking at a blank sheet of drawing paper; but presently his pencil began to move in light strokes at the corner. He watched it idly, impersonally, as though it were a motion of his fingers imposed on him from outside. Finally he looked at the result with disapproval, scratched it out and then blocked it in again in exactly the same way.

Suddenly he chose a new pencil, picked up his ruler and made a measurement on the paper, and then another. An hour passed. The sketch took shape and outline, varied itself slightly, yielded in part to an eraser and appeared in an improved form. After two hours, he raised his head, and catching sight of his tense, absorbed face he started with surprise. There were a dozen half-smoked cigarettes in the tray beside him.

When he turned out his light at last it was half past five. The milk wagons were rumbling through the twilit streets outside, and the first sunshine streaming pink over the roofs of the houses across the way fell upon the board which bore his night's work. It was the plan of a suburban bungalow.

III

As the August days passed, Llewellyn continued to think of Lucy with a certain anger and contempt. If she could accept so lightly what had happened just two months ago, he had wasted his emotion upon a girl who was essentially shallow. It cheapened his conception of her, of himself, of the whole affair. Again the idea came to him of leaving Philadelphia and making a new start farther west, but his interest in the outcome of the competition decided him to postpone his departure for a few weeks more.

The blueprints of his design were made and dispatched. Mr Garnett cautiously refused to make any prophecies, but Llewellyn knew that everyone in the office who had seen the drawing felt a vague excitement about it. Almost literally he had drawn a bungalow in the air – a bungalow that had never been lived in before. It was neither Italian, Elizabethan, New England or California Spanish, nor a mongrel form with features from each one. Someone dubbed it the tree house, and there was a certain happiness in the label; but its charm proceeded less from any bizarre quality than from the virtuosity of the conception as a whole – an unusual length here and there, an odd, tantalizing familiar slope of the roof, a door that was like the door to the secret places of a dream. Chauncey Garnett remarked that it was the first skyscraper he had ever seen built with one storey, but he recognized that Llewellyn's unquestionable talent had matured overnight. Except that the organizers of the competition were probably seeking something more adapted to standardization, it might have had a chance for the award.

Only Llewellyn was sure. When he was reminded that he was only twenty-one, he kept silent, knowing that, whatever his years, he would never again be twenty-one at heart. Life had betrayed him. He had squandered himself on a worthless girl and the world had punished him for it, as ruthlessly as though he had spent spiritual coin other than his own. Meeting Lucy on the street again, he passed her without a flicker of his eye – and returned to his room, his day spoiled by the sight of that young distant face, the insincere reproach of those dark haunting eyes.

A week or so later arrived a letter from New York informing him that from four hundred plans submitted the judges of the competition had chosen his for the prize. Llewellyn walked into Mr Garnett's office without excitement, but with a strong sense of elation, and laid the letter on his employer's desk.

'I'm especially glad,' he said, 'because before I go away I wanted to do something to justify your belief in me.'

Mr Garnett's face assumed an expression of concern.

'It's this business of Lucy Wharton, isn't it?' he demanded. 'It's still on your mind?'

'I can't stand meeting her,' said Llewellyn. 'It always make me feel – like the devil.'

'But you ought to stay till they put up your house for you.'

'I'll come back for that, perhaps. I want to leave tonight.'

Garnett looked at him thoughtfully.

'I don't like to see you go away,' he said. 'I'm going to tell you something I didn't intend to tell you. Lucy needn't worry you a bit any more – your responsibility is absolutely over.'

'Why's that?' Llewellyn felt his heart quicken.

'She's going to marry another man.'

'Going to marry another man!' repeated Llewellyn mechanically.

'She's going to marry George Hemmick, who represents her father's business in Chicago. They're going out there to live.'

'I see.'

'The Whartons are delighted,' continued Garnett. 'I think they've felt this thing pretty deeply – perhaps more deeply than it deserves. And I've been sorry all along that the brunt of it fell on you. But you'll find the girl you really want one of these days, Llewellyn, and meanwhile the sensible thing for everyone concerned is to forget that it happened at all.'

'But I can't forget,' said Llewellyn in a strained voice. 'I don't understand what you mean by all that – you people – you and Lucy and her father and mother. First it was such a tragedy, and now it's something to forget! First I was this vicious young man and now I'm to go ahead and find the girl I want. Lucy's going to marry somebody and live in Chicago. Her father and mother feel fine because our elopement didn't get in the newspapers and hurt their social position. It came out "all right"!'

Llewellyn stood there speechless, aghast and defeated by this manifestation of the world's indifference. It was all about nothing – his very self-reproaches had been pointless and in vain.

'So that's that,' he said finally in a new and hard voice. 'I realize now that from beginning to end I was the only one who had any conscience in this affair after all.'

IV

The little house, fragile yet arresting, all aglitter like a toy in its fresh coat of robin's-egg blue, stood out delicately against the clear sky. Set upon new-laid sod between two other bungalows, it swung the eye sharply towards itself, held your glance for a moment, then turned up the corners of your lips with the sort of smile reserved for children. Something went on in it, you imagined; something charming and not quite real. Perhaps the whole front opened up like the front of a doll's house; you were tempted to hunt for the catch because you felt an irresistible inclination to peer inside.

Long before the arrival of Llewellyn Clark and Mr Garnett a small crowd had gathered – the constant efforts of two policemen were required to keep people from breaking through the strong fence and trampling the tiny garden. When Llewellyn's eye first fell upon it, as their car rounded a corner, a lump rose in his throat. That was his own – something that had come alive out of his mind. Suddenly he realized that it was not for sale, that he wanted it more than anything in the world. It could mean to him what love might have meant, something always bright and warm where he could rest from whatever disappointments life might have in store. And unlike love, it would set no traps for him. His career opened up before him in a shining path and for the first time in months he was radiantly happy.

The speeches, the congratulations, passed in a daze. When he got up to make a stumbling but grateful acknowledgement, even the sight of Lucy standing close to another man on the edge of the crowd failed to send a pang through him, as it would have a month before. That was the past, and only the future counted. He hoped with all his heart, without reservations now, or bitterness, that she would be happy.

Afterwards, when the crowd melted away, he felt the necessity of being alone. Still in a sort of trance, he went inside the house again and wandered from room to room, touching the walls, the furniture, the window casements, with almost a caress. He pulled aside curtains and gazed out; he stood for a while in the kitchen and seemed to see the fresh bread and butter on the white boards of the table, and hear the kettle, murmurous on the stove. Then back through the dining-room – he remembered planning that the evening light should fall through the window just so – and into the bedroom, where he watched a breeze ruffle the edge of a curtain faintly, as if someone already lived here. He would sleep in this room tonight, he thought. He would buy things for a cold supper from a corner store. He was sorry for everyone who was not an architect, who could not make their own houses; he wished he could have set up every stick and stone with his own hands.

The September dusk fell. Returning from the store, he set out his purchases on the dining-room table – cold roast chicken, bread and jam, and a bottle of milk. He ate lingeringly, then he sat back in his chair and smoked a cigarette, his eyes wandering about the walls. This was home. Llewellyn, brought up by a series of aunts, scarcely remembered ever having had a home before – except, of course, where he had lived with Lucy. Those barren rooms in which they were so miserable together had been, never-theless, a sort of home. Poor children – he looked back on them both, him-self as well as her, from a great distance. Little wonder their love had made a faint, frail effort, a gesture, and then, unprepared for the oppression of those stifling walls, starved quickly to death.

Half an hour passed. Outside, the silence was heavy except for the complaint of some indignant dog far down the street. Llewellyn's mind, detached by the unfamiliar, almost mystical surroundings, drifted away from the immediate past; he was thinking of the day when he had first met Lucy, a year before. Little Lucy Wharton – how touched he had been by her trust in him, by her confidence that, at twenty, he was experienced in the ways of the world.

He got to his feet and began to walk slowly up and down the room – starting suddenly as the front doorbell pealed through the house for the first time. He opened the door and Mr Garnett stepped inside.

'Good evening, Llewellyn,' he said. 'I came back to see if the king was happy in his castle.'

'Sit down,' said Llewellyn tensely. 'I've got to ask you something. Why is Lucy marrying this man? I want to know.'

'Why, I think I told you that he's a good deal older,' answered Garnett quietly. 'She feels that he understands.'

'I want to see her!' Llewellyn cried. He leaned miserably against the mantelpiece. 'I don't know what to do. Mr Garnett, we're in love with each other, don't you realize that? Can you stay in this house and not realize it? It's her house and mine. Why, every room in it is haunted with Lucy! She came in when I was at dinner and sat with me – just now I saw her in front of the mirror in the bedroom, brushing her hair—'

'She's out on the porch,' interrupted Garnett quietly. 'I think she wants to talk to you. In a few months she's going to have a child.'

For a few minutes Chauncey Garnett moved about the empty room, looking at this feature or that, here and there, until the walls seemed to fade out and melt into the walls of the little house where he had brought his own wife more than forty years ago. It was long gone, that house – the gift of his father-in-law; it would have seemed an atrocity to this generation. Yet on many a forgotten late afternoon when he had turned in at its gate, and the gas had flamed out at him cheerfully from its windows, he had got from it a moment of utter peace that no other house had given him since.

Until this house. The same quiet secret thing was here. Was it that his old mind was confusing the two, or that love had built this out of the tragedy in Llewellyn's heart? Leaving the question unanswered he found his hat and walked out on the dark porch, scarcely glanced at the single shadow on the porch chair a few yards away.

"You see, I never bothered to get that annulment, after all,' he said as if he were talking to himself. 'I thought it over carefully and I saw that you two were good people. And I had an idea that eventually you'd do the right thing. Good people – so often do.'

When he reached the kerb he looked back at the house. Again his mind – or his eyes – blurred and it seemed to him that it was that other house of forty years ago. Then, feeling vaguely ineffectual and a little guilty because he had meddled in other people's affairs, he turned and walked off hastily down the street.

YOUR WAY AND MINE

Woman's Home Companion, May 1927

'Your Way and Mine' was written in February 1926 at Salies-de-Bearn, a spa in the French Pyrenees where the Fitzgeralds spent two months while Zelda was taking a cure for digestive problems. In his cover letter Fitzgerald informed Harold Ober:

This is one of the lowsiest stories I've ever written Just terrible! I lost interest in the middle (by the way the last part is typed triple space because I thought I could fix it – but I couldn't)

Please – and I mean this – don't offer it to the Post. I think that as things are now it would be wretched policy. Nor to the Red Book. It hasn't one redeeming touch of my usual spirit in it. I was desperate to begin a story + invented a business plot – the kind I can't handle. I'd rather have $1000 for it from some obscure place than twice that + have it seen. I feel very strongly about this!

Woman's Home Companion *paid $1750, featuring it on the cover; and it was syndicated by the Metro Newspaper Service.*

One spring afternoon in the first year of the present century a young man was experimenting with a new typewriter in a brokerage office on lower Broadway. At his elbow lay an eight-line letter and he was endeavouring to make a copy on the machine but each attempt was marred by a monstrous capital rising unexpectedly in the middle of a word or by the disconcerting intrusion of some symbol such as $ or % into an alphabet whose membership was set at twenty-six many years ago. Whenever he detected a mistake he made a new beginning with a fresh sheet but after the fifteenth try he was aware of a ferocious instinct to cast the machine from the window.

The young man's short blunt fingers were too big for the keys. He was big all over; indeed his bulky body seemed to be in the very process of growth for it had ripped his coat at the back seam, while his trousers clung to thigh and calf like skin tights. His hair was yellow and tousled – you could see the paths of his broad fingers in it – and his eyes were of a hard brilliant blue but the lids drooping a little over them reinforced an impression of legarthy that the clumsy body conveyed. His age was twenty-one.

'What do you think the eraser's for, McComas?'

The young man looked around.

'What's that?' he demanded brusquely.

'The eraser,' repeated the short alert human fox who had come in the outer door and paused behind him. 'That there's a good copy except for one word. Use your head or you'll be sitting there until tomorrow.'

The human fox moved on into his private office. The young man sat for a moment, motionless, sluggish. Suddenly he grunted, picked up the eraser referred to and flung it savagely out of the window.

Twenty minutes later he opened the door of his employer's office. In his hand was the letter, immaculately typed, and the addressed envelope.

'Here it is, sir,' he said, frowning a little from his late concentration.

The human fox took it, glanced at it and then looked at McComas with a peculiar smile.

'You didn't use the eraser?'

'No, I didn't, Mr Woodley.'

'You're one of those thorough young men, aren't you?' said the fox sarcastically.

'What?'

'I said "thorough" but since you weren't listening I'll change it to "pig-headed". Whose time did you waste just to avoid a little erasure that the best typists aren't too proud to make? Did you waste your time or mine?'

'I wanted to make one good copy,' answered McComas steadily. 'You see, I never worked a typewriter before.'

'Answer my question,' snapped Mr Woodley. 'When you sat there making two dozen copies of that letter were you wasting your time or mine?'

'It was mostly my lunchtime,' McComas replied, his big face flushing to an angry pink. 'I've got to do things my own way or not at all.'

For answer Mr Woodley picked up the letter and envelope, folded them, tore them once and again and dropped the pieces into the wastepaper basket with a toothy little smile.

'That's my way,' he announced. 'What do you think of that?'

Young McComas had taken a step forward as if to snatch the fragments from the fox's hand.

'By golly,' he cried. 'By golly. Why, for two cents I'd spank you!'

With an angry snarl Mr Woodley sprang to his feet, fumbled in his pocket and threw a handful of change upon his desk.

Ten minutes later the outside man coming in to report perceived that neither young McComas nor his hat were in their usual places. But in the private office he found Mr Woodley, his face crimson and foam bubbling between his teeth, shouting frantically into the telephone. The outside man noticed to his surprise that Mr Woodley was in daring dishabille and that there were six suspender buttons scattered upon the office floor.

In 1902 Henry McComas weighed 196 pounds. In 1905 when he journeyed back to his home town, Elmira, to marry the love of his boyhood he tipped accurate beams at 210. His weight remained constant for two years but after the panic of 1907 it bounded to 220, about which comfortable figure it was apparently to hover for the rest of his life.

He looked mature beyond his years – under certain illuminations his yellow hair became a dignified white – and his bulk added to the impression of authority that he gave. During his first five years off the farm there was never a time when he wasn't scheming to get into business for himself.

For a temperament like Henry McComas', which insisted on running at a pace of its own, independence was an utter necessity. He must make his own rules, willy-nilly, even though he join the ranks of those many abject failures who have also tried. Just one week after he had achieved his emancipation from other people's hierarchies he was moved to expound his point to Theodore Drinkwater, his partner – this because Drinkwater had wondered aloud if he intended never to come downtown before eleven.

'I doubt it,' said McComas.

'What's the idea?' demanded Drinkwater indignantly. 'What do you think the effect's going to be on our office force?'

'Does Miss Johnston show any sign of being demoralized?'

'I mean after we get more people. It isn't as if you were an old man, Mac, with your work behind you. You're only twenty-eight, not a day older than I. What'll you do at forty?'

'I'll be downtown at eleven o'clock,' said McComas, 'every working day of my life.'

Later in the week one of their first clients invited them to lunch at a celebrated business club; the club's least member was a rajah of the swelling, expanding empire.

'Look around, Ted,' whispered McComas as they left the dining-room. 'There's a man looks like a prizefighter, and there's one who looks like a ham actor. That's a plumber there behind you; there's a coal heaver and a couple of cowboys – do you see ? There's a chronic invalid and a confidence man, a pawnbroker – that one on the right. By golly, where are all the big businessmen we came to see ?'

The route back to their office took them by a small restaurant where the clerks of the district flocked to lunch.

'Take a look at them, Ted, and you'll find the men who know the rules – and think and act and look like just what they are.'

'I suppose if they put on pink moustaches and came to work at five in the afternoon they'd get to be great men,' scoffed Drinkwater.

'Posing is exactly what I don't mean. Just accept yourself. We're brought up on fairy stories about the new leaf, but who goes on believing them except those who have to believe and have to hope or else go crazy. I think America will be a happier country when the individual begins to look his personal limitations in the face. Anything that's in your character at twenty-one is usually there to stay.'

In any case what was in Henry McComas' was there to stay. Henry McComas wouldn't dine with a client in a bad restaurant for a proposition of three figures, wouldn't hurry his luncheon for a proposition of four, wouldn't go without it for a proposition of five. And in spite of these pecularities the exporting firm in which he owned forty-nine per cent of the stock began to pepper South America with locomotives, dynamos, barb wire, hydraulic engines, cranes, mining machinery, and other appurtenances of civilization. In 1913 when Henry McComas was thirty-four he owned a house on Ninety-second Street and calculated that his income for the next year would come to thirty thousand dollars. And because of a sudden and unexpected demand from Europe which was not for pink lemonade, it came to twice that. The buying agent for the British government arrived, followed by the buying agents for the French, Belgian, Russian and Serbian governments, and a share of the commodities required was assembled under the stewardship of Drinkwater and McComas. There was a chance that they would be rich men. Then suddenly this eventually began to turn on the woman Henry McComas had married.

Stella McComas was the daughter of a small hay and grain dealer of upper New York. Her father was unlucky and always on the verge of failure, so she grew up in the shadow of worry. Later, while Henry McComas got his start in New York, she earned her living by teaching physical culture in the public schools of Utica. In consequence she brought to her marriage a belief in certain stringent rules for the care of the body and an exaggerated fear of adversity.

For the first years she was so impressed with her husband's rapid rise and so absorbed in her babies that she accepted Henry as something infallible and protective, outside the scope of her provincial wisdom. But as her little girl grew into short dresses and hair ribbons, and her little boy into the custody of an English nurse she had more time to look closely at her husband. His leisurely ways, his corpulency, his sometimes maddening deliberateness, ceased to be the privileged idiosyncrasies of success, and became only facts.

For a while he paid no great attention to her little suggestions as to his diet, her occasional crankiness as to his hours, her invidious comparisons between his habits and the fancied habits of other men. Then one morning a peculiar lack of taste in his coffee precipitated the matter into the light.

'I can't drink the stuff – it hasn't had any taste for a week,' he complained. 'And why is it brought in a cup from the kitchen ? I like to put the cream and sugar in myself.'

Stella avoided an answer but later he reverted to the matter.

'About my coffee. You'll remember – won't you ?– to tell Rose.'

Suddenly she smiled at him innocently.

'Don't you feel better, Henry ?' she asked eagerly.

'What ?'

'Less tired, less worried ?'

'Who said I was tired and worried ? I never felt better in my life.'

'There you are.' She looked at him triumphantly. 'You laugh at my theories but this time you'll have to admit there's something in them. You feel better because you haven't had sugar in your coffee for over a week.'

He looked at her incredulously.

'What have I had ?'

'Saccharine.'

He got up indignantly and threw his newspaper on the table.

'I might have known it,' he broke out. 'All that bringing it out from the kitchen. What the devil is saccharine ?'

'It's a substitute, for people who have a tendency to run to fat.'

For a moment he hovered on the edge of anger, then he sat down shaking with laughter.

'It's done you good,' she said reproachfully.

'Well, it won't do me good any more,' he said grimly. 'I'm thirty-four years old and I haven't been sick a day in ten years. I've forgotten more about my constitution than you'll ever know.'

'You don't live a healthy life, Henry. It's after forty that things begin to tell.'

'Saccharine!' he exclaimed, again breaking into laughter. 'Saccharine! I thought perhaps it was something to keep me from drink. You know they have these—'

Suddenly she grew angry.

'Well why not? You ought to be ashamed to be so fat at your age. You wouldn't be if you took a little exercise and didn't lie around in bed all morning.'

Words utterly failed her.

'If I wanted to be a farmer,' said her husband quietly, 'I wouldn't have left home. This saccharine business is over today – do you see?'

Their financial situation rapidly improved. By the second year of the war they were keeping a limousine and chauffeur and began to talk vaguely of a nice summer house on Long Island Sound. Month by month a swelling stream of materials flowed through the ledgers of Drinkwater and McComas to be dumped on the insatiable bonfire across the ocean. Their staff of clerks tripled and the atmosphere of the office was so charged with energy and achievement that Stella herself often liked to wander in on some pretext during the afternoon.

One day early in 1916 she called to learn that Mr McComas was out and was on the point of leaving when she ran into Ted Drinkwater coming out of the elevator.

'Why, Stella,' he exclaimed, 'I was thinking about you only this morning.'

The Drinkwaters and the McComases were close if not particularly spontaneous friends. Nothing but their husbands' intimate association would have thrown the two women together, yet they were 'Henry, Ted, Mollie, and Stella' to each other and in ten years scarcely a month had passed without their partaking in a superficially cordial family dinner. The dinner being over, each couple indulged in an unsparing post-mortem over the other without, however, any sense of disloyalty. They were used to each other – so Stella was somewhat surprised by Ted Drinkwater's personal eagerness at meeting her this afternoon.

'I want to see you,' he said in his intent direct way. 'Have you got a minute, Stella? Could you come into my office?'

'Why, yes.'

As they walked between rows of typists towards the glassed privacy of THEODORE DRINKWATER, PRESIDENT, Stella could not help thinking that he made a more appropriate business figure than her husband. He was lean, terse, quick. His eye glanced keenly from right to left as if taking the exact measure of every clerk and stenographer in sight.

'Sit down, Stella.'

She waited, a feeling of vague apprehension stealing over her.

Drinkwater frowned

'It's about Henry,' he said.

'Is he sick?' she demanded quickly.

'No. Nothing like that.' He hesitated. 'Stella, I've always thought you were a woman with a lot of common sense.'

She waited.

'This is a thing that's been on my mind for over a year,' he continued. 'He and I have battled it out so often that – that a certain coldness has grown up between us.'

'Yes?' Stella's eyes blinked nervously.

'It's about the business,' said Drinkwater abruptly. 'A coldness with a business partner is a mighty unpleasant thing.'

'What's the matter?'

'The old story, Stella. These are big years for us and he thinks business is going to wait while he carries on in the old country-store way. Down at eleven, hour and a half for lunch, won't be nice to a man he doesn't like for love or money. In the last six months he's lost us about three sizable orders by things like that.'

Instinctively she sprang to her husband's defence.

'But hasn't he saved money too by going slow? On that thing about the copper, you wanted to sign right away and Henry—'

'Oh, that—' He waved it aside a little hurriedly. 'I'm the last man to deny that Henry has a wonderful instinct in certain ways—'

'But it was a great big thing,' she interrupted. 'It would have practically ruined you if he hadn't put his foot down. He said—'

She pulled herself up short.

'Oh, I don't know,' said Drinkwater with an expression of annoyance, 'perhaps not so bad as that. Anyway, we all make mistakes and that's aside from the question. We have the opportunity right now of jumping into Class A. I mean it. Another two years of this kind of business and we can each put away our first million dollars. And, Stella, whatever happens, I am determined to put away mine. Even—' He considered his words for a moment. 'Even if it comes to breaking with Henry.'

'Oh!' Stella exclaimed. 'I hope—'

'I hope not too. That's why I wanted to talk to you. Can't you do something, Stella? You're about the only person he'll listen to. He's so darn pig-headed he can't understand how he disorganizes the office. Get him up in the morning. No man ought to lie in bed till eleven.'

'He gets up at half past nine.'

'He's down here at eleven. That's what counts. Stir him up. Tell him you want more money. Orders are more money and there are lots of orders around for anyone who goes after them.'

'I'll see what I can do,' she said anxiously. 'But I don't know – Henry's difficult – very set in his ways.'

'You'll think of something. You might—' He smiled grimly. 'You might give him a few more bills to pay. Sometimes I think an extravagant wife's the best inspiration a man can have. We need more pep down here. I've got to be the pep for two. I mean it, Stella, I can't carry this thing alone.'

Stella left the office with her mind in a panic. All the fears and uncertainties of her childhood had been brought suddenly to the surface. She saw Henry cast off by Ted Drinkwater and trying unsuccessfully to run a business of his own. With his easy-going ways! They would slide down hill, giving up the servants one by one, the car, the house. Before she reached home her imagination had envisaged poverty, her children at work – starvation. Hadn't Ted Drinkwater just told her that he himself was the life of the concern – that he kept things moving? What would Henry do alone?

For a week she brooded over the matter, guarding her secret but looking with a mixture of annoyance and compassion at Henry over the dinner table. Then she mustered up her resolution. She went to a real estate agent and handed over her entire bank account of nine thousand dollars as the first payment on a house they had fearfully coveted on Long Island . . . That night she told Henry.

'Why, Stella, you must have gone crazy,' he cried aghast. 'You must have gone crazy. Why didn't you ask me?'

He wanted to take her by the shoulders and shake her.

'I was afraid, Henry,' she answered truthfully.

He thrust his hands despairingly through his yellow hair.

'Just at this time, Stella. I've just taken out an insurance policy that's more than I can really afford – we haven't paid for the new car – we've had a new front put on this house – last week your sable coat. I was going to devote tonight to figuring just how close we were running on money.'

'But can't you – can't you take something out of the business until things get better ?' she demanded in alarm.

'That's just what I can't do. It's impossible. I can't explain because you don't understand the situation down there. You see Ted and I – can't agree on certain things—'

Suddenly a new light dawned on her and she felt her body flinch. Supposing that by bringing about this situation she had put her husband into his partner's hands. Yet wasn't that what she wanted— wasn't it necessary for the present that Henry should conform to Drinkwater's methods ?

'Sixty thousand dollars,' repeated Henry in a frightened voice that made her want to cry. 'I don't know where I am going to get enough to buy it on mortgage.' He sank into a chair. 'I might go and see the people you dealt with tomorrow and make a compromise – let some of your nine thousand go.'

'I don't think they would,' she said, her face set. 'They were awfully anxious to sell – the owner's going away.'

She had acted on impulse, she said, thinking that in their increasing prosperity the money would be available. He had been so generous about the new car – she supposed that now at last they could afford what they wanted.

It was typical of McComas that after the first moment of surprise he wasted no energy in reproaches. But two days later he came home from work with such a heavy and dispirited look on his face that she could not help but guess that he and Ted Drinkwater had had it out – and that what she had wanted had come true. That night in shame and pity she cried herself to sleep.

A new routine was inaugurated in Henry McComas' life. Each morning Stella woke him at eight and he lay for fifteen minutes in an unwilling trance, as if his body were surprised at this departure from the custom of a decade. He reached the office at nine-thirty as promptly as he had once reached it at eleven – on the first morning his appearance caused a flutter of astonishment among the older employees – and he limited his lunchtime to a conscientious hour. No longer could he be found asleep on his office couch between two and three o'clock on summer afternoons – the couch itself vanished into that limbo which held his leisurely periods of digestion and his cherished surfeit of sleep. These were his concessions to Drinkwater in exchange for the withdrawal of sufficient money to cover his immediate needs.

Drinkwater of course could have bought him out, but for various reasons the senior partner did not consider this advisable. One of them, though he didn't admit it to himself, was his absolute reliance on McComas in all matters of initiative and decision. Another reason was the tumultuous condition of the market, for as 1916 boomed on with the tragic battle of the Somme the allied agents sailed once more to the city of plenty for the wherewithal of another year. Coincidentally Drinkwater and McComas moved into a suite that was like a floor in a country club and there they sat all day while anxious and gesticulating strangers explained what they must have, helplessly pledging their peoples to thirty years of economic depression. Drinkwater and McComas farmed out a dozen contracts a week and started the movement of countless tons towards Europe. Their names were known up and down the Street now – they had forgotten what it was to be kept waiting on a telephone.

But though profits increased and Stella, settled in the Long Island house, seemed for the first time in years perfectly satisfied, Henry McComas found himself growing irritable and nervous. What he missed most was the sleep for which his body hungered and which seemed to descend upon him at its richest just as he was shocked back into the living world each morning. And in spite of all material gains he was always aware that he was walking in his own paths no longer.

Their interests broadened and Drinkwater was frequently away on trips to the industrial towns of New England or the South. In consequence the detail of the office fell upon McComas – and he took it hard. A man capable of enormous concentration, he had previously harvested his power for hours of importance. Now he was inclined to fritter it away upon things that in perspective often proved to be inessentials. Sometimes he was engaged in office routine until six, then at home working until midnight when he tumbled, worn out but often still wide-eyed, into his beleaguered bed.

The firm's policy was to slight their smaller accounts in Cuba and the West Indies and concentrate upon the tempting business of the war, and all though the summer they were hurrying to clear the scenes for the arrival of a new purchasing commission in September. When it arrived it unexpectedly found Drinkwater in Pennsylvania, temporarily out of reach. Time was short and the orders were to be placed in bulk. After much anxious parley over the telephone McComas persuaded four members of the commission to meet him for an hour at his own house that night.

Thanks to his foresight everything was in order. If he hadn't been able to be specific over the phone the *coup* towards which he had been working would have ended in failure. When it was brought off he was due for a rest and he knew it acutely. He'd had sharp fierce headaches in the past few weeks – he had never known a headache before.

The commissioners had been indefinite as to what time he could expect them that night. They were engaged for dinner and would be free somewhere between nine and eleven. McComas reached home at six, rested for a half-hour in a steaming bath and then stretched himself gratefully on his bed. Tomorrow he would join Stella and the children in the country. His weekends had been too infrequent in this long summer of living alone in the Ninety-second Street house with a deaf housekeeper. Ted Drinkwater would have nothing to say now, for this deal, the most ambitious of all, was his own. He had originated and engineered it – it seemed as if fate had arranged Drinkwater's absence in order to give him the opportunity of concluding it himself.

He was hungry. He considered whether to take cold chicken and buttered toast at the hands of the housekeeper or to dress and go out to the little restaurant on the corner. Idly he reached his hand towards the bell, abandoned the attempt in the air, overcome by a pleasing languor which dispelled the headache that had bothered him all day.

That reminded him to take some aspirin and as he got up to go towards the bureau he was surprised at the weakened condition in which the hot bath had left him. After a step or two he turned about suddenly and plunged rather than fell back upon the bed. A faint feeling of worry passed over him and then an iron belt seemed to wind itself around his head and tighten, sending a spasm of pain through his body. He would ring for Mrs Corcoran, who would call a doctor to fix him up. In a minute – he wondered at his indecision – then he cried out sharply as he realized the cause of it. His will had already given his brain the order and his brain had signalled it to his hand. It was his hand that would not obey.

He looked at his hand. Rather white, relaxed, motionless, it lay upon the counterpane. Again he gave it a command, felt his neck cords tighten with the effort. It did not move.

'It's asleep,' he thought, but with rising alarm. 'It'll pass off in a minute.' Then he tried to reach his other hand across his body to massage away

251

the numbness but the other hand remained with a sort of crazy indifference on its own side of the bed. He tried to lift his foot – his knees . . .

After a few seconds he gave a snort of nervous laughter. There was something ridiculous about not being able to move your own foot. It was like someone else's foot, a foot in a dream. For a moment he had the fantastic notion that he must be asleep. But no – the unmistakable sense of reality was in the room.

'This is the end,' he thought, without fear, almost without emotion. 'This thing, whatever it is, is creeping over me. In a minute I shall be dead.'

But the minute passed and another minute, and nothing happened, nothing moved except the hand of the little leather clock on his dresser which crept slowly over the point of seven minutes to seven. He turned his head quickly from side to side, shaking it as a runner kicks his legs to warm up. But there was no answering response from the rest of his body, only a slight rise and fall between belly and chest as he breathed out and in and a faint tremble of his helpless limbs from the faint tremble of the bed.

'Help!' he called out. 'Mrs Corcoran. Mrs Cor-cor-an, help! Mrs Corcor—'

There was no answer. She was in the kitchen probably. No way of calling her except by the bell, two feet over his head. Nothing to do but lie there until this passed off, or until he died, or until someone inquired for him at the front door.

The clock ticked past nine o'clock. In a house two blocks away the four members of the commission finished dinner, looked at their watches and issued forth into the September night with briefcases in their hands. Outside a private detective nodded and took his place beside the chauffeur in the waiting limousine. One of the men gave an address on Ninety-second Street.

Ten minutes later Henry McComas heard the doorbell ring through the house. If Mrs Corcoran was in the kitchen she would hear it too. On the contrary if she was in her room with the door shut she would hear nothing.

He waited, listening intently for the sound of footsteps. A minute passed. Two minutes. The doorbell rang again.

'Mrs Corcoran!' he cried desperately.

Sweat began to roll from his forehead and down the folds of his neck. Again he shook his head desperately from side to side, and his will made a last mighty effort to kick his limbs into life. Not a movement, not a sound, except a third peal of the bell, impatient and sustained this time and singing like a trumpet of doom in his ear.

Suddenly he began to swear at the top of his voice calling in turn upon Mrs Corcoran, upon the men in the street, asking them to break down the door, reassuring, imprecating, explaining. When he finished, the bell had stopped ringing; there was silence once more within the house.

A few minutes later the four men outside re-entered their limousine and drove south and west towards the docks. They were to sleep on board ship that night. They worked late for there were papers to go ashore but long after the last of them was asleep Henry McComas lay awake and felt the sweat rolling from his neck and forehead. Perhaps all his body was sweating. He couldn't tell.

For a year and a half Henry McComas lay silent in hushed and darkened rooms and fought his way back to life. Stella listened while a famous specialist explained that certain nervous systems were so constituted that only the individual could judge what was, or wasn't, a strain. The specialist realized that a host of hypochondriacs imposed upon this fact to nurse and pamper themselves through life when in reality they were as hardy and phlegmatic as the policeman on the corner, but it was nevertheless a fact. Henry McComas' large, lazy body had been the protection and insulation of a nervous intensity as fine and taut as a hair wire. With proper rest it functioned brilliantly for three or four hours a day – fatigued ever so slightly over the danger line it snapped like a straw.

Stella listened, her face wan and white. Then a few weeks later she went to Ted Drinkwater's office and told him what the specialist had said. Drinkwater frowned uncomfortably – he remarked that specialists were paid to invent consoling nonsense. He was sorry but business must go on, and he thought it best for everyone, including Henry, that the partnership be dissolved. He didn't blame Henry but he couldn't forget that just because his partner didn't see fit to keep in good condition they had missed the opportunity of a lifetime.

After a year Henry McComas found one day that he could move his arms down to the wrists; from that hour onward he grew rapidly well. In 1919 he went into business for himself with very little except his abilities and his good name and by the time this story ends, in 1926, his name alone was good for several million dollars.

What follows is another story. There are different people in it and it takes place when Henry McComas' personal problems are more or less satisfactorily solved; yet it belongs to what has gone before. It concerns Henry McComas' daughter.

Honoria was nineteen, with her father's yellow hair (and, in the current fashion, not much more of it), her mother's small pointed chin and eyes that she might have invented herself, deep-set yellow eyes with short stiff eyelashes that sprang from them like the emanations from a star in a picture. He figure was slight and childish and when she smiled you were afraid that she might expose the loss of some baby teeth, but the teeth were there, a complete set, little and white. Many men had looked upon Honoria in flower. She expected to be married in the fall.

Whom to marry was another matter. There was a young man who travelled incessantly back and forth between London and Chicago playing in golf tournaments. If she married him she would at least be sure of seeing her husband every time he passed through New York. There was Max Van Camp who was unreliable, she thought, but good-looking in a brisk sketchy way. There was a dark man named Strangler who played polo and would probably beat her with a riding crop like the heroes of Ethel M. Dell. And there was Russel Codman, her father's right-hand man, who had a future and whom she liked best of all.

He was not unlike her father in many ways – slow in thought, leisurely and inclined to stoutness – and perhaps these qualities had first brought him to Henry McComas' favour. He had a genial manner and a hearty confident smile, and he had made up his mind about Honoria when he first saw her stroll into her father's office one day three years before. But so far he hadn't asked her to marry him, and though this annoyed Honoria she liked him for it too – he wanted to be secure and successful before he asked her to share his life. Max Van Camp, on the other hand, had asked her a dozen times. He was a quick-witted 'alive' young man of the new school, continually bubbling over with schemes that never got beyond McComas' wastepaper basket – one of those curious vagabonds of business who drift from position to position like strolling minstrels and yet manage to keep moving in an upward direction all their lives. He had appeared in McComas' office the year before bearing an introductory letter from a friend.

He got the position. For a long while neither he nor his employer, nor anyone in the office, was quite sure what the position was. McComas at that time was interested in exporting, in real estate developments and, as a venture, in the possibilities of carrying the chain store idea into new fields.

Van Camp wrote advertising, investigated properties and accomplished such vague duties as might come under the phrase, 'We'll get Van Camp to do that.' He gave the effect always of putting much more clamour and energy into a thing than it required and there were those who, because he was somewhat flashy and often wasted himself like an unemployed dynamo, called him a bluff and pronounced that he was usually wrong.

'What's the matter with you young fellows?' Henry McComas said to him one day. 'You seem to think business is some sort of trick game, discovered about 1910, that nobody ever heard of before. You can't even look at a proposition unless you put it into this new language of your own. What do you mean you want to "sell" me this proposition? Do you want to suggest it – or are you asking money for it?'

'Just a figure of speech, Mr McComas.'

'Well, don't fool yourself that it's anything else. Business sense is just common sense with your personal resources behind it – nothing more.'

'I've heard Mr Codman say that,' agreed Max Van Camp meekly.

'He's probably right. See here—' he looked keenly at Van Camp; 'how would you like a little competition with that same gentleman? I'll put up a bonus of five hundred dollars on who comes in ahead.'

'I'd like nothing better, Mr McComas.'

'All right. Now listen. We've got retail hardware stores in every city of over a thousand population in Ohio and Indiana. Some fellow named McTeague is horning in on the idea – he's taken the towns of twenty thousand and now he's got a chain as long as mine. I want to fight him in the towns of that size. Codman's gone to Ohio. Suppose you take Indiana. Stay six weeks. Go to every town of over twenty thousand in the state and buy up the best hardware stores in sight.'

'Suppose I can only get the second-best?'

'Do what you can. There isn't any time to waste because McTeague's got a good start on us. Think you can leave tonight?'

He gave some further instructions while Van Camp fidgeted impatiently. His mind had grasped what was required of him and he wanted to get away. He wanted to ask Honoria McComas one more question, the same one, before it was time to go.

He received the same answer because Honoria knew she was going to marry Russel Codman, just as soon as he asked her to. Sometimes when she was alone with Codman she would shiver with excitement, feeling that now surely the time had come at last – in a moment the words would flow romantically from his lips. What the words would be she didn't know, couldn't imagine, but they would be thrilling and extraordinary, not like the spontaneous appeals of Max Van Camp which she knew by heart.

She waited excitedly for Russel Codman's return from the West. This time, unless he spoke, she would speak herself. Perhaps he didn't want her after all, perhaps there was someone else. In that case she would marry Max Van Camp and make him miserable by letting him see that he was getting only the remnants of a blighted life.

Then before she knew it the six weeks were up and Russel Codman came back to New York. He reported to her father that he was going to see her that night. In her excitement Honoria found excuses for being near the front door. The bell rang finally and a maid stepped past her and admitted a visitor into the hall.

'Max,' she cried.

He came towards her and she saw that his face was tired and white.

'Will you marry me?' he demanded without preliminaries.

She sighed.

'How many times, Max?'

'I've lost count,' he said cheerfully. 'But I haven't even begun. Do I understand that you refuse?'

'Yes, I'm sorry.'

'Waiting for Codman?'

She grew annoyed.

'That's not your affair.'

'Where's your father?'

She pointed, not deigning to reply.

Max entered the library where McComas rose to meet him.

'Well?' inquired the older man. 'How did you make out?'

'How did Codman make out?' demanded Van Camp.

'Codman did well. He bought about eighteen stores – in several cases the very stores McTeague was after.'

'I knew he would,' said Van Camp.

'I hope you did the same.'

'No,' said Van Camp unhappily. 'I failed.'

'What happened?' McComas slouched his big body reflectively back in his chair and waited.

'I saw it was no use,' said Van Camp after a moment. 'I don't know what sort of places Codman picked up in Ohio but if it was anything like Indiana they weren't worth buying. These towns of twenty thousand haven't got three good hardware stores. They've got one man who won't sell out on account of the local wholesaler; then there's one man that McTeague's got, and after that only little places on the corner. Anything else you'll have to build up yourself. I saw right away that it wasn't worth while.' He broke off. 'How many places did Codman buy ?

'Eighteen or nineteen.'

'I bought three.'

McComas looked at him impatiently.

'How did you spend your time ?' he asked. 'Take you two weeks apiece to get them ?'

'Took me two days,' said Van Camp gloomily. 'Then I had an idea.'

'What was that ?' McComas' voice was ironical.

'Well – McTeague had all the good stores.'

'Yes.'

'So I thought the best thing was to buy McTeague's company over his head.'

'What ?'

'Buy his company over his head,' and Van Camp added with seeming irrelevance, 'you see, I heard that he'd had a big quarrel with his uncle who owned fifteen percent of the stock.'

'Yes,' McComas was leaning forward now – the sarcasm gone from his face.

'McTeague only owned twenty-five per cent and the storekeepers themselves owned forty. So if I could bring round the uncle we'd have a majority. First I convinced the uncle that his money would be safer with McTeague as a branch manager in our organization—'

'Wait a minute – wait a minute,' said McComas. 'You go too fast for me. You say the uncle had fifteen per cent – how'd you get the other forty ?'

'From the owners. I told them the uncle had lost faith in McTeague and I offered them better terms. I had all their proxies on condition that they would be voted in a majority only.'

'Yes,' said McComas eagerly. Then he hesitated. 'But it didn't work, you say. What was the matter with it ? Not sound ?'

'Oh, it was a sound scheme all right.'

'Sound schemes always work.'

'This one didn't.'

'Why not ?'

'The uncle died.'

McComas laughed. Then he stopped suddenly and considered.

'So you tried to buy McTeague's company over his head ?'

'Yes,' said Max with a shamed look. 'And I failed.'

The door flew open suddenly and Honoria rushed into the room.

'Father,' she cried. At the sight of Max she stopped, hesitated, and then carried away by her excitement continued:

'Father – did you ever tell Russel how you proposed to Mother?'

'Why, let me see – yes, I think I did.'

Honoria groaned.

'Well, he tried to use it again on me.'

'What do you mean?'

'All these months I've been waiting' – she was almost in tears – 'waiting to hear what he'd say. And then – when it came – it sounded *familiar* – as if I'd heard it before.'

'It's probably one of my proposals,' suggested Van Camp. 'I've used so many.'

She turned on him quickly.

'Do you mean to say you've ever proposed to any other girl but me?'

'Honoria – would you mind?'

'Mind. Of course I wouldn't mind. I'd never speak to you again as long as I lived.'

'You say Codman proposed to you in the words I used to your mother?' demanded McComas.

'Exactly,' she wailed. 'He knew them by heart.'

'That's the trouble with him,' said McComas thoughtfully. 'He always was my man and not his own. You'd better marry Max, here.'

'Why—' she looked from one to the other, 'why – I never knew you liked Max, Father. You never showed it.'

'Well, that's just the difference,' said her father, 'between your way and mine.'

THE LOVE BOAT

Saturday Evening Post, 8 October 1927

'The Love Boat' was written in August 1927 at Ellerslie, a rented mansion near Wilmington, Delaware. Fitzgerald had returned to America to write Tender Is the Night, *but the work on the novel was interrupted and postponed while he wrote money-making stories. The* Post *paid $3500 for it, a raise of $500 over Fitzgerald's previous story price.*

Written at a time when Fitzgerald's life was increasingly undisciplined, 'The Love Boat' treats a search for the lost hopes or ideals of youth. It belongs to a group of retrospective stories he wrote at Ellerslie, notably the Basil Duke Lee stories about a boy growing up in St Paul and going off to boarding school in the East. Fitzgerald's attempt to reorganize his life abroad had proved a failure, and these retrospective stories represent a return to American experience by a return to youth.

The boat floated down the river through the summer night like a Fourth of July balloon footloose in the heavens. The decks were brightly lit and restless with dancers, but bow and stern were in darkness; so the boat had no more outline than an accidental cluster of stars. Between the black banks it floated, softly parting the mild dark tide from the sea and leaving in its wake small excited gusts of music – 'Babes in the Woods' over and over, and 'Moonlight Bay'. Past the scattered lights of Pokus Landing, where a poet in an attic window saw yellow hair gleam in the turn of a dance. Past Ulm, where the moon came up out of a boiler works, and West Esther, where it slid, unregretted, behind a cloud.

The radiance of the boat itself was enough for, among others, the three young Harvard graduates; they were weary and a little depressed and they gave themselves up promptly to its enchantment. Their own boat was casually drifting and a collision was highly possible, but no one made a movement to start the engine and get out of the way.

'It makes me very sad,' one of them said. 'It is so beautiful that it makes me want to cry.'

'Go on and cry, Bill.'

'Will you cry too?'

'We'll all cry.'

His loud, facetious 'Boo-hoo!' echoed across the night, reached the steamer and brought a small lively crowd to the rail.

'Look! It's a launch.'

'Some guys in a launch.'

Bill got to his feet. The two crafts were scarcely ten feet apart.

'Throw us a hempen rope,' he pleaded eloquently. 'Come on – be impulsive. Please do.'

Once in a hundred years there would have been a rope at hand. It was there that night. With a thud the coil struck the wooden bottom and in an instant the motorboat was darting along behind the steamer, as if in the wake of a harpooned whale.

Fifty high-school couples left the dance and scrambled for a place around the suddenly interesting stern rail. Fifty girls gave forth immemorial small cries of excitement and sham fright. Fifty young men forgot the mild exhibitionism which had characterized their manner of the evening and looked grudgingly at the more effectual show-off of three others. Mae Purley, without the involuntary quiver of an eyelash, fitted the young man standing in the boat into her current dream, where he displaced Al Fitzpatrick with laughable ease. She put her hand on Al Fitzpatrick's arm and squeezed it a little because she had stopped thinking about him entirely and felt that he must be aware of it. Al, who had been standing with his eyes squinted up, watching the towed boat, looked tenderly at Mae and tried to put his arm about her shoulder. But Mae Purley and Bill Frothington, handsome and full of all the passionate promise in the world, had locked eyes across the intervening space.

They made love. For a moment they made love as no one ever dares to do after. Their glance was closer than an embrace, more urgent than a call. There were no words for it. Had there been, and had Mae heard them, she would have fled to the darkest corner of the ladies' washroom and hid her face in a paper towel.

'We want to come on board!' Bill called. 'We're life-preserver salesmen! How about pulling us around to the side?'

Mr McVitty, the principal, arrived on the scene too late to interfere. The three young Harvard graduates – Ellsworth Ames soaking wet, unconsciously Byronic with his dark curls plastered damply to his forehead, Hamilton Abbot and Bill Frothington surer-footed and dry – climbed and were hoisted over the side. The motorboat bobbed on behind.

With a sort of instinctive reverence for the moment, Mae Purley hung back in the shadow, not through lack of confidence but through excess of it. She knew that he would come straight to her. That was never the trouble and never had been – the trouble was in keeping up her own interest after she had satisfied the deep but casual curiosity of her lips. But tonight was going to be different. She knew this when she saw that he was in no hurry; he was leaning against the rail making a couple of high-school seniors – who suddenly seemed very embryonic to themselves – feel at ease.

He looked at her once.

'It's all right,' his eyes said, without a movement of his face, 'I understand as well as you. I'll be there in just a minute.'

Life burned high in them both; the steamer and its people were at a distance and in darkness. It was one of those times.

'I'm a Harvard man,' Mr McVitty was saying, 'class of 1907.' The three young men nodded with polite indifference. 'I'm glad to know we won the race,' continued the principal, simulating a reborn enthusiasm which had never existed. 'I haven't been to New London in fifteen years.'

'Bill here rowed Number Two,' said Ames. 'That's a coaching launch we've got.'

'Oh. You were on the crew ?'

'Crew's over now,' said Bill impatiently. 'Everything's over.'

'Well, let me congratulate you.'

Shortly they froze him into silence. They were not his sort of Harvard man; they wouldn't have known his name in four years there together. But they would have been much more gracious and polite about it had it not been this particular night. They hadn't broken away from the hilarious mobs of classmates and relatives at New London to exchange discomfort with the master of a mill-town high school.

'Can we dance ?' they demanded.

A few minutes later Bill and Mae Purley were walking down the deck side by side. Life had met over the body of Al Fitzpatrick, engulfing him. The two clear voices:

'Perhaps you'll dance with me,' with the soft assurance of the moonlight itself, and: 'I'd love to,' were nothing that could be argued about, not by twice what Al Fitzpatrick pretended to be. The most consoling thought in Al's head was that they might be fought over.

What was it they said? Did you hear it? Can you remember? Later that night she remembered only his pale wavy hair and the long limbs that she followed around the dancing floor.

She was thin, a thin burning flame, colourless yet fresh. Her smile came first slowly, then with a rush, pouring out of her heart, shy and bold, as if all the life of that little body had gathered for a moment around her mouth and the rest of her was a wisp that the least wind would blow away. She was a changeling whose lips alone had escaped metamorphosis, whose lips were the only point of contact with reality.

'Then you live near?'

'Only about twenty-five miles from you,' Bill said. 'Isn't it funny?'

'Isn't it funny?'

They looked at each other, a trifle awed in the face of such manifest destiny. They stood between two lifeboats on the top deck. Mae's hand lay on his arm, playing with a loose ravel of his tweed coat. They had not kissed yet – that was coming in a minute. That was coming any time now, as soon as every cup of emotional moonlight had been drained of its possibilities and cast aside. She was seventeen.

'Are you glad I live near?'

She might have said 'I'm delighted' or 'Of course I am.' But she whispered, 'Yes; are you?'

'Mae – with an *e*,' he said and laughed in a husky whisper. Already they had a joke together. 'You look so darn beautiful.'

She accepted the compliment in silence, meeting his eyes. He pressed her to him by her merest elbow in a way that would have been impossible had she not been eager too. He never expected to see her after tonight.

'Mae.' His whisper was urgent. Mae's eyes came nearer, grew larger, dissolved against his face, like eyes on a screen. Her frail body breathed imperceptibly in his arms.

A dance stopped. There was clapping for an encore. Then clapping for another encore with what had seemed only a poor bar of music in between. There was another dance, scarcely longer than a kiss. They were heavily endowed for love, these two, and both of them had played with it before.

Down below, Al Fitzpatrick's awareness of time and space had reached a pitch that would have been invaluable to an investigator of the new mathematics. Bit by bit the boat presented itself to him as it really was, a wooden hulk garish with forty-watt bulbs, peopled by the commonplace young people of a commonplace town. The river was water, the moon was a flat meaningless symbol in the sky. He was in agony – which is to speak tritely. Rather, he was in deadly fear; his throat was dry, his mouth drooped into a hurt half moon as he tried to talk to some of the other boys – shy unhappy boys, who loitered around the stern.

Al was older than the rest – he was twenty-two, and out in the world for seven years. He worked in the Hammacker Mills and attended special high-school classes at night. Another year might see him assistant manager of the shops, and Mae Purley, with about as much eagerness as was to be expected in a girl who was having everything her own way, had half promised to marry him when she was eighteen. His wasn't a temperament to go to pieces. When he had brooded up to the limit of his nature he felt a necessity for action. Miserably and desperately he climbed up to the top deck to make trouble.

Bill and Mae were standing close together by the lifeboat, quiet, absorbed and happy. They moved a little apart as he came near. 'Is that you, Mae?' called Al in a hard voice. 'Aren't you going to come down and dance?'

'We were just coming.'

They walked towards him in a trance.

'What's the idea?' Al said hoarsely. 'You've been up here over two hours.'

At their indifference he felt pain swelling and spreading inside him, constricting his breath.

'Have you met Mr Frothington?' She laughed shyly at the unfamiliar name.

'Yeah,' said Al rudely. 'I don't see the idea of his keeping you up here.'

'I'm sorry,' said Bill. 'We didn't realize.'

'Oh, you didn't?' Well, I did.' His jealousy cut through their absorption. They acknowledged it by an effort to hurry, to be impersonal, to defer to his wishes. Ungraciously he followed and the three of them came in a twinkling upon a scene that had suddenly materialized on the deck below.

Ellsworth Ames, smiling, but a little flushed, was leaning against the rail while Ham Abbot attempted to argue with a distraught young husky who kept trying to brush past him and get at Ames. Near them stood an indignant girl with another girl's soothing arm around her waist.

'What is it?' demanded Bill quickly.

The distraught young man glared at him. 'Just a couple of snobs that come here and try to spoil everybody else's good time!' he cried wildly.

'He doesn't like me,' said Ellsworth lightly. 'I invited his girl to dance.'

'She didn't want to dance with you!' shouted the other. 'You think you're so damn smart – ask her if she wanted to dance with you.'

The girl murmured indistinguishable words and disclaimed all responsibility by beginning to cry.

'You're too fresh, that's the trouble!' continued her defender. 'I know what you said to her when you danced with her before. What do you think these girls are ? They're just as good as anybody, see ?'

Al Fitzpatrick moved in closer.

'Let's put 'em all off the boat,' he suggested, stubborn and ashamed. 'They haven't got any business butting in here.'

A mild protest went up from the crowd, especially from the girls, and Abbot put his hand conciliatingly on the husky's shoulder. But it was too late.

'You'll put me off?' Ellsworth was saying coldly. 'If you try to lay your hands on me I'll rearrange your whole face.'

'Shut up, Ellie!' snapped Bill. 'No use getting disagreeable. They don't want us; we'd better go.' He stepped close to Mae, and whispered, 'Good night. Don't forget what I said. I'll drive over and see you Sunday afternoon.'

As he presssed her hand quickly and turned away he saw the argumentative boy swing suddenly at Ames, who caught the blow with his left arm. In a moment they were slugging and panting, knee to knee in the shall space left by the gathering crowd. Simultaneously Bill felt a hand pluck at his sleeve and he turned to face Al Fitzpatrick. Then the deck was in an uproar. Abbot's attempt to separate Ames and his antagonist was misinterpreted; instantly he was involved in a battle of his own, cannonading against the other pairs, slipping on the smooth deck, bumping against noncombatants and scurrying girls who sent up shrill cries. He saw Al Fitzpatrick slap the deck suddenly with his whole body, not to rise again. He heard calls of 'Get Mr McVitty!' and then his own opponent was dropped by a blow he did not strike, and Bill's voice said: 'Come on to the boat!'

The next few minutes streaked by in wild confusion. Avoiding Bill, whose hammerlike arms had felled their two champions, the high-school boys tried to pull down Ham and Ellie, and the harassed group edged and revolved towards the stern rail.

'Hidden-ball stuff!' Bill panted. 'Save it for Haughton. I'm G-Gardner, you're Bradlee and Mahan – hip!'

Mr McVitty's alarmed face appeared above the combat, and his high voice, ineffectual at first, finally pierced the heat of battle.

'Aren't you ashamed of yourselves! Bob – Cecil – George Roberg! Let go, I say!'

Abruptly the battle was over and the combatants, breathing hard, eyed one another impassively in the moonlight.

Ellie laughed and held out a pack of cigarettes. Bill untied the motorboat and walked forward with the painter to bring it alongside.

'They claim you insulted one of the girls,' said Mr McVitty uncertainly. 'Now that's no way to behave after we took you aboard.'

'That's nonsense,' snapped Ellie, between gasps. 'I only told her I'd like to bite her neck.'

'Do you think that was a very gentlemanly thing to say?' demanded Mr McVitty heatedly.

'Come on, Ellie!' Bill cried. 'Good-bye, everybody! Sorry there was such a row!'

They were already shadows of the past as they slipped one by one over the rail. The girls were turning cautiously back to their own men, and not one of them answered, and not one of them waved farewell.

'A bunch of meanies,' remarked Ellie ironically. 'I wish all you ladies had one neck so I could bite it all at once. I'm a glutton for ladies' necks.'

Feeble retorts went up here and there like muffled pistol shots.

'*Good night, ladies,*' Ham sang, as Bill shoved away from the side:

Good night, ladies,
Good night, ladies,
We're going to leave you now-ow-ow.

The boat moved up the river through the summer night, while the launch, touched by its swell, rocked to and fro gently in the wide path of the moon.

II

On the following Sunday afternoon Bill Frothington drove over from Truro to the isolated rural slum known as Wheatly Village. He had stolen away from a house full of guests, assembled for his sister's wedding, to pursue what his mother would have called an 'unworthy affair'. But behind him lay an extremely successful career at Harvard and a youth somewhat more austere than the average, and this fall he would disappear for life into the banking house of Read, Hoppe and Company in Boston. He felt that the summer was his own. And had the purity of his intentions towards Mae Purley been questioned he would have defended himself with righteous anger. He had been thinking of her for five days. She attracted him violently, and he was following the attraction with eyes that did not ask to see.

Mae lived in the less offensive quarter of town on the third floor of its only apartment house, an unsuccessful relic of those more prosperous days of New England textile weaving that ended twenty years ago. Her father was a timekeeper who had fallen out of the white-collar class; Mae's two older brothers were working at the loom, and Bill's only impression as he entered the dingy flat was one of hopeless decay. The mountainous, soiled mother, at once suspicious and deferential, and the anaemic, beaten Anglo-Saxon asleep on the couch after his Sunday dinner were no more than shadows against the poor walls. But Mae was clean and fresh. No breath of squalor touched her. The pale pure youth of her cheeks, and her thin childish body shining through a new organdie dress, measured up full to the summer day.

'Where you going to take my little girl ?' Mrs Purley asked anxiously.

'I'm going to run away with her,' he said, laughing.

'Not with my little girl.'

'Oh, yes, I am. I don't see why she hasn't been run away with before.'

'Not my little girl.'

They held hands going downstairs, but not for an hour did the feeling of being intimate strangers pass. When the first promise of evening blew into the air at five o'clock and the light changed from white to yellow, their eyes met once in a certain way and Bill knew that it was time. They turned up a side road and down a wagon track, and in a moment the spell was around them again – the equal and opposite urge that drew them together. They talked about each other and then their voices grew quiet and they kissed, while chestnut blossoms slid in white diagonals through the air and fell across the car. After a long while an instinct told her that they had stayed long enough. He drove her home.

It went on like that for two months. He would come for her in the late afternoon and they would go for dinner to the shore. Afterwards they would drive around until they found the centre of the summer night and park there while the enchanted silence spread over them like leaves over the babes in the wood. Some day, naturally, they were going to marry. For the present it was impossible; he must go to work in the fall. Vaguely and with more than a touch of sadness both of them realized that this wasn't true; that if Mae had been of another class an engagement would have been arranged at once. She knew that he lived in a great country house with a park and a caretaker's lodge, that there were stables full of cars and horses, and that house parties and dances took place there all summer. Once they had driven past the gate and Mae's heart was leaden in her breast as she saw that those wide acres would lie between them all her life.

On his part Bill knew that it was impossible to marry Mae Purley. He was an only son and he wore one of those New England names that are carried with one always. Eventually he broached the subject to his mother.

'It isn't her poverty and ignorance,' his mother said, among other things. 'It's her lack of any standards – common women are common for life. You'd see her impressed by cheap and shallow people, by cheap and shallow things.'

'But, Mother, this isn't 1850. It isn't as if she were marrying into the royal family.'

'If it were, it wouldn't matter. But you have a name that for many generations has stood for leadership and self-control. People who have given up less and taken fewer responsibilities have had nothing to say aloud when men like your father and your Uncle George and your Great-grandfather Frothington held their heads high. Toss your pride away and see what you've left at thirty-five to take you through the rest of your life.'

'But you can only live once,' he protested – knowing, nevertheless, that what she said was, for him, right. His youth had been pointed to make him understand that exposition of superiority. He knew what it was to be the best, at home, at school, at Harvard. In his senior year he had known men to dodge behind a building and wait in order to walk with him across the Harvard Yard, not to be seen with him out of mere poor snobbishness, but to get something intangible, something he carried within him of the less obvious, less articulate experience of the race.

Several days later he went to see Mae and met her coming out of the flat. They sat on the stairs in the half darkness.

'Just think of these stairs,' he said huskily. 'Think how many times you've kissed me on these stairs. At night when I've brought you home. On every landing. Last month when we walked up and down together five times before we could say good night.'

'I hate these stairs. I wish I never had to go up them any more.'

'Oh, Mae, what are we doing to do?'

She didn't answer for a moment. 'I've been thinking a lot these last three days,' she said. 'I don't think it's fair to myself to go on like this – or to Al.'

'To Al,' he said startled. 'Have you been seeing Al?'

'We had a long talk last night.'

'Al!' he repeated incredulously.

'He wants to get married. He isn't mad any more.'

Bill tried suddenly to face the situation he had been dodging for two months, but the situation, with practised facility, slid around the corner. He moved up a step till he was beside Mae, and put his arm around her.

'Oh, let's get married!' she cried desperately. 'You can. If you want to, you can.'

'I do want to.'

'Then why can't we?'

'We can, but not yet.'

'Oh, God, you've said that before.'

For a tragic week they quarrelled and came together over the bodies of unresolved arguments and irreconcilable facts. They parted finally on a trivial question as to whether he had once kept her waiting half an hour.

Bill went to Europe on the first possible boat and enlisted in an ambulance unit. When America went into the war he transferred to the aviation and Mae's pale face and burning lips faded off, faded out, against the wild dark background of the war.

III

In 1919 Bill fell romantically in love with a girl of his own set. He met her on the Lido and wooed her on golf courses and in fashionable speakeasies and in cars parked at night, loving her much more from the first than he had ever loved Mae. She was a better person, prettier and more intelligent and with a kindlier heart. She loved him; they had much the same tastes and more than ample money.

There was a child, after a while there were four children, then only three again. Bill grew a little stout after thirty, as athletes will. He was always going to take up something strenuous and get into real condition. He worked hard and drank a little too freely every weekend. Later he inherited the country house and lived there in the summer.

When he and Stella had been married eight years they felt safe for each other, safe from the catastrophes that had overtaken the majority of their friends. To Stella this brought relief; Bill, once he had accepted the idea of their safety, was conscious of a certain discontent, a sort of chemical restlessness. With a feeling of disloyalty to Stella, he shyly sounded his friends on the subject and found that in men of his age the symptoms were almost universal. Some blamed it on the war: 'There'll never be anything like the war.'

It was not variety of woman that he wanted. The mere idea appalled him. There were always women around. If he took a fancy to someone Stella invited her for a weekend, and men who liked Stella fraternally, or even somewhat sentimentally, were as often in the house. But the feeling persisted and grew stronger. Sometimes it would steal over him at dinner – a vast nostalgia – and the people at table would fade out and odd memories of his youth would come back to him. Sometimes a familiar taste or a smell would give him this sensation. Chiefly it had to do with the summer night.

One evening, walking down the lawn with Stella after dinner, the feeling seemed so close that he could almost grasp it. It was in the rustle of the pines, in the wind, in the gardener's radio down behind the tennis court.

'Tomorrow,' Stella said, 'there'll be a full moon.'

She had stopped in a broad path of moonlight and was looking at him. Her hair was pale and lovely in the gentle light. She regarded him for a moment oddly, and he took a step forward as if to put his arms around her; then he stopped, unresponsive and dissatisfied. Stella's expression changed slightly and they walked on.

'That's too bad,' he said suddenly. 'Because tomorrow I've got to go away.'

'Where?'

'To New York. Meeting of the trustees of school. Now that the kids are entered I feel I should.'

'You'll be back Sunday?'

'Unless something comes up and I telephone.'

'Ad Haughton's coming Sunday, and maybe the Ameses.'

'I'm glad you won't be alone.'

Suddenly Bill had remembered the boat floating down the river and Mae Purley on the deck under the summer moon. The image became a symbol of his youth, his introduction to life. Not only did he remember the deep excitement of that night but felt it again, her face against his, the rush of air about them as they stood by the lifeboat and the feel of its canvas cover to his hand.

When his car dropped him at Wheatly Village next afternoon he experienced a sensation of fright. Eleven years – she might be dead; quite possibly she had moved away. Any moment he might pass her on the street, a tired, already faded woman pushing a baby carriage and leading an extra child.

'I'm looking for a Miss Mae Purley,' he said to a taxi driver. 'It might be Fitzpatrick now.'

'Fitzpatrick up at the works?'

Inquiries within the station established the fact that Mae Purley was indeed Mrs Fitzpatrick. They lived just outside of town.

Ten minutes later the taxi stopped before a white Colonial house.

'They made it over from a barn,' volunteered the taxi man. 'There was a picture of it in one of them magazines.'

Bill saw that someone was regarding him from behind the screen door. It was Mae. The door opened slowly and she stood in the hall, unchanged, slender as of old. Instinctively he raised his arms and then, as he took another step forward, instinctively he lowered them.

'Mae.'

'Bill.'

She was there. For a moment he possessed her, her frailty, her thin smouldering beauty; then he had lost her again. He could no more have embraced her than he could have embraced a stranger.

On the sun porch they stared at each other. 'You haven't changed,' they said together.

It was gone from her. Words, casual, trivial, and insincere, poured from her mouth as if to fill the sudden vacancy in his heart:

'Imagine seeing you – know you anywhere – thought you'd forgotten me – talking about you only the other night.'

Suddenly he was without any inspiration. His mind became an utter blank, and try as he might, he could summon up no attitude to fill it.

'It's a nice place you have here,' he said stupidly.

'We like it. You'd never guess it, but we made it out of an old barn.'

'The taxi driver told me.'

'—stood here for a hundred years empty – got it for almost nothing – pictures of it before and after in *Home and Country Side*.'

Without warning his mind went blank again. What was the matter? Was he sick? He had even forgotten why he was here.

He knew only that he was smiling benevolently and that he must hang on to that smile, for if it passed he could never recreate it. What did it mean when one's mind went blank? He must see a doctor tomorrow.

'—since Al's done so well. Of course Mr Kohlsatt leans on him, so he don't get away much. I get away to New York sometimes. Sometimes we both get away together.'

'Well, you certainly have a nice place here,' he said desperately. He must see a doctor in the morning. Doctor Flynn or Doctor Keyes or Doctor Given who was at Harvard with him. Or perhaps that specialist who was recommended to him by that woman at the Ameses'; or Doctor Gross or Doctor Studeford or Doctor de Martel—

'—I never touch it, but Al always keeps something in the house. Al's gone to Boston, but I think I can find the key.'

—or Doctor Ramsay or old Doctor Ogden, who had brought him into the world. He hadn't realized that he knew so many doctors. He must make a list.

'—you're just exactly the same.'

Suddenly Bill put both hands on his stomach, gave a short coarse laugh and said, 'Not here.' His own act startled and surprised him, but it dissipated the blankness for a moment and he began to gather up the pieces of his afternoon. From her chatter he discovered her to be under the impression that in some vague and sentimental past she had thrown him over. Perhaps she was right. Who was she anyhow – this hard, commonplace article wearing Mae's body for a mask of life ? Defiance rose in him.

'Mae, I've been thinking about that boat,' he said desperately.

'What boat ?'

'The steamboat on the Thames, Mae. I don't think we should let ourselves get old. Get your hat, Mae. Let's go for a boat ride tonight.'

'But I don't see the point,' she protested. 'Do you think just riding on a boat keeps people young ? Maybe if it was salt water—'

'Don't you remember that night on the boat ?' he said, as if he were talking to a child. 'That's how we met. Two months later you threw me over and married Al Fitzpatrick.'

'But I didn't marry Al then,' she said. 'It wasn't till two years later when he got a job as superintendent. There was a Harvard man I used to go around with that I almost married. He knew you. His name was Abbot – Ham Abbot.'

'Ham Abbot – you saw him again ?'

'We went around for almost a year. I remember Al was wild. He said if I had any more Harvard men around he'd shoot them. But there wasn't anything wrong with it. Ham was just cuckoo about me and I used to let him rave.'

Bill had read somewhere that every seven years a change is completed in the individual that makes him different from his self of seven years ago.

He clung to the idea desperately. Dimly he saw this person pouring him an enormous glass of applejack, dimly he gulped it down and, through a description of the house, fought his way to the front door.

'Notice the original beams. The beams were what we liked best—' She broke off suddenly. 'I remember now about the boat. You were in a launch and you got on board with Ham Abbot that night.'

The applejack was strong. Evidently it was fragrant also, for as they started off, the taxi driver volunteered to show him where the gentleman could get some more. He would give him a personal introduction in a place down by the wharf.

Bill sat at a dingy table behind swinging doors and, while the sun went down behind the Thames, disposed of four more applejacks. Then he remembered that he was keeping the taxi waiting. Outside a boy told him that the driver had gone home to supper and would be back in half an hour.

He sauntered over to a bale of goods and sat down, watching the mild activity of the docks. It was dusk presently. Stevedores appeared momentarily against the lighted hold of a barge and jerked quickly out of sight down an invisible incline. Next to the barge lay a steamer and people were going aboard; first a few people and then an increasing crowd. There was a breeze in the air and the moon came up rosy gold with a haze around.

Someone ran into him precipitately in the darkness, tripped, swore and staggered to his feet.

'I'm sorry,' said Bill cheerfully. 'Hurt yourself?'

'Pardon me,' stuttered the young man. 'Did I hurt you?'

'Not at all. Here, have a light.'

They touched cigarettes.

'Where's the boat going?'

'Just down the river. It's the high-school picnic tonight.'

'What?'

'The Wheatly High School picnic. The boat goes down to Groton, then it turns around and comes back.'

Bill thought quickly. 'Who's the principal of the high school?'

'Mr McVitty.' The young man fidgeted impatiently. 'So long, bud. I got to go aboard.'

'Me too,' whispered Bill to himself. 'Me too.'

Still he sat there lazily for a moment, listening to the sounds clear and distinct now from the open deck: the high echolalia of the girls, the boys calling significant but obscure jokes to one another across the night. He was feeling fine. The air seemed to have distributed the applejack to all the rusty and unused corners of his body. He bought another pint, stowed it in his hip pocket and walked on board with all the satisfaction, the insouciance of a transatlantic traveller.

A girl standing in a group near the gangplank raised her eyes to him as he went past. She was slight and fair. Her mouth curved down and then broke upward as she smiled, half at him, half at the man beside her. Someone made a remark and the group laughed. Once again her glance slipped sideways and met his for an instant as he passed by.

Mr McVitty was on the top deck with half a dozen other teachers, who moved aside at Bill's breezy approach.

'Good evening, Mr McVitty. You don't remember me.'

'I'm afraid I don't, sir.' The principal regarded him with tentative noncommittal eyes.

'Yet I took a trip with you on this same boat, exactly eleven years ago tonight.'

'This boat, sir, was only built last year.'

'Well, a boat like it,' said Bill. 'I wouldn't have known the difference myself.'

Mr McVitty made no reply. After a moment Bill continued confidently, 'We found that night that we were both sons of John Harvard.'

'Yes ?'

'In fact on that very day I had been pulling an oar against what I might refer to as dear old Yale.'

Mr McVitty's eyes narrowed. He came closer to Bill and his nose wrinkled slightly.

'Old Eli,' said Bill; 'in fact, Eli Yale.'

'I see,' said Mr McVitty dryly. 'And what can I do for you tonight ?'

Someone came up with a question and in the enforced silence it occurred to Bill that he was present on the slightest of all pretexts – a previous and unacknowledged acquaintance. He was relieved when a dull rumble and a quiver of the deck indicated that they had left the shore.

Mr McVitty, disengaged, turned towards him with a slight frown. 'I seem to remember you now,' he said. 'We took three of you aboard from a motorboat and we let you dance. Unfortunately the evening ended in a fight.'

Bill hesitated. In eleven years his relation to Mr McVitty had somehow changed. He recalled Mr McVitty as a more negligible, more easily dealt with person. There had been no such painful difficulties before.

'Perhaps you wonder how I happen to be here ?' he suggested mildly.

'To be frank, I do, Mr—'

'Frothington,' supplied Bill, and he added brazenly, 'It's rather a sentimental excursion for me. My greatest romance began on the evening you speak of. That was when I first met – my wife.'

Mr McVitty's attention was caught at last. 'You married one of our girls ?'

Bill nodded. 'That's why I wanted to take this trip tonight.'

'Your wife's with you ?'

'No.'

'I don't understand—' He broke off, and suggested gently, 'Or maybe I do. Your wife is dead ?'

After a moment Bill nodded. Somewhat to his surprise two great tears rolled suddenly down his face.

Mr McVitty put his hand on Bill's shoulder. 'I'm sorry,' he said. 'I understand your feeling, Mr Frothington, and I respect it. Please make yourself at home.'

After a nibble at his bottle Bill stood in the door of the *salon* watching the dance. It might have been eleven years ago. There were the high-school characters that he and Ham and Ellie had laughed at afterwards – the fat boy who surely played centre on the football team and the adolescent hero with the pompadour and the blatant good manners, president of his class. The pretty girl who had looked at him by the gangplank danced past him, and with a quick lift of his heart he placed her, too; her confidence and the wide but careful distribution of her favours – she was the popular girl, as Mae had been eleven years before.

Next time she went past he touched the shoulder of the boy she was dancing with. 'May I have some of this ?' he said.

'What ?' her partner gasped.

'May I have some of this dance ?'

The boy stared at him without relinquishing his hold.

'Oh, it's all right, Red,' she said impatiently. 'That's the way they do now.'

Red stepped sulkily aside. Bill bent his arm as nearly as he could into the tortuous clasp that they were all using, and started.

'I saw you talking to Mr McVitty,' said the girl, looking up into his face with a bright smile. 'I don't know you, but I guess it's all right.'

'I saw you before that.'

'When ?'

'Getting on the boat.'

'I don't remember.'

'What's your name?' he asked.

'May Schaffer. What's the matter?'

'Do you spell it with an *e*?'

'No; why?'

A quartet of boys had edged towards them. One of its members suddenly shot out as if propelled from inside the group and bumped awkwardly against Bill.

'Can I have part of this dance?' asked the boy with a sort of giggle.

Without enthusiasm Bill let go. When the next dance began he cut in again. She was lovely. Her happiness in herself, in the evening, would have transfigured a less pretty girl. He wanted to talk to her alone and was about to suggest that they go outside when there was a repetition of what had happened before – a young man was apparently shot by force from a group to Bill's side.

'Can I have part of this dance?'

Bill joined Mr McVitty by the rail. 'Pleasant evening,' he remarked. 'Don't you dance?'

'I enjoy dancing,' said Mr McVitty; and he added pointedly, 'In my position it doesn't seem quite the thing to dance with young girls.'

'That's nonsense,' said Bill pleasantly. 'Have a drink?'

Mr McVitty walked suddenly away.

When he danced with May again he was cut in on almost immediately. People were cutting in all over the floor now – evidently he had started something. He cut back, and again he started to suggest that they go outside, but he saw that her attention was held by some horseplay going on across the room.

'I got a swell love nest up in the Bronx,' somebody was saying.

'Won't you come outside?' said Bill. 'There's the most wonderful moon.'

'I'd rather dance.'

'We could dance out there.'

She leaned away from him and looked up with innocent scorn into his eyes.

'Where'd you get it?' she said.

'Get what?'

'All the happiness.'

Before he could answer, someone cut in. For a moment he imagined that the boy had said, 'Part of this dance, daddy?' but his annoyance at May's indifference drove the idea from his mind. Next time he went to the point at once.

'I live near here,' he said. 'I'd be awfully pleased if I could call and drive you over for a weekend sometime.'

'What?' she asked vaguely. Again she was listening to a miniature farce being staged in the corner.

'My wife would like so much to have you,' went on Bill. Great dreams of what he could do for this girl for old times' sake rose in his mind.

Her head swung towards him curiously. 'Why, Mr McVitty told somebody your wife was dead.'

'She isn't,' said Bill.

Out of the corner of his eye he saw the inevitable catapult coming and danced quickly away from it.

A voice rang out: 'Just look at old daddy step.'

'Ask him if I can have some of this dance.'

Afterwards Bill only remembered the evening up to that point. A crowd swirled around him and someone kept demanding persistently who was a young boiler maker.

He decided, naturally enough, to teach them a lesson, as he had done before, and he told them so. Then there was a long discussion as to whether he could swim. After that the confusion deepened; there were blows and a short sharp struggle. He picked up the story himself in what must have been several minutes later, when his head emerged from the cool waters of the Thames River.

The river was white with the moon, which had changed from rosy gold to a wafer of shining cheese on high. It was some time before he could locate the direction of the shore, but he moved around unworried in the water. The boat was a mere speck now, far down the river, and he laughed to think how little it all mattered, how little anything mattered. Then, feeling sure that he had his wind and wondering if the taxi was still waiting at Wheatly Village, he struck out for the dark shore.

IV

He was worried as he drew near home next afternoon, possessed of a dark, unfounded fear. It was based, of course, on his own silly transgression. Stella would somehow hear of it. In his reaction from the debonair confidence of last night, it seemed inevitable that Stella would hear of it.

'Who's here?' he asked the butler immediately.

'No one, sir. The Ameses came about an hour ago, but there was no word, so they went on. They said—'

'Isn't my wife here?'

'Mrs Frothington left yesterday just after you.'

The whips of panic descended upon him.

'How long after me?'

'Almost immediately, sir. The telephone rang and she answered it, and almost immediately she had her bag packed and left the house.'

'Mr Ad Haughton didn't come?'

'I haven't seen Mr Haughton.'

It had happened. The spirit of adventure had seized Stella too. He knew that her life had been not without a certain pressure from sentimental men, but that she would ever go anywhere without telling him—

He threw himself face downward on a couch. What had happened? He had never meant things to happen. Was that what she had meant when she had looked at him in that peculiar way the other night?

He went upstairs. Almost as soon as he entered the big bedroom he saw the note, written on blue stationery lest he miss it against the white pillow. In his misery an old counsel of his mother's came back to him: 'The more terrible things seem the more you've got to keep yourself in shape.'

Trembling, he divested himself of his clothes, turned on a bath and lathered his face. Then he poured himself a drink and shaved. It was like a dream, this change in his life. She was no longer his; even if she came back she was no longer his. Everything was different – this room, himself, everything that had existed yesterday. Suddenly he wanted it back. He got out of the bathtub and knelt down on the bath mat beside it and prayed. He prayed for Stella and himself and Ad Haughton; he prayed crazily for the restoration of his life – the life that he had just as crazily cut in two. When he came out of the bathroom with a towel around him, Ad Haughton was sitting on the bed.

'Hello, Bill. Where's your wife?'

'Just a minute,' Bill answered. He went back into the bathroom and swallowed a draught of rubbing alcohol guaranteed to produce violent gastric disturbances. Then he stuck his head out of the door casually.

'Mouthful of gargle,' he explained. 'How are you, Ad? Open that envelope on the pillow and we'll see where she is.'

'She's gone to Europe with a dentist. Or rather her dentist is going to Europe, so she had to dash to New York—'

He hardly heard. His mind, released from worry, had drifted off again. There would be a full moon tonight, or almost a full moon. Something had happened under a full moon once. What it was he was unable for the moment to remember.

His long, lanky body, his little lost soul in the universe, sat there on the bathroom window seat.

'I'm probably the world's worst guy,' he said, shaking his head at himself in the mirror – 'probably the world's worst guy. But I can't help it. At my age you can't fight against what you know you are.'

Trying his best to be better, he sat there faithfully for an hour. Then it was twilight and there were voices downstairs, and suddenly there it was, in the sky over his lawn, all the restless longing after fleeing youth in all the world – the bright uncapturable moon.

THE BOWL

Saturday Evening Post, 21 January 1928*

*'The Bowl' was written in September–November 1927 at Ellerslie. It
began as what Fitzgerald described as a 'two part sophisticated football
story' and gave him considerable trouble as he tried to rush it for publication
during the football season. After Fitzgerald cut it, Thomas Costain, fiction
editor of the* Post, *was happy to buy it for $3500, informing Harold Ober
that Fitzgerald had 'got the real spirit of the game as it has perhaps never
been done before'.*

*Given Fitzgerald's dreams of gridiron glory ('the shoulder pads worn for
one day on the Princeton freshman football field') and his admiration for the
Ivy League football gods of his youth (Hobey Baker and Buz Law of
Princeton and Ted Coy of Yale), it is surprising that he did not write more
football fiction. The game as it was played before the First World War
appealed to his romantic instincts – a gentleman's sport dominated by Ivy
League aristocrats. Fitzgerald's second story, 'Reade, Substitute Right Half'
(St Paul Academy Now and Then, February 1910) expressed Fitzgerald's
hopes for football recognition; but except for two Basil stories with football
scenes, 'The Bowl' is Fitzgerald's only professionally published football story.
This story is also about something else: Fitzgerald's respect for disciplined
young women. Daisy Cary, the actress, is a proper mate for Dolly Harlan
because she understands the responsibilities of being a public figure. Daisy is
obviously a trial sketch for Rosemary Hoyt of* Tender Is the Night,
*for both were based on Lois Moran, the actress Fitzgerald met in
Hollywood in 1927.*

There was a man in my class at Princeton who never went to football
games. He spent his Saturday afternoons delving for minutiae about

---

*'The Bowl' is in *The Bodley Head Scott Fitzgerald*, Vol. V (London: Bodley
Head, 1963) but has not been collected in an American edition.

Greek athletics and the somewhat fixed battles between Christians and wild beasts under the Antonines. Lately – several years out of college – he has discovered football players and is making etchings of them in the manner of the late George Bellows. But he was once unresponsive to the very spectacle at his door, and I suspect the originality of his judgements on what is beautiful, what is remarkable and what is fun.

I revelled in football, as audience, amateur statistician and foiled participant – for I had played in prep school, and once there was a headline in the school newspaper: 'Deering and Mullins Star Against Taft in Stiff Game Saturday'. When I came in to lunch after the battle the school stood up and clapped and the visiting coach shook hands with me and prophesied – incorrectly – that I was going to be heard from. The episode is laid away in the most pleasant lavender of my past. That year I grew very tall and thin, and when at Princeton the following fall I looked anxiously over the freshman candidates and saw the polite disregard with which they looked back at me, I realized that that particular dream was over. Keene said he might make me into a very fair pole vaulter – and he did – but it was a poor substitute; and my terrible disappointment that I wasn't going to be a great football player was probably the foundation of my friendship with Dolly Harlan. I want to begin this story about Dolly with a little rehashing of the Yale game up at New Haven, sophomore year.

Dolly was started at half back; this was his first big game. I roomed with him and I had scented something peculiar about his state of mind, so I didn't let him out of the corner of my eye during the whole first half. With field glasses I could see the expression on his face; it was strained and incredulous, as it had been the day of his father's death, and it remained so, long after any nervousness had had time to wear off. I thought he was sick and wondered why Keene didn't see and take him out; it wasn't until later that I learned what was the matter.

It was the Yale Bowl. The size of it or the inclosed shape of it or the height of the sides had begun to get on Dolly's nerves when the team practised there the day before. In that practice he dropped one or two punts, for almost the first time in his life, and he began thinking it was because of the Bowl.

There is a new disease called agoraphobia – afraid of crowds – and another called siderodromophobia – afraid of railroad travelling – and my friend Doctor Glock, the psychoanalyst, would probably account easily for Dolly's state of mind. But here's what Dolly told me afterwards:

'Yale would punt and I'd look up. The minute I looked up, the sides of that damn pan would seem to go shooting up too. Then when the ball started to come down, the sides began leaning forward and bending over me until I could see all the people on the top seats screaming at me and shaking their fists. At the last minute I couldn't see the ball at all, but only the Bowl; every time it was just luck that I was under it and every time I juggled it in my hands.'

To go back to the game. I was in the cheering section with a good seat on the forty-yard line – good, that is, except when a very vague graduate, who had lost his friends and his hat, stood up in front of me at intervals and faltered, 'Stob Ted Coy!' under the impression that we were watching a game played a dozen years before. When he realized finally that he was funny he began performing for the gallery and roused a chorus of whistles and boos until he was dragged unwillingly under the stand.

It was a good game – what is known in college publications as a historic game. A picture of the team that played it now hangs in every barber shop in Princeton, with Captain Gottlieb in the middle wearing a white sweater, to show that they won a championship. Yale had had a poor season, but they had the breaks in the first quarter, which ended 3 to 0 in their favour.

Between quarters I watched Dolly. He walked around panting and sucking a water bottle and still wearing that strained stunned expression. Afterwards he told me he was saying over and over to himself: 'I'll speak to Roper. I'll tell him between halves. I'll tell him I can't go through this any more.' Several times already he had felt an almost irresistible impulse to shrug his shoulders and trot off the field, for it was not only this un-expected complex about the Bowl; the truth was that Dolly fiercely and bitterly hated the game.

He hated the long, dull period of training, the element of personal con-flict, the demand on his time, the monotony of the routine and the nervous apprehension of disaster just before the end. Sometimes he imagined that all the others detested it as much as he did, and fought down their aversion as he did and carried it around inside them like a cancer that they were afraid to recognize. Sometimes he imagined that a man here and there was about to tear off the mask and say, 'Dolly, do you hate this lousy business as much as I do?'

His feeling had begun back at St Regis' School and he had come up to Princeton with the idea that he was through with football for ever. But upper classmen from St Regis kept stopping him on the campus and asking him how much he weighed, and he was nominated for vice-president of our class on the strength of his athletic reputation – and it was autumn, with achievement in the air. He wandered down to freshman practice one afternoon, feeling oddly lost and dissatisfied, and smelled the turf and smelled the thrilling season. In half an hour he was lacing on a pair of borrowed shoes and two weeks later he was captain of the freshman team.

Once committed, he saw that he had made a mistake; he even considered leaving college. For, with his decision to play, Dolly assumed a moral responsibility, personal to him, besides. To lose or to let down, or to be let down, was simply intolerable to him. It offended his Scot's sense of waste. Why sweat blood for an hour with only defeat at the end?

Perhaps the worst of it was that he wasn't really a star player. No team in the country could have spared using him, but he could do no spectacular thing superlatively well, neither run, pass nor kick. He was five-feet-eleven and weighed a little more than a hundred and sixty; he was a first-rate defensive man, sure in interference, a fair line plunger and a fair punter. He never fumbled and he was never inadequate; his presence, his constant cold sure aggression, had a strong effect on other men. Morally, he captained any team he played on and that was why Roper had spent so much time trying to get length in his kicks all season – he wanted him in the game.

In the second quarter Yale began to crack. It was a mediocre team composed of flashy material, but uncoordinated because of injuries and impending changes in the Yale coaching system. The quarterback, Josh Logan, had been a wonder at Exeter – I could testify to that – where games can be won by the sheer confidence and spirit of a single man. But college teams are too highly organized to respond so simply and boyishly, and they recover less easily from fumbles and errors of judgement behind the line.

So, with nothing to spare, with much grunting and straining, Princeton moved steadily down the field. On the Yale twenty-yard line things suddenly happened. A Princeton pass was intercepted; the Yale man, excited by his own opportunity, dropped the ball and it bobbed leisurely in the general direction of the Yale goal. Jack Devlin and Dolly Harlan of Princeton and somebody – I forget who – from Yale were all about the same distance from it. What Dolly did in that split second was all instinct; it presented no problem to him. He was a natural athlete and in a crisis his nervous system thought for him. He might have raced the two others for the ball; instead, he took out the Yale man with savage precision while Devlin scooped up the ball and ran ten yards for a touchdown.

This was when the sports writers still saw games through the eyes of Ralph Henry Barbour. The press box was right behind me, and as Princeton lined up to kick goal I heard the radio man ask:

'Who's Number Twenty-two?'

'Harlan.'

'Harlan is going to kick goal. Devlin, who made the touchdown, comes from Lawrenceville School. He is twenty years old. The ball went true between the bars.'

Between the halves, as Dolly sat shaking with fatigue in the locker room, Little, the back-field coach, came and sat beside him.

'When the ends are right on you, don't be afraid to make a fair catch,' Little said. 'That big Havemeyer is liable to jar the ball right out of your hands.'

Now was the time to say it: 'I wish you'd tell Bill—' But the words twisted themselves into a trivial question about the wind. His feeling would have to be explained, gone into, and there wasn't time. His own self seemed less important in this room, redolent with the tired breath, the ultimate effort, the exhaustion of ten other men. He was shamed by a harsh sudden quarrel that broke out between an end and tackle; he resented the former players in the room – especially the graduate captain of two years before, who was a little tight and over-vehement about the referee's favouritism. It seemed terrible to add one more jot to all this train and annoyance. But he might have come out with it all the same if Little hadn't kept saying in a low voice: 'What a take-out, Dolly! What a beautiful take-out!' and if Little's hand hadn't rested there, patting his shoulder.

II

In the third quarter Joe Dougherty kicked an easy field goal from the twenty-yard line and we felt safe, until towards twilight a series of desperate forward passes brought Yale close to a score. But Josh Logan had exhausted his personality in sheer bravado and he was outguessed by the defence at the last. As the substitutes came running in, Princeton began a last march down the field. Then abruptly it was over and the crowd poured from the stands, and Gottlieb, grabbing the ball, leaped up in the air. For a while everything was confused and crazy and happy; I saw some freshmen try to carry Dolly, but they were shy and he got away.

We all felt a great personal elation. We hadn't beaten Yale for three years and now everything was going to be all right. It meant a good winter at college, something pleasant and slick to think back upon in the damp cold days after Christmas, when a bleak futility settles over a university town. Down on the field, an improvised and uproarious team ran through plays with a derby, until the snake dance rolled over them and blotted them out. Outside the Bowl, I saw two abysmally gloomy and disgusted Yale men get into a waiting taxi and in a tone of final abnegation tell the driver, 'New York.' You couldn't find Yale men; in the manner of the vanquished, they had absolutely melted away.

I begin Dolly's story with my memories of this game because that evening the girl walked into it. She was a friend of Josephine Pickman's and the four of us were going to drive up to the Midnight Frolic in New York. When I suggested to him that he'd be too tired he laughed drily – he'd have gone anywhere that night to get the feel and rhythm of football out of his head. He walked into the hall of Josephine's house at half past six, looking as if he'd spent the day in the barber shop save for a small and fetching strip of court plaster over one eye. He was one of the handsomest men I ever knew, anyhow; he appeared tall and slender in street clothes, his hair was dark, his eyes big and sensitive and dark, his nose aquiline and, like all his features, somehow romantic. It didn't occur to me then, but I suppose he was pretty vain – not conceited, but vain – for he always dressed in brown or soft light grey, with black ties, and people don't match themselves so successfully by accident.

He was smiling a little to himself as he came in. He shook my hand buoyantly and said, 'Why, what a surprise to meet you here, Mr Deering,' in a kidding way. Then he saw the two girls through the long hall, one dark and shining, like himself, and one with gold hair that was foaming and frothing in the firelight, and said in the happiest voice I've ever heard, 'Which one is mine ?'

'Either you want, I guess.'

'Seriously, which is Pickman ?'

'She's light.'

'Then the other one belongs to me. Isn't that the idea ?'

'I think I'd better warn them about the state you're in.'

Miss Thorne, small, flushed and lovely, stood beside the fire. Dolly went right up to her.

'You're mine,' he said; 'you belong to me.'

She looked at him coolly, making up her mind; suddenly she liked him and smiled. But Dolly wasn't satisfied. He wanted to do something incredibly silly or startling to express his untold jubilation that he was free.

'I love you,' he said. He took her hand, his brown velvet eyes regarding her tenderly, unseeingly, convincingly. 'I love you.'

For a moment the corners of her lips fell as if in dismay that she had met someone stronger, more confident, more challenging than herself. Then, as she drew herself together visibly, he dropped her hand and the little scene in which he had expended the tension of the afternoon was over.

It was a bright cold November night and the rush of air past the open car brought a vague excitement, a sense that we were hurrying at top speed towards a brilliant destiny. The roads were packed with cars that came to long inexplicable halts while police, blinded by the lights, walked up and down the line giving obscure commands. Before we had been gone an hour New York began to be a distant hazy glow against the sky.

Miss Thorne, Josephine told me, was from Washington, and had just come down from a visit in Boston.

'For the game?' I said.

'No; she didn't go to the game.'

'That's too bad. If you'd let me know I could have picked up a seat—'

'She wouldn't have gone. Vienna never goes to games.'

I remembered now that she hadn't even murmured the conventional congratulations to Dolly.

'She hates football. Her brother was killed in a prep-school game last year. I wouldn't have brought her tonight, but when we got home from the game I saw she'd been sitting there holding a book open at the same page all afternoon. You see, he was this wonderful kid and her family saw it happen and naturally never got over it.'

'But does she mind being with Dolly?'

'Of course not. She just ignores football. If anyone mentions it she simply changes the subject.'

I was glad that it was Dolly and not, say, Jack Devlin who was sitting back there with her. And I felt rather sorry for Dolly. However strongly he felt about the game, he must have waited for some acknowledgement that his effort had existed.

He was probably giving her credit for a subtle consideration, yet, as the images of the afternoon flashed into his mind he might have welcomed a compliment to which he could respond, 'What nonsense!' Neglected entirely, the images would become insistent and obtrusive.

I turned around and was somewhat startled to find that Miss Thorne was in Dolly's arms; I turned quickly back and decided to let them take care of themselves.

As we waited for a traffic light on upper Broadway, I saw a sporting extra headlined with the score of the game. The green sheet was more real than the afternoon itself – succinct, condensed and clear:

PRINCETON CONQUERS YALE 10–3

SEVENTY THOUSAND WATCH TIGER TRIM

BULLDOG

DEVLIN SCORES ON YALE FUMBLE

There it was – not like the afternoon, muddled, uncertain, patchy and scrappy to the end, but nicely mounted now in the setting of the past:

PRINCETON, 10; YALE, 3

Achievement was a curious thing, I thought. Dolly was largely responsible for that. I wondered if all things that screamed in the headlines were simply arbitrary accents. As if people should ask, 'What does it look like?'

'It looks most like a cat.'

'Well, then, let's call it a cat.'

My mind, brightened by the lights and the cheerful tumult, suddenly grasped the fact that all achievement was a placing of emphasis – a moulding of the confusion of life into form.

Josephine stopped in front of the New Amsterdam Theater, where her chauffeur met us and took the car. We were early, but a small buzz of excitement went up from the undergraduates waiting in the lobby – 'There's Dolly Harlan' – and as we moved towards the elevator several acquaintances came up to shake his hand. Apparently oblivious to these ceremonies, Miss Thorne caught my eye and smiled. I looked at her with curiosity; Josephine had imparted the rather surprising information that she was just sixteen years old. I suppose my return smile was rather patronizing, but instantly I realized that the fact could not be imposed on. In spite of all the warmth and delicacy of her face, the figure that somehow reminded me of an exquisite, romanticized little ballerina, there was a quality in her that was as hard as steel. She had been brought up in Rome, Vienna and Madrid, with flashes of Washington; her father was one of those charming American diplomats who, with fine obstinacy, try to recreate the Old World in their children by making their education rather more royal than that of princes. Miss Thorne was sophisticated. In spite of all the abandon of American young people, sophistication is still a Continental monopoly.

We walked in upon a number in which a dozen chorus girls in orange and black were racing wooden horses against another dozen dressed in Yale blue. When the lights went on, Dolly was recognized and some Princeton students set up a clatter of approval with the little wooden hammers given out for applause; he moved his chair unostentatiously into a shadow.

Almost immediately a flushed and very miserable young man appeared beside our table. In better form he would have been extremely pre-possessing; indeed, he flashed a charming and dazzling smile at Dolly, as if requesting his permission to speak to Miss Thorne.

Then he said, 'I thought you weren't coming to New York tonight.'

'Hello, Carl.' She looked up at him coolly.

'Hello, Vienna. That's just it; "Hello Vienna – Hello Carl." But why? I thought you weren't coming to New York tonight.'

Miss Thorne made no move to introduce the man, but we were conscious of his somewhat raised voice.

'I thought you promised me you weren't coming.'

'I didn't expect to, child. I just left Boston this morning.'

'And who did you meet in Boston – the fascinating Tunti?' he demanded.

'I didn't meet anyone, child.'

'Oh, yes, you did! You met the fascinating Tunti and you discussed living on the Riviera.' She didn't answer. 'Why are you so dishonest, Vienna?' he went on. 'Why did you tell me on the phone—'

'I am not going to be lectured,' she said, her tone changing suddenly. 'I told you if you took another drink I was through with you. I'm a person of my word and I'd be enormously happy if you went away.'

'Vienna!' he cried in a sinking, trembling voice.

At this point I got up and danced with Josephine. When we came back there were people at the table – the men to whom we were to hand over Josephine and Miss Thorne, for I had allowed for Dolly being tired, and several others. One of them was Al Ratoni, the composer, who, it appeared, had been entertained at the embassy in Madrid. Dolly Harlan had drawn his chair aside and was watching the dancers. Just as the lights went down for a new number a man came up out of the darkness and leaning over Miss Thorne whispered in her ear. She started and made a motion to rise, but he put his hand on her shoulder and forced her down. They began to talk together in low excited voices.

The tables were packed close at the old Frolic. There was a man rejoining the party next to us and I couldn't help hearing what he said:

'A young fellow just tried to kill himself down in the wash room. He shot himself through the shoulder, but they got the pistol away before—' A minute later his voice again: 'Carl Sanderson, they said.'

When the number was over I looked around. Vienna Thorne was staring very rigidly at Miss Lillian Lorraine, who was rising towards the ceiling as an enormous telephone doll. The man who had leaned over Vienna was gone and the others were obliviously unaware that anything had happened. I turned to Dolly and suggested that he and I had better go, and after a glance at Vienna in which reluctance, weariness and then resignation were mingled, he consented. On the way to the hotel I told Dolly what had happened.

'Just some souse,' he remarked after a moment's fatigued consideration. 'He probably tried to miss himself and get a little sympathy. I suppose those are the sort of things a really attractive girl is up against all the time.'

This wasn't my attitude. I could see that mussed white shirt front with very young blood pumping over it, but I didn't argue, and after a while Dolly said, 'I suppose that sounds brutal, but it seems a little soft and weak, doesn't it? Perhaps that's just the way I feel tonight.'

When Dolly undressed I saw that he was a mass of bruises, but he assured me that none of them would keep him awake. Then I told him why Miss Thorne hadn't mentioned the game and he woke up suddenly; the familiar glitter came back into his eyes.

'So that was it! I wondered. I thought maybe you'd told her not to say anything about it.'

Later, when the lights had been out half an hour, he suddenly said, 'I see,' in a loud clear voice. I don't know whether he was awake or asleep.

III

I've put down as well as I can everything I can remember about the first meeting between Dolly and Miss Vienna Thorne. Reading it over, it sounds casual and insignificant, but the evening lay in the shadow of the game and all that happened seemed like that. Vienna went back to Europe almost immediately and for fifteen months passed out of Dolly's life.

It was a good year – it still rings true in my memory as a good year. Sophomore year is the most dramatic at Princeton, just as junior year is at Yale. It's not only the elections to the upperclass clubs but also everyone's destiny begins to work itself out. You can tell pretty well who's going to come through, not only by their immediate success but by the way they survive failure. Life was very full for me. I made the board of the Princetonian, and our house burned down out in Dayton, and I had a silly half-hour fist fight in the gymnasium with a man who later became one of my closest friends, and in March Dolly and I joined the upperclass club we'd always wanted to be in. I fell in love, too, but it would be an irrelevancy to tell about that here.

April came and the first real Princeton weather, the lazy green-and-gold afternoons and the bright thrilling nights haunted with the hour of senior singing. I was happy, and Dolly would have been happy except for the approach of another football season. He was playing baseball, which excused him from spring practice, but the bands were beginning to play faintly in the distance. They rose to concert pitch during the summer, when he had to answer the question 'Are you going back early for football?' a dozen times a day. On the fifteenth of September he was down in the dust and heat of late-summer Princeton, crawling over the ground on all fours, trotting through the old routine and turning himself into just the sort of specimen that I'd have given ten years of my life to be.

From first to last, he hated it, and never let down for a minute. He went into the Yale game that fall weighing a hundred and fifty-three pounds, though that wasn't the weight printed in the paper, and he and Joe McDonald were the only men who played all through that disastrous game. He could have been captain by lifting his finger – but that involves some stuff that I know confidentially and can't tell. His only horror was that by some chance he'd have to accept it. Two seasons! He didn't even talk about it now. He left the room or the club when the conversation veered around to football. He stopped announcing to me that he 'wasn't going through that business any more'. This time it took the Christmas holidays to drive that unhappy look from his eyes.

Then at the New Year Miss Vienna Thorne came home from Madrid and in February a man named Case brought her down to the Senior Prom.

IV

She was even prettier than she had been before, softer, externally at least, and a tremendous success. People passing her on the street jerked their heads quickly to look at her – a frightened look, as if they realized that they had almost missed something. She was temporarily tired of European men, she told me, letting me gather that there had been some sort of unfortunate love affair. She was coming out in Washington next fall.

Vienna and Dolly. She disappeared with him for two hours the night of the club dances, and Harold Case was in despair. When they walked in again at midnight I thought they were the handsomest pair I saw. They were both shining with that peculiar luminosity that dark people sometimes have. Harold Case took one look at them and went proudly home.

Vienna came back a week later, solely to see Dolly. Late that evening I had occasion to go up to the deserted club for a book and they called me from the rear terrace, which opens out to the ghostly stadium and to an unpeopled sweep of night. It was an hour of thaw, with spring voices in the warm wind, and wherever there was light enough you could see drops glistening and falling. You could feel the cold melting out of the stars and the bare trees and shrubbery towards Stony Brook turning lush in the darkness.

They were sitting together on a wicker bench, full of themselves and romantic and happy.

'We had to tell someone about it,' they said.

'Now can I go?'

'No, Jeff,' they insisted; 'stay here and envy us. We're in the stage where we want someone to envy us. Do you think we're a good match?'

What could I say?

'Dolly's going to finish at Princeton next year,' Vienna went on, 'but we're going to announce it after the season in Washington in the autumn.'

I was vaguely relieved to find that it was going to be a long engagement.

'I approve of you, Jeff,' Vienna said.

'I want Dolly to have more friends like you. You're stimulating for him – you have ideas. I told Dolly he could probably find others like you if he looked around his class.'

Dolly and I both felt a little uncomfortable.

'She doesn't want me to be a Babbitt,' he said lightly.

'Dolly's perfect,' asserted Vienna. 'He's the most beautiful thing that ever lived, and you'll find I'm very good for him, Jeff. Already I've helped him make up his mind about one important thing.' I guessed what was coming. 'He's going to speak a little piece if they bother him about playing football next autumn, aren't you, child?'

'Oh, they won't bother me,' said Dolly uncomfortably. 'It isn't like that—'

'Well, they'll try to bully you into it, morally.'

'Oh, no,' he objected. 'It isn't like that. Don't let's talk about it now, Vienna. It's such a swell night.'

Such a swell night! When I think of my own love passages at Princeton,

I always summon up that night of Dolly's, as if it had been I and not he who sat there with youth and hope and beauty in his arms.

Dolly's mother took a place on Ram's Point, Long Island, for the summer, and late in August I went East to visit him. Vienna had been there a week when I arrived, and my impressions were: first, that he was very much in love; and, second, that it was Vienna's party. All sorts of curious people used to drop in to see Vienna. I wouldn't mind them now – I'm more sophisticated – but then they seemed rather a blot on the summer. They were all slightly famous in one way or another, and it was up to you to find out how. There was a lot of talk, and especially there was much discussion of Vienna's personality. Whenever I was alone with any of the other guests we discussed Vienna's sparkling personality. They thought I was dull, and most of them thought Dolly was dull. He was better in his line than any of them were in theirs, but his was the only specialty that wasn't mentioned. Still, I felt vaguely that I was being improved and I boasted about knowing most of those people in the ensuing year, and was annoyed when people failed to recognize their names.

The day before I left, Dolly turned his ankle playing tennis, and afterwards he joked about it to me rather sombrely.

'If I'd only broken it things would be so much easier. Just a quarter of an inch more bend and one of the bones would have snapped. By the way, look here.'

He tossed me a letter. It was a request that he report at Princeton for practice on September fifteenth and that meanwhile he begin getting himself in good condition.

'You're not going to play this fall?'

He shook his head.

'No. I'm not a child any more. I've played for two years and I want this year free. If I went through it again it'd be a piece of moral cowardice.'

'I'm not arguing, but – would you have taken this stand if it hadn't been for Vienna?'

'Of course I would. If I let myself be bullied into it I'd never be able to look myself in the face again.'

Two weeks later I got the following letter:

Dear Jeff: When you read this you'll be somewhat surprised. I have, actually, this time, broken my ankle playing tennis. I can't even walk with crutches at present; it's on a chair in front of me swollen up and wrapped up as big as a house as I write. No one, not even Vienna, knows about our conversation on the same subject last summer and so let us both absolutely forget it. One thing, though – an ankle is a darn hard thing to break, though I never knew it before.

I feel happier than I have for years – no early-season practice, no sweat and suffer, a little discomfort and inconvenience, but free. I feel as if I've outwitted a whole lot of people, and it's nobody's business but that of your

Machiavellian (sic) friend,

DOLLY.

PS You might as well tear up this letter.

It didn't sound like Dolly at all.

V

Once down at Princeton I asked Frank Kane – who sells sporting goods on Nassau Street and can tell you offhand the name of the scrub quarterback in 1901 – what was the matter with Bob Tatnall's team senior year.

'Injuries and tough luck,' he said. 'They wouldn't sweat after the hard games. Take Joe McDonald, for instance, All-American tackle the year before; he was slow and stale, and he knew it and didn't care. It's a wonder Bill got that outfit through the season at all.'

I sat in the stands with Dolly and watched them beat Lehigh 3–0 and tie Bucknell by a fluke. The next week we were trimmed 14–0 by Notre Dame. On the day of the Notre Dame game Dolly was in Washington with Vienna, but he was awfully curious about it when he came back next day. He had all the sporting pages of all the papers and he sat reading them and shaking his head. Then he stuffed them suddenly into the wastepaper basket.

'This college is football crazy,' he announced. 'Do you know that English teams don't even train for sports?'

I didn't enjoy Dolly so much in those days. It was curious to see him with nothing to do. For the first time in his life he hung around – around the room, around the club, around casual groups – he who had always been going somewhere with dynamic indolence. His passage along a walk had once created groups – groups of classmates who wanted to walk with him, of underclassmen who followed with their eyes a moving shrine. He became democratic, he mixed around, and it was somehow not appropriate. He explained that he wanted to know more men in his class.

But people want their idols a little above them, and Dolly had been a sort of private and special idol. He began to hate to be alone, and that, of course, was most apparent to me. If I got up to go out and he didn't happen to be writing a letter to Vienna, he'd ask, 'Where are you going?' in a rather alarmed way and make an excuse to limp along with me.

'Are you glad you did it, Dolly?' I asked him suddenly one day.

He looked at me with reproach behind the defiance in his eyes.

'Of course I'm glad.'

'I wish you were in that back field, all the same.'

'It wouldn't matter a bit. This year's game's in the Bowl. I'd probably be dropping kicks for them.'

The week of the Navy game he suddenly began going to all the practices. He worried; that terrible sense of responsibility was at work. Once he had hated the mention of football; now he thought and talked of nothing else. The night before the Navy game I woke up several times to find the lights burning brightly in his room.

We lost 7 to 3 on Navy's last-minute forward pass over Devlin's head. After the first half Dolly left the stands and sat down with the players on the field. When he joined me afterwards his face was smudgy and dirty as if he had been crying.

The game was in Baltimore that year. Dolly and I were going to spend the night in Washington with Vienna, who was giving a dance. We rode over there in an atmosphere of sullen gloom and it was all I could do to keep him from snapping out at two naval officers who were holding an exultant post-mortem in the seat behind.

The dance was what Vienna called her second coming-out party. She was having only the people she liked this time, and these turned out to be chiefly importations from New York. The musicians, the playwrights, the vague supernumeraries of the arts, who had dropped in at Dolly's house on Ram's Point, were here in force. But Dolly, relieved of his obligations as host, made no clumsy attempt to talk their language that night. He stood moodily against the wall with some of that old air of superiority that had first made me want to know him. Afterwards, on my way to bed, I passed Vienna's sitting-room and she called me to come in. She and Dolly, both a little white, were sitting across the room from each other and there was tensity in the air.

'Sit down, Jeff,' said Vienna wearily. 'I want you to witness the collapse of a man into a schoolboy.' I sat down reluctantly. 'Dolly's changed his mind,' she said. 'He prefers football to me.'

'That's not it,' said Dolly stubbornly.

'I don't see the point,' I objected. 'Dolly can't possibly play.'

'But he thinks he can. Jeff, just in case you imagine I'm being pig-headed about it, I want to tell you a story. Three years ago, when we first came back to the United States, father put my young brother in school. One afternoon we all went out to see him play football. Just after the game started he was hurt, but father said, "It's all right. He'll be up in a minute. It happens all the time." But, Jeff, he never got up. He lay there, and finally they carried him off the field and put a blanket over him. Just as we got to him he died.'

She looked from one to the other of us and began to sob convulsively. Dolly went over, frowning, and put his arm around her shoulder.

'Oh, Dolly,' she cried, 'won't you do this for me – just this one little thing for me ?'

He shook his head miserably. 'I tried, but I can't,' he said. 'It's my stuff, don't you understand, Vienna ? People have got to do their stuff.'

Vienna had risen and was powdering her tears at a mirror; now she flashed around angrily.

'Then I've been labouring under a misapprehension when I supposed you felt about it much as I did.'

'Let's not go over all that. I'm tired of talking, Vienna; I'm tired of my own voice. It seems to me that no one I know does anything but talk any more.'

'Thanks. I suppose that's meant for me.'

'It seems to me your friends talk a great deal. I've never heard so much jabber as I've listened to tonight. Is the idea of actually doing anything repulsive to you, Vienna ?'

'It depends upon whether it's worth doing.'

'Well, this is worth doing – to me.'

'I know your trouble, Dolly,' she said bitterly. 'You're weak and you want to be admired. This year you haven't had a lot of little boys following you around as if you were Jack Dempsey, and it almost breaks your heart. You want to get out in front of them all and make a show of yourself and hear the applause.'

He laughed shortly. 'If that's your idea of how a football player feels—'

'Have you made up your mind to play ?' she interrupted.

'If I'm any use to them – yes.'

'Then I think we're both wasting our time.'

Her expression was ruthless, but Dolly refused to see that she was in earnest. When I got away he was still trying to make her 'be rational', and next day on the train he said that Vienna had been 'a little nervous'. He was deeply in love with her, and he didn't dare think of losing her; but he was still in the grip of the sudden emotion that had decided him to play, and his confusion and exhaustion of mind made him believe vainly that everything was going to be all right. But I had seen that look on Vienna's face the night she talked with Mr Carl Sanderson at the Frolic two years before.

Dolly didn't get off the train at Princeton Junction, but continued on to New York. He went to two orthopaedic specialists and one of them arranged a bandage braced with a whole little fence of whalebones that he was to wear day and night. The probabilities were that it would snap at the first brisk encounter, but he could run on it and stand on it when he kicked. He was out on University Field in uniform the following afternoon.

His appearance was a small sensation. I was sitting in the stands watching practice with Harold Case and young Daisy Cary. She was just beginning to be famous then, and I don't know whether she or Dolly attracted the most attention. In those times it was still rather daring to bring down a moving-picture actress; if that same young lady went to Princeton today she would probably be met at the station with a band.

Dolly limped around and everyone said, 'He's limping!' He got under a punt and everyone said, 'He did that pretty well!' The first team were laid off after the hard Navy game and everyone watched Dolly all afternoon. After practice I caught his eye and he came over and shook hands. Daisy asked him if he'd like to be in a football picture she was going to make. It was only conversation, but he looked at me with a dry smile.

When he came back to the room his ankle was swollen up as big as a stove pipe, and next day he and Keene fixed up an arrangement by which the bandage would be loosened and tightened to fit its varying size. We called it the balloon. The bone was nearly healed, but the little bruised sinews were stretched out of place again every day. He watched the Swarthmore game from the sidelines and the following Monday he was in scrimmage with the second team against the scrubs.

In the afternoons sometimes he wrote to Vienna. His theory was that they were still engaged, but he tried not to worry about it, and I think the very pain that kept him awake at night was good for that. When the season was over he would go and see.

We played Harvard and lost 7 to 3. Jack Devlin's collar bone was broken and he was out for the season, which made it almost sure that Dolly would play. Amid the rumours and fears of mid-November the news aroused a spark of hope in an otherwise morbid undergraduate body – hope all out of proportion to Dolly's condition. He came back to the room the Thursday before the game with his face drawn and tired.

'They're going to start me,' he said, 'and I'm going to be back for punts. If they only knew—'

'Couldn't you tell Bill how you feel about that?'

He shook his head and I had a sudden suspicion that he was punishing himself for his 'accident' last August. He lay silently on the couch while I packed his suitcase for the team train.

The actual day of the game was, as usual, like a dream – unreal with its crowds of friends and relatives and the inessential trappings of a gigantic show. The eleven little men who ran out on the field at last were like bewitched figures in another world, strange and infinitely romantic, blurred by a throbbing mist of people and sound. One aches with them intolerably, trembles with their excitement, but they have no traffic with us now, they are beyond help, consecrated and unreachable – vaguely holy.

The field is rich and green, the preliminaries are over and the teams trickle out into position. Head guards are put on; each man claps his hands and breaks into a lonely little dance. People are still talking around you, arranging themselves, but you have fallen silent and your eye wanders from man to man. There's Jack Whitehead, a senior, at end; Joe McDonald, large and reassuring, at tackle; Toole, a sophomore, at guard; Red Hopman, centre; someone you can't identify at the other guard – Bunker probably – he turns and you see his number – Bunker; Bean Gile, looking unnaturally dignified and significant at the other tackle; Poore, another sophomore at end. Back of them is Wash Sampson at quarter – imagine how he feels! But he runs here and there on light feet, speaking to his man and that, trying to communicate his alertness and his confidence of success. Dolly Harlan stands motionless, his hands on his hips, watching the Yale kicker tee up the ball; near him is Captain Bob Tatnall—

There's the whistle! The line of the Yale team sways ponderously forward from its balance and a split second afterwards comes the sound of the ball. The field streams with running figures and the whole Bowl strains forward as if thrown by the current of an electric chair.

Suppose we fumbled right away.

Tatnall catches it, goes back ten yards, is surrounded and blotted out of sight. Spears goes through centre for three. A short pass, Sampson to Tatnall, is completed, but for no gain. Harlan punts to Devereaux, who is downed in his tracks on the Yale forty-yard line.

Now we'll see what they've got.

It developed immediately that they had a great deal. Using an effective crisscross and a short pass over centre, they carried the ball fifty-four yards to the Princeton six-yard line, where they lost it on a fumble, recovered by Red Hopman. After a trade of punts, they began another push, this time to the fifteen-yard line, where, after four hair-raising forward passes, two of them batted down by Dolly, we got the ball on downs. But Yale was still fresh and strong, and with a third onslaught the weaker Princeton line began to give way. Just after the second quarter began Devereaux took the ball over for a touchdown and the half ended with Yale in possession of the ball on our ten-yard line. Score: Yale, 7; Princeton, 0.

We hadn't a chance. The team was playing above itself, better than it had played all year, but it wasn't enough. Save that it was the Yale game, when anything could happen, anything *had* happened, the atmosphere of gloom would have been deeper than it was, and in the cheering section you could cut it with a knife.

Early in the game Dolly Harlan had fumbled Devereaux's high punt, but recovered without gain; towards the end of the half another kick slipped through his fingers, but he scooped it up, and slipping past the end, went back twelve yards. Between halves he told Roper he couldn't seem to get under the ball, but they kept him there. His own kicks were carrying well and he was essential in the only back-field combination that could hope to score.

After the first play of the game he limped slightly, moving around as little as possible to conceal the fact. But I knew enough about football to see that he was in every play, starting at that rather slow pace of his and finishing with a quick side lunge that almost always took out his man. Not a single Yale forward pass was finished in his territory, but towards the end of the third quarter he dropped another kick – backed around in a confused little circle under it, lost it and recovered on the five-yard line just in time to avert a certain score. That made the third time, and I saw Ed Kimball throw off his blanket and begin to warm up on the sidelines.

Just at that point our luck began to change. From a kick formation, with Dolly set to punt from behind our goal, Howard Bement, who had gone in for Wash Sampson at quarter, took the ball through the centre of the line, got by the secondary defence and ran twenty-six yards before he was pulled down. Captain Tasker, of Yale, had gone out with a twisted knee, and Princeton began to pile plays through his substitute, between Bean

Gile and Hopman, with George Spears and sometimes Bob Tatnall carrying the ball. We went up to the Yale forty-yard line, lost the ball on a fumble and recovered it on another as the third quarter ended. A wild ripple of enthusiasm ran through the Princeton stands. For the first time we had the ball in their territory with first down and the possibility of tying the score. You could hear the tenseness growing all around you in the intermission; it was reflected in the excited movements of the cheer leaders and the uncontrollable patches of sound that leaped out of the crowd, catching up voices here and there and swelling to an undisciplined roar.

I saw Kimball dash out on the field and report to the referee and I thought Dolly was through at last, and was glad, but it was Bob Tatnall who came out, sobbing, and brought the Princeton side cheering to its feet.

With the first play pandemonium broke loose and continued to the end of the game. At intervals it would swoon away to a plaintive humming; then it would rise to the intensity of wind and rain and thunder, and beat across the twilight from one side of the Bowl to the other like the agony of lost souls swinging across a gap in space.

The teams lined up on Yale's forty-one yard line and Spears immediately dashed off tackle for six yards. Again he carried the ball – he was a wild unpopular southerner with inspired moments – going through the same hole for five more and a first down. Dolly made two on a cross buck and Spears was held at centre. It was third down, with the ball on Yale's twenty-nine-yard line and eight to go.

There was some confusion immediately behind me, some pushing and some voices; a man was sick or had fainted – I never discovered which. Then my view was blocked out for a minute by rising bodies and then everything went definitely crazy. Substitutes were jumping around down on the field, waving their blankets, the air was full of hats, cushions, coats and a deafening roar. Dolly Harlan, who had scarcely carried the ball a dozen times in his Princeton career, had picked a long pass from Kimball out of the air and, dragging a tackler, struggled five yards to the Yale goal.

VI

Some time later the game was over. There was a bad moment when Yale began another attack, but there was no scoring and Bob Tatnall's eleven had redeemed a mediocre season by tying a better Yale team. For us there was the feel of victory about it, the exaltation if not the jubilance, and the Yale faces issuing from out the Bowl wore the look of defeat. It would be a good year, after all – a good fight at the last, a tradition for next year's team. Our class – those of us who cared – would go out from Princeton without the taste of final defeat. The symbol stood – such as it was; the banners blew proudly in the wind. All that is childish? Find us something to fill the niche of victory.

I waited for Dolly outside the dressing-rooms until almost everyone had come out; then, as he still lingered, I went in. Someone had given him a little brandy, and since he never drank much, it was swimming in his head.

'Have a chair, Jeff.' He smiled, broadly and happily. 'Rubber! Tony! Get the distinguished guest a chair. He's an intellectual and he wants to interview one of the bone-headed athletes. Tony, this is Mr Deering. They've got everything in this funny Bowl but armchairs. I love this Bowl. I'm going to build here.'

He fell silent, thinking about all things happily. He was content. I persuaded him to dress – there were people waiting for us. Then he insisted on walking out upon the field, dark now, and feeling the crumbled turf with his shoe.

He picked up a divot from a cleat and let it drop, laughed, looked distracted for a minute, and turned away.

With Tad Davis, Daisy Cary and another girl, we drove to New York. He sat beside Daisy and was silly, charming and attractive. For the first time since I'd known him he talked about the game naturally, even with a touch of vanity.

'For two years I was pretty good and I was always mentioned at the bottom of the column as being among those who played. This year I dropped three punts and slowed up every play till Bob Tatnall kept yelling at me, "I don't see why they won't take you out!" But a pass not even aimed at me fell in my arms and I'll be in the headlines tomorrow.'

He laughed. Somebody touched his foot; he winced and turned white.

'How did you hurt it?' Daisy asked. 'In football?'

'I hurt it last summer,' he said shortly.

'It must have been terrible to play on it.'

'It was.'

'I suppose you had to.'

'That's the way sometimes.'

They understood each other. They were both workers; sick or well, there were things that Daisy also had to do. She spoke of how, with a vile cold, she had had to fall into an open-air lagoon out in Hollywood the winter before.

'Six times – with a fever of a hundred and two. But the production was costing ten thousand dollars a day.'

'Couldn't they use a double ?'

'They did whenever they could – I only fell in when it had to be done.'

She was eighteen and I compared her background of courage and independence and achievement, of politeness based upon the realities of cooperation, with that of most society girls I had known. There was no way in which she wasn't inestimably their superior – if she had looked for a moment my way – but it was Dolly's shining velvet eyes that signalled to her own.

'Can't you go out with me tonight ?' I heard her ask him.

He was sorry, but he had to refuse. Vienna was in New York; she was going to see him. I didn't know, and Dolly didn't know, whether there was to be a reconciliation or a good-bye.

When she dropped Dolly and me at the Ritz there was real regret, that lingering form of it, in both their eyes.

'There's a marvellous girl,' Dolly said. I agreed. 'I'm going up to see Vienna. Will you get a room for us at the Madison ?'

So I left him. What happened between him and Vienna I don't know; he has never spoken about it to this day. But what happened later in the evening was brought to my attention by several surprised and even indignant witnesses to the event.

Dolly walked into the Ambassador Hotel about ten o'clock and went to the desk to ask for Miss Cary's room. There was a crowd around the desk, among them some Yale or Princeton undergraduates from the game. Several of them had been celebrating and evidently one of them knew Daisy and had tried to get her room by phone. Dolly was abstracted and he must have made his way through them in a somewhat brusque way and asked to be connected with Miss Cary.

One young man stepped back, looked at him unpleasantly and said, 'You seem to be in an awful hurry. Just who are you ?'

There was one of those slight silent pauses and the people near the desk all turned to look. Something happened inside Dolly; he felt as if life had arranged his role to make possible this particular question – a question that now he had no choice but to answer. Still, there was silence. The small crowd waited.

'Why, I'm Dolly Harlan,' he said deliberately. 'What do you think of that ?'

It was quite outrageous. There was a pause and then a sudden little flurry and chorus: 'Dolly Harlan! What? What did he say?'

The clerk had heard the name; he gave it as the phone was answered from Miss Cary's room.

'Mr Harlan's to go right up, please.'

Dolly turned away, alone with his achievement, taking it for once to his breast. He found suddenly that he would not have it long so intimately; the memory would outlive the triumph and even the triumph would outlive the glow in his heart that was best of all. Tall and straight, an image of victory and pride, he moved across the lobby, oblivious alike to the fate ahead of him or the small chatter behind.

AT YOUR AGE

Saturday Evening Post, 17 August 1929

'At Your Age' was written in Paris in June 1929. Tranquillity had eluded the Fitzgeralds at Ellerslie, and he returned to France in the spring of 1929 with Tender Is the Night *still unfinished. The departure from America was motivated by Zelda's desire to study ballet in Paris as well as by Fitzgerald's feeling that he would be able to work on his novel more effectively in its setting.*

Harold Ober's response to 'At Your Age' was: 'At this minute it seems to me the finest story you have ever written – and the finest I have ever read.' His enthusiasm brought a raise to $4000 from the Post, *Fitzgerald's peak story price. Ober was probably responsible for its selection for the* Modern Library *Great Modern Short Stories (1930) because 'At Your Age' was not among the five stories Fitzgerald nominated.*

Tom Squires came into the drug store to buy a toothbrush, a can of talcum, a gargle, Castile soap, Epsom salts and a box of cigars. Having lived alone for many years, he was methodical, and while waiting to be served he held the list in his hand. It was Christmas week and Minneapolis was under two feet of exhilarating, constantly refreshed snow; with his cane Tom knocked two clean crusts of it from his overshoes. Then, looking up, he saw the blonde girl.

She was a rare blonde, even in that Promised Land of Scandinavians, where pretty blondes are not rare. There was warm colour in her cheeks, lips and pink little hands that folded powders into papers; her hair, in long braids twisted about her head, was shining and alive. She seemed to Tom suddenly the cleanest person he knew of, and he caught his breath as he stepped forward and looked into her grey eyes.

'A can of talcum.'

'What kind?'

'Any kind . . . That's fine.'

She looked back at him apparently without self-consciousness, and, as the list melted away, his heart raced with it wildly.

'I am not old,' he wanted to say. 'At fifty I'm younger than most men of forty. Don't I interest you at all?'

But she only said, 'What kind of gargle?'

And he answered, 'What can you recommend? . . . That's fine.'

Almost painfully he took his eyes from her, went out and got into his coupé.

'If that young idiot only knew what an old imbecile like me could do for her,' he thought humorously – 'what worlds I could open out to her!'

As he drove away into the winter twilight he followed this train of thought to a totally unprecedented conclusion. Perhaps the time of day was the responsible stimulant, for the shop windows glowing into the cold, the tinkling bells of a delivery sleigh, the white gloss left by shovels on the sidewalks, the enormous distance of the stars, brought back the feel of other nights thirty years ago. For an instant the girls he had known then slipped like phantoms out of their dull matronly selves of today and fluttered past him with frosty, seductive laughter, until a pleasant shiver crawled up his spine.

'Youth! Youth! Youth!' he apostrophized with conscious lack of originality, and, as a somewhat ruthless and domineering man of no morals whatsoever, he considered going back to the drug store to seek the blonde girl's address. It was not his sort of thing, so the half-formed intention passed; the idea remained.

'Youth, by heaven – youth!' he repeated under his breath. 'I want it near me, all around me, just once more before I'm too old to care.'

He was tall, lean and handsome, with the ruddy, bronzed face of a sportsman and a just faintly greying moustache. Once he had been among the city's best beaux, organizer of cotillions and charity balls, popular with men and women, and with several generations of them. After the war he had suddenly felt poor, gone into business, and in ten years accumulated nearly a million dollars. Tom Squires was not introspective, but he perceived now that the wheel of his life had revolved again, bringing up forgotten, yet familiar, dreams and yearnings. Entering his house, he turned suddenly to a pile of disregarded invitations to see whether or not he had been bidden to a dance tonight.

Throughout his dinner, which he ate alone at the Downtown Club, his eyes were half closed and on his face was a faint smile. He was practising so that he would be able to laugh at himself painlessly, if necessary.

'I don't even know what they talk about,' he admitted. 'They pet – prominent broker goes to petting party with débutante. What is a petting party? Do they serve refreshments? Will I have to learn to play a saxophone?'

These matters, lately as remote as China in a newsreel, came alive to him. They were serious questions. At ten o'clock he walked up the steps of the College Club to a private dance with the same sense of entering a new world as when he had gone into a training camp back in '17. He spoke to a hostess of his generation and to her daughter, overwhelmingly of another, and sat down in a corner to acclimate himself.

He was not alone long. A silly young man named Leland Jaques, who lived across the street from Tom, remarked him kindly and came over to brighten his life. He was such an exceedingly fatuous young man that, for a moment, Tom was annoyed, but he perceived craftily that he might be of service.

'Hello, Mr Squires. How are you, sir?'

'Fine, thanks, Leland. Quite a dance.'

As one man of the world with another, Mr Jaques sat, or lay, down on the couch and lit – or so it seemed to Tom – three or four cigarettes at once.

'You should of been here last night, Mr Squires. Oh, boy, that was a party and a half! The Caulkins. Hap-past five!'

'Who's that girl who changes partners every minute?' Tom asked . . . 'No, the one in white passing the door.'

'That's Annie Lorry.'

'Arthur Lorry's daughter?'

'Yes.'

'She seems popular.'

'About the most popular girl in town – anyway, at a dance.'

'Not popular except at dances?'

'Oh, sure, but she hangs around with Randy Cambell all the time.'

'What Cambell?'

'D. B.'

There were new names in town in the last decade.

'It's a boy-and-girl affair.' Pleased with this phrase, Jaques tried to repeat it: 'One of those boy-and-girls affair – boys-and-girl affairs—' He gave it up and lit several more cigarettes, crushing out the first series on Tom's lap.

'Does she drink?'

'Not especially. At least I never saw her passed out . . . That's Randy Cambell just cut in on her now.'

They were a nice couple. Her beauty sparkled bright against his strong, tall form, and they floated hoveringly, delicately, like two people in a nice, amusing dream. They came near and Tom admired the faint dust of powder over her freshness, the guarded sweetness of her smile, the fragility of her body calculated by nature to a millimetre to suggest a bud, yet guarantee a flower. Her innocent, passionate eyes were brown, perhaps; but almost violet in the silver light.

'Is she out this year?'

'Who?'

'Miss Lorry.'

'Yes.'

Although the girl's loveliness interested Tom, he was unable to picture himself as one of the attentive, grateful queue that pursued her around the room. Better meet her when the holidays were over and most of these young men were back in college 'where they belonged'. Tom Squires was old enough to wait.

He waited a fortnight while the city sank into the endless northern midwinter, where grey skies were friendlier than metallic blue skies, and dusk, whose lights were a reassuring glimpse into the continuity of human cheer, was warmer than the afternoons of bloodless sunshine. The coat of snow lost its press and became soiled and shabby, and ruts froze in the street; some of the big houses on Crest Avenue began to close as their occupants went South. In those cold days Tom asked Annie and her parents to go as his guests to the last Bachelors' Ball.

The Lorrys were an old family in Minneapolis, grown a little harassed and poor since the war. Mrs Lorry, a contemporary of Tom's, was not surprised that he should send mother and daughter orchids and dine them luxuriously in his apartment on fresh caviar, quail and champagne. Annie saw him only dimly – he lacked vividness, as the old do for the young – but she perceived his interest in her and performed for him the traditional ritual of young beauty – smiles, polite, wide-eyed attention, a profile held obligingly in this light or in that. At the ball he danced with her twice, and, though she was teased about it, she was flattered that such a man of the world – he had become that instead of a mere old man – had singled her out. She accepted his invitation to the symphony the following week, with the idea that it would be uncouth to refuse.

There were several 'nice invitations' like that. Sitting beside him, she dozed in the warm shadow of Brahms and thought of Randy Cambell and other romantic nebulosities who might appear tomorrow. Feeling casually mellow one afternoon, she deliberately provoked Tom to kiss her on the way home, but she wanted to laugh when he took her hands and told her fervently he was falling in love.

'But how could you?' she protested. 'Really, you mustn't say such crazy things. I won't go out with you any more, and then you'll be sorry.'

A few days later her mother spoke to her as Tom waited outside in his car:

'Who's that, Annie?'

'Mr Squires.'

'Shut the door a minute. You're seeing him quite a bit.'

'Why not?'

'Well, dear, he's fifty years old.'

'But, mother, there's hardly anybody else in town.'

'But you mustn't get any silly ideas about him.'

'Don't worry. Actually, he bores me to extinction most of the time.' She came to a sudden decision: 'I'm not going to see him any more. I just couldn't get out of going with him this afternoon.'

And that night, as she stood by her door in the circle of Randy Cambell's arm, Tom and his single kiss had no existence for her.

'Oh, I do love you so,' Randy whispered. 'Kiss me once more.'

Their cool cheeks and warm lips met in the crisp darkness, and, watching the icy moon over his shoulder, Annie knew that she was his surely and, pulling his face down, kissed him again, trembling with emotion.

'When'll you marry me then?' he whispered.

'When can you – we afford it?'

'Couldn't you announce our engagement? If you knew the misery of having you out with somebody else and then making love to you.'

'Oh, Randy, you ask so much.'

'It's so awful to say good night. Can't I come in for a minute?'

'Yes.'

Sitting close together in a trance before the flickering, lessening fire, they were oblivious that their common fate was being coolly weighed by a man of fifty who lay in a hot bath some blocks away.

II

Tom Squires had guessed from Annie's extremely kind and detached manner of the afternoon that he had failed to interest her. He had promised himself that in such an eventuality he would drop the matter, but now he found himself in no such humour. He did not want to marry her; he simply wanted to see her and be with her a little; and up to the moment of her sweetly casual, half-passionate, yet wholly unemotional kiss, giving her up would have been easy, for he was past the romantic age; but since that kiss the thought of her made his heart move up a few inches in his chest and beat there steady and fast.

'But this is the time to get out,' he said to himself. 'My age; no possible right to force myself into her life.'

He rubbed himself dry, brushed his hair before the mirror, and, as he laid down the comb, said decisively: 'That is that.' And after reading for an hour he turned out the lamp with a snap and repeated aloud: 'That is that.'

In other words, that was not that at all, and the click of material things did not finish Annie Lorry as a business decision might be settled by the tap of a pencil on the table.

'I'm going to carry this matter a little further,' he said to himself about half past four; on that acknowledgement he turned over and found sleep.

In the morning she had receded somewhat, but by four o'clock in the afternoon she was all around him – the phone was for calling her, a woman's footfalls passing his office were her footfalls, the snow outside the window was blowing, perhaps, against her rosy face.

'There is always the little plan I thought of last night,' he said to himself. 'In ten years I'll be sixty, and then no youth, no beauty for me ever any more.'

In a sort of panic he took a sheet of note paper and composed a carefully phrased letter to Annie's mother, asking permission to pay court to her daughter. He took it himself into the hall, but before the letter slide he tore it up and dropped the pieces in a cuspidor.

'I couldn't do such an underhand trick,' he told himself, 'at my age.' But this self-congratulation was premature, for he rewrote the letter and mailed it before he left his office that night.

Next day the reply he had counted on arrived – he could have guessed its very words in advance. It was a curt and indignant refusal.

It ended:

I think it best that you and my daughter meet no more.

Very Sincerely Yours,

    MABEL TOLLMAN LORRY.

'And now,' Tom thought coolly, 'we'll see what the girl says to that.'

He wrote a note to Annie. Her mother's letter had surprised him, it said, but perhaps it was best that they should meet no more, in view of her mother's attitude.

By return post came Annie's defiant answer to her mother's fiat: 'This isn't the Dark Ages. I'll see you whenever I like.' She named a rendezvous for the following afternoon. Her mother's short-sightedness brought about what he failed to achieve directly; for where Annie had been on the point of dropping him, she was now determined to do nothing of the sort. And the secrecy engendered by disapproval at home simply contributed the missing excitement. As February hardened into deep, solemn, interminable winter, she met him frequently and on a new basis. Sometimes they drove over to St Paul to see a picture or to have dinner; sometimes they parked far out on a boulevard in his coupé, while the bitter sleet glazed the windshield to opacity and furred his lamps with ermine. Often he brought along something special to drink – enough to make her gay, but, carefully, never more; for mingled with his other emotions about her was something paternally concerned.

Laying his cards on the table, he told her that it was her mother who had unwittingly pushed her towards him, but Annie only laughed at his duplicity.

She was having a better time with him than with anyone else she had ever known. In place of the selfish exigency of a younger man, he showed her a never-failing consideration. What if his eyes were tired, his cheeks a little leathery and veined, if his will was masculine and strong. Moreover, his experience was a window looking out upon a wider, richer world; and with Randy Cambell next day she would feel less taken care of, less valued, less rare.

It was Tom now who was vaguely discontented. He had what he wanted – her youth at his side – and he felt that anything further would be a mistake. His liberty was precious to him and he could offer her only a dozen years before he would be old, but she had become something precious to him and he perceived that drifting wasn't fair. Then one day late in February the matter was decided out of hand.

They had ridden home from St Paul and dropped into the College Club for tea, breaking together through the drifts that masked the walk and rimmed the door. It was a revolving door; a young man came around in it, and stepping into his space, they smelt onions and whisky. The door revolved again after them, and he was back within, facing them. It was Randy Cambell; his face was flushed, his eyes dull and hard.

'Hello, beautiful,' he said, approaching Annie.

'Don't come so close,' she protested lightly. 'You smell of onions.'

'You're particular all of a sudden.'

'Always. I'm always particular.' Annie made a slight movement back towards Tom.

'Not always,' said Randy unpleasantly. Then, with increased emphasis and a fractional glance at Tom: 'Not always.' With his remark he seemed to join the hostile world outside. 'And I'll just give you a tip,' he continued: 'Your mother's inside.'

The jealous ill-temper of another generation reached Tom only faintly, like the protest of a child, but at this impertinent warning he bristled with annoyance.

'Come on, Annie,' he said brusquely. 'We'll go in.'

With her glance uneasily averted from Randy, Annie followed Tom into the big room.

It was sparsely populated; three middle-aged women sat near the fire. Momentarily Annie drew back, then she walked towards them.

'Hello, mother . . . Mrs Trumble . . . Aunt Caroline.'

The two latter responded; Mrs Trumble even nodded faintly at Tom. But Annie's mother got to her feet without a word, her eyes frozen, her mouth drawn. For a moment she stood staring at her daughter; then she turned abruptly and left the room.

Tom and Annie found a table across the room.

'Wasn't she terrible ?' said Annie, breathing aloud. He didn't answer.

'For three days she hasn't spoken to me.' Suddenly she broke out: 'Oh, people can be so small! I was going to sing the leading part in the Junior League show, and yesterday Cousin Mary Betts, the president, came to me and said I couldn't.'

'Why not ?'

'Because a representative Junior League girl mustn't defy her mother. As if I were a naughty child!'

Tom stared on at a row of cups on the mantelpiece – two or three of them bore his name. 'Perhaps she was right,' he said suddenly. 'When I begin to do harm to you it's time to stop.'

'What do you mean ?'

At her shocked voice his heart poured a warm liquid forth into his body, but he answered quietly: 'You remember I told you I was going South ? Well, I'm going tomorrow.'

There was an argument, but he had made up his mind. At the station next evening she wept and clung to him.

'Thank you for the happiest month I've had in years,' he said.

'But you'll come back, Tom.'

'I'll be two months in Mexico; then I'm going East for a few weeks.'

He tried to sound fortunate, but the frozen city he was leaving seemed to be in blossom. Her frozen breath was a flower on the air, and his heart sank as he realized that some young man was waiting outside to take her home in a car hung with blooms.

'Good-bye, Annie. Good-bye, sweet!'

Two days later he spent the morning in Houston with Hal Meigs, a classmate at Yale.

'You're in luck for such an old fella,' said Meigs at luncheon, 'because I'm going to introduce you to the cutest little travelling companion you ever saw, who's going all the way to Mexico City.'

The lady in question was frankly pleased to learn at the station that she was not returning alone. She and Tom dined together on the train and later played rummy for an hour; but when, at ten o'clock, standing in the door of the stateroom, she turned back to him suddenly with a certain look, frank and unmistakable, and stood there holding that look for a long moment, Tom Squires was suddenly in the grip of an emotion that was not the one in question. He wanted desperately to see Annie, call her for a second on the phone, and then fall asleep, knowing she was young and pure as a star, and safe in bed.

'Good night,' he said, trying to keep any repulsion out of his voice.

'Oh! Good night.'

Arriving in El Paso next day, he drove over the border to Juarez. It was bright and hot, and after leaving his bags at the station he went into a bar for an iced drink; as he sipped it a girl's voice addressed him thickly from the table behind:

'You'n American?'

He had noticed her slumped forward on her elbows as he came in; now, turning, he faced a young girl of about seventeen, obviously drunk, yet with gentility in her unsteady, sprawling voice. The American bartender leaned confidentially forward.

'I don't know what to do about her,' he said. 'She come in about three o'clock with two young fellows – one of them her sweetie. They had a fight and the men went off, and this one's been here ever since.'

A spasm of distaste passed over Tom – the rules of his generation were outraged and defied. That an American girl should be drunk and deserted in a tough foreign town – that such things happened, might happen to Annie. He looked at his watch, hesitated.

'Has she got a bill ? 'he asked.

'She owes for five gins. But suppose her boy friends come back ?'

'Tell them she's at the Roosevelt Hotel in El Paso.'

Approaching, he put his hand on her shoulder. She looked up.

'You look like Santa Claus,' she said vaguely. 'You couldn't possibly be Santa Claus, could you ?'

'I'm going to take you to El Paso.'

'Well,' she considered, 'you look perfectly safe to me.'

She was so young – a drenched little rose. He could have wept for her wretched unconsciousness of the old facts, the old penalties of life. Jousting at nothing in an empty tilt yard with a shaking spear. The taxi moved too slowly through the suddenly poisonous night.

Having explained things to a reluctant night clerk, he went out and found a telegraph office.

'Have given up Mexican trip,' he wired. 'Leaving here tonight. Please meet train in the St Paul station at three o'clock and ride with me to Minneapolis, as I can't spare you for another minute. All my love.'

He could at least keep an eye on her, advise her, see what she did with her life. That silly mother of hers!

On the train, as the baked tropical lands and green fields fell away and the North swept near again with patches of snow, then fields of it, fierce winds in the vestibule and bleak, hibernating farms, he paced the corridors with intolerable restlessness. When they drew into the St Paul station he swung himself off like a young man and searched the platform eagerly, but his eyes failed to find her. He had counted on those few minutes between the cities; they had become a symbol of her fidelity to their friendship, and as the train started again he searched it desperately from smoker to observation car. But he could not find her, and now he knew that he was mad for her; at the thought that she had taken his advice and plunged into affairs with other men, he grew weak with fear.

Drawing into Minneapolis, his hands fumbled so that he must call the porter to fasten his baggage. Then there was an interminable wait in the corridor while the baggage was taken off and he was pressed up against a girl in a squirrel-trimmed coat.

'Tom!'

'Well, I'll be—'

Her arms went up around his neck. 'But, Tom,' she cried, 'I've been right here in this car since St Paul!'

His cane fell in the corridor, he drew her very tenderly close and their lips met like starved hearts.

III

The new intimacy of their definite engagement brought Tom a feeling of young happiness. He awoke on winter mornings with the sense of undeserved joy hovering in the room; meeting young men, he found himself matching the vigour of his mind and body against theirs. Suddenly his life had a purpose and a background; he felt rounded and complete. On grey March afternoons when she wandered familiarly in his apartment the warm sureties of his youth flooded back – ecstasy and poignancy, the mortal and the eternal posed in their immemorially tragic juxtaposition and, a little astounded, he found himself relishing the very terminology of young romance. But he was more thoughtful than a younger lover; and to Annie he seemed to 'know everything', to stand holding open the gates for her passage into the truly golden world.

'We'll go to Europe first,' he said.

'Oh, we'll go there a lot, won't we? Let's spend our winters in Italy and the spring in Paris.'

'But, little Annie, there's business.'

'Well, we'll stay away as much as we can anyhow. I hate Minneapolis.'

'Oh, no.' He was a little shocked. 'Minneapolis is all right.'

'When you're here it's all right.'

Mrs Lorry yielded at length to the inevitable. With ill grace she acknowledged the engagement, asking only that the marriage should not take place until fall.

'Such a long time,' Annie sighed.

'After all, I'm your mother. It's so little to ask.'

It was a long winter, even in a land of long winters. March was full of billowy drifts, and when it seemed at last as though the cold must be defeated, there was a series of blizzards, desperate as last stands. The people waited; their first energy to resist was spent, and man, like weather, simply hung on. There was less to do now and the general restlessness was expressed by surliness in daily contacts. Then, early in April, with a long sigh the ice cracked, the snow ran into the ground and the green, eager spring broke up through.

One day, riding along a slushy road in a fresh, damp breeze with a little starved, smothered grass in it, Annie began to cry. Sometimes she cried for nothing, but this time Tom suddenly stopped the car and put his arm round her.

'Why do you cry like that? Are you unhappy?'

'Oh, no, no!' she protested.

'But you cried yesterday the same way. And you wouldn't tell me why. You must always tell me.'

'Nothing, except the spring. It smells so good, and it always has so many sad thoughts and memories in it.'

'It's our spring, my sweetheart,' he said. 'Annie, don't let's wait. Let's be married in June.'

'I promised mother, but if you like we can announce our engagement in June.'

The spring came fast now. The sidewalks were damp, then dry, and the children roller-skated on them and boys played baseball in the soft, vacant lots. Tom got up elaborate picnics of Annie's contemporaries and encouraged her to play golf and tennis with them. Abruptly, with a final, triumphant lurch of nature, it was full summer.

On a lovely May evening Tom came up the Lorry's walk and sat down beside Annie's mother on the porch.

'It's so pleasant,' he said, 'I thought Annie and I would walk instead of driving this evening. I want to show her the funny old house I was born in.'

'On Chambers Street, wasn't it? Annie'll be home in a few minutes. She went riding with some young people after dinner.'

'Yes, on Chambers Street.'

He looked at his watch presently, hoping Annie would come while it was still light enough to see. Quarter of nine. He frowned. She had kept him waiting the night before, kept him waiting an hour yesterday afternoon.

'If I was twenty-one,' he said to himself, 'I'd make scenes and we'd both be miserable.'

He and Mrs Lorry talked; the warmth of the night precipitated the vague evening lassitude of the fifties and softened them both, and for the first time since his attentions to Annie began, there was no unfriendliness between them. By and by long silences fell, broken only by the scratch of a match or the creak of her swinging settee. When Mr Lorry came home Tom threw away his second cigar in surprise and looked at his watch; it was after ten.

'Annie's late,' Mrs Lorry said.

'I hope there's nothing wrong,' said Tom anxiously. 'Who is she with?'

'There were four when they started out. Randy Cambell and another couple – I didn't notice who. They were only going for a soda.'

'I hope there hasn't been any trouble. Perhaps— Do you think I ought to go and see?'

'Ten isn't late nowadays. You'll find—' Remembering that Tom Squires was marrying Annie, not adopting her, she kept herself from adding: 'You'll get used to it.'

Her husband excused himself and went up to bed, and the conversation became more forced and desultory. When the church clock over the way struck eleven they both broke off and listened to the beats. Twenty minutes later just as Tom impatiently crushed out his last cigar, an automobile drifted down the street and came to rest in front of the door.

For a minute no one moved on the porch or in the auto. Then Annie, with a hat in her hand, got out and came quickly up the walk. Defying the tranquil night, the car snorted away.

'Oh, hello!' she cried. 'I'm so sorry! What time is it? Am I terribly late?'

Tom didn't answer. The street lamp threw wine colour upon her face and expressed with a shadow the heightened flush of her cheek. Her dress was crushed, her hair was in brief, expressive disarray. But it was the strange little break in her voice that made him afraid to speak, made him turn his eyes aside.

'What happened?' Mrs Lorry asked casually.

'Oh, a blow-out and something wrong with the engine – and we lost our way. Is it terribly late?'

And then, as she stood before them, her hat still in her hand, her breast rising and falling a little, her eyes wide and bright, Tom realized with a shock that he and her mother were people of the same age looking at a person of another. Try as he might, he could not separate himself from Mrs Lorry. When she excused herself he suppressed a frantic tendency to say, 'But why should you go now? After sitting here all evening?'

They were alone. Annie came up to him and pressed his hand. He had never been so conscious of her beauty; her damp hands were touched with dew.

'You were out with young Cambell,' he said.

'Yes. Oh, don't be mad. I feel – I feel so upset tonight.'

'Upset?'

She sat down, whimpering a little.

'I couldn't help it. Please don't ₁be mad. He wanted so for me to take a ride with him and it was such a wonderful night, so I went just for an hour. And we began talking and I didn't realize the time. I felt so sorry for him.'

'How do you think I felt?' He scorned himself, but it was said now.

'Don't, Tom. I told you I was terribly upset. I want to go to bed.'

'I understand. Good night, Annie.'

'Oh, please don't act that way, Tom. Can't you understand?'

But he could, and that was just the trouble. With the courteous bow of another generation, he walked down the steps and off into the obliterating moonlight. In a moment he was just a shadow passing the street lamps and then a faint footfall up the street.

IV

All through that summer he often walked abroad in the evenings. He liked to stand for a minute in front of the house where he was born, and then in front of another house where he had been a little boy. On his customary routes there were other sharp landmarks of the nineties, converted habitats of gaieties that no longer existed – the shell of Jansen's Livery Stables and the old Nushka Rink, where every winter his father had curled on the well-kept ice.

'And it's a darn pity,' he would mutter. 'A darn pity.'

He had a tendency, too, to walk past the lights of a certain drug store, because it seemed to him that it had contained the seed of another and nearer branch of the past. Once he went in, and inquiring casually about the blonde clerk, found that she had married and departed several months before. He obtained her name and on an impulse sent her a wedding present 'from a dumb admirer', for he felt he owed something to her for his happiness and pain. He had lost the battle against youth and spring, and with his grief paid the penalty for age's unforgivable sin – refusing to die. But he could not have walked down wasted into the darkness without being used up a little; what he had wanted, after all, was only to break his strong old heart. Conflict itself has a value beyond victory and defeat, and those three months – he had them for ever.

INDECISION

Saturday Evening Post, 16 May 1931

'Indecision' was written in January–February 1931 – probably in Lausanne, Switzerland, where Fitzgerald was staying at the Hôtel de la Paix while Zelda Fitzgerald was under treatment at the Prangins clinic.* The Post *paid $4000 for it. After Zelda's breakdown in April 1930 Fitzgerald concentrated on short stories – instead of his novel – for two years, writing sixteen stories to earn the money for hospital bills. In 1931 – his most lucrative year before Hollywood – his income from nine stories was $36,000 (less ten per cent commission), whereas his total royalties from seven books was $100. Although the 1930–31 stories include two intensely personal masterpieces, 'One Trip Abroad' and 'Babylon Revisited', most of them are clearly contrived.*

The Switzerland of 'Indecision' and 'Hotel Child' is largely populated with unattractive people. Fitzgerald had little reason to write pleasant stories about Switzerland because for him it was a land of illness and despair. 'A country where few things begin, but many things end' – as he noted in 'One Trip Abroad'.

In May 1931 Harold Ober relayed the Post's *reservations about Fitzgerald's recent stories, adding: 'These last three stories of yours, "Flight and Pursuit", "A New Leaf", and "Indecision", have been interesting to me because they were very vivid bits of life but I do feel that in these three stories you have failed to make the reader care about any one of the characters.'*

This one was dressed in a horizon-blue Swiss skiing suit with, however, the unmistakable touch of a Paris shears about it. Above it shone her

---

*It is difficult to be exact about Fitzgerald's residences in 1931. While Zelda Fitzgerald was at Prangins clinic, he stayed at hotels in Switzerland and visited his daughter Scottie in Paris.

snow-warm cheeks and her eyes that were less confident than brave. With his hat, Tommy McLane slapped snow from his dark, convictlike costume. He was already reflecting that he might have been out with Rosemary, dancing around Rosemary and the two 'ickle durls' down at the other hotel, amid the gleam of patent Argentine hair, to the soothing whispers of 'I'm Getting Myself Ready for You'. When he was with Emily he felt always a faint nostalgia for young Rosemary and for the sort of dance that seemed to go on inside and all around Rosemary and the two 'ickle durls'. He knew just how much happened there – not much; just a limited amount of things, just a pleasant lot of little things strung into hours, moving to little melodies hither and thither. But he missed it; it was new to him again after four years, and he missed it. Likewise when he was with Rosemary, making life fun with jokes for her, he thought of Emily, who was twenty-five and carried space around with her into which he could step and be alone with their two selves, mature and complicated and trusting, and almost in love.

Out the window, the snow on the pine trees was turning lilac in the first dusk; and because the world was round, or for some such reason, there was rosy light still on that big mountain, the Dent de Something. Bundled-up children were splattering back to their hotels for tea as if the outdoors were tired of them and wanted to change its dress in quiet dignity. Down in the valley there were already bright windows and misty glows from the houses and hotels of the town.

He left Emily at her hotel door. She had never seemed so attractive, so good, so tranquil a person, given a half-decent chance. He was annoyed that he was already thinking of Rosemary.

'We'll meet in the bar down there at 7.30,' he said, 'and don't dress.'

Putting on his jacket and flat cap, Tommy stepped out into the storm. It was a welcome blizzard and he inhaled damp snowflakes that he could no longer see against the darkening sky. Three flying kids on a sledge startled him with a warning in some strange language and he just managed to jump out of their path. He heard them yell at the next bend, and then, a little farther on, he heard sleigh bells coming up the hill in the dark. It was all very pleasant and familiar, yet it did not remind him of Minneapolis, where he was born, because the automobile had spoiled all that side of north-western life while he was still a baby. It was pleasant and familiar because these last five days here among alien mountains held some of the happiest moments of his life.

He was twenty-seven; he was assistant manager and slated for manager of a New York bank in Paris, or else he would be offered the option of Chicago next spring at a larger salary. He had come up here to one of the gayest places in Switzerland with the idea that if he had nothing else to think of for ten days he might fall in love. He could afford to fall in love, but in Paris the people he saw all knew it, and he had instinctively become analytical and cagy. Here he felt free; the first night had seen at least a dozen girls and women, 'any one of whom'; on the second night, there had still been half a dozen; the third night there were three, with one new addition – Emily Elliot from the other hotel. Now, on the day after Christmas, it had narrowed down to two – Emily and Rosemary Merriweather. He had actually written all this down on a blotter as if he were in his office in the Place Vendome, added and subtracted them, listed points.

'Two really remarkable girls,' he said to himself in a tone not unlike the clumping squeak of his big shoes on the snow. 'Two absolutely good ones.'

Emily Elliot was divorced and twenty-five. Rosemary was eighteen.

He saw her immediately as he went into his hotel – a blonde, ravishing, southern beauty like so many that had come before her and so many yet to be born. She was from 'N'Awlins 'rigin'ly', but now from 'Athens, Joja'. He had first spoken to her on Christmas Eve, after an unavailing search for someone to introduce him, some means to pierce the wall of vacationing boys within which she seemed hermetically sealed. Sitting with another man, he stared at her across the room, admiring her with his eyes, frankly and tauntingly. Presently she spoke to her escort; they crossed the room and sat down at the table next to him, with Rosemary's back just one inch from him. She sent her young man for something; Tommy spoke. The next day, at the risk of both their lives, he took her down the big bob run.

Rosemary saw him now as he came in. She was revolving slowly through the last of the tea hour with a young Levantine whom he disliked. She wore white and her face lighted up white, like an angel under an arc lamp. 'Where you been?' her big eyes said.

But Tommy was shrewd, and he merely nodded to her and to the two 'ickle durls' who danced by, and found a seat in a far corner. He knew that a surfeit of admiration such as Rosemary's breeds an appreciation of indifference. And presently she came over to him, dragging her bridling partner by an interlaced little finger.

'Where you been?' she demanded.

'Tell that Spic to go count his piastres and I'll talk turkey with you.'

She bestowed upon the puzzled darkling a healing smile.

'You don't mind, honey, if I sit this out? See you later.'

When he had departed, Tommy protested, ' "Honey"! Do you call him "honey"? Why don't you call him "greasy"?'

She laughed sweetly.

'Where you been?'

'Skiing. But every time I go away, that doesn't mean you can go dance with a whole lot of gigolo numbers from Cairo. Why does he hold his hand parallel to the floor when he dances? Does he think he's stilling the waves? Does he think the floor's going to swing up and crack him?'

'He's a Greek, honey.'

'That's no reason. And you better get that word "honey" cleaned and pressed before you use it on me again.' He felt very witty. 'Let's go to my boudoir,' he suggested.

He had a bedroom and bath and a tiny *salon*. Once inside the door of the latter, he shot the bolt and took her in his arms, but she drew away from him.

'You been up at that other hotel,' she said.

'I had to invite a girl to dinner. Did you know you're having dinner with me tonight? . . . You're beautiful.'

It was true. Her face, flushed with cold and then warmed again with the dance, was a riot of lovely, delicate pinks, like many carnations, rising in many shades from the white of her nose to the high spot of her cheeks. Her breathing was very young as she came close to him – young and eager and exciting. Her lips were faintly chapped, but soft in the corners.

After a moment she sat with him in a single chair. And just for a second words formed on his lips that it was hard not to utter. He knew she was in love with him and would probably marry him, but the old terror of being held rose in him. He would have to tell this girl so many things. He looked closely at her, holding her face under his, and if she had said one wise or witty thing he might have spoken, but she only looked up with a glaze of childish passion in her eyes and said: 'What are you thinking, honey?'

The moment passed. She fell back smoothly into being only a part of the day's pleasure, the day's excitement. She was desirable here, but she was desirable downstairs too. The mountains were bewitching his determinations out of him.

Drawing her close to him, lightly he said: 'So you like the Spics, eh? I suppose the boys are all Spics down in New Orleans?'

As she squeezed his face furiously between thumb and finger, his mind was already back with Emily at the other hotel a quarter of a mile away.

Tommy's dinner was not to be at his hotel. After meeting in the bar they sledged down into the village to a large old-fashioned Swiss taproom, a thing of woodwork, clocks, steins, kegs and antlers. There were other parties like their own, bound together by the common plan of eating *fondue* – a peculiarly indigestible form of welsh rabbit – and drinking spiced wine, and then hitching on the backs of sleighs to Doldorp several miles away, where there was a townspeople's ball.

His own party included Emily; her cousin, young Frank Forrester; young Count de Caros Moros, a friend of Rosemary's – she played ping-pong with him and harked to his guitar and to his tales of machine-gunning his discontented fellow countrymen in Andalusia – a Cambridge University hockey hero named Harry Whitby, and lastly the two 'ickle durls' – Californians who were up from a Montreux school for the holidays and very anxious to be swept off their feet. Six Americans, two Europeans.

It was a good party. Some grey-haired men of the golden nineties sang ancient glees at the piano, the *fondue* was fun, the wine was pert and heady, and smoke swirled out of the brown walls and toned the bright costumes into the room. They were all on a ship going somewhere, with the port just ahead; the faces of girls and young men bore the same innocent and un-lined expectations of the great possibilities inherent in the situation and the night. The Latins became Americans easily, the English with more effort. Then it was over and one hundred five-pound boots stamped towards the sleighs that waited at the door.

For a moment Tommy lingered, engrossed in conversation with Emily, yet with sudden twinges of conscience about Rosemary. She had been on his left; he had last seen her listening to young Caros Moros perform upon his extremely portable guitar. Outside in the crisp moonlight he saw her tying her sledge to one of the sleighs ahead. The sleighs were moving off; he and Emily caught one, and at the crisp-cracking whips the horses pulled, breasting the dark air. Past them figures ran and scrambled, the younger people pushing one another off, landing in a cloud of soft snow, then panting after the horses, to fling themselves exhausted on a sledge, or else wail that they were being left behind. On either side the fields were tranquil; the space through which the cavalcade moved was high and limit-less. After they were in the country there was less noise; perhaps ears were listening atavistically for wolves howling in the clumps of trees far across the snow.

At Doldorp he stood with Emily in the doorway, watching the others go in.

'Everybody's first husband with everybody's first wife,' she remarked. 'Who believes in marriage? I do. A plucky girl – takes the count of nine and comes up for more. But not for two years; I'm over here to do some straight thinking.'

It occurred to Tommy that two years was a long time, but he knew that girls so frequently didn't mean what they said. He and Emily watched the entrance of Mr Cola, nicknamed Capone, with his harem, consisting of wife, daughters, wife's friend and three Siamese. Then they went inside.

The crowd was enormous – peasants, servants from the hotels, shop-keepers, guides, outlanders, cow herders, ski teachers and tourists. They all got seats where they could, and Tommy saw Rosemary with a crowd of young people across the room; she seemed a little tired and pale, sitting back with her lips apart and her eyes fixed and sleepy. When someone waltzed off with Emily, he went over and asked her to dance.

'I don't want to dance. I'm tired.'

'Let's got sit where we can hear the yodelling.'

'I can hear it here.'

'What am I accused of?' he demanded.

'Nothing. I haven't even seen you.'

Her current partner smiled at him ingratiatingly, but Tommy was growing annoyed:

'Didn't I explain that this dinner was for a girl who'd been particularly nice to me? I told you I'd have to devote a lot of the evening to her.'

'Go on devote it, then. I'm leaving soon.'

'Who with?'

'Capone has a sleigh.'

'Yes, you're leaving with him. He'll take you for a ride; you'll be on the spot if you don't look out.'

He felt a touch of uneasiness. The mystery she had lacked this afternoon was strong in her now. Before he should be so weak as to grant her another advantage, he turned and asked one of the 'ickle durls' to dance.

The 'ickle durl' bored him. She admired him; she was used to clasping her hands together in his wake and heaving audible sighs. When the music stopped he gave her an outrageous compliment to atone for his preoccupation and left her at her table. The night was ruined. He realized that it was Rosemary who moved him most deeply, and his eyes wandered to her across the room. He told himself that she was playing him jealously, but he hated the way she was fooling with young Caros Moros; and he liked it still less when he glanced over a little later and found that the two of them were gone.

He sprang up and dashed out of the door; there was the snow, lightly falling, there were the waiting sleighs, the horses patient in their frozen harness, and there was a small, excited crowd of Swiss gathered around Mr Cola's sleigh.

'*Salaud !*' he heard. '*Salaud Français !*'

It appeared that the French courier, long accepted as a member of the Cola *ménage*, had spent the afternoon tippling with his master; the courier had not survived. Cola had been compelled to assist him outdoors, where he promptly gave tongue to a series of insults directed at the Swiss. They were all *boches*. Why hadn't they come in the war? A crowd gathered, and as it included several Swiss who were in the same state as the Frenchman, the matter was growing complicated; the women were uncomfortable, the Siamese were smiling diplomatically among themselves. One of the Swiss was on the runner of the sleigh, leaning over Mrs Cola and shaking his fist in the courier's face. Mr Cola stood up in the sleigh and addressed them in hoarse American as to 'the big idea ?'

'Dirty Frenchmen!' cried the Swiss. 'Yes, and during your Revolution did you not cut the Swiss Guards down to the last man ?'

'Get out of here!' shouted Cola. 'Hey, coachman, drive right over 'em! You guys go easy there! Take your hands off the sleigh . . . Shut up, you!' – this to the courier, who was still muttering wildly. Cola looked at him as if he contemplated throwing him to the crowd. In a moment Tommy edged himself between the outraged Swiss patriot and the sleigh.

'Ne'mine what they say! Drive on!' cried Cola again. 'We got to get these girls out of here!'

Conscious of Rosemary's eyes staring at him out of a bearskin robe, and of Caros Moros next to her, Tommy raised his voice:

'*Ce sont des dames Américaines; il n'y a qu'un Français. Voyons ! Qu'est-ce que vous voulez ?*'

But the massacre of the Swiss Guards was not to be disposed of so lightly.

Tommy had an inspiration. 'But who tried to save the Swiss Guards ? Answer me that!' he shouted. 'An American – Benjamin Franklin! He almost saved them!'

His preposterous statement rang out strong and true upon the electric air. The protagonist of the martyrs was momentarily baffled.

'An American saved them!' Tommy cried. 'Hurray for America and Switzerland!' And he added quickly, to the coachman, 'Drive on now – and fast!'

The sleigh started with a lurch. Two men clung to it for a moment and then let go, and the conveyance slid free behind the swiftly trotting horses.

'*Vive l'Amérique! Vive la Suisse!*' Tommy shouted.

'*Vive la Fra—*' began the courier, but Cola put his fur glove in the man's mouth. They drove rapidly for a few minutes.

'Drop me here,' Tommy said. 'I have to go back to the dance.' He looked at Rosemary, but she would not meet his eye. She was a bundle of fur next to Caros Moros, and he saw the latter drop his arm around her till they were one mass of fur together. The sight was horrible; of all the people in the world she had become the most desirable, and he wanted every bit of her youth and freshness. He wanted to jerk Caros Moros to his feet and pull him from the sleigh. He saw how stupid it had been to play so long with her innocence and sincerity, until now she scarcely saw him any more, scarcely knew he was there.

As he swung himself off the sleigh, Rosemary and Caros Moros were singing softly:

... I wouldn't stoop
To onion soup;
With corn-beef hash I'm all
  through—

and the Spaniard winked at Tommy as if to say, 'We know how to handle this little girl, don't we?'

The courier struggled and then cried in a blurred voice: 'Beeb wa Fwance.'

'Keep your glove in his mouth,' said Tommy savagely. 'Choke him to death.'

He walked off down the road, utterly miserable.

III

His first instinct next morning was to phone her immediately; his second was to sulk proudly in his room, hoping against hope that his own phone would ring. After luncheon he went downstairs, where he was addressed by the objectionable Greek who had danced with her at tea yesterday afternoon – ages ago.

'Tell me; you like to play the ping-pong?'

'It depends who with,' Tommy answered rudely. Immediately he was so sorry that he went downstairs with the man and batted the white puff-balls for half an hour.

At four he skied over to Emily's hotel, resolving to drive the other and more vivid image from his mind. The lobby was filled with children in fancy dress, who had gathered there from many hotels for the children's Christmas ball.

Emily was a long time coming down, and when she did she was hurried and distracted.

'I'm so sorry. I've been costuming my children, and now I've got to get them launched into this orgy, because they're both very shy.'

'Sit and get your breath a minute. We'll talk about love.'

'Honestly, I can't, Tommy. I'll see you later.' And she added quickly, 'Can't you get your little southern girl? She seemed to worry you a lot last night.'

After half an hour of diffident grand marches, Emily came back to him, but Tommy's patience was exhausted and he was on his feet to go. Even now she showed him that he was asking for time and attention out of turn, and, being unavailable, she had again grown as mysterious as Rosemary.

'It's been a hard day in lots of ways,' she explained as she walked with him to the door. 'Things I can't tell you about.'

'Oh, yes?' People had so many affairs. You never knew how much space you actually occupied in their lives.

Outdoors he came across her young cousin, Frank Forrester, buckling on his skis. Pushing off together, they drifted slowly down a slushy hill.

'Let me tell you something,' Frank burst out. 'I'm never going to get married. I've seen too much of it. And if any girl asked my advice, I'd tell her to stay out.' He was full of the idea: 'There's my mother, for instance. She married a second husband, and what does he do but have her spied on and bribe her maids to open her mail? Then there's Emily. You know what happened to her; one night her husband came home and told her she was acting cold to him, but that he'd fix that up. So he built a bonfire under her bed, made up of shoes and things, and set fire to it. And if the leather hadn't smelled so terrible she'd have been burned to death.'

'That's just two marriages.'

'Two!' said Frank resentfully. 'Isn't that enough? Now we think Emily's husband is having her spied on. There's a man keeps watching us in the dining-room.'

As Tommy stemmed into the driveway of his hotel, he wondered if he was really attractive to women at all. Yesterday he had been sure of these two, holding them in the hollow of his hand. As he dressed for dinner he realized that he wanted them both. It was an outrage that he couldn't have them both. Wouldn't a girl rather have half of him than all of Harry Whitby, or a whole Spic with a jar of pomade thrown in? Life was so badly arranged – better no women at all than only one woman.

He shouted 'Come in!' to a knock at his salon door, and leaning around the corner, his hand on his dress tie, found the two 'ickle durls'.

He started. Had they inherited him from Rosemary? Had he been theirs since the superior pair seemed to have relinquished their claims? Were they really presuming that he might escort them to the fancy-dress ball tonight?

Slipping on his coat, he went into his parlour. They were got up as Arlésienne peasant girls, with high black bonnets and starched aprons.

'We've come about Rosemary,' they said directly. 'We wanted to see if you won't do something about it. She's been in bed all day and she says she isn't coming to the party tonight. Couldn't you at least call her up?'

'Why should I call her up?'

'You know she's perfectly crazy about you, and last night was the most miserable she ever spent in her life. After she broke Caros Moros' guitar, we couldn't stop her crying.'

A contented glow spread over Tommy. His instinct was to telephone at once, but, curiously enough, to telephone Emily, so that he could talk to her with his newborn confidence.

The 'ickle durls' moved towards the door. 'You will call her up,' they urged him respectfully.

'Right now.' He took them each in one arm, like a man in a musical comedy, and kissed the rouge on their cheeks. When they were gone, he telephoned Rosemary. Her 'hello' was faint and frightened.

'Are you sorry you were so terrible to me last night, baby?' he demanded. 'No real pickaninny would—'

'You were the terrible one.'

'Are you coming to the party tonight?'

'Oh, I will if you'll act differently. But I'll be hours; I'm still in bed. I can't get down till after dinner.'

With Rosemary safely locked up again in the tranquil cells of his mind, he rang up Emily.

'I'm sorry I was so short with you this afternoon,' she said immediately.

'Are you in love with me?'

'Why, no; I don't think so.'

'Aren't you a little bit in love with me ?'

'I like you a lot.'

'Dear Emily. What's this about being spied on ?'

'Oh, there's a man here who walked into my room – maybe by accident. But he always watches us.'

'I can't stand having you annoyed,' he said. 'Please call on me if anything definite happens. I'd be glad to come up and rub his face in the snow.'

There was a pregnant telephone silence.

'I wish I was with you now,' he said gently.

After a moment she whispered, 'I do too.'

He had nothing to complain of; the situation was readjusted; things were back where they had been twenty-four hours ago. Eating dinner alone, he felt that in reality both girls were beside him, one on either hand. The dining room was shimmering with unreality for the fancy-dress party, for tonight was the last big event of the Christmas season. Most of the younger people who gave it its real colour would start back to school tomorrow.

And Tommy felt that in the evening somewhere – but in whose company he couldn't say – there would come a moment; perhaps the moment. Probably very late, when the orchestra and what remained of the party – the youth and cream of it – would move into the bar, and Abdul, with Oriental delight in obscurity, would manipulate the illumination in a sort of counterpoint whose other tone was the flashing moon from the ice rink, bouncing in the big windows. Tommy had danced with Rosemary in that light a few hours after their first meeting; he remembered the mysterious darkness, with the cigarette points turning green or silver when the lights shone red, the sense of snow outside and the occasional band of white falling across the dancers as a door was opened and shut. He remembered her in his arms and the plaint of the orchestra playing:

That's why mother made me
Promise to be true

and the other vague faces passing in the darkness.

She knew I'd meet someone
Exactly like you.

He thought now of Emily. They would have a very long, serious conversation, sitting in the hall. Then they would slip away and talk even more seriously, but this time with her very close to him. Anything might happen – anything.

But he was thinking of the two apart; and tonight they would both be here in full view of each other. There must be no more complications like last evening; he must dovetail the affairs with skill and thought.

Emerging from dinner, he strolled down the corridor, already filled with graces and grotesques, conventional clouds of columbines, clowns, peasants, pirates and ladies of Spain. He never wore costume himself and the sight of a man in motley made him sad, but some of the girls were lovelier than in life, and his heart jumped as he caught sight of a snow-white ballet dancer at the end of the corridor, and recognized Rosemary. But almost as he started towards her, another party emerged from the cloakroom, and in it was Emily.

He thought quickly. Neither one had seen him, and to greet one with the other a few yards away was to get off on the wrong foot, for he had invented opening remarks for each one – remarks which must be made alone. With great presence of mind, he dove for the men's wash room and stood there tensely.

Emerging in a few minutes, he hovered cautiously along the hall. Passing the lounge, he saw, in a side glance, that Caros Moros was with Rosemary and that she was glancing about impatiently. Emily looked up from her table, saw him and beckoned. Without moving a muscle of his face, Tommy stared above her and passed on. He decided to wait in the bar until the dancing actually started; it would be easier when the two were separated in the crowd. In the bar he was hailed gratefully by Mr Cola; Mr Cola was killing time there desperately, with his harem waiting outside.

'I'm having them all psychoanalysed,' he said. 'I got a guy down from Zurich, and he's doing one a day. I never saw such a gloomy bunch of women; always bellyaching wherever I take 'em. A man I knew told me he had his wife psychoanalysed and she was easier to be with afterwards.'

Tommy heard only vaguely. He had become aware that, as if they had planned it in collusion, Emily and Rosemary had sauntered simultaneously into the bar. Blind-eyed and breathless, he strode out and into the ballroom. One of the 'ickle durls' danced by him and he seized her gratefully.

'Rosemary was looking for you,' she told him, turning up the flattered face of seventeen.

Presently he felt silly dancing with her, but, perhaps because of her admirers' deference to his maturer years, three encores passed and no one cut in. He began to feel like a man pushing a baby carriage. He took a dislike to her colonial costume, the wig of which sent gusts of powder up his nose. She even smelled young – of very pure baby soap and peppermint candy. Like almost every act he had performed in the last two days, he was unable to realize why he had cut in on her at all.

He saw Rosemary dancing with Caros Moros, then with other partners, and then again with Caros Moros. He had now been a half-hour with the 'ickle durl'; his gaiety was worn thin and his smile was becoming strained when at last he was cut in on. Feeling ruffled and wilted, he look around, to find that Rosemary and Caros Moros had disappeared. With the discovery, he came to the abrupt decision that he would ask her to marry him.

He went searching; ploughing brusquely through crowds like a swimmer in surf. Just as, finally, he caught sight of the white-pointed cap and escaping yellow curls, he was accosted by Frank Forrester:

'Emily sent me to look for you. Her maid telephoned that somebody tried to get into her room, and we think it's the man who keeps watching her in the dining-room.'

Tommy stared at him vaguely, and Frank continued:

'Don't you think you and I ought to go up there now and rub his face in the snow?'

'Where?'

'To our hotel.'

Tommy's eyes begged around him. There was nothing he wanted less.

'We'd like to find out one way or another.' And then, as Tommy still hesitated: 'You haven't lost your nerve, have you? About rubbing his face in the snow?'

Evasion was impossible. Tommy threw a last quick glance at Rosemary, who was moving with Caros Moros back towards the dancing floor.

At Emily's hotel the maid waited in the lower hall. It seemed that the bedroom door had opened slowly a little way; then closed again quickly. She had fled downstairs. Silently Tommy and Frank mounted the stairs and approached the room; they breathed quietly at the threshold and flung open the door. The room was empty.

'I think this was a great flight of the imagination,' Tommy scolded. 'We might as well go back—'

He broke off, as there were light footsteps in the corridor and a man walked coolly into the room.

'*Ach je !*' he exclaimed sharply.

'Aha!' Frank stepped behind him and shut the door. 'We got you.'

The man looked from one to the other in alarm.

'I must be in the wrong room!' he exclaimed, and then, with an uncomfortable laugh: 'I see! My room is just above this and I got the wrong floor again. In my last hotel I was on the third floor, so I got the habit—'

'Why do you always listen to every word we say at table?' demanded Frank.

'I like to look at you because you are such nice, handsome, wealthy American people. I've come to this hotel for years.'

'We're wasting time,' said Tommy impatiently. 'Let's go to the manager.'

The intruder was more than willing. He proved to be a coal dealer from Berlin, an old and valued client of the house. They apologized; there was no hard feeling; they must join him in a drink. It was ten minutes before they got away, and Tommy led a furious pace back towards the dance. He was chiefly furious at Emily. Why should people be spied upon? What sort of women were spied upon? He felt as if this were a plan of Emily's to keep him away from Rosemary, who with every instant was dancing farther and farther off with Caros Moros into a youthful Spanish dream. At the drive of the hotel Frank said good night.

'You're not going back to the dance?'

'It's finished; the ballroom's dark. Everybody's probably gone to Doldorp, because here it always closes early on Sunday night.'

Tommy dashed up the drive to the hotel. In the gloomy half light of the office a last couple were struggling into overshoes; the dance was over.

'For you, Mr McLane.' The night concierge handed him a telegram. Tommy stared at it for a moment before he tore it open.

GENEVA SWITZERLAND 2/1/31

H.P. EASTBY ARRIVED TONIGHT FROM PARIS STOP ABSOLUTELY ESSENTIAL
YOU BE HERE FOR EARLY LUNCH MONDAY STOP AFTERWARDS
ACCOMPANYING HIM TO DIJON
SAGE.

For a moment he couldn't understand. When he had grasped the utterly unarguable dictum, he took the concierge by both arms.

'You know Miss Merriweather. Did she go to Doldorp?'

'I think she did.'

'Get me a sleigh.'

'Every sleigh in town has gone over there; some with ten people in them. These last people here couldn't get sleighs.'

'Any price!' cried Tommy fiercely. 'Think!'

He threw down five large silver wheels on the desk.

'There's the station sleigh, but the horses have got to be out at seven in the morning. If you went to the stables and asked Eric—'

Half an hour later the big, glassed-in carryall jingled out on the Doldorp road with a solitary passenger. After a mile a first open sleigh dashed past them on its way home, and Tommy leaned out and glared into the anonymous bundles of fur and called 'Rosemary!' in a firm but unavailing voice. When they had gone another mile, sleighs began to pass in increasing numbers. Sometimes a taunting shout drifted back to him; sometimes his voice was drowned in a chorus of 'Jingle Bells' or 'Merrily We Roll Along'. It was hopeless; the sleighs were coming so fast now that he couldn't examine the occupants; and then there were no more sleighs and he sat upright in the great, hearselike vehicle, rocking on towards a town that he knew no longer held what he was after. A last chorus rang in his ears:

Good night, ladies,
Good night, ladies,
Good night, lay-de-es,
I'm going to leave you now.

IV

He was awake at seven with the *valet de chambre* shaking his shoulders. The sun was waving gold, green and white flags on the Wildstrubel as he fumbled clumsily for his razor. The great fiasco of the night before drifted over him, and he could hear even the great blackbirds cawing, 'You went away too far,' on the white balcony outside.

Desperately he considered telephoning her, wondering if he could explain to a girl still plunged in drowsiness what he would have had trouble in explaining in person. But it was already time to go; he drove off in a crowded sleigh with other faces wan in the white morning.

They were passing the crisp pale green rink where Wiener waltzes blared all day and the blazing colours of many schools flashed against pale blue skies. Then there was the station full of frozen breath; he was in the first-class carriage of the train drawing away from the little valley, past pink pines and fresh, diamond-strewn snow.

Across from him women were weeping softly for temporarily lost children whom they had left up there for another term at school. And in a compartment farther up he suddenly glimpsed the two 'ickle durls'. He drew back; he couldn't stand that this morning. But he was not to escape so readily. As the train passed Caux, high on its solitary precipice, the 'ickle durls' came along the corridor and spied him.

'Hey, there!' They exchanged glances. 'We didn't think you were on the train.'

'Do you know,' began the older one – the one he had danced with last night – 'what we'd like?'

It was something daring evidently, for they went off into spasms of suppressed giggles.

'What we'd like,' the 'ickle durl' continued, 'is to ask you if – we wondered if you would send us a photo.'

'Of what?' asked Tommy.

'Of yourself.'

'She's asking for herself,' declared the other 'ickle durl' indignantly. 'I wouldn't be so darn fresh.'

'I haven't had a photo taken for years.'

'Even an old one,' pursued the 'ickle durl' timidly.

'And listen,' said the other one: 'Won't you come up for just a minute and say good-bye to Rosemary? She's still crying her eyes out, and I think she'd like it if you even came up to say good-bye.'

He jerked forward as if thrown by the train.

'Rosemary!'

'She cried all the way to Doldorp and all the way back, and then she broke Caros Moros' other guitar that he keeps in reserve; so he feels awful, being up there another month without any guitar.'

But Tommy was gone. As the train began traversing back and forth towards Lake Geneva, the two 'ickle durls' sat down resignedly in his compartment.

'So then—' he was saying at the moment. 'No, don't move; I don't mind a bit. I like you like that. Use my handkerchief . . . Listen. If you've got to go to Paris, can't you possibly come by way of Geneva and Dijon?'

'Oh, I'd love to. I don't want to let you out of my sight – not now, anyhow.'

At that moment – perhaps out of habit, perhaps because the two girls had become almost indissolubly wedded in his mind – he had a sharp, vivid impression of Emily. Wouldn't it be better for him to see them both together before coming to such an important decision?

'Will you marry me?' he cried desperately. 'Are we engaged? Can't we put it in writing?'

With the sound of his own voice the other image faded from his mind for ever.

FLIGHT AND PURSUIT

Saturday Evening Post, 14 May 1932

*'Flight and Pursuit' was probably written in Switzerland in April 1931.
The* Post *bought the story with some reluctance for $4000, and Harold
Ober reported to Fitzgerald: 'The* Post *are taking "Flight and Pursuit"
but they want me to tell you that they do not feel that your last three
stories have been up to the best you can do. They think it might be a good
idea for you to write some American stories – that is stories laid on this side
of the Atlantic and they feel that the last stories have been lacking in plot.'
The* Post *indicated its reservations about this story by holding it for a year
before publishing it in fourth position and leaving Fitzgerald's name off
the cover. (His name appeared on the cover only once again, for the 4 June
1932 issue.)*

*'Flight and Pursuit' again drew on Fitzgerald's unhappy impressions
of Switzerland. As he commented in 'The Hotel Child', 'this corner of
Europe does not draw people; rather, it accepts them without too many
inconvenient questions'.*

In 1918, a few days before the Armistice, Caroline Martin, of Derby, in
Virginia, eloped with a trivial young lieutenant from Ohio. They were
married in a town over the Maryland border and she stayed there until
George Corcoran got his discharge – then they went to his home in the
North.

It was a desperate, reckless marriage. After she had left her aunt's house
with Corcoran, the man who had broken her heart realized that he had
broken his own too; he telephoned, but Caroline had gone, and all that he
could do that night was to lie awake and remember her waiting in the front
yard, with the sweetness draining down into her out of the magnolia trees,
out of the dark world, and remember himself arriving in his best uniform,
with boots shining and with his heart full of selfishness that, from shame,

turned into cruelty. Next day he learned that she had eloped with Corcoran and, as he had deserved, he had lost her.

In Sidney Lahaye's overwhelming grief, the petty reasons for his act disgusted him – the alternative of a long trip around the world or of a bachelor apartment in New York with four Harvard friends; more positively the fear of being held, of being bound. The trip – they could have taken it together. The bachelor apartment – it had resolved into its bare, cold constituent parts in a single night. Being held? Why, that was all he wanted – to be close to that freshness, to be held in those young arms for ever.

He had been an egoist, brought up selfishly by a selfish mother; this was his first suffering. But like his small, wiry, handsome person, he was all knit of one piece and his reaction were not trivial. What he did he carried with him always, and he knew he had done a contemptible and stupid thing. He carried his grief around, and eventually it was good for him. But inside of him, utterly unassimilable, indigestible, remained the memory of the girl.

Meanwhile, Caroline Corcoran, lately the belle of a Virginia town, was paying for the luxury of her desperation in a semi-slum of Dayton, Ohio.

II

She had been three years in Dayton and the situation had become intolerable. Brought up in a district where everyone was comparatively poor, where not two gowns out of fifty at country-club dances cost more than thirty dollars, lack of money had not been formidable in itself. This was very different. She came into a world not only of straining poverty but of a commonness and vulgarity that she had never touched before. It was in this regard that George Corcoran had deceived her. Somewhere he had acquired a faint patina of good breeding and he had said or done nothing to prepare her for his mother, into whose two-room flat he introduced her. Aghast, Caroline realized that she had stepped down several floors. These people had no position of any kind; George knew no one; she was literally alone in a strange city. Mrs Corcoran disliked Caroline – disliked her good manners, her southern ways, the added burden of her presence. For all her airs, she had brought them nothing save, eventually, a baby. Meanwhile George got a job and they moved to more spacious quarters, but mother came, too, for she owned her son, and Caroline's months went by in unimaginable dreariness. At first she was too ashamed and too poor to go home, but at the end of a year her aunt sent her money for a visit and she spent a month in Derby with her little son, proudly reticent, but unable to keep some of the truth from leaking out to her friends. Her friends had done well, or less well, but none of them had fared quite so ill as she.

But after three years, when Caroline's child became less dependent, and when the last of her affection for George had been frittered away, as his pleasant manners became debased with his own inadequacies, and when her bright, unused beauty still plagued her in the mirror, she knew that the break was coming. Not that she had specific hopes of happiness – for she accepted the idea that she had wrecked her life, and her capacity for dreaming had left her that November night three years before – but simply because conditions were intolerable. The break was heralded by a voice over the phone – a voice she remembered only as something that had done her terrible injury long ago.

'Hello,' said the voice – a strong voice with strain in it. 'Mrs George Corcoran?'

'Yes.'

'Who was Caroline Martin?'

'Who is this?'

'This is someone you haven't seen for years. Sidney Lahaye.'

After a moment she answered in a different tone: 'Yes?'

'I've wanted to see you for a long time,' the voice went on.

'I don't see why,' said Caroline simply.

'I want to see you. I can't talk over the phone.'

Mrs Corcoran, who was in the room, asked, 'Who is it?' forming the words with her mouth. Caroline shook her head slightly.

'I don't see why you want to see me,' she said, 'and I don't think I want to see you.' Her breath came quicker; the old wound opened up again, the injury that had changed her from a happy young girl in love into whatever vague entity in the scheme of things she was now.

'Please don't ring off,' Sidney said. 'I didn't call you without thinking it over carefully. I heard things weren't going well with you.'

'That's not true.' Caroline was very conscious now of Mrs Corcoran's craning neck. 'Things are going well. And I can't see what possible right you have to intrude in my affairs.'

'Wait, Caroline! You don't know what happened back in Derby after you left. I was frantic—'

'Oh, I don't care—' she cried. 'Let me alone; do you hear?'

She hung up the receiver. She was outraged that this man, almost forgotten now save as an instrument of her disaster, should come back into her life!

'Who was it?' demanded Mrs Corcoran.

'Just a man – a man I loathe.'

'Who?'

'Just an old friend.'

Mrs Corcoran looked at her sharply. 'It wasn't that man, was it?' she asked.

'What man?'

'The one you told Georgie about three years ago, when you were first married – it hurt his feelings. The man you were in love with that threw you over.'

'Oh, no,' said Caroline. 'That is my affair.'

She went to the bedroom that she shared with George. If Sidney should persist and come here, how terrible – to find her sordid in a mean street.

When George came in, Caroline heard the mumble of his mother's conversation behind the closed door; she was not surprised when he asked at dinner:

'I hear that an old friend called you up.'

'Yes. Nobody you know.'

'Who was it?'

'It was an old acquaintance, but he won't call again,' she said.

'I'll bet he will,' guessed Mrs Corcoran. 'What was it you told him wasn't true?'

'That's my affair.'

Mrs Corcoran glanced significantly at George, who said:

'It seems to me if a man calls up my wife and annoys her, I have a right to know about it.'

'You won't, and that's that.' She turned to his mother: 'Why did you have to listen, anyhow?'

'I was there. You're my son's wife.'

'You make trouble,' said Caroline quietly; 'you listen and watch me and make trouble. How about the woman who keeps calling up George – you do your best to hush that up.'

'That's a lie!' George cried. 'And you can't talk to my mother like that! If you don't think I'm sick of your putting on a lot of dog when I work all day and come home to find—'

As he went off into a weak, raging tirade, pouring out his own self-contempt upon her, Caroline's thoughts escaped to the fifty-dollar bill, a present from her grandmother hidden under the paper in a bureau drawer. Life had taken much out of her in three years; she did not know whether she had the audacity to run away – it was nice, though, to know the money was there.

Next day, in the spring sunlight, things seemed better – and she and George had a reconciliation. She was desperately adaptable, desperately sweet-natured, and for an hour she had forgotten all the trouble and felt the old emotion of mingled passion and pity for him. Eventually his mother would go; eventually he would change and improve; and meanwhile there was her son with her own kind, wise smile, turning over the pages of a linen book on the sunny carpet. As her soul sank into a helpless, feminine apathy, compounded of the next hour's duty, of a fear of further hurt or incalculable change, the phone rang sharply through the flat.

Again and again it rang, and she stood rigid with terror. Mrs Corcoran was gone to market, but it was not the old woman she feared. She feared the black cone hanging from the metal arm, shrilling and shrilling across the sunny room. It stopped for a minute, replaced by her heartbeats; then began again. In a panic she rushed into her room, threw little Dexter's best clothes and her only presentable dress and shoes into a suitcase and put the fifty-dollar bill in her purse. Then taking her son's hand, she hurried out of the door, pursued down the apartment stairs by the persistent cry of the telephone. The windows were open, and as she hailed a taxi and directed it to the station, she could still hear it clamouring out into the sunny morning.

III

Two years later, looking a full two years younger, Caroline regarded herself in the mirror, in a dress that she had paid for. She was a stenographer, employed by an importing firm in New York; she and young Dexter lived on her salary and on the income of ten thousand dollars in bonds, a legacy from her aunt. If life had fallen short of what it had once promised, it was at least livable again, less than misery. Rising to a sense of her big initial lie, George had given her freedom and the custody of her child. He was in kindergarten now, and safe until 5.30, when she would call for him and take him to the small flat that was at least her own. She had nothing warm near her, but she had New York, with its diversion for all purses, its curious yielding up of friends for the lonely, its quick metropolitan rhythm of love and birth and death that supplied dreams to the unimaginative, pageantry and drama to the drab.

But though life was possible it was less than satisfactory. Her work was hard, she was physically fragile; she was much more tired at the day's end than the girls with whom she worked. She must consider a precarious future when her capital should be depleted by her son's education. Thinking of the Corcoran family, she had a horror of being dependent on her son; and she dreaded the day when she must push him from her. She found that her interest in men had gone. Her two experiences had done something to her; she saw them clearly and she saw them darkly, and that part of her life was sealed up, and it grew more and more faint, like a book she had read long ago. No more love.

Caroline saw this with detachment, and not without a certain, almost impersonal, regret. In spite of the fact that sentiment was the legacy of a pretty girl, it was just one thing that was not for her. She surprised herself by saying in front of some other girls that she disliked men, but she knew it was the truth. It was an ugly phrase, but now, moving in an approximately foursquare world, she detested the compromises and evasions of her marriage. 'I hate men – I, Caroline, hate men. I want from them no more than courtesy and to be left alone. My life is incomplete, then, but so be it. For others it is complete, for me it is incomplete.'

The day that she looked at her evening dress in the mirror, she was in a country house on Long Island – the home of Evelyn Murdock, the most spectacularly married of all her old Virginia friends. They had met in the street, and Caroline was there for the weekend, moving unfamiliarly through a luxury she had never imagined, intoxicated at finding that in her new evening dress she was as young and attractive as these other women, whose lives had followed more glamorous paths. Like New York the rhythm of the weekend, with its birth, its planned gaieties and its announced end, followed the rhythm of life and was a substitute for it. The sentiment had gone from Caroline, but the patterns remained. The guests, dimly glimpsed on the veranda, were prospective admirers. The visit to the nursery was a promise of future children of her own; the descent to dinner was a promenade down a marriage aisle, and her gown was a wedding dress with an invisible train.

'The man you're sitting next to,' Evelyn said, 'is an old friend of yours. Sidney Lahaye – he was at Camp Rosecrans.'

After a confused moment she found that it wasn't going to be difficult at all. In the moment she had met him – such a quick moment that she had no time to grow excited – she realized that he was gone for her. He was only a smallish, handsome man, with a flushed, dark skin, a smart little black moustache and very fine eyes. It was just as gone as gone. She tried to remember why he had once seemed the most desirable person in the world, but she could only remember that he had made love to her, that he had made her think of them as engaged, and then that he had acted badly and thrown her over – into George Corcoran's arms. Years later he had telephoned like a travelling salesman remembering a dalliance in a casual city. Caroline was entirely unmoved and at her ease as they sat down at table.

But Sidney Lahaye was not relinquishing her so easily.

'So I called you up that night in Derby,' he said; 'I called you for half an hour. Everything had changed for me in that ride out to camp.'

'You had a beautiful remorse.'

'It wasn't remorse; it was self-interest. I realized I was terribly in love with you. I stayed awake all night—'

Caroline listened indifferently. It didn't even explain things; nor did it tempt her to cry out on fate – it was just a fact.

He stayed near her, persistently. She knew no one else at the party; there was no niche in any special group for her. They talked on the veranda after dinner, and once she said coolly:

'Women are fragile that way. You do something to them at certain times and literally nothing can ever change what you've done.'

'You mean that you definitely hate me.'

She nodded. 'As far as I feel actively about you at all.'

'I suppose so. It's awful, isn't it?'

'No. I even have to think before I can really remember how I stood waiting for you in the garden that night, holding all my dreams and hopes in my arms like a lot of flowers – they were that to me, anyhow. I thought I was pretty sweet. I'd saved myself up for that – all ready to hand it all to you. And then you came up to me and kicked me.' She laughed incredulously. 'You behaved like an awful person. Even though I don't care any more, you'll always be an awful person to me. Even if you'd found me that night, I'm not at all sure that anything could have been done about it. Forgiveness is just a silly word in a matter like that.'

Feeling her own voice growing excited and annoyed, she drew her cape around her and said in an ordinary voice:

'It's getting too cold to sit here.'

'One more thing before you go,' he said. 'It wasn't typical of me. It was so little typical that in the last five years I've never spent an unoccupied moment without remembering it. Not only I haven't married, I've never even been faintly in love. I've measured up every girl I've met to you, Caroline – their faces, their voices, the tips of their elbows.'

'I'm sorry I had such a devastating effect on you. It must have been a nuisance.'

'I've kept track of you since I called you in Dayton; I knew that, sooner or later, we'd meet.'

'I'm going to say good night.'

But saying good night was easier than sleeping, and Caroline had only an hour's haunted doze behind her when she awoke at seven. Packing her bag, she made up a polite, abject letter to Evelyn Murdock, explaining why she was unexpectedly leaving on Sunday morning. It was difficult and she disliked Sidney Lahaye a little bit more intensely for that.

IV

Months later Caroline came upon a streak of luck. A Mrs O'Connor, whom she met through Evelyn Murdock, offered her a post as private secretary and travelling companion. The duties were light, the travelling included an immediate trip abroad, and Caroline, who was thin and run down from work, jumped at the chance. With astonishing generosity the offer included her boy.

From the beginning Caroline was puzzled as to what had attracted Helen O'Connor to her. Her employer was a woman of thirty, dissipated in a discreet way, extremely worldly and, save for her curious kindness to Caroline, extremely selfish. But the salary was good and Caroline shared in every luxury and was invariably treated as an equal.

The next three years were so different from anything in her past that they seemed years borrowed from the life of someone else. The Europe in which Helen O'Connor moved was not one of tourists but of seasons. Its most enduring impression was a phantasmagoria of the names of places and people – of Biarritz, of Mme de Colmar, of Deauville, of the Comte de Berme, of Cannes, of the Derehiemers, of Paris and the Château de Madrid. They lived the life of casinos and hotels so assiduously reported in the Paris American papers – Helen O'Connor drank and sat up late, and after a while Caroline drank and sat up late. To be slim and pale was fashionable during those years, and deep in Caroline was something that had become directionless and purposeless, that no longer cared. There was no love; she sat next to many men at table, appreciated compliments, courtesies and small gallantries, but the moment something more was hinted, she froze very definitely. Even when she was stimulated with excitement and wine, she felt the growing hardness of her sheath like a breastplate. But in other ways she was increasingly restless.

At first it had been Helen O'Connor who urged her to go out; now it became Caroline herself for whom no potion was too strong or any evening too late. There began to be mild lectures from Helen.

'This is absurd. After all, there's such a thing as moderation.'

'I suppose so, if you really want to live.'

'But you want to live; you've got a lot to live for. If my skin was like yours, and my hair— Why don't you look at some of the men that look at you ?'

'Life isn't good enough, that's all,' said Caroline. 'For a while I made the best of it, but I'm surer every day that it isn't good enough. People get through by keeping busy; the lucky ones are those with interesting work. I've been a good mother, but I'd certainly be an idiot putting in a sixteen-hour day mothering Dexter into being a sissy.'

'Why don't you marry Lahaye ? He has money and position and everything you could want.'

There was a pause. 'I've tried men. To hell with men.'

Afterwards she wondered at Helen's solicitude, having long realized that the other woman cared nothing for her. They had not even mutual tastes; often they were openly antipathetic and didn't meet for days at a time. Caroline wondered why she was kept on, but she had grown more self-indulgent in these years and she was not inclined to quibble over the feathers that made soft her nest.

One night on Lake Maggiore things changed in a flash. The blurred world seen from a merry-go-round settled into place; the merry-go-round suddenly stopped.

They had gone to the hotel in Locarno because of Caroline. For months she had had a mild but persistent asthma and they had come there for rest before the gaieties of the fall season at Biarritz. They met friends, and with them Caroline wandered to the Kursaal to play mild *boule* at a maximum of two Swiss francs. Helen remained at the hotel.

Caroline was sitting in the bar. The orchestra was playing a *Wiener Walzer*, and suddenly she had the sensation that the chords were extending themselves, that each bar of three-four time was bending in the middle, dropping a little and thus drawing itself out, until the waltz itself, like a phonograph running down, became a torture. She put her fingers in her ears; then suddenly she coughed into her handkerchief.

She gasped.

The man with her asked: 'What is it? Are you sick?'

She leaned back against the bar, her handkerchief with the trickle of blood clasped concealingly in her hand. It seemed to her half an hour before she answered, 'No, I'm all right,' but evidently it was only a few seconds, for the man did not continue his solicitude.

'I must get out,' Caroline thought. 'What is it?' Once or twice before she had noticed tiny flecks of blood, but never anything like this. She felt another cough coming and, cold with fear and weakness, wondered if she could get to the wash room.

After a long while the trickle stopped and someone wound the orchestra up to normal time. Without a word she walked slowly from the room, holding herself delicately as glass. The hotel was not a block away; she set out along the lamplit street. After a minute she wanted to cough again, so she stopped and held her breath and leaned against the wall. But this time it was no use; she raised her handkerchief to her mouth and lowered it after a minute, this time concealing it from her eyes. Then she walked on.

In the elevator another spell of weakness overcame her, but she managed to reach the door of her suite, where she collapsed on a little sofa in the antechamber. Had there been room in her heart for any emotion except terror, she would have been surprised at the sound of an excited dialogue in the *salon*, but at the moment the voices were part of a nightmare and only the shell of her ear registered what they said.

'I've been six months in Central Asia, or I'd have caught up with this before,' a man's voice said, and Helen answered, 'I've no sense of guilt whatsoever.'

'I don't suppose you have. I'm just panning myself for having picked you out.'

'May I ask who told you this tale, Sidney?'

'Two people. A man in New York had seen you in Monte Carlo and said for a year you'd been doing nothing but buying drinks for a bunch of cadgers and spongers. He wondered who was backing you. Then I saw Evelyn Murdock in Paris, and she said Caroline was dissipating night after night; she was thin as a rail and her face looked like death. That's what brought me down here.'

'Now listen, Sidney. I'm not going to be bullied about this. Our arrangement was that I was to take Caroline abroad and give her a good time, because you were in love with her or felt guilty about her, or something. You employed me for that and you backed me. Well, I've done just what you wanted. You said you wanted to her meet lots of men.'

'I said men.'

'I've rounded up what I could. In the first place, she's absolutely indifferent, and when men find that out, they're liable to go away.'

He sat down. 'Can't you understand that I wanted to do her good, not harm ? She's had a rotten time; she's spent most of her youth paying for something that was my fault, so I wanted to make it up the best way I could. I wanted her to have two years of pleasure; I wanted her to learn not to be afraid of men and to have some of the gaiety that I cheated her out of. With the result that you led her into two years of dissipation—' He broke off: 'What was that ?' he demanded.

Caroline had coughed again, irrepressibly. Her eyes were closed and she was breathing in little gasps as they came into the hall. Her hand opened and her handkerchief dropped to the floor.

In a moment she was lying on her own bed and Sidney was talking rapidly into the phone. In her dazed state the passion in his voice shook her like a vibration, and she whispered, 'Please! Please!' in a thin voice. Helen loosened her dress and took off her slippers and stockings.

The doctor made a preliminary examination and then nodded formidably at Sidney. He said that by good fortune a famous Swiss specialist on tuberculosis was staying at the hotel; he would ask for an immediate consultation.

The specialist arrived in bedroom slippers. His examination was as thorough as possible with the instruments at hand. Then he talked to Sidney in the *salon*.

'So far as I can tell without an X-ray, there is a sudden and widespread destruction of tissue on one side – sometimes happens when the patient is run down in other ways. If the X-ray bears me out, I would recommend an immediate artificial pnemothorax. The only chance is to completely isolate the left lung.'

'When could it be done ?'

The doctor considered. 'The nearest centre for this trouble is Montana Vermala, about three hours from here by automobile. If you start immediately and I telephone to a colleague there, the operation might be performed tomorrow morning.'

In the big, springy car Sidney held her across his lap, surrounding with his arms the mass of pillows. Caroline hardly knew who held her, nor did her mind grasp what she had overheard. Life jostled you around so – really very tiring. She was so sick, and probably going to die, and that didn't matter, except that there was something she wanted to tell Dexter.

Sidney was conscious of a desperate joy in holding her, even though she hated him, even though he had brought her nothing but harm. She was his in these night hours, so fair and pale, dependent on his arms for protection from the jolts of the rough road, leaning on his strength at last, even though she was unaware of it; yielding him the responsibility he had once feared and ever since desired. He stood between her and disaster.

Past Dome d'Ossola, a dim, murkily lighted Italian town; past Brig, where a kindly Swiss official saw his burden and waved him by without demanding his passport; down the valley of the Rhône, where the growing stream was young and turbulent in the moonlight. Then Sierre, and the haven, the sanctuary in the mountains, two miles above, where the snow gleamed. The funicular waited: Caroline sighed a little as he lifted her from the car.

'It's very good of you to take all this trouble,' she whispered formally.

V

For three weeks she lay perfectly still on her back. She breathed and she saw flowers in her room. Eternally her temperature was taken. She was delirious after the operation and in her dreams she was again a girl in Virginia, waiting in the yard for her lover. Dress stay crisp for him – button stay put – bloom magnolia – air stay still and sweet. But the lover was neither Sidney Lahaye nor an abstraction of many men – it was herself, her vanished youth lingering in that garden, unsatisfied and unfulfilled; in her dream she waited there under the spell of eternal hope for the lover that would never come, and who now no longer mattered.

The operation was a success. After three weeks she sat up, in a month her fever had decreased and she took short walks for an hour every day. When this began, the Swiss doctor who had performed the operation talked to her seriously.

'There's something you ought to know about Montana Vermala; it applies to all such places. It's a well-known characteristic of tuberculosis that it tends to hurt the morale. Some of these people you'll see on the streets are back here for the third time, which is usually the last time. They've grown fond of the feverish stimulation of being sick; they come up here and live a life almost as gay as life in Paris – some of the champagne bills in this sanatorium are amazing. Of course, the air helps them, and we manage to exercise a certain salutary control over them, but that kind are never really cured, because in spite of their cheerfulness they don't want the normal world of responsibility. Given the choice, something in them would prefer to die. On the other hand, we know a lot more than we did twenty years ago, and every month we send away people of character completely cured. You've got that chance because your case is fundamentally easy; your right lung is utterly untouched. You can choose; you can run with the crowd and perhaps linger along three years, or you can leave in one year as well as ever.'

Caroline's observation confirmed his remarks about the environment. The village itself was like a mining town – hasty, flimsy buildings dominated by the sinister bulk of four or five sanatoriums; chastely cheerful when the sun glittered on the snow, gloomy when the cold seeped through the gloomy pines. In contrast were the flushed, pretty girls in Paris clothes whom she passed on the street, and the well-turned-out men. It was hard to believe they were fighting such a desperate battle, and as the doctor had said, many of them were not. There was an air of secret ribaldry – it was considered funny to send miniature coffins to new arrivals, and there was a continual undercurrent of scandal. Weight, weight, weight; everyone talked of weight – how many pounds one had put on last month or lost the week before.

She was conscious of death around her, too, but she felt her own strength returning day by day in the high, vibrant air, and she knew she was not going to die.

After a month came a stilted letter from Sidney. It said:

I stayed only until the immediate danger was past. I knew that, feeling as you do, you wouldn't want my face to be the first thing you saw. So I've been down here in Sierre at the foot of the mountain, polishing up my Cambodge diary. If it's any consolation for you to have someone who cares about you within call, I'd like nothing better than to stay on here. I hold myself utterly responsible for what happened to you, and many times I've wished I had died before I came into your life. Now there's only the present – to get you well.

About your son – once a month I plan to run up to his school in Fontainebleau and see him for a few days – I've seen him once now and we like each other. This summer I'll either arrange for him to go to a camp or take him through the Norwegian fjords with me, whichever plan seems advisable.

The letter depressed Caroline. She saw herself sinking into a bondage of gratitude to this man – as though she must thank an attacker for binding up her wounds. Her first act would be to earn the money to pay him back. It made her tired even to think of such things now, but it was always present in her subconscious, and when she forgot it she dreamed of it. She wrote:

Dear Sidney: It's absurd your staying there and I'd much rather you didn't. In fact, it makes me uncomfortable. I am, of course, enormously grateful for all you've done for me and for Dexter. If it isn't too much trouble, will you come up here before you go to Paris, as I have some things to send him?

Sincerely,

CAROLINE M. CORCORAN.

He came a fortnight later, full of a health and vitality that she found as annoying as the look of sadness that was sometimes in his eyes. He adored her and she had no use for his adoration. But her strongest sensation was one of fear – fear that since he had made her suffer so much, he might be able to make her suffer again.

'I'm doing you no good, so I'm going away,' he said. 'The doctors seem to think you'll be well by September. I'll come back and see for myself. After that I'll never bother you again.'

If he expected to move her, he was disappointed.

'It may be some time before I can pay you back,' she said.

'I got you into this.'

'No, I got myself into it . . . Good-bye, and thank you for everything you've done.'

Her voice might have been thanking him for bringing a box of candy. She was relieved at his departure. She wanted only to rest and be alone.

The winter passed. Towards the end she skied a little, and then spring came sliding up the mountain in wedges and spear points of green. Summer was sad, for two friends she had made there died within a week and she followed their coffins to the foreigners' graveyard in Sierre. She was safe now. Her affected lung had again expanded; it was scarred, but healed; she had no fever, her weight was normal and there was a bright mountain colour in her cheeks.

October was set as the month of her departure, and as autumn approached, her desire to see Dexter again was overwhelming. One day a wire came from Sidney in Tibet stating that he was starting for Switzerland.

Several morning later the floor nurse looked in to toss her a copy of the *Paris Herald* and she ran her eyes listlessly down the columns. Then she sat up suddenly in bed.

AMERICAN FEARED LOST IN BLACK SEA

Sidney Lahaye, Millionaire Aviator, and Pilot Missing Four Days.

Teheran, Persia, 5 October—

Caroline sprang out of bed, ran with the paper to the window, looked away from it, then looked at it again.

AMERICAN FEARED LOST IN BLACK SEA

Sidney Lahaye, Millionaire Aviator—

'The Black Sea,' she repeated, as if that was the important part of the affair – 'in the Black Sea.'

She stood there in the middle of an enormous quiet. The pursuing feet that had thundered in her dream had stopped. There was a steady, singing silence.

'Oh-h-h!' she said.

AMERICAN FEARED LOST IN BLACK SEA

Sidney Lahaye, Millionaire Aviator, and Pilot Missing Four Days.

Teheran, Persia, 5 October—

Caroline began to talk to herself in an excited voice.

'I must get dressed,' she said; 'I must get to the telegraph and see whether everything possible has been done. I must start for there.' She moved around the room, getting into her clothes. 'Oh-h-h!' she whispered. 'Oh-h-h!' With one shoe on, she fell face downward across the bed. 'Oh, Sidney – Sidney!' she cried, and then again, in terrible protest: 'Oh-h-h!' She rang for the nurse. 'First, I must eat and get some strength; then I must find out about trains.'

She was so alive now that she could feel parts of herself uncurl, unroll. Her heart picked up steady and strong, as if to say, 'I'll stick by you,' and her nerves gave a sort of jerk as all the old fear melted out of her. Suddenly she was grown, her broken girlhood dropped away from her, and the startled nurse answering her ring was talking to someone she had never seen before.

'It's all so simple. He loved me and I loved him. That's all there is. I must get to the telephone. We must have a consul there somewhere.'

For a fraction of a second she tried to hate Dexter because he was not Sidney's son, but she had no further reserve of hate. Living or dead, she was with her love now, held close in his arms. The moment that his footsteps stopped, that there was no more menace, he had overtaken her. Caroline saw that what she had been shielding was valueless – only the little girl in the garden, only the dead, burdensome past.

'Why I can stand anything,' she said aloud – 'anything – even losing him.'

The doctor, alarmed by the nurse, came hurrying in.

'Now, Mrs Corcoran, you're to be quiet. No matter what news you've had, you— Look here, this may have some bearing on it, good or bad.'

He handed her a telegram, but she could not open it, and she handed it back to him mutely. He tore the envelope and held the message before her:

PICKED UP BY COALER CITY OF CLYDE STOP ALL WELL—

The telegram blurred; the doctor too. A wave of panic swept over her as she felt the old armour clasp her metallically again. She waited a minute, another minute; the doctor sat down.

'Do you mind if I sit in your lap a minute?' she said. 'I'm not contagious any more, am I?'

With her head against his shoulder, she drafted a telegram with his fountain pen on the back of the one she had just received. She wrote:

PLEASE DON'T TAKE ANOTHER AEROPLANE BACK HERE. WE'VE GOT EIGHT YEARS TO MAKE UP, SO WHAT DOES A DAY OR TWO MATTER? I LOVE YOU WITH ALL MY HEART AND SOUL.

ON YOUR OWN

(unpublished)

'On Your Own' was written as 'Home to Maryland' in the spring of
1931 after Fitzgerald's return to Europe from his father's funeral, a strongly
emotional event for him. Edward Fitzgerald was buried in the little
cemetery of St Mary's Catholic Church on Rockville, Maryland – changed
to 'Rocktown' in the story – now a suburb of Washington, but then the
sleepy county seat where he had been raised during and after the Civil War.
'Then it was over,' the story says, 'and the country doctor lay among a
hundred Lovejoys and Dorseys and Crawshaws.'

This story shows the way Fitzgerald took an emotion and wove his
hyperbolic magic around it. Though he had no ancestors named Lovejoy or
Crawshaw, he was indeed descended from a long line of imposing Dorseys
going back to the original Edward, who moved to Maryland from Virginia
in 1650. Not a Dorsey is buried at St Mary's but a few Scotts, with
whom they intermarried, are, inspiring the line repeated in Tender Is the
Night, 'It was very friendly leaving him there with all his relations
around him.' Later in the story, the heroine is asked why she doesn't buy
and restore 'a fine old house called Lovejoy Hall' in 'St Charles County',
which had belonged to one of her Lovejoy forebears. This is a reference to
'Tudor Hall', home of Fitzgerald's great-great-grandfather Philip Key, a
member of the Continental Congress, in the southern Maryland county of
St Mary's. It was for sale at that time, as he must have heard from
relatives at the funeral.

Over the five years after it was written, 'On Your Own' was declined by
seven magazines, the first time this had happened to a Fitzgerald story
since his apprentice days. It is one of the stories he 'stripped' for his
Notebooks, salvaging favourite passages for later use. 'On Your Own' is
included here because it is the only remaining unpublished story bearing,
in his words, that 'one little drop of something . . . the extra I had.'

The third time he walked around the deck Evelyn stared at him. She stood leaning against the bulwark and when she heard his footsteps again she turned frankly and held his eyes for a moment until his turned away, as a woman can when she has the protection of other men's company. Barlotto, playing ping-pong with Eddie O'Sullivan, noticed the encounter. 'Aha!' he said, before the stroller was out of hearing, and when the rally was finished: 'Then you're still interested even if it's not the German Prince.'

'How do you know it's not the German Prince?' Evelyn demanded.

'Because the German Prince is the horse-faced man with white eyes. This one' – he took a passenger list from his pocket – 'is either Mr George Ives, Mr Jubal Early Robbins and valet, or Mr Joseph Widdle with Mrs Widdle and six children.'

It was a medium-sized German boat, five days westbound from Cherbourg. The month was February and the sea was dingy grey and swept with rain. Canvas sheltered all the open portions of the promenade deck, even the ping-pong table was wet.

K'*tap* K'*tap* K'*tap* K'*tap*. Barlotto looked like Valentino – since he got fresh in the rumba number she had disliked playing opposite him. But Eddie O'Sullivan had been one of her best friends in the company.

Subconsciously she was waiting for the solitary promenader to round the deck again but he didn't. She faced about and looked at the sea through the glass windows; instantly her throat closed and she held herself close to the wooden rail to keep her shoulders from shaking. Her thoughts rang aloud in her ears: My father is dead – when I was little we would walk to town on Sunday morning, I in my starched dress, and he would buy the Washington paper and a cigar and he was so proud of his pretty little girl. He was always so proud of me – he came to New York to see me when I opened with the Marx Brothers and he told everybody in the hotel he was my father, even the elevator boys. I'm glad he did, it was so much pleasure for him, perhaps the best time he ever had since he was young. He would like it if he knew I was coming all the way from London.

'Game and set,' said Eddie.

She turned around.

'We'll go down and wake up the Barneys and have some bridge, eh?' suggested Barlotto.

Evelyn led the way, pirouetting once and again on the moist deck, then breaking into an 'Off to Buffalo' against a sudden breath of wet wind. At the door she slipped and fell inward down the stair, saved herself by a perilous one-arm swing – and was brought up against the solitary promenader. Her mouth fell open comically – she balanced for a moment. Then the man said, 'I beg your pardon,' in an unmistakably southern voice. She met his eyes again as the three of them passed on.

The man picked up Eddie O'Sullivan in the smoking room the next afternoon.

'Aren't you the London cast of *Chronic Affection* ?'

'We were until three days ago. We were going to run another two weeks but Miss Lovejoy was called to America so we closed.'

'The whole cast on board ?' The man's curiosity was inoffensive, it was a really friendly interest combined with a polite deference to the romance of the theatre. Eddie O'Sullivan liked him.

'Sure, sit down. No, there's only Barlotto, the juvenile, and Miss Lovejoy and Charles Barney, the producer, and his wife. We left in twenty-four hours – the others are coming on the *Homeric*.'

'I certainly did enjoy seeing your show. I've been on a trip around the world and I turned up in London two weeks ago just ready for something American – and you had it.'

An hour later Evelyn poked her head around the corner of the smoking-room door and found them there.

'Why are you hiding out on us ?' she demanded. 'Who's going to laugh at my stuff ? That bunch of card sharps down there ?'

Eddie introduced Mr George Ives. Evelyn saw a handsome, well-built man of thirty with a firm and restless face. At the corners of his eyes two pairs of fine wrinkles indicated an effort to meet the world on some other basis than its own. On his part George Ives saw a rather small dark-haired girl of twenty-six, burning with a vitality that could only be described as 'professional'. Which is to say it was not amateur – it could never use itself up upon any one person or group. At moments it possessed her so entirely, turning every shade of expression, every casual gesture, into a thing of such moment that she seemed to have no real self of her own. Her mouth was made of two small intersecting cherries pointing off into a bright smile; she had enormous, dark brown eyes. She was not beautiful but it took her only about ten seconds to persuade people that she was. Her body was lovely with little concealed muscles of iron. She was in black now and overdressed – she was always very chic and a little overdressed.

'I've been admiring you ever since you hurled yourself at me yesterday afternoon,' he said.

'I had to make you some way or other, didn't I? What's a girl going to do with herself on a boat – fish?'

They sat down.

'Have you been in England long?' George asked.

'About five years – I go bigger over there.' In its serious moments her voice had the ghost of a British accent. 'I'm not really very good at anything – I sing a little, dance a little, clown a little, so the English think they're getting a bargain. In New York they want specialists.'

It was apparent that she would have preferred an equivalent popularity in New York.

Barney, Mrs Barney and Barlotto came into the bar.

'Aha!' Barlotto cried when George Ives was introduced. 'She won't believe he's not the Prince.' He put his hand on George's knee. 'Miss Lovejoy was looking for the Prince the first day when she heard he was on board. We told her it was you.'

Evelyn was weary of Barlotto, weary of all of them, except Eddie O'Sullivan, though she was too tactful to have shown it when they were working together. She looked around. Save for two Russian priests playing chess their party was alone in the smoking-room – there were only thirty first-class passengers, with accommodations for two hundred. Again she wondered what sort of an America she was going back to. Suddenly the room depressed her – it was too big, too empty to fill and she felt the necessity of creating some responsive joy and gaiety around her.

'Let's go down to my *salon*,' she suggested, pouring all her enthusiasm into her voice, making them a free and thrilling promise. 'We'll play the phonograph and send for the handsome doctor and the chief engineer and get them in a game of stud. I'll be the decoy.'

As they went downstairs she knew she was doing this for the new man. She wanted to play to him, show him what a good time she could give people. With the phonograph wailing 'You're driving me crazy' she began building up a legend. She was a 'gun moll' and the whole trip had been a frame to get Mr Ives into the hands of the mob. Her throaty mimicry flicked here and there from one to the other; two ship's officers coming in were caught up in it and without knowing much English still understood the verve and magic of the impromptu performance. She was Anne Pennington, Helen Morgan, the effeminate waiter who came in for an order, she was everyone there in turn, and all in pace with the ceaseless music.

Later George Ives invited them all to dine with him in the upstairs restaurant that night. And as the party broke up and Evelyn's eyes sought his approval he asked her to walk with him before dinner.

The deck was still damp, still canvassed in against the persistent spray of rain. The lights were a dim and murky yellow and blankets tumbled awry on empty deck chairs.

'You were a treat,' he said. 'You're like – Mickey Mouse.'

She took his arm and bent double over it with laughter.

'I like being Mickey Mouse. Look – there's where I stood and stared at you every time you walked around. Why didn't you come around the fourth time?'

'I was embarrassed so I went up to the boat deck.'

As they turned at the bow there was a great opening of doors and a flooding out of people who rushed to the rail.

'They must have had a poor supper,' Evelyn said. 'No – look!'

It was the *Europa* – a moving island of light. It grew larger minute by minute, swelled into a harmonious fairyland with music from its deck and searchlights playing on its own length. Through field-glasses they could discern figures lining the rail and Evelyn spun out the personal history of a man who was pressing his own pants in a cabin. Charmed they watched its sure matchless speed.

'Oh, Daddy, buy me that!' Evelyn cried, and then something suddenly broke inside her – the sight of beauty, the reaction to her late excitement choked her up and she thought vividly of her father. Without a word she went inside.

Two days later she stood with George Ives on the deck while the gaunt scaffolding of Coney Island slid by.

'What was Barlotto saying to you just now?' she demanded.

George laughed.

'He was saying just about what Barney said this afternoon, only he was more excited about it.'

She groaned.

'He said that you played with everybody – and that I was foolish if I thought this little boat flirtation meant anything – everybody had been through being in love with you and nothing ever came of it.'

'He wasn't in love with me,' she protested. 'He got fresh in a dance we had together and I called him for it.'

'Barney was wrought up too – said he felt like a father to you.'

'They make me tired,' she exclaimed. 'Now they think they're in love with me just because—'

352

'Because they see I am.'

'Because they think I'm interested in you. None of them were so eager until two days ago. So long as I make them laugh it's all right but the minute I have any impulse of my own they all bustle up and think they're being so protective. I suppose Eddie O'Sullivan will be next.'

'It was my fault telling them we found we lived only a few miles from each other in Maryland.'

'No, it's just that I'm the only decent-looking girl on an eight-day boat, and the boys are beginning to squabble among themselves. Once they're in New York they'll forget I'm alive.'

Still later they were together when the city burst thunderously upon them in the early dusk – the high white range of lower New York swooping down like a strand of a bridge, rising again into uptown New York, hallowed with diadems of foamy light, suspended from the stars.

'I don't know what's the matter with me,' Evelyn sobbed. 'I cry so much lately. Maybe I've been handling a parrot.'

The German band started to play on deck but the sweeping majesty of the city made the march trivial and tinkling; after a moment it died away.

'Oh, God! It's so beautiful,' she whispered brokenly.

If he had not been going south with her the affair would probably have ended an hour later in the customs shed. And as they rode south to Washington next day he receded for the moment and her father came nearer. He was just a nice American who attracted her physically – a little necking behind a lifeboat in the darkness. At the iron grating in the Washington station where their ways divided she kissed him good-bye and for the time forgot him altogether as her train shambled down into the low-forested clayland of southern Maryland. Screening her eyes with her hands Evelyn looked out upon the dark infrequent villages and the scattered farm lights. Rocktown was a shrunken little station and there was her brother with a neighbour's Ford – she was ashamed that her luggage was so good against the exploded upholstery. She saw a star she knew and heard Negro laughter from out of the night; the breeze was cool but in it there was some smell she recognized – she was home.

At the service next day in the Rocktown churchyard, the sense that she was on a stage, that she was being watched, froze Evelyn's grief – then it was over and the country doctor lay among a hundred Lovejoys and Dorseys and Crawshaws. It was very friendly leaving him there with all his relations around him. Then as they turned from the graveside her eyes fell on George Ives who stood a little apart with his hat in his hand. Outside the gate he spoke to her.

'You'll excuse my coming. I had to see that you were all right.'

'Can't you take me away somewhere now?' she asked impulsively. 'I can't stand much of this. I want to go to New York tonight.'

His face fell. 'So soon?'

'I've got to be learning a lot of new dance routines and freshening up my stuff. You get sort of stale abroad.'

He called for her that afternoon, crisp and shining as his coupé. As they started off she noticed that the men in the gasoline stations seemed to know him with liking and respect. He fitted into the quickening spring landscape, into a legendary Maryland of graciousness and gallantry. He had not the range of a European; he gave her little of that constant reassurance as to her attractiveness – there were whole half-hours when he seemed scarcely aware of her at all.

They stopped once more at the churchyard – she brought a great armful of flowers to leave as a last offering on her father's grave. Leaving him at the gate she went in.

The flowers scattered on the brown unsettled earth. She had no more ties here now and she did not know whether she would come back any more. She knelt down. All these dead, she knew them all, their weather-beaten faces with hard blue flashing eyes, their spare violent bodies, their souls made of new earth in the long forest-heavy darkness of the seventeenth century. Minute by minute the spell grew on her until it was hard to struggle back to the old world where she had dined with kings and princes, where her name in letters two feet high challenged the curiosity of the night. A line of William McFee's surged through her:

O staunch old heart that toiled so long for me
I waste my years sailing along the sea.

The words released her – she broke suddenly and sat back on her heels, crying.

How long she was staying she didn't know; the flowers had grown invisible when a voice called her name from the churchyard and she got up and wiped her eyes.

'I'm coming.' And then, 'Good-bye then Father, all my fathers.'

George helped her into the car and wrapped a robe around her. Then he took a long drink of country rye from his flask.

'Kiss me before we start,' he said suddenly.

She put up her face towards him.

'No, really kiss me.'

'Not now.'

'Don't you like me?'

'I don't feel like it, and my face is dirty.'

'As if that mattered.'

His persistence annoyed her.

'Let's go on,' she said.

He put the car into gear.

'Sing me a song.'

'Not now, I don't feel like it.'

He drove fast for half an hour – then he stopped under thick sheltering trees.

'Time for another drink. Don't you think you better have one – it's getting cold.'

'You know I don't drink. You have one.'

'If you don't mind.'

When he had swallowed he turned towards her again.

'I think you might kiss me now.'

Again she kissed him obediently but he was not satisfied.

'I mean really,' he repeated. 'Don't hold away like that. You know I'm in love with you and you say you like me.'

'Of course I do,' she said impatiently, 'but there are times and times. This isn't one of them. Let's go on.'

'But I thought you liked me.'

'I won't if you act this way.'

'You don't like me then.'

'Oh don't be absurd,' she broke out, 'of course I like you, but I want to get to Washington.'

'We've got lots of time.' And then as she didn't answer, 'Kiss me once before we start.'

She grew angry. If she had liked him less she could have laughed him out of this mood. But there was no laughter in her – only an increasing distaste for the situation.

'Well,' he said with a sigh, 'this car is very stubborn. It refuses to start until you kiss me.' He put his hand on hers but she drew hers away.

'Now look here.' Her temper mounted into her cheeks, her forehead. 'If there was anything you could do to spoil everything it was just this. I thought people only acted like this in cartoons. It's so utterly crude and' – she searched for a word – 'and *American*. You only forgot to call me "baby".'

'Oh.' After a minute he started the engine and then the car. The lights of Washington were a red blur against the sky.

'Evelyn,' he said presently. 'I can't think of anything more natural than wanting to kiss you, I—'

'Oh, it was so clumsy,' she interrupted. 'Half a pint of corn whisky and then telling me you wouldn't start the car unless I kissed you. I'm not used to that sort of thing. I've always had men treat me with the greatest delicacy. Men have been challenged to duels for staring at me in a casino – and then you, that I liked so much, try a thing like that. I can't stand it—' And again she repeated, bitterly, 'It's so American.'

'Well, I haven't any sense of guilt about it but I'm sorry I upset you.'

'Don't you *see*?' she demanded. 'If I'd wanted to kiss you I'd have managed to let you know.'

'I'm terribly sorry,' he repeated.

They had dinner in the station buffet. He left her at the door of her pullman car.

'Good-bye,' she said, but coolly now, 'Thank you for an awfully interesting trip. And call me up when you come to New York.'

'Isn't this silly,' he protested. 'You're not even going to kiss me good-bye.'

She didn't want to at all now and she hesitated before leaning forward lightly from the step. But this time he drew back.

'Never mind,' he said. 'I understand how you feel. I'll see you when I come to New York.'

He took off his hat, bowed politely and walked away. Feeling very alone and lost Evelyn went on into the car. That was for meeting people on boats, she thought, but she kept on feeling strangely alone.

II

She climbed a network of steel, concrete and glass, walked under a high echoing dome and came out into New York. She was part of it even before she reached her hotel. When she saw mail waiting for her and flowers around her suite, she was sure she wanted to live and work here with this great current of excitement flowing through her from dawn to dusk.

Within two days she was putting in several hours a morning limbering up neglected muscles, an hour of new soft-shoe stuff with Joe Crusoe, and making a tour of the city to look at every entertainer who had something new.

Also she was weighing the prospects for her next engagement. In the background was the chance of going to London as a co-featured player in a Gershwin show then playing New York. Yet there was an air of repetition about it. New York excited her and she wanted to get something here. This was difficult – she had little following in America, show business was in a bad way – after a while her agent brought her several offers for shows that were going into rehearsal this fall. Meanwhile she was getting a little in debt and it was convenient that there were almost always men to take her to dinner and the theatre.

March blew past. Evelyn learned new steps and performed in half a dozen benefits; the season was waning. She dickered with the usual young impresarios who wanted to 'build something around her', but who seemed never to have the money, the theatre and the material at one and the same time. A week before she must decide about the English offer she heard from George Ives.

She heard directly, in the form of a telegram announcing his arrival, and indirectly in the form of a comment from her lawyer when she mentioned the fact. He whistled.

'Woman, have you snared George Ives ? You don't need any more jobs. A lot of girls have worn out their shoes chasing him.'

'Why, what's his claim to fame ?'

'He's rich as Croesus – he's the smartest young lawyer in the South, and they're trying to run him now for governor of his state. In his spare time he's one of the best polo players in America.'

Evelyn whistled.

'This is news,' she said.

She was startled. Her feelings about him suddenly changed – everything he had done began to assume significance. It impressed her that while she had told him all about her public self he had hinted nothing of this. Now she remembered him talking aside with some ship reporters at the dock.

He came on a soft poignant day, gentle and spirited. She was engaged for lunch but he picked her up at the Ritz afterwards and they drove in Central Park. When she saw in a new revelation his pleasant eyes and his mouth that told how hard he was on himself, her heart swung towards him – she told him she was sorry about that night.

'I didn't object to what you did but to the way you did it,' she said. 'It's all forgotten. Let's be happy.'

'It all happened so suddenly,' he said. 'It was disconcerting to look up suddenly on a boat and see the girl you've always wanted.'

'It was nice, wasn't it?'

'I thought that anything so like a casual flower needn't be respected. But that was all the more reason for treating it gently.'

'What nice words,' she teased him. 'If you keep on I'm going to throw myself under the wheels of the cab.'

Oh, she liked him. They dined together and went to a play and in the taxi going back to her hotel she looked up at him and waited.

'Would you consider marrying me?'

'Yes, I'd consider marrying you.'

'Of course if you married me we'd live in New York.'

'Call me Mickey Mouse,' she said suddenly.

'Why?'

'I don't know – it was fun when you called me Mickey Mouse.'

The taxi stopped at her hotel.

'Won't you come in and talk for a while?' she asked. Her bodice was stretched tight across her heart.

'Mother's here in New York with me and I promised I'd go and see her for a while.'

'Oh.'

'Will you dine with us tomorrow night?'

'All right.'

She hurried in and up to her room and put on the phonograph.

'Oh, gosh, he's going to respect me,' she thought. 'He doesn't know anything about me, he doesn't know anything about women. He wants to make a goddess out of me and I want to be Mickey Mouse.' She went to the mirror swaying softly before it.

Lady play your mandolin
Lady let that tune begin.

At her agent's next morning she ran into Eddie O'Sullivan.

'Are you married yet?' he demanded. 'Or did you ever see him again?'

'Eddie, I don't know what to do. I think I'm in love with him but we're always out of step with each other.'

'Take him in hand.'

'That's just what I don't want to do. I want to be taken in hand myself.'

'Well, you're twenty-six – you're in love with him. Why don't you marry him? It's a bad season.'

'He's so American,' she answered.

'You've lived abroad so long that you don't know what you want.'

'It's a man's place to make me certain.'

It was in a mood of revolt against what she felt was to be an inspection that she made a midnight rendezvous for afterwards to go to Chaplin's film with two other men – 'because I frightened him in Maryland and he'll only leave me politely at my door'. She pulled all her dresses out of her wardrobe and defiantly chose a startling gown from Vionnet; when George called for her at seven she summoned him up to her suite and displayed it, half hoping he would protest.

'Wouldn't you rather I'd go as a convent girl?'

'Don't change anything. I worship you.'

But she didn't want to be worshipped.

It was still light outside and she liked being next to him in the car. She felt fresh and young under the fresh young silk – she would be glad to ride with him for ever, if only she were sure they were going somewhere.

. . . The suite at the Plaza closed around them; lamps were lighted in the *salon*.

'We're really almost neighbours in Maryland,' said Mrs Ives. 'Your name's familiar in St Charles county and there's a fine old house called Lovejoy Hall. Why don't you buy it and restore it?'

'There's no money in the family,' said Evelyn bluntly. 'I'm the only hope, and actresses never save.'

When the other guest arrived Evelyn started. Of all shades of her past – Colonel Cary. She wanted to laugh, or else hide – for an instant she wondered if this had been calculated. But she saw in his surprise that it was impossible.

'Delighted to see you again,' he said simply.

As they sat down at table Mrs Ives remarked:

'Miss Lovejoy is from our part of Maryland.'

'I see,' Colonel Cary looked at Evelyn with the equivalent of a wink. His expression annoyed her and she flushed. Evidently he knew nothing about her success on the stage, remembered only an episode of six years ago. When champagne was served she let a waiter fill her glass lest Colonel Cary think that she was playing an unsophisticated role.

'I thought you were a teetotaller,' George observed.

'I am. This is about the third drink I ever had in my life.'

The wine seemed to clarify matters; it made her see the necessity of anticipating whatever the Colonel might afterwards tell the Ives. Her glass was filled again. A little later Colonel Cary gave an opportunity when he asked:

'What have you been doing all these years?'

'I'm on the stage.' She turned to Mrs Ives. 'Colonel Cary and I met in my most difficult days.'

'Yes?'

The Colonel's face reddened but Evelyn continued steadily.

'For two months I was what used to be called a "party girl".'

'A party girl?' repeated Mrs Ives puzzled.

'It's a New York phenomenon,' said George.

Evelyn smiled at the Colonel. 'It used to amuse me.'

'Yes, very amusing,' he said.

'Another girl and I had just left school and decided to go on the stage. We waited around agencies and offices for months and there were literally days when we didn't have enough to eat.'

'How terrible,' said Mrs Ives.

'Then somebody told us about "party girls". Businessmen with clients from out of town sometimes wanted to give them a big time – singing and dancing and champagne, all that sort of thing, make them feel like regular fellows seeing New York. So they'd hire a room in a restaurant and invite a dozen party girls. All it required was to have a good evening dress and to sit next to some middle-aged man for two hours and laugh at his jokes and maybe kiss him good night. Sometimes you'd find a fifty-dollar bill in your napkin when you sat down at table. It sounds terrible, doesn't it – but it was salvation to us in that awful three months.'

A silence had fallen, short as far as seconds go but so heavy that Evelyn felt it on her shoulders. She knew that the silence was coming from some deep place in Mrs Ives's heart, that Mrs Ives was ashamed for her and felt that what she had done in the struggle for survival was unworthy of the dignity of woman. In those same seconds she sensed the Colonel chuckling maliciously behind his bland moustache, felt the wrinkles beside George's eyes straining.

'It must be terribly hard to get started on the stage,' said Mrs Ives. 'Tell me – have you acted mostly in England?'

'Yes.'

What had she said? Only the truth and the whole truth in spite of the old man leering there. She drank off her glass of champagne.

George spoke quickly, under the Colonel's roar of conversation: 'Isn't that a lot of champagne if you're not used to it?'

She saw him suddenly as a man dominated by his mother; her frank little reminiscence had shocked him. Things were different for a girl on her own and at least he should see that it was wiser than that Colonel Cary might launch dark implications thereafter. But she refused further champagne.

After dinner she sat with George at the piano.

'I suppose I shouldn't have said that at dinner,' she whispered.

'Nonsense! Mother know everything's changed nowadays.'

'She didn't like it,' Evelyn insisted. 'And as for that old boy that looks like a Peter Arno cartoon!'

Try as she might Evelyn couldn't shake off the impression that some slight had been put upon her. She was accustomed only to having approval and admiration around her.

'If you had to choose again would you choose the stage?' Mrs Ives asked.

'It's a nice life,' Evelyn said emphatically. 'If I had daughters with talent I'd choose it for them. I certainly wouldn't want them to be society girls.'

'But we can't all have talent,' said Colonel Cary.

'Of course most people have the craziest prejudices about the stage,' pursued Evelyn.

'Not so much nowadays,' said Mrs Ives. 'So many nice girls go on the stage.'

'Girls of position,' added Colonel Cary.

'They don't usually last very long,' said Evelyn. 'Every time some débutante decides to dazzle the world there's another flop due on Broadway. But the thing that makes me maddest is the way people condescend. I remember one season on the road – all the small-town social leaders inviting you to parties and then whispering and snickering in the corner. Snickering at Gladys Knowles!' Evelyn's voice rang with indignation: 'When Gladys goes to Europe she dines with the most prominent people in every country, the people who don't know these backwoods social leaders exist—'

'Does she dine with their wives too?' asked Colonel Cary.

'With their wives too.' She glanced sharply at Mrs Ives. 'Let me tell you that girls on the stage don't feel a bit inferior, and the really fashionable people don't think of patronizing them.'

The silence was there again heavier and deeper, but this time excited by her own words Evelyn was unconscious of it.

'Oh, it's American women,' she said. 'The less they have to offer the more they pick on the ones that have.'

She drew a deep breath, she felt that the room was stifling.

'I'm afraid I must go now,' she said.

'I'll take you,' said George.

They were all standing. She shook hands. She liked George's mother, who after all had made no attempt to patronize her.

'It's been very nice,' said Mrs Ives.

'I hope we'll meet soon. Good night.'

With George in a taxi she gave the address of a theatre on Broadway.

'I have a date,' she confessed.

'I see.'

'Nothing very important.' She glanced at him, and put her hand on his. Why didn't he ask her to break the date? But he only said:

'He better go over Forty-fifth Street.'

Ah, well, maybe she'd better go back to England – and be Mickey Mouse. He didn't know anything about women, anything about love, and to her that was the unforgivable sin. But why in a certain set of his face under the street lamps did he remind her of her father?

'Won't you come to the picture?' she suggested.

'I'm feeling a little tired – I'm turning in.'

'Will you phone me tomorrow?'

'Certainly.'

She hesitated. Something was wrong and she hated to leave him. He helped her out of the taxi and paid it.

'Come with us?' she asked almost anxiously. 'Listen, if you like—'

'I'm going to walk for a while!'

She caught sight of the men waiting for her and waved to them.

'George, is anything the matter?' she said.

'Of course not.'

He had never seemed so attractive, so desirable to her. As her friends came up, two actors, looking like very little fish beside him, he took off his hat and said:

'Good night, I hope you enjoy the picture.'

'George—'

—and a curious thing happened. Now for the first time she realized that her father was dead, that she was alone. She had thought of herself as being self-reliant, making more in some seasons than his practice brought him in five years. But he had always been behind her somewhere, his love had always been behind her— She had never been a waif, she had always had a place to go.

And now she was alone, alone in the swirling indifferent crowd. Did she expect to love this man, who offered her so much, with the naïve romantics of eighteen. He loved her – he loved her more than any one in the world loved her. She wasn't ever going to be a great star, she knew that, and she had reached the time when a girl had to look out for herself.

'Why, look,' she said, 'I've got to go. Wait – or don't wait.'

Catching up her long gown she sped up Broadway. The crowd was enormous as theatre after theatre eddied out to the sidewalks. She sought for his silk hat as for a standard, but now there were many silk hats. She peered frantically into groups and crowds as she ran. An insolent voice called after her and again she shuddered with a sense of being unprotected.

Reaching the corner she peered hopelessly into the tangled mass of the block ahead. But he had probably turned off Broadway so she darted left down the dimmer alley of Forty-eighth Street. Then she saw him, walking briskly, like a man leaving something behind – and overtook him at Sixth Avenue.

'George,' she cried.

He turned; his face looking at her was hard and miserable.

'George, I didn't want to go to that picture, I wanted you to make me not go. Why didn't you ask me not to go?'

'I didn't care whether you went or not.'

'Didn't you?' she cried. 'Don't you care for me any more?'

'Do you want me to call you a cab?'

'No, I want to be with you.'

'I'm going home.'

'I'll walk with you. What is it, George? What have I done?'

They crossed Sixth Avenue and the street became darker.

'What is it, George? Please tell me. If I did something wrong at your mother's why didn't you stop me?'

He stopped suddenly.

'You were our guest,' he said.

'What did I do?'

'There's no use going into it.' He signalled a passing taxi. 'It's quite obvious that we look at things differently. I was going to write you to-morrow but since you ask me it's just as well to end it today.'

'But why, George?' She wailed, 'What did I do?'

'You went out of your way to make a preposterous attack on an old gentlewoman who had given you nothing but courtesy and consideration.'

'Oh, George, I didn't, I didn't. I'll go to her and apologize. I'll go tonight.'

'She wouldn't understand. We simply look at things in different ways.'

'Oh – h-h.' She stood aghast.

He started to say something further, but after a glance at her he opened the taxi door.

'It's only two blocks. You'll excuse me if I don't go with you.'

She had turned and was clinging to the iron railing of a stair.

'I'll go in a minute,' she said. 'Don't wait.'

She wasn't acting now. She wanted to be dead. She was crying for her father, she told herself – not for him but for her father.

His footsteps moved off, stopped, hesitated – came back.

'Evelyn.'

His voice was close beside her.

'Oh, poor baby,' it said. He turned her about gently in his arms and she clung to him.

'Oh yes,' she cried in wild relief. 'Poor baby – just your poor baby.'

She didn't know whether this was love or not but she knew with all her heart and soul that she wanted to crawl into his pocket and be safe for ever.

BETWEEN THREE AND FOUR

Saturday Evening Post, 5 September 1931

*'Between Three and Four' was written in June 1931, probably in
Switzerland. The* Post *paid $4000 for it. This story was the first in which
Fitzgerald treated the Depression scene in response to the* Post's *request
for stories with American settings. Other stories in this collection which deal
with the Depression are 'A Change of Class', 'Diagnosis', 'The Rubber
Cheque', 'The Family Bus', 'No Flowers', and 'New Types'. Although
Fitzgerald began writing these stories in Europe, he had observed the effects
of the Depression when he went to America for his father's funeral in
January. He included none of these stories in* Taps at Reveille *(1935),
indicating his recognition that he had not succeeded with this new material.
Because of the requirements of the mass-circulation magazines, all of these
Depression stories have happy endings – which did not accord with the
experiences of readers who did not always have a nickel to buy the* Post.*

This happened nowadays, with everyone somewhat discouraged. A lot of
less fortunate spirits cracked when money troubles came to be added to
all the nervous troubles accumulated in the prosperity – neurosis being a
privilege of people with a lot of extra money. And some cracked merely
because it was in the air, or because they were used to the great, golden
figure of plenty standing behind them, as the idea of prudence and glory
stands behind the French, and the idea of 'the thing to do' used to stand
behind the English. Almost everyone cracked a little.

Howard Butler had never believed in anything, including himself,
except the system, and had not believed in that with the intensity of men
who were its products or its prophets. He was a quiet, introverted man, not
at all brave or resilient and, except in one regard, with no particular harm
in him. He thought a lot without much apparatus for thinking, and in
normal circumstances one would not expect him to fly very high or sink

very low. Nevertheless, he had a vision, which is the matter of this story.

Howard Butler stood in his office on the ninth floor of a building in New York, deciding something. It was a branch and a showroom of B. B. Eddington's Sons, office furniture and supplies, of which he was a branch manager – a perfect office ceremoniously equipped throughout, though now a little empty because of the decreased personnel due to hard times. Miss Wiess had just telephoned the name of an unwelcome caller, and he was deciding whether he hadn't just as well see the person now; it was a question of sooner or later. Mrs Summer was to be shown in.

Mrs Summer did not need to be shown in, since she had worked there for eight years, up until six months ago. She was a handsome and vital lady in her late forties, with golden-greyish hair, a stylish-stout figure with a reminiscent touch of the Gibson Girl bend to it, and fine young eyes of bright blue. To Howard Butler she was still as vivid a figure as when, as Sarah Belknap, she had declined to marry him nearly thirty years ago – with the essential difference that he hated her.

She came into his private office with an alert way she had and, in a clear, compelling voice that always affected him, said, 'Hello, Howard,' as if, without especially liking him, she didn't object to him at all. This time there was just a touch of strain in her manner.

'Hello, Sarah.'

'Well,' she breathed, 'it's very strange to be back here. Tell me you've got a place for me.'

He pursed his lips and shook his head. 'Things don't pick up.'

'H'm.' She nodded and blinked several times.

'Cancellations, bad debts – we've closed two branches and there've been more pay cuts since you left. I've had to take one.'

'Oh, I wouldn't expect the salary I used to get. I realize how things are. But, literally, I can't find anything. I thought, perhaps, there might be an opening, say as office manager or head stenographer, with full responsibility. I'd be very glad of fifty dollars a week.'

'We're not paying anything like that.'

'Or forty-five. Or even forty. I had a chance at twenty-five when I first left here and, like an idiot, I let it go. It seemed absurd after what I'd been getting; I couldn't keep Jack at Princeton on that. Of course, he's partly earning his way, but even in the colleges the competition is pretty fierce now – so many boys need money. Anyhow, last week I went back and tried to get the job at twenty-five, and they just laughed at me.' Mrs Summer smiled grimly, but with full control over herself; yet she could only hold the smile a minute and she talked on to conceal its disappearance: 'I've been eating at the soup kitchens to save what little I've got left. When I think that a woman of my capacity— That's not conceit, Howard; you know I've got capacity. Mr Eddington always thought so. I never quite understood—'

'It's tough, Sarah,' he said quickly. He looked at her shoes – they were still good shoes – on top anyhow. She had always been well turned out.

'If I had left earlier, if I'd been let out before the worst times came, I could have placed myself; but when I started hunting, everyone had got panicky.'

'We had to let Muller go too.'

'Oh, you did,' she said, with interest; the news restored her a measure of self-respect.

'A week ago.'

Six months before, the choice had been between Mr Muller and Mrs Summer, and Sarah Summer knew, and Howard Butler knew that she knew, that he had made a ticklish decision. He had satisfied an old personal grudge by keeping Muller, who was a young man, clearly less competent and less useful to the firm than Mrs Summer, and who received the same salary.

Now they stared at each other; she trying to fix on him, to pin him down, to budge him; he trying to avoid her, and succeeding, but only by retreating into recently hollowed out cavities in his soul, but safe cavities, from which he could even regard her plight with a certain satisfaction. Yet he was afraid of what he had done; he was trying to be hard, but in her actual presence the sophistries he had evolved did not help him.

'Howard, you've got to give me a job,' she broke out. 'Anything – thirty dollars, twenty-five dollars. I'm desperate. I haven't thirty dollars left. I've got to get Jack through this year – his junior year. He wants to be a doctor. He thinks he can hold out till June on his own, but someone drove him down to New York on Washington's Birthday, and he saw the way I was living. I tried to lie to him, but he guessed, and now he says he's going to quit and get a job. Howard, I'd rather be dead than stand in his way. I've been thinking of nothing else for a week. I'd be better dead. After all, I've had my life – and a lot of happiness.'

For an instant Butler wavered. It could be done, but the phrase 'a lot of happiness' hardened him, and he told himself how her presence in the office now would be a continual reproach.

Thirty years ago, on the porch of a gabled house in Rochester, he had sat in misery while John Summer and Sarah Belknap had told him moonily about their happiness. 'I wanted you to be the first to know, Howard,' Sarah had said. Butler had blundered into it that evening, bringing flowers and a new offer of his heart; then he was suddenly made aware that things were changed, that he wasn't very alive for either of them. Later, something she had said was quoted or misquoted to him – that if John Summer had not come along, she'd have been condemned to marry Howard Butler.

Years later he had walked into the office one morning to find her his subordinate. This time there was something menacing and repellent in his wooing, and she had put a stop to it immediately, definitely and finally. Then, for eight years, Butler had suffered her presence in the office, drying out in the sunshine of her vitality, growing bitter in the shadow of her indifference; aware that, despite her widowhood, her life was more complete than his.

'I can't do it,' he said, as if regretfully. 'Things are stripped to the bone here. There's no one you could displace. Miss Wiess has been here twelve years.'

'I wonder if it would do any good to talk to Mr Eddington.'

'He's not in New York, and it wouldn't do any good.'

She was beaten, but she went on evenly, 'Is there any likelihood of a change, in the next month, say ?'

Butler shrugged his shoulders. 'How does anybody know when business will pick up ? I'll keep you in mind if anything turns up.' Then he added, in a surge of weakness: 'Come back in a week or so, some afternoon between three and four.'

Mrs Summer got up; she looked older than when she had come into the office.

'I'll come back then.' She stood twisting her gloves, and her eyes seemed to stare out into more space than the office enclosed. 'If you haven't anything for me then, I'll probably just – quit permanently.'

She walked quickly to the window, and he half rose from his chair.

'Nine floors is a nice height,' she remarked. 'You could think things out one more time on the way down.'

'Oh, don't talk that way. You'll get a break any day now.'

'Businesswoman Leaps Nine Floors to Death,' said Mrs Summer, her eyes still fixed out the window. She sighed in a long, frightened breath, and turned towards the door. 'Good-bye, Howard. If you think things over, you'll see I was right in not even trying to love you. I'll be back some day next week, between three and four.'

He thought of offering her five dollars, but that would break down something inside him, so he let her go like that.

II

He saw her through the transparent place where the frosting was rubbed from the glass of his door. She was thinner than she had been last week, and obviously nervous, starting at anyone coming in or going out. Her foot was turned sideways under the chair and he saw where an oval hole was stopped with a piece of white cardboard. When her name was telephoned, he said, 'Wait,' letting himself be annoyed that she had come slightly before three; but the real cause of his anger lay in the fact that he wasn't up to seeing her again. To postpone his realization of the decision made in his subconscious, he dictated several letters and held a telephone conversation with the head office. When he had finished, he found it was five minutes to four; he hadn't meant to detain her an hour. He phoned Miss Wiess that he had no news for Mrs Summer and couldn't see her.

Through the glass he watched her take the news. It seemed to him that she swayed as she got up and stood blinking at Miss Wiess.

'I hope she's gone for good,' Butler said to himself. 'I can't be responsible for everybody out of work in this city. I'd go crazy.'

Later he came downstairs into a belt of low, stifling city heat; twice on his way home he stopped at soda fountains for cold drinks. In his apartment he locked the door, as he so often did lately, as if he were raising a barrier against all the anxiety outside. He moved about, putting away some laundry, opening bills, brushing his coat and hanging it up – for he was very neat – and singing to himself:

I can't give you anything but love, baby,
That's the only thing I've plenty of, baby—

He was tired of the song, but he continually caught himself humming it. Or else he talked to himself, like many men who live alone.

'Now, that's two coloured shirts and two white ones. I'll wear this one out first, because it's almost done. Almost done . . . Seven, eight, and two in the wash – ten—'

Six o'clock. All the offices were out now; people hurrying out of elevators, swarming down the stairs. But the picture came to Butler tonight with a curious addition; he seemed to see someone climbing up the stairs, too, passing the throng, climbing very slowly and resting momentarily on the landings.

'Oh, what nonsense!' he thought impatiently. 'She'd never do it. She was just trying to get my goat.'

But he kept on climbing up flights of stairs with her, the rhythm of the climbing as regular and persistent as the beat of fever. He grabbed his hat suddenly and went out to get dinner.

There was a storm coming; the sultry dust rose in swirls along the street. The people on the street seemed a long way removed from him in time and space. It seemed to him that they were all sad, all walking with their eyes fixed on the ground, save for a few who were walking and talking in pairs. These latter seemed absurd, with their obliviousness of the fact that they were making a show of themselves with those who were walking as it was fitting – silent and alone.

But he was glad that the restaurant where he went was full. Sometimes, when he read the newspapers a lot, he felt that he was almost the only man left with enough money to get along with; and it frightened him, because he knew pretty well that he was not much of a man and they might find it out and take his position away from him. Since he was not all right with himself in his private life, he had fallen helplessly into the clutches of the neurosis that gripped the nation, trying to lose sight of his own insufficiencies in the universal depression.

'Don't you like your dinner?' the waitress asked.

'Yes, sure.' He began to eat self-consciously.

'It's the heat. I just seen by the papers another woman threw herself out of a ninth-storey window this afternoon.'

Butler's fork dropped to the floor.

'Imagine a woman doing that,' she went on, as she stooped for the fork. 'If I ever wanted to do that, I'd go drown myself.'

'What did you say?'

'I say I'd go drown myself. I can't swim anyhow. But I said if—'

'No, before that – about a woman.'

'About a woman that threw herself out of a ninth-storey window. I'll get the paper.'

He tried to stop her; he couldn't look at the paper. With trembling fingers he laid a dollar on the table and hurried out of the restaurant.

It couldn't possibly be her, because he had seen her at four, and it was now only twenty after seven. Three hours. A news stand drifted up to him, piled with late editions. Forming the sound of 'agh' in his throat, he hurried past, hurried on, into exile.

He had better look. It couldn't be Sarah.

But he knew it was Sarah. BUSINESSWOMAN, DISPIRITED, LEAPS NINE FLOORS TO DEATH. He passed another news stand and, turning into Fifth Avenue, walked north. The rain began in large drops that sent up whiffs of dust, and Butler, looking at the crawling sidewalk, suddenly stopped, unable to go forward or to retrace his steps.

'I'll have to get a paper,' he muttered. 'Otherwise I won't sleep.'

He walked to Madison Avenue and found a news-stand; his hand felt over the stacked papers and picked up one of each; he did not look at them, but folded them under his arm. He heard the rain falling on them in crisp pats, and then more softly, as if it was shredding them away. When he reached his door, he suddenly flung the soggy bundle down a basement entrance and hurried inside. Better wait till morning.

He undressed excitedly, as if he hadn't a minute to lose. 'It's probably not her,' he kept repeating aloud. 'And if it is, what did I have to do with it? I can't be responsible for everybody out of work in this city.' With the help of this phrase and a hot double gin, he fell into a broken sleep.

He awoke at five, after a dream which left him shaken with its reality. In the dream he was talking to Sarah Belknap again. She lay in a hammock on a porch, young once more, and with a childish wistfulness. But she knew what was going to happen to her presently – she was going to be thrown from a high place and be broken and dead. Butler wanted to help her – tears were running out of his eyes and he was wringing his hands – but there was nothing he could do now; it was too late. She did not say that it was all his fault, but her eyes, grieving silently and helplessly about what was going to happen, reproached him for not having prevented it.

The sound that had awakened him was the plop of his morning paper against the door. The resurgent dream, heartbreaking and ominous, sank back into the depths from which it came, leaving him empty; and now his consciousness began to fill up with all the miserable things that made their home there. Torn between the lost world of pity and the world of meanness where he lived, Butler sprang out of bed, opened the door and took up the paper. His eyes, blurred with sleep, ran across the columns:

BUSINESSWOMAN, DISPIRITED, LEAPS NINE FLOORS TO DEATH

For a moment he thought it was an illusion. The print massed solidly below the headline; the headline itself disappeared. He rubbed his eyes with one fist; then he counted the columns over, and found that two columns were touching that should have flanked the story – but, no; there it was:

BUSINESSWOMAN, DISPIRITED, LEAPS NINE FLOORS TO DEATH

He heard the cleaning woman moving about in the hall, and going to the door, he flung it open.

'Mrs Thomas!'

A pale Negress with corded glasses looked up at him from her pail.

'Look at this, Mrs Thomas!' he cried. 'My eyes are bad! I'm sick! I've got to know! Look!'

He held the paper before her; he felt his voice quivering like a muscle: 'Now, you tell me. Does it say, "Businesswoman Leaps to Death"? Right there! Look, can't you?'

The Negress glanced at him curiously, bent her head obediently to the page.

'Indeed it does, Mr Butler.'

'Yes?' He passed his hand across his eyes. 'Now, below that. Does it say, "Mrs John Summer"? Does it say, "Mrs John Summer"? Look carefully now.'

Again she glanced sharply at him before looking at the paper. 'Indeed it does, Mr Butler. "Mrs John Summer".' After a minute she added, 'Man, you're sick.'

Butler closed his door, got back into bed and lay staring at the ceiling. After a while he began repeating his formulas aloud:

'I mustn't get to thinking that I had anything to do with it, because I didn't. She'd been offered another job, but she thought she was too good for it. What would she have done for me if she'd been in my place?'

He considered telephoning the office that he was ill, but young George Eddington was expected back any day, and he did not dare. Miss Wiess had gone on her vacation yesterday, and there was a substitute to be broken in. The substitute had not known Mrs Summer, so there would be no discussion of what had happened.

It was a day of continuing heat, wasted unprolific heat that cradled the groans of the derrick and the roar of the electric riveters in the building going up across the street. In the heat every sound was given its full discordant value, and by early afternoon Butler was sick and dizzy. He had made up his mind to go home, and was walking restlessly about his office when the thing began to happen. He heard the clock outside his office ticking loud in the hot silence, heard the little, buzzing noise it made, passing the hour; and at the same moment he heard the sigh of pneumatic hinges, as the corridor door swung open and someone came into the outer office. Then there wasn't a sound.

For a moment he hoped that it was someone he would have to see; then he shivered and realized that he was afraid – though he did not know why – and walked towards his own door. Before reaching it, he stopped. The noise of the riveting machine started again, but it seemed farther away now. For an instant he had the impression that the clock in the next room had stopped, too, but there it was again, marking rather long seconds against the silence.

Suddenly he did not want to know who had come into the next room; yet he was irresistibly impelled to find out. In one corner of his door was the transparent spot through which almost the whole outer office was visible, but now Butler discovered a minute scrape in the painted letter B of his name. Through it he could see the floor, and the dark little hall giving on the corridor where chairs for visitors were placed. Clamping his teeth together, he put his eye to this crack.

Tucked beneath the chair and criss-crossing the chair legs were a pair of woman's tan shoes. The sole of one shoe turned towards him, and he made out a grey oval in the centre. Breathlessly he moved until his eye was at the other hole. There was something sitting in the chair – rather, slumped in it, as if it had been put down there and had immediately crumpled. A dangling hand and what he could see of the face were of a diaphanous pallor, and the whole attitude was one of awful stillness. With a little, choking noise, Butler sprang back from the door.

III

It was several minutes before he was able to move from the wall against which he had backed himself. It was as if there was a sort of bargain between himself and the thing outside that, by staying perfectly still, playing dead, he was safe. But there was not a sound, not a movement, in the outer office and, after a while, a surface rationality asserted itself. He told himself that this was all the result of strain; that the frightening part of it was not the actual phantom, but that his nerves should be in a state to conjure it up. But he drew little consolation from this; if the terror existed, it was immaterial whether it originated in another world or in the dark places of his own mind.

He began making a systematic effort to pull himself together. In the first place, the noises outside were continuing as before; his office, his own body, were tangible as ever, and people were passing in the street; Miss Rousseau would answer the pressure of a bell which was within reach of his hand. Secondly, there could, conceivably, be some natural explanation of the thing outside; he had not been able to see the whole face and he could not be absolutely sure that it was what he thought it was; any number of people had cardboard in their shoes these days. In the third place – and he astonished himself at the coolness with which he deliberated this – if the matter reached an intolerable point, one could always take one's own life, thus automatically destroying whatever horror had come into it.

It was this last thought that caused him to go to the window and look down at the people passing below. He stood there for a minute, never quite turning his back on the door, and watched the people passing and the work-men on the steel scaffolding over the way. His heart tried to go out to them, and he struggled desperately to assert the common humanity he shared with them, the joys and griefs they had together, but it was impossible. Fundamentally, he despised them and – that is to say, he could make no connection with them, while his connection with the thing in the next room was manifest and profound.

Suddenly Butler wrenched himself around, walked to the door and put his eye to the aperture. The figure had moved, had slumped farther side-ways, and the blood rushed up, tingling, into his head as he saw that the face, now turned sightlessly toward him, was the face of Sarah Summer.

He found himself sitting at his desk, bent over it in a fit of uncontrollable laughter.

How long he had sat there he did not know, when suddenly he heard a noise, and recognized it, after a moment, as the swishing sigh of the hinges on the outer door. Looking at his watch, he saw that it was four o'clock.

He rang for Miss Rousseau, and when she came, asked: 'Is anyone waiting to see me?'

'No, Mr Butler.'

'Was there someone earlier?'

'No, sir.'

'Are you sure?'

'I've been in the filing room, but the door was open; if anyone had come in I'd surely have heard them.'

'All right. Thanks.'

As she went out, he looked after her through the open door. The chair was now empty.

IV

He took a strong bromide that night and got himself some sleep, and his reasoning reassumed, with dawn, a certain supremacy. He went to the office, not because he felt up to it but because he knew he would never be able to go again. He was glad he had gone, when Mr George Eddington came in late in the morning.

'Man, you look sick,' Eddington said.

'It's only the heat.'

'Better see a doctor.'

'I will,' said Butler, 'but it's nothing.'

'What's happened here the last two weeks ?'

BUSINESSWOMAN, DISPIRITED, LEAPS NINE FLOORS TO DEATH

'Very little,' he said aloud. 'We've moved out of the Two Hundredth Street warehouse.'

'Whose idea was that ?'

'Your brother's.'

'I'd rather you'd refer all such things to me for confirmation. We may have to move in again.'

'I'm sorry.'

'Where's Miss Wiess ?'

'Her mother's sick; I gave her three days' vacation.'

'And Mrs Summer's left . . . Oh, by the way, I want to speak to you about that later.'

Butler's heart constricted suddenly. What did he mean ? Had he seen the papers ?

'I'm sorry Miss Wiess is gone,' said Eddington. 'I wanted to go over all this last month's business.'

'I'll take the books home tonight,' Butler offered conciliatingly. 'I can be ready to go over them with you tomorrow.'

'Please do.'

Eddington left shortly. Butler found something in his tone disquieting – the shortness of a man trying to prepare one for even harsher eventualities. There was so much to worry about now, Butler thought; it hardly seemed worth while worrying about so many things. He sat at his desk in a sort of despairing apathy, realizing at lunchtime that he had done nothing all morning.

At 1.30, on his way back to the office, a chill wave of terror washed suddenly over him. He walked blindly as the remorseless sun led him along a path of flat black and hostile grey. The clamour of a fire engine plunging through the quivering air had the ominous portent of things in a nightmare. He found that someone had closed his windows, and he flung them open to the sweltering machines across the street. Then, with an open ledger before him, he sat down to wait.

Half an hour passed. Butler heard Miss Rousseau's muffled typewriter in the outer office, and her voice making a connection on the phone. He heard the clock move over two o'clock with a rasping sound; almost immediately he looked at his watch and found it was 2.30. He wiped his forehead, finding how cold sweat can be. Minutes passed. Then he started bolt upright as he heard the outer door open and close slowly, with a sigh.

Simultaneously he felt something change in the day outside – as if it had turned away from him, foreshortening and receding like a view from a train. He got up with difficulty, walked to the door and peered through the transparent place into the outer office.

She was there; her form cut the shadow of the corner; he knew the line of her body under her dress. She was waiting to see if he could give her a job, so that she could keep herself, and her son might not have to give up his ambitions.

'I'm afraid there's nothing. Come back next week. Between three and four.'

'I'll come back.'

With a struggle that seemed to draw his last reserve of strength up from his shoes, Butler got himself under control and picked up the phone. Now he would see – he would see.

'Miss Rousseau.'

'Yes, Mr Butler.'

'If there's anyone waiting to see me, please send them in.'

'There's no one waiting to see you, Mr Butler. There's—'

Uttering a choked sound, he hung up the phone and walked to the door and flung it open.

It was no use; she was there, clearly discernible, distinct and vivid as in life. And as he looked, she rose slowly, her dark garments falling about her like cerements – arose and regarded him with a wan smile, as if, at last and too late, he was going to help her. He took a step backward.

Now she came towards him slowly, until he could see the lines in her face, the wisps of grey-gold hair under her hat.

With a broken cry, he sprang backward so that the door slammed. Simultaneously he knew, with a last fragment of himself, that there was something wrong in the very nature of the logic that had brought him to this point, but it was too late now. He ran across the office like a frightened cat, and with a sort of welcome apprehension of nothingness, stepped out into the dark air beyond his window. Even had he grasped the lost fact that he sought for – the fact that the cleaning woman who had read him the newspaper could neither read nor write – it was too late for it to affect him. He was already too much engrossed in death to connect it with anything or to think what bearing it might have on the situation.

V

Mrs Summer did not go on into Butler's office. She had not been waiting to see him, but was here in answer to a summons from Mr Eddington, and she was intercepted by Eddington himself, who took her aside, talking:

'I'm sorry about all this.' He indicated Butler's office. 'We're letting him go. We've only recently discovered that he fired you practically on his own whim. Why, the number of your ideas we're using— We never considered letting you go. Things have been so mixed up.'

'I came to see you yesterday,' Mrs Summer said. 'I was all in and there was no one in the office at the moment. I must have fainted in the chair, because it was an hour later when I remembered anything, and then I was too tired to do anything except go home.'

'We'll see about all this,' Eddington said grimly. 'We'll— It's one of those things—' He broke off. The office was suddenly full of confusion; there was a policeman and, behind him, many curious peering faces. 'What's the matter ? . . . Hello, there seems to be something wrong here. What is it, officer ?'

A CHANGE OF CLASS

Saturday Evening Post, 26 September 1931

'A Change of Class' was written in July 1931 – probably in Switzerland. The Post *paid $4000. During the Depression the magazine required hopeful or encouraging stories conveying the message that, even if prosperity wasn't just around the corner, the crash could be regarded as a correction of the excesses of the twenties. The plot is not far-fetched: fortunes were made during the boom on stock-market tips, and reports about rich bartenders or wealthy bootblacks were commonplace. As Fitzgerald noted in 'My Lost City', 'My barber retired on a half-million bet in the market and I was conscious that the head waiters who bowed me, or failed to bow me, to my table were far, far wealthier than I.' The setting of 'A Change of Class' is Wilmington, Delaware, where the Fitzgeralds had lived at Ellerslie between 1927 and 1929.*

Not to identify the city too closely, it is in the East and not far from New York, and its importance as a financial centre is out of proportion to its small population. Three families, with their many ramifications and the two industries they all but control, are responsible for this; there is a Jadwin Street and a Jadwin Hotel, a Dunois Park and a Dunois Fountain, a Hertzog Hospital and a Hertzog Boulevard.

The Jadwins are the wealthiest; within miles of the city one cannot move out of their shadow. Only one of the many brothers and cousins is concerned with this story.

He wanted a haircut and, of course, went to Earl, in the barber shop of the Jadwin Hotel. A black porter sprang out of his lethargy, the barbers at work paid him the tribute of a secret stare, the proprietor's eyes made a quick pop at the sight of him. Only Earl, cutting a little boy's hair, kept his dignity. He tapped his shears against his comb and went over to Philip Jadwin.

'It'll be five minutes, Mr Jadwin,' he said withot obsequiousness. 'If you don't want to wait here, I can telephone up to your office.'

'That's all right, Earl; I'll wait.'

Philip Jadwin sat with glazed eyes. He was thirty-one, stiffly handsome, industrious and somewhat shy. He was in love with a typist in his office, but afraid to do anything about it, and sometimes it made him miserable. Lately it was a little better; he had himself in hand, but as he receded from the girl her face reproached him. At twenty-one or forty he might have dashed away with her to Elkton, Maryland, but he was at a conventional age, very much surrounded by the most conservative branch of his family. It wouldn't do.

As he seated himself in Earl's chair a swarthy man with long prehensile arms entered the barber shop, said, 'Hello, Earl,' flicked his eyes over Jadwin and went on towards the manicurist. When he had passed, Earl threw after him the smile that functions in the wake of notoriety.

'He gave me a half-bottle of rye today,' said Earl. 'It was open and he didn't like to carry it with him.'

'Well, don't cut my ear off,' said Jadwin.

'Don't you worry about that,' Earl glanced towards the rear of the shop and frowned. 'He gets a lot of manicures.'

'That's a pretty manicurist.'

Earl hesitated. 'I'll tell you confidentially, Mr Jadwin, she's my wife – has been for a month – but being both in the same shop, we thought we wouldn't say anything as long as we're here. The boss might not like it.'

Jadwin congratulated him: 'You've got a mighty pretty wife.'

'I don't like her manicuring bootleggers. This Berry, now, he's all right – he just gave me a half-bottle of rye, if that coon ain't drunk it up – but I tell you, I like nice people.'

As Jadwin didn't answer, Earl realized he had gone beyond the volubility he permitted himself. He worked silently and well, with deft, tranquillizing hands. He was a dark-haired, good-looking young man of twenty-six, a fine barber, steady and with no bad habits save the horses, which he had given up when he married. But after the hot towel an idea which had been with him since Jadwin came in came to the surface with the final, stimulating flicker of the drink in his veins. He might be snubbed, he might even lose a customer, but this was the year 1926 and the market had already grasped the imagination of many classes. Also he had been prompted to this by many people, among them his wife.

'Hert-win preferred seems to be going up, Mr Jadwin,' he ventured.

'Yes.' Jadwin was thinking again of the girl in his office or her wouldn't have broken a principle of his family by saying: 'But watch it next week when—' He broke off.

'Going up more?' Earl's eyes lit excitedly, but his hands applying the bay rum were strong and steady.

'Naturally, I believe in it,' said Jadwin with caution, 'but only as an out-and-out buy.'

'Of course,' agreed Earl piously. 'No face powder, that's right.'

Going home in the street car that night, he told Violet about it: 'We got two thousand dollars. With that I think I can get the new shop in the Cornwall Building, with three chairs. There's about twenty regular customers I'd be taking with me. What I could do, see, is buy this stock and then borrow money on it to buy the shop with. Or else I could take a chance on what he told me and buy it on margin. Let me tell you he ain't putting out much; he's vice-president of Hert-win. His old man is Cecil Jadwin, you know . . . What would you do?'

'It would be nice to make a lot,' said Violet, 'but we don't want to lose the money.'

'That helps.'

'Well, it would be nice to have a lot of money. But you decide.'

He decided conservatively, content with his prospects, liking his work in the cheerful, gossipy shop, loving his wife and his new existence with her in a new little apartment. He decided conservatively, and then Hert-win moved up twenty points in as many hours. If he had played on margin, as had one of the barbers in whom he had confided the tip, he would have more than doubled his two thousand.

'Why don't you ask him for another tip?' suggested Violet.

'He wouldn't like it.'

'It don't hurt him. I think you're crazy if you don't ask him again.'

'I don't dare.'

Nevertheless, he delayed the negotiations about the shop in the Cornwall Building.

One day about a week later, Philip Jadwin came into the shop in a wretched humour. The girl in his office had announced that she was quitting, and he knew it was the end of something, and how much he cared.

Earl, cutting his hair and shaving him, was conscious of a sinking sensation; he felt exactly as if he were going to ask Mr Jadwin for money. The shave was over, the hot towel – in a moment it would be too late.

'I wonder if Hert-win is going to make another quick rise,' Earl said in a funny voice.

Then Jadwin flared out at him. Sitting up in the chair, he said, in a low, angry voice: 'What do you take me for – a race-track tipster? I don't come here to be annoyed. If you want to keep your customers—'

He got out of the chair and began putting on his collar. For Earl that was plenty. Against his own better tact and judgement, he had blundered, and now he grew red and his mouth quivered as he stood there with the apron in his hand.

Jadwin, tying his tie at the mirror, was suddenly sorry; he had snapped at three persons this morning, and now he realized that it must be his own fault. He liked Earl; for three years he had been his customer, and there was a sort of feeling between them; a physical sympathy in the moments when Earl's hands were passing over his face, in the fine razor respecting its sensibility, or the comb, which seemed proud in the last fillip with which it finished him. Earl's chair was a place to rest, a sanctuary, once he was hidden under an apron and a lather of soap, his eyes trustfully closed, his senses awake to the pleasant smells of lotions and soap. He always remembered Earl handsomely at Christmas. And he knew that Earl liked him and respected him.

'Look here,' he said gruffly. 'I'll tell you one thing, but don't go lose your shirt on it, because nothing's certain in this world. Look at the paper tomorrow; if the appellate-court decision in the Chester case is against the railroads, you can expect a lot of activity in all Hert-win interests.' And he added carefully, 'I think. Now don't ever ask me anything again.'

And so Earl blundered into the golden age.

II

'See that fellow going out?' the barbers said to their customers three years later. 'Used to work here, but quit last year to take care of all his money. Philip Jadwin gave him some tips . . . G'bye, Earl. Come in more often.'

He came often. He liked the familiar cosmetic smell from the manicure corner, where the girls sat in white uniforms, freshly clean and faintly sweating lip rouge and cologne; he liked the gleaming nickel of the chairs, the sight of a case of keen razors, the joking abuse of the coloured porter that made the hours pass. Sometimes he just sat around and read a paper. But he was hurried tonight, going to a party, so he got into his car and drove home.

It was a nice house in a new development, not large or lavish, for Earl wasn't throwing away his money. In fact, he had worked in the barber shop two years after he needed to, taking ten-cent tips from men he could have bought out a dozen times over. He quit because Violet insisted on it. His trade didn't go with the coloured servant and the police dog, the big machine for outdoors and the many small noisy machines for the house. The Johnsons knew how to play bridge and they went quite often to New York. He was worth more than a hundred thousand dollars.

In his front yard he paused, thinking to himself that it was like a dream. That was as near as he could analyse his feelings; he was not even sure whether the dream was happy or unhappy – Violet was sure for both of them that it was happy.

She was dressing. She took very good care of herself; her nails were fever-coloured and she had a water wave or a marcel every day. She had been sedate as a manicurist, but she was very lively as a young wife; she had forgotten that their circumstances had ever been otherwise and regarded each step up as a return to the world in which she belonged, just as we often deceive ourselves into thinking that we appertain to the milieu of our most distinguished friend.

'I heard something funny today—' Earl said.

But Violet interrupted sharply: 'You better start putting on your tuxedo. It's half past six.'

They were short and inattentive with each other, because the world in which they moved was new and distracting. They were always rather pathetically ashamed of each other in public, though Earl still boasted of his wife's chic and she of his ability to make money. From the day when they moved into the new house, Violet adopted the manner of one following a code, a social rite, plain to herself but impossible for Earl to understand. She herself failed to understand that from their position in mid-air they were constrained merely to observe myopically and from a distance, and then try to imitate. Their friends were in the same position. They all tried to bolster up one another's lack of individuality by saying that So-and-So had a great sense of humour, or that So-and-So had a real knack of wearing clothes, but they were all made sterile and devitalized by their new environments, paying the price exacted for a passage into the middle class.

'But I heard something funny,' insisted Earl, undressing, 'about Howard Shalder. I heard downtown that he was a bootlegger; that he was Berry's boss.'

'Did you ?' she said indifferently.

'Well, what do you think about it?'

'I knew about it. Lots of nice people are bootleggers now – society people even.'

'Well, I don't see why we should be friends with a bootlegger.'

'But he isn't like a bootlegger,' she said. 'They have a beautiful home, and they're more refined than most of the people we know.'

'Well, look here, Violet. Would you go to the home of that Ed that used to sell us corn when we lived on—'

Indignantly she turned around from the mirror: 'You don't think Mr Shalder peddles bottles at back doors, do you?'

'If he's a bootlegger we oughtn't to go round with them,' Earl continued stubbornly. 'Nice people won't have anything to do with us.'

'You said your own self what a lovely girl she was. She never even takes a drink. You were the one that made friends with them.'

'Well, anyhow, I'm not going to the home of a bootlegger.'

'You certainly are tonight.'

'I suppose we got to tonight,' he said unwillingly, 'but I don't like to see you sitting next to him and holding hands – even in kidding. His wife didn't like it either.'

'Oh, sign off!' cried Violet impatiently. 'Can't we ever go out without your trying to spoil it? If you don't like the ones we know, why don't you get to know some others? Why don't you invite some of the Jadwins and the Hertzogs to dinner, if you're so particular?'

'We ought to be able to have friends without their being boot—'

'If you say that again, I'll scream.'

As they went down their walk half an hour later, they could hear the radio playing 'The Breakaway' in Shalder's house. It was a fine machine, but to Earl it did not sound like the promise of a particularly good time, since if he turned on his radio he could have the same music. There were three fine cars in front of the house; one had just driven up, and they recognized a couple they had met there before – an Italian-American, Lieutenant Spirelli, and his wife. Lieutenant Spirelli wore an officer's uniform. Howard Shalder, a big, tough young man with a twice-a-day beard and a hearty voice, stood hospitably on his front steps. Like all people who have lived by rendering personal service, Earl had a sharp sense of the relative importance of people; because he was a really kind man, this didn't show itself in snobbishness. Nevertheless, as they crossed the street the sight of the broken-English Italian in his inappropriate uniform depressed him, and he felt a renewed doubt as to whether he had risen in the world. In the barber shop both Shalder and Spirelli would have been part of the day's work; meeting them this way seemed to imply that they were on the same level, that this was the way he was. He didn't like it. He felt he was in Mr Jadwin's class – not Mr Jadwin's equal but a part of the structure to which Mr Jadwin belonged.

He crossed the street a little behind Violet. The sun was still yellow, but the tranquillity of evening was already in the air, with the cries of birds and children softened and individualized. Not the most bored captive of society had any more sense of being in a cage than had Earl as he walked into that house to have fun.

That was, a little later in the evening, the exact mood of Mr Philip Jadwin, but he was escaping instead of entering. The dinner dance at the country club had affected him as singularly banal; it was an exceptionally wet, prenuptial affair, and he was on the wagon, so a moment arrived when he could stand it no longer. His very leaving was fraught with nuisances – he was lapelled by a bore who told him of a maudlin personal grief; he was cornered by a woman who insisted on walking down the drive with him to talk about investments, in spite of the cloying fact that couples in every second parked car were in various stages of intimacy. Alone at last, he drove into the main white road and breathed in the fine June night.

He was rather bored with life, interested in business, but feeling somewhat pointless lately in making more money for himself, already so rich. Apparently the boom was going on for ever and things could take care of themselves; he wished he had devoted more attention to his personal desires. Three years ago he should have married that girl in his office who had made him tremble whenever she came near. He had been afraid. Now three of the relatives of whom he had been afraid were dead and a cousin of his had since married his stenographer and had not been very strongly persecuted, and she was making him a fine wife too.

This very morning Jadwin had discovered that the girl he had wanted and had been too cautious to take was now married and had a baby. He encountered her on the street; she was shy, she seemed disinclined to give him either her new name or her address. He did not know if he still loved her, but she seemed real to him, or at least someone from a time when everything seemed more real. The carefully brought-up children of wealthy easterners grow old early; at thirty-four Philip Jadwin wasn't sure he had any emotions at all.

But he had enough sentiment to make him presently stop under the bright moonlight, look at an address in a notebook and turn his car in a new direction. He wanted to see where she lived, he wanted to eavesdrop on her; perhaps, if the lights were on, stare in on some happy domestic scene. Again, if her surroundings were squalid, he might give her husband a lift. A great girl; there was something about her that always moved him – only once in a lifetime perhaps—

He drove into a new street laid out with pleasant red-brick houses: it seemed to Jadwin that he had owned this land or the adjoining parcel himself a few years back. He drove slowly along between the lighted houses, peering for the number. It was a little after ten.

No. 42, 44, 46 – there. He slowed down further, looking at a brightly lit house which poured radio music out into the night. He drove a little past it and cut off his motor; then he could hear festive voices inside, and in a window he saw a man's black back against a yellow mushroom lamp. No poverty there; the house looked comfortable, the lawn well kept, and it was a pleasant neighbourhood. Jadwin was glad.

He got out of his car and sauntered cautiously along the sidewalk towards the house, stopping in the shadow of the hedge as the front door opened, gleamed, slammed, and left a man standing on the steps. He was in a dinner coat and hatless. He came down the walk, and as Jadwin resumed his saunter they came face to face. At once they recognized each other.

'Why, hello, Mr Jadwin.'

'Hello, there, Earl.'

'Well, well, well,' Earl was a little tight and he took a long breath as if it was medicine. 'They're having a party in there, but I quit.'

'Isn't that where the Shalders live?'

'Sure. Big bootlegger.'

Jadwin started. 'Bootlegger?'

'Sure, but if he thinks he can—' He broke off and resumed with dignity: 'I live over the way. The house with the col— columnade.' Then he remembered that Mr Jadwin had started him towards the acquisition of that house, and the fact sobered him further: 'Maybe you remember—' he began, but Jadwin interrupted:

'Are you sure Shalder's a bootlegger?'

'Dead sure. Admits it himself.'

'What does – how does his wife like it?'

'She didn't know till they were married. She told me that tonight after she had a cocktail – I made her take a cocktail because she was upset, because Shalder and my—' Again he changed the subject suddenly: 'Would you care to come over to my house and smoke a cigar and have a drink?'

'Why, not tonight, thanks. I must get along.'

'I don't know whether you remember the tip on the market you gave me three years ago, Mr Jadwin. That was the start of all this.' He waved his hand towards the house and brought it around as if to include the other house and his wife too.

A wave of distaste passed over Jadwin. He remembered the incident, and if this was the result, he regretted it. He was a simple man with simple tastes; his love for Irene had been founded upon them in reaction against the complicated surfaces of the girls he knew. It shocked him to find her in this atmosphere which, at best, was only a shoddy imitation of the other. He winced as bursts of shrill laughter volleyed out into the night.

'And believe me, I'm very grateful to you, Mr Jadwin,' continued Earl. 'I always said that if we ever had a son—'

'How are things going with you?' Jadwin asked hastily.

'Oh, going great. I've been making a lot of money.'

'What are you doing?'

'Just watching the board,' said Earl apologetically. 'As a matter of fact, I'd like to get a nice position. I had to quit the barber business; it didn't seem to go with all the jack I made. But I've always been sort of sorry. There's Doctor Jordan, for instance. He tells me he's got over three hundred thousand dollars on paper and he still keeps on making five-dollar visits. Then there's a porter in the First National—'

They both turned around suddenly; a woman carrying a small bag was coming down the gravel path from the rear of the house. Where it met the sidewalk she stood for a moment in the moonlight, looking at the house; then, with a curious, despairing gesture of her shoulders, she set off quickly along the sidewalk. Before either Jadwin or Earl could move, the front door opened and a large man in a dinner coat dashed out and after her. When he caught up to her they heard fragments of conversation; excited and persuasive on his part, quiet and scornful on hers:

'You're acting crazy, I tell you!'

'I'm only going to my sister's. I'm glad I took the baby there.'

'I tell you I didn't—'

'You can't kiss a woman before my eyes in my own house and have your friends go to sleep on my bed.'

'Now, look here, Irene!'

After a moment she gave up, shrugged her shoulders contemptuously and dropped her bag. He picked it up, and together they went up the gravel path by which she had come out.

'That was her. That was Mrs Shalder,' said Earl.

'I recognized her.'

'She's a fine young woman too. That Shalder – somebody ought to do something to him. I'd like to go in there now and get my wife.'

'Why don't you ?' asked Jadwin.

Earl sighed. 'What's the use ? There'd just be a quarrel and they'd all make it up tomorrow. I've been to a lot of parties like this since I moved out here, Mr Jadwin. They all make it up tomorrow.'

And now the house gave forth another guest. It was Violet, who marked her exit by some shrill statement to people inside before she slammed the door. It was as if the others, entering through the kitchen, had forced her out in front. Coming down the walk, she saw Earl.

'Well, I never want to see that bunch again,' she began angrily.

'Sh!' Earl warned her. 'Look, Vi; I want you to meet Mr Jadwin. You've heard me speak of him. This is my wife, Violet, Mr Jadwin.'

Violet's manner changed. Her hand leaped at her hair, her lips parted in an accommodating smile.

'Why, how do you do, Mr Jadwin; it's a pleasure indeed. I hope you'll excuse my looks; I've been—' She broke off discreetly. 'Earl, why can't you ask Mr Jadwin over to our home for a drink ?'

'Oh, you're very kind, but—'

'That's our home across the way. I don't suppose it looks so very much to you.'

'It looks very nice.'

'Yes,' said Violet, combing her mind for topics . . . 'I saw in the papers that your sister is getting married. I know a woman who knows her very well – a Mrs Lemmon. Do you know her ?'

'I'm afraid I—'

'She's very nice. She has a nice home on Penn Street.' Again she smoothed her hair. 'My, I must look a sight – and I had a wave this afternoon.'

'I've got to be going along,' said Jadwin.

'You sure you don't want a drink ?' asked Earl.

'No, another time.'

'Well, good night then,' said Violet. 'Any time you're passing by and want a drink, we'd be very happy if you just dropped in informally.'

They went across the street together, and he saw that the encounter with him had temporarily driven the unpleasant evening from their minds. Earl walked alertly and Violet kept patting at various parts of her person. Neither of them looked around, as if that wasn't fair. The party in the Shalders' house was still going on, but there was a light now in a bedroom upstairs, and as Jadwin started his car he stared at it for a moment.

'It's all awfully mixed up,' he said.

III

Nowhere in America was the drop in the market felt more acutely than in that city. Since it was the headquarters of the Hert-win industries, and since everyone had the sense of being somehow on the inside, the plunging had been enormous. In the dark autumn it seemed that every person in town was more or less involved.

Earl Johnson took the blow on his chin. Two-thirds of his money melted away in the first slumps while he looked on helplessly, grasping at every counsel in the newspapers, every wild rumour in the crowd. He felt that there was one man who might have been able to help him; if he had been still a barber and shaving Mr Philip Jadwin, he might have asked, 'What had I better do now?' and got the right answer. Once he even called at his office, but Mr Jadwin was busy. He didn't go back.

When he met a barber from the Jadwin Hotel shop, he could not help noticing the grin back of the sympathetic words; it was human to regard his short-lived soar as comic. But he didn't really understand what had happened until several months later, when his possessions began to peel away. The automobile went, the mortgaged house went, though they continued to live there on a rental, pending its resale. Violet suggested selling her pearl necklace, but when he consented, she became so bitter that he told her not to.

These few things were literally all they had – old washing machines, radios, electric refrigerators were a drug on the market. As 1930 wobbled its way downhill Earl saw that they had salvaged nothing – not the love with which, under happy auspices, they had started life, no happy memories, only a few transient exhilarations; no new knowledge or capability – not a thing – simply a space where three years had been. In the spring of 1930 he went back to work. He had his old chair, and it was exciting when his old customers came in one by one.

'What? Earl! Well, this is like old times.'

Some of them didn't know of his prosperity, and of those who did, some were delicately silent, others made only a humorously sympathetic reference to it, no one was unpleasant. Within a month personal appointments took up half his time, as in the old days – people popping in the door and saying, 'In half an hour, Earl?' He was again the most popular barber, the best workman in the city. His fingers grew supple and soft, the rhythm of the shop entered into him, and something told him that he was now a barber for life. He didn't mind; the least pleasant parts of his life were hangovers from his prosperity.

For one thing, there was Mr Jadwin. Once his most faithful customer, he had come into the shop the first day of Earl's return, startled at the sight of him and gone to another barber. Earl's chair had been empty. The other barber was almost apologetic about it afterwards. 'He's your customer,' he told Earl. 'He's just got used to coming to the rest of us while you were gone, and he don't want to let us down right away.' But Jadwin never came to Earl; in fact, he obviously avoided him, and Earl felt it deeply and didn't understand.

But his worst trouble was at home; home had become a nightmare. Violet was unable to forgive him for having caused the collapse in Wall Street, after having fooled her with the boom. She even made herself believe that she had married him when he was rich and that he had dragged her down from a higher station. She saw that life would never bounce him very high again and she was ready to get out.

Earl woke up one April morning, aware, with the consciousness that floats the last edge of sleep, that she had been up and at the window for perhaps ten minutes, perhaps a half-hour.

'What is it, Vi?' he asked. 'What are you looking for?'

She started and turned around. 'Nothing. I was just standing here.'

He went downstairs for the newspaper. When he returned she was again at the window in the attitude of watching, and she threw a last glance towards it before she went down to get breakfast. He joined her ten minutes later.

'One thing's settled,' he said. 'I was going to sell the Warren Files common for what I could get, but this morning it ain't even in the list of stocks at all. What do you know about that?'

'I suppose it's just as good as the rest of your investments?'

'I haven't got any more investments. Here's what I'm going to do: I'm going to take what cash I got left, which is just about enough, and buy the concession for the new barber shop in the Hertzog Building. And I'm going to do it now.'

'You've got some cash?' Violet demanded. 'How much?'

'There's two thousand in the savings bank. I didn't tell you because I thought we ought to have something to fall back on.'

'And yet you sell the car!' Violet said. 'You let me do the housework and talk about selling my jewellery!'

'Keep your shirt on, Vi. How long do you think two thousand would last, living the way we were? You better be glad we got it now, because if I have this barber shop, then it's mine, and nobody can lose me my job, no matter what happens.'

He broke off. She had left the breakfast table and gone to the front window.

'What's the matter out there? You'd think there was a street parade.'

'I was just wondering about the postman.'

'He'll be another hour,' said Earl. 'Anyhow, about a month ago I took an option on this shop for two hundred dollars. I've been waiting to see if the market was ever going to change.'

'How much did you say was in the bank?' she asked suddenly.

'About two thousand dollars.'

When he had gone, Violet left the dishes on the table and went out on the porch, where she sat down and fixed her eyes on the Shalder house across the way. The postman passed, but, she scarcely saw him. After half an hour Irene Shalder emerged and hurried towards the street car. Still Violet waited.

At half past ten a taxi drew up in front of the Shalder house and a few minutes later Shalder came out carrying a pair of suitcases. This was her signal. She hurried across the street and caught him as he was getting into the cab.

'I got a new idea,' she said.

'Yes, but I got to go, Violet. I got to catch a train.'

'Never mind. I got a new idea. Something for both of us.'

'I told you we could settle that later – when I get things straightened out. I'll write you next week; I swear I will.'

'But this is something for right now. It's real cash; we could get it today.'

Shalder hesitated. 'If you mean that necklace of yours, it wouldn't much more than get us to the Coast.'

'This is two thousand dollars cash I'm talking about.'

Shalder spoke to the taxi man and went across the street with her. They sat down in the parlour.

'If I get this two thousand,' said Violet, 'will you take me with you?'

'Where'll you get it?'

'I can get it. But you answer me first.'

'I don't know,' he said hesitantly. 'Like I told you, that Philadelphia mob gave me twenty-four hours to get out of town. Do you think I'd go otherwise just when I'm short of money? Irene went out looking for her old job this morning.'

'Does she know you're going?'

'She thinks I'm going to Chicago. I told her I'd send for her and the kid when I get started.'

Violet wet her lips. 'Well, how about it? Two thousand dollars would give you a chance to look around – something to get started with.'

'Where you can get it?'

'It's in a bank, and it's as much mine as it is Earl's, because it's in a joint account. But you better think quick, because he wants to put it into a barber shop. Next he'd want me to go back to manicuring. I tell you I can't stand this life much longer.'

Shalder walked up and down, considering. 'All right. Make me out a cheque,' he said. 'And go pack your grips.'

At that moment Irene Shalder was talking to Philip Jadwin in his office in the Hertzog Building.

'Of course you can have your position back,' he said. 'We've missed you. Sit down a minute and tell me what you've been doing.'

She sat down, and as she talked he watched her. There was a faint mask of unhappiness and fright on her face, but underneath it he felt the quiet charm that had always moved him. She spoke frankly of all that she had hoarded up inside her in two years.

'And when he sends for you?' he asked when she had finished.

'He won't send for me.'

'How do you know?'

'I just know. He – well, I don't think he's going alone. There's a woman he likes. He doesn't think I know, but I couldn't help knowing. Oh, it's all just terrible. Anyhow, if he sends for anybody, it'll be for this woman. I think he'd take her with him now if he had the money.'

Philip Jadwin wanted to put his arm around her and whisper, 'Now you've got a friend. All this trouble is over.' But he only said: 'Maybe it's better for him to go. Where's your baby?'

'She's been at my sister's since Monday; I was afraid to keep her in the house. You see, Howard has been threatened by some people he used to do business with and I didn't know what they might do. That's why he's leaving town.'

'I see.'

Several hours later Jadwin's secretary brought in a note:

Dear Mr Jadwin: As you probably know, I took an option on the new barber shop, depositing two hundred with Mr Edsall. Well, I have decided to take it up and I understand Mr Edsall is out of town, and I would like to close the deal now, if you could see me.

Respectfully,

EARL JOHNSON.

Jadwin had not known that Earl held the option, and the news was unwelcome. He felt guilty about Earl, and from feeling guilty about him, it was only a step to disliking him. He had grown to think of him as the type of all the speculation for which big business was blamed, and having had a glimpse afterwards at the questionable paradise that Earl had bought with his money, he looked at the story and at its victim himself with distaste. Having avoided Earl in the other barber shop, he was now faced with having him in the building where he had his own offices.

'I'll see if I can talk him out of it,' he thought.

When Earl came in he kept him standing. 'Your note was rather a surprise to me,' he began.

'I only just decided,' said Earl humbly.

'I mean I'm surprised that you're going on your own again so quickly. I shouldn't think you'd plunge into another speculation just at this time.'

'This isn't a speculation, Mr Jadwin. I understand the barber business. Always when the boss was gone I took charge; he'll tell you that himself.'

'But any business requires a certain amount of financial experience, a certain ability to figure costs and profits. There've been a lot of failures in this town because of people starting something they couldn't handle. You'd better think it over carefully before you rush into this.'

'I have thought it over carefully, Mr Jadwin. I was going to buy a shop three years ago, but I put the money into Hert-win when I got that tip from you.'

'You remember I didn't want to give you the tip and I told you you'd probably lose your shirt.'

'I never blamed you, Mr Jadwin – never. It was something I oughtn't to have meddled with. But the barber business is something I know.'

'Why should you blame me?'

'I shouldn't. But when you avoided my chair I thought maybe you thought I did.'

This was too close to home to be pleasant.

'Look here, Earl,' said Jadwin hurriedly. 'We've almost closed with another party about this barber shop. Would you consider giving up your option if we forfeit, say, two hundred dollars?'

Earl rubbed his chin. 'I tell you, Mr Jadwin, I got just two thousand dollars and I don't know what to do with it. If I knew any other way of making it work for me – but nowadays it's dangerous for a man to speculate unless he's got inside information.'

'It's dangerous for everybody always,' remarked Jadwin impatiently. 'Then, do I understand that you insist on going into this?'

'Unless you could suggest something else,' said Earl hesitantly.

'Unless I give you another tip, eh?' Jadwin smiled in spite of himself. 'Well, if that's the way it is— Have you got the money here?'

'It's in the savings bank. I can write you a cheque.'

Jadwin rang for his secretary and gave her a scribbled note to telephone the bank and see if the money was actually on deposit. In a few minutes she sent word that it was.

'All right, Earl,' said Jadwin. 'It's your barber shop. I suppose in a few months you'll be sold out for laundry bills, but that's your affair.'

The phone on his desk rang and his secretary switched him on to the teller at the savings bank:

'Mr Jadwin, just a few minutes after your secretary called, a party presented a cheque drawn on Earl Johnson's account.'

'Well?'

'If we honour it, it leaves him a balance of only sixty-six dollars instead of two thousand and sixty-six. It's a joint account and this cheque is signed by Violet Johnson. The party wishing to cash it is Howard Shalder. It's made out to his order.'

'Wait a minute,' said Jadwin quickly, and he leaned back in his chair to think. What Irene Shalder had said came back to him: 'There's a woman he likes . . . he'd take her with him now if he had the money.' Now evidently the woman had found the money.

'This is a damn serious thing,' he thought. 'If I tell them to cash that cheque, Earl probably loses his wife, and with my connivance.' But in the back of his mind he knew that it would set Irene Shalder free.

Philip Jadwin came to a decision and leaned forward to the receiver:

'All right, cash it.' He rang off and turned to Earl. 'Well, make out your cheque. For two thousand dollars.'

He stood up, terribly aware of what he had done. He watched Earl bent over his cheque book, not knowing that the cheque would come back unhonoured and that the whole transaction was meaningless. And watching the fingers twisted clumsily about the fountain pen, he thought how deft those same fingers were with a razor, handling it so adroitly that there was no pull or scrape; of those fingers manipulating a hot towel that never scalded, spreading a final, smooth lotion—

'Earl,' he said suddenly, 'if somebody told you that your wife was running away with another man – that she was on her way to the station – what would you do?'

Earl looked at him steadily. 'Mr Jadwin, I'd thank God,' he said.

A minute later he handed the cheque to Jadwin and received a signed paper; the transaction was complete.

'I hope you'll patronize us sometime, Mr Jadwin.'

'What? Oh, yes, Earl. Certainly I will.'

'Thank you, Mr Jadwin. I'm going to do my best.'

When he had gone, Jadwin looked at the cheque and tore it into small pieces. By this time Shalder and Earl's wife were probably at the station.

'I wonder what the devil I've done,' he brooded.

IV

So that is how Earl Johnson happens to have the barber shop in the Hertzog Building. It is a cheerful shop, bright and modern; probably the most prosperous shop in town, although a large number of the clients insist on Earl's personal attentions. Earl is constitutionally a happy and a sociable man; eventually he will marry again. He knows his staff and sticks to it, and that is not the least important or least creditable thing that can be said about him.

Once in a while he plays the horses on tips that he gets from the paper the shop subscribes to.

'All right, sir,' he says,' in twenty minutes then. I'll wait for you, Mr Jadwin.'

And, then, back at his chair: 'That's Philip Jadwin. He's a nice fellow. I got to admit I like nice people.'

The soul of a slave, says the Marxian. Anyhow that's the sort of soul that Earl has, and he's pretty happy with it. I like Earl.

SIX OF ONE—

Redbook, February 1932

'Six of One—' was written as 'Half a Dozen of the Other', probably in Switzerland in July 1931. It is not known why the Post declined this story, but Redbook paid $3000 for it.

'Six of One—' is an indirect response to the Depression in that it excoriates 'all that waste at the top' and expressed confidence in the Alger types. This story is one of Fitzgerald's rare expressions of open hostility towards the rich, mixed with a sense of regret that seriousness and privilege or ambition and glamour do not often inhabit the same skin, 'Six of One—' is significant in terms of Fitzgerald's personal politics. Despite his image as the chronicler of the very rich, he regarded himself as a liberal and developed an interest in Marxism at this time. (He had listed himself as a socialist in his first Who's Who entry.) Nonetheless, the story is obviously not a call to class warfare, for Fitzgerald was keenly sensitive to the attractions of the aristocracy: 'The young princes in velvet gathered in lovely domesticity around the queen amid the hush of rich draperies may presently grow up to be Pedro the Cruel or Charles the Mad, but the moment of beauty was there.'

Barnes stood on the wide stairs looking down through a wide hall into the living-room of the country place and at the group of youths. His friend Schofield was addressing some benevolent remarks to them, and Barnes did not want to interrupt; as he stood there, immobile, he seemed to be drawn suddenly into rhythm with the group below; he perceived them as statuesque beings, set apart, chiselled out of the Minnesota twilight that was setting on the big room.

In the first place all five, the two young Schofields and their friends, were fine-looking boys, very American, dressed in a careless but not casual way over well-set-up bodies, and with responsive faces open to all four winds. Then he saw that they made a design, the faces profile upon profile, the heads blond and dark, turning towards Mr Schofield, the erect yet vaguely lounging bodies, never tense but ever ready under the flannels and the soft angora wool sweaters, the hands placed on other shoulders, as if to bring each one into the solid freemasonry of the group. Then suddenly, as though a group of models posing for a sculptor were being dismissed, the composition broke and they all moved towards the door. They left Barnes with a sense of having seen something more than five young men between sixteen and eighteen going out to sail or play tennis or golf, but having gained a sharp impression of a whole style, a whole mode of youth, something different from his own less assured, less graceful generation, something unified by standards that he didn't know. He wondered vaguely what the standards of 1920 were, and whether they were worth anything – had a sense of waste, of much effort for a purely esthetic achievement. Then Schofield saw him and called him down into the living-room.

'Aren't they a fine bunch of boys?' Schofield demanded. 'Tell me, did you ever see a finer bunch?'

'A fine lot,' agreed Barnes, with a certain lack of enthusiasm. He felt a sudden premonition that his generation in its years of effort had made possible a Periclean age, but had evolved no prospective Pericles. They had set the scene: was the cast adequate?

'It isn't just because two of them happen to be mine,' went on Schofield. 'It's self-evident. You couldn't match that crowd in any city in the country. First place, they're such a husky lot. Those two little Kavenaughs aren't going to be big men – more like their father; but the oldest one could make any college hockey-team in the country right now.'

'How old are they?' asked Barnes.

'Well, Howard Kavenaugh, the oldest, is nineteen – going to Yale next year. Then comes my Wister – he's eighteen, also going to Yale next year. You liked Wister, didn't you? I don't know anybody who doesn't. He'd make a great politician, that kid. Then there's a boy named Larry Patt who wasn't here today – he's eighteen too, and he's state golf champion. Fine voice too; he's trying to get in Princeton.'

'Who's the blond-haired one who looks like a Greek god?'

'That's Beau Lebaume. He's going to Yale, too, if the girls will let him leave town. Then there's the other Kavenaugh, the stocky one – he's going to be an even better athlete than his brother. And finally there's my youngest, Charley; he's sixteen.' Schofield sighed reluctantly. 'But I guess you've heard all the boasting you can stand.'

'No, tell me more about them – I'm interested. Are they anything more than athletes?'

'Why, there's not a dumb one in the lot, except maybe Beau Lebaume; but you can't help liking him anyhow. And every one of them's a natural leader. I remember a few years ago a tough gang tried to start something with them, calling them "candies" – well, that gang must be running yet. They sort of remind me of young knights. And what's the matter with their being athletes? I seem to remember you stroking the boat at New London and that didn't keep you from consolidating railroad systems and—'

'I took up rowing because I had a sick stomach,' said Barnes. 'By the way, are these boys all rich?'

'Well, the Kavenaughs are, of course; and my boys will have something.' Barnes' eyes twinkled.

'So I suppose since they won't have to worry about money, they're brought up to serve the state,' he suggested. 'You spoke of one of your sons having a political talent and their all being like young knights, so I suppose they'll go out for public life and the army and navy.'

'I don't know about that,' Schofield's voice sounded somewhat alarmed. 'I think their fathers would be pretty disappointed if they didn't go into business. That's natural, isn't it?'

'It's natural, but it isn't very romantic,' said Barnes good-humouredly.

'You're trying to get my goat,' said Schofield. 'Well, if you can match that—'

'They're certainly an ornamental bunch,' admitted Barnes. 'They've got what you call glamour. They certainly look like the cigarette ads in the magazines; but—'

'But you're an old sour-belly,' interrupted Schofield. 'I've explained that these boys are all well-rounded. My son Wister led his class at school this year, but I was a darn sight prouder that he got the medal for best all-round boy.'

The two men faced each other with the uncut cards of the future on the table before them. They had been in college together, and were friends of many years' standing. Barnes was childless, and Schofield was inclined to attribute his lack of enthusiasm to that.

'I somehow can't see them setting the world on fire, doing better than their fathers,' broke out Barnes suddenly. 'The more charming they are, the harder it's going to be for them. In the East people are beginning to realize what wealthy boys are up against. Match them? Maybe not now.' He leaned forward, his eyes lighting up. 'But I could pick six boys from any high school in Cleveland, give them an education, and I believe that ten years from this time your young fellows here would be utterly outclassed. There's so little demanded of them, so little expected of them – what could be softer than just to have to go on being charming and athletic?'

'I know your idea,' objected Schofield scoffingly. 'You'd go to a big municipal high school and pick out the six most brilliant scholars—'

'I'll tell you what I'll do—' Barnes noticed that he had unconsciously substituted 'I will' for 'I would', but he didn't correct himself. 'I'll go to the little town in Ohio, where I was born – there probably aren't fifty or sixty boys in the high school there, and I wouldn't be likely to find six geniuses out of that number.'

'And what?'

'I'll give them a chance. If they fail, the chance is lost. That is a serious responsibility, and they 've got to take it seriously. That's what these boys haven't got – they're only asked to be serious about trivial things.' He thought for a moment. 'I'm going to do it.'

'Do what?'

'I'm going to see.'

A fortnight later he was back in the small town in Ohio where he had been born, where, he felt, the driving emotions of his own youth still haunted the quiet streets. He interviewed the principal of the high school, who made suggestions; then by the, for Barnes, difficult means of making an address and afterwards attending a reception, he got in touch with teachers and pupils. He made a donation to the school, and under cover of this found opportunities of watching the boys at work and at play.

It was fun – he felt his youth again. There were some boys that he liked immediately, and he began a weeding-out process, inviting them in groups of five or six to his mother's house, rather like a fraternity rushing freshmen. When a boy interested him, he looked up his record and that of his family – and at the end of a fortnight he had chosen five boys.

In the order in which he chose them, there was first Otto Schlach, a farmer's son who had already displayed extraordinary mechanical aptitude and a gift for mathematics. Schlach was highly recommended by his teachers, and he welcomed the opportunity offered him of entering the Massachusetts Institute of Technology.

A drunken father left James Matsko as his only legacy to the town of Barnes' youth. From the age of twelve, James had supported himself by keeping a newspaper-and-candy store with a three-foot frontage; and now at seventeen he was reputed to have saved five hundred dollars. Barnes found it difficult to persuade him to study money and banking at Columbia, for Matsko was already assured of his ability to make money. But Barnes had prestige as the town's most successful son, and he convinced Matsko that otherwise he would lack frontage, like his own place of business.

Then there was Jack Stubbs, who had lost an arm hunting, but in spite of this handicap played on the high-school football team. He was not among the leaders in studies; he had developed no particular bent; but the fact that he had overcome that enormous handicap enough to play football – to tackle and to catch punts – convinced Barnes that no obstacles would stand in Jack Stubbs' way.

The fourth selection was George Winfield, who was almost twenty. Because of the death of his father, he had left school at fourteen, helped to support his family for four years, and then, things being better, he had come back to finish high school. Barnes felt, therefore, that Winfield would place a serious value on an education.

Next came a boy whom Barnes found personally antipathetic. Louis Ireland was at once the most brilliant scholar and most difficult boy at school. Untidy, insubordinate and eccentric, Louis drew scurrilous caricatures behind his Latin book, but when called upon inevitably produced a perfect recitation. There was a big talent nascent somewhere in him – it was impossible to leave him out.

The last choice was the most difficult. The remaining boys were mediocrities, or at any rate they had so far displayed no qualities that set them apart. For a time Barnes, thinking patriotically of his old university, considered the football captain, a virtuostic half back who would have been welcome on any eastern squad; but that would have destroyed the integrity of the idea.

He finally chose a younger boy, Gordon Vandervere, of a rather higher standing than the others. Vandervere was the handsomest and one of the most popular boys in school. He had been intended for college, but his father, a harassed minister, was glad to see the way made easy.

Barnes was content with himself; he felt godlike in being able to step in to mould these various destinies. He felt as if they were his own sons, and he telegraphed Schofield in Minneapolis:

HAVE CHOSEN HALF A DOZEN OF THE OTHER, AND AM BACKING THEM AGAINST THE WORLD.

And now, after all this biography, the story begins . . .

The continuity of the frieze is broken. Young Charley Schofield had been expelled from Hotchkiss. It was a small but painful tragedy – he and four other boys, nice boys, popular boys, broke the honour system as to smoking. Charley's father felt the matter deeply, varying between disappointment about Charley and anger at the school. Charley came home to Minneapolis in a desperate humour and went to the country day-school while it was decided what he was to do.

It was still undecided in midsummer. When school was over, he spent his time playing golf, or dancing at the Minnekada Club – he was a handsome boy of eighteen, older than his age, with charming manners, with no serious vices, but with a tendency to be easily influenced by his admirations. His principal admiration at the time was Gladys Irving, a young married woman scarcely two years old than himself. He rushed her at the club dances, and felt sentimentally about her, though Gladys on her part was in love with her husband and asked from Charley only the confirmation of her own youth and charm that a belle often needs after her first baby.

Sitting out with her one night on the veranda of the Lafayette Club, Charley felt a necessity to boast to her, to pretend to be more experienced, and so more potentially protective.

'I've seen a lot of life for my age,' he said. 'I've done things I couldn't even tell you about.'

Gladys didn't answer.

'In fact last week—' he began, and thought better of it. 'In any case I don't think I'll go to Yale next year – I'd have to go East right away, and tutor all summer. If I don't go, there's a job open in Father's office; and after Wister goes back to college in the fall, I'll have the roadster to myself.'

'I thought you were going to college,' Gladys said coldly.

'I was. But I've thought things over, and now I don't know. I've usually gone with older boys, and I feel older than boys my age. I like older girls, for instance.' When Charley looked at her then suddenly, he seemed unusually attractive to her – it would be very pleasant to have him here, to cut in on her at dances all summer. But Gladys said:

'You'd be a fool to stay here.'

'Why?'

'You started something – you ought to go through with it. A few years running around town, and you won't be good for anything.'

'You think so,' he said indulgently.

Gladys didn't want to hurt him or to drive him away from her; yet she wanted to say something stronger.

'Do you think I'm thrilled when you tell me you've had a lot of dissipated experience? I don't see how anybody could claim to be your friend and encourage you in that. If I were you, I'd at least pass your examinations for college. Then they can't say you just lay down after you were expelled from school.'

'You think so?' Charley said, unruffled, and in his grave, precocious manner, as though he were talking to a child. But she had convinced him, because he was in love with her and the moon was around her. 'Oh me, oh my, oh you' was the last music they had danced to on the Wednesday before, and so it was one of those times.

Had Gladys let him brag to her, concealing her curiosity under a mask of companionship, if she had accepted his own estimate of himself as a man formed, no urging of his father's would have mattered. As it was, Charley passed into college that fall, thanks to a girl's tender reminiscences and her own memories of the sweetness of youth's success in young fields.

And it was well for his father that he did. If he had not, the catastrophe of his older brother Wister that autumn would have broken Schofield's heart. The morning after the Harvard game the New York papers carried a headline:

YALE BOYS AND FOLLIES GIRLS IN
MOTOR CRASH NEAR RYE
IRENE DALEY IN GREENWICH HOSPITAL
THREATENS BEAUTY SUIT
MILLIONAIRE'S SON INVOLVED

The four boys came up before the dean a fortnight later. Wister Schofield, who had driven the car, was called first.

'It was not your car, Mr Schofield,' the dean said. 'It was Mr Kavenaugh's car, wasn't it?'

'Yes sir.'

'How did you happen to be driving?'

'The girls wanted me to. They didn't feel safe.'

'But you'd been drinking too, hadn't you?'

'Yes, but not so much.'

'Tell me this,' asked the dean: 'Haven't you ever driven a car when you'd been drinking – perhaps drinking even more than you were that night?'

'Why – perhaps once or twice, but I never had any accidents. And this was so clearly unavoidable—'

'Possibly,' the dean agreed; 'but we'll have to look at it this way: Up to this time you had no accidents even when you deserved to have them. Now you've had one when you didn't deserve it. I don't want you to go out of here feeling that life or the University or I myself haven't given you a square deal, Mr Schofield. But the newspapers have given this a great deal of prominence, and I'm afraid that the University will have to dispense with your presence.'

Moving along the frieze to Howard Kavenaugh, the dean's remarks to him were substantially the same.

'I am particularly sorry in your case, Mr Kavenaugh. Your father has made substantial gifts to the University, and I took pleasure in watching you play hockey with your usual brilliance last winter.'

Howard Kavenaugh left the office with uncontrollable tears running down his cheeks.

Since Irene Daley's suit for her ruined livelihood, her ruined beauty, was directed against the owner and the driver of the automobile, there were lighter sentences for the other two occupants of the car. Beau Lebaume came into the dean's office with his arm in a sling and his handsome head swathed in bandages and was suspended for the remainder of the current year. He took it jauntily and said good-bye to the dean with as cheerful a smile as could show through the bandages. The last case, however, was the most difficult. George Winfield, who had entered high school late because work in the world had taught him the value of an education, came in looking at the floor.

'I can't understand your participation in this affair,' said the dean. 'I know your benefactor, Mr Barnes, personally. He told me how you left school to go to work, and how you came back to it four years later to continue your education, and he felt that your attitude towards life was essentially serious. Up to this point you have a good record here at New Haven, but it struck me several months ago that you were running with a rather gay crowd, boys with a great deal of money to spend. You are old enough to realize that they couldn't possibly give you as much in material ways as they took away from you in others. I've got to give you a year's suspension. If you come back, I have every hope you'll justify the confidence that Mr Barnes reposed in you.'

'I won't come back,' said Winfield. 'I couldn't face Mr Barnes after this. I'm not going home.'

At the suit brought by Irene Daley, all four of them lied loyally for Wister Schofield. They said that before they hit the gasoline pump they had seen Miss Daley grab the wheel. But Miss Daley was in court, with her face, familiar to the tabloids, permanently scarred; and her counsel exhibited a letter cancelling her recent moving-picture contract. The students' case looked bad; so in the intermission, on their lawyer's advice, they settled for forty thousand dollars. Wister Schofield and Howard Kavenaugh were snapped by a dozen photographers leaving the court-room, and served up in flaming notoriety next day.

That night, Wister, the three Minneapolis boys, Howard and Beau Lebaume started for home. George Winfield said good-bye to them in the Pennsylvania station; and having no home to go to, walked out into New York to start life over.

Of all Barnes' protégés, Jack Stubbs with his one arm was the favourite. He was the first to achieve fame – when he played on the tennis team at Prince, the rotogravure section carried pictures showing how he threw the ball from his racket in serving. When he was graduated, Barnes took him into his own office – he was often spoken of as an adopted son. Stubbs, together with Schlach, now a prominent consulting engineer, were the most satisfactory of his experiments, although James Matsko at twenty-seven had just been made a partner in a Wall Street brokerage house. Financially he was the most successful of the six, yet Barnes found himself somewhat repelled by his hard egoism. He wondered, too, if he, Barnes, had really played any part in Matsko's career – did it after all matter whether Matsko was a figure in metropolitan finance or a big merchant in the Mid-west, as he would have undoubtedly become without any assistance at all.

One morning in 1930 he handed Jack Stubbs a letter that led to a balancing up of the book of boys.

'What do you think of this?'

The letter was from Louis Ireland in Paris. About Louis they did not agree, and as Jack read, he prepared once more to intercede in his behalf.

My dear Sir: After your last communication, made through your bank here and enclosing a cheque which I hereby acknowledge, I do not feel that I am under any obligation to write you at all. But because the concrete fact of an object's commercial worth may be able to move you, while you remain utterly insensitive to the value of an abstract idea – because of this I write to tell you that my exhibition was an unqualified success. To bring the matter even nearer to your intellectual level, I may tell you that I sold two pieces – a head of Lallette, the actress, and a bronze animal group – for a total of seven thousand francs :$280.00).

Moreover I have commissions which will take me all summer – I enclose a piece about me cut from *Cahiers d'Art*, which will show you that whatever your estimate of my abilities and my career, it is by no means unanimous.

This is not to say that I am ungrateful for your well-intentioned attempt to 'educate' me. I suppose that Harvard was no worse than any other polite finishing school – the year that I wasted there gave me a sharp and well-documented attitude on American life and institutions. But your suggestions that I come to America and make standardized nymphs for profiteers' fountains was a little too much—

Stubbs looked up with a smile.

'Well,' Barnes said, 'what do you think? Is he crazy – or now that he has sold some statues, does it prove that I'm crazy?'

'Neither one,' laughed Stubbs. 'What you objected to in Louis wasn't his talent. But you never got over that year he tried to enter a monastery and then got arrested in the Sacco-Vanzetti demonstrations, and then ran away with the professor's wife.'

'He was just forming himself,' said Barnes dryly, 'just trying his little wings. God knows what he's been up to abroad.'

'Well, perhaps he's formed now,' Stubbs said lightly. He had always liked Louis Ireland – privately he resolved to write and see if he needed money.

'Anyhow, he's graduated from me,' announced Barnes. 'I can't do any more to help him or hurt him. Suppose we call him a success, though that's pretty doubtful – let's see how we stand. I'm going to see Schofield out in Minneapolis next week, and I'd like to balance accounts. To my mind, the successes are you, Otto Schlach, James Matsko – whatever you and I may think of him as a man – and let's assume that Louis Ireland is going to be a great sculptor. That's four. Winfield's disappeared. I've never had a line from him.'

'Perhaps he's doing well somewhere.'

'If he were doing well, I think he'd let me know. We'll have to count him as a failure so far as my experiment goes. Then there's Gordon Vandervere.'

Both were silent for a moment.

'I can't make it out about Gordon,' Barnes said. 'He's such a nice fellow, but since he left college, he doesn't seem to come through. He was younger than the rest of you, and he had the advantage of two years at Andover before he went to college, and at Princeton he knocked them cold, as you say. But he seems to have worn his wings out – for four years now he's done nothing at all; he can't hold a job; he can't get his mind on his work, and he doesn't seem to care. I'm about through with Gordon.'

At this moment Gordon was announced over the phone.

'He asked for an appointment,' explained Barnes. 'I suppose he wants to try something new.'

A personable young man with an easy and attractive manner strolled in to the office.

'Good afternoon, Uncle Ed. Hi there, Jack!' Gordon sat down. 'I'm full of news.'

'About what?' asked Barnes.

'About myself.'

'I know. You've just been appointed to arrange a merger between J. P. Morgan and the Queensborough Bridge.'

'It's a merger,' agreed Vandervere, 'but those are not the parties to it. I'm engaged to be married.'

Barnes glowered.

'Her name,' continued Vandervere, 'is Esther Crosby.'

'Let me congratulate you,' said Barnes ironically. 'A relation of H. B. Crosby, I presume.'

'Exactly,' said Vandervere unruffled. 'In fact, his only daughter.'

For a moment there was silence in the office. Then Barnes exploded.

'*You're* going to marry H. B. Crosby's daughter? Does he know that last month you retired by request from one of his banks?'

'I'm afraid he knows everything about me. He's been looking me over for four years. You see, Uncle Ed,' he continued cheerfully, 'Esther and I got engaged during my last year at Princeton – my room mate brought her down to a house-party, but she switched over to me. Well, quite naturally Mr Crosby wouldn't hear of it until I'd proved myself.'

'Proved yourself!' repeated Barnes. 'Do you consider that you've proved yourself?'

'Well – yes.'

'How?'

'By waiting four years. You see, either Esther or I might have married anybody else in that time, but we didn't. Instead we sort of wore him away. That's really why I haven't been able to get down to anything. Mr Crosby is a strong personality, and it took a lot of time and energy wearing him away. Sometimes Esther and I didn't see each other for months, so she couldn't eat; so then thinking of that I couldn't eat, so then I couldn't work—'

'And you mean he's really given his consent?'

'He gave it last night.'

'Is he going to let you loaf?'

'No. Esther and I are going into the diplomatic service. She feels that the family has passed through the banking phase.' He winked at Stubbs. 'I'll look up Louis Ireland when I get to Paris, and send Uncle Ed a report.'

Suddenly Barnes roared with laughter.

'Well, it's all in the lottery-box,' he said. 'When I picked out you six, I was a long way from guessing—' He turned to Stubbs and demanded: 'Shall we put him under *failure* or under *success*?'

'A howling success,' said Stubbs. 'Top of the list.'

A fortnight later Barnes was with his old friend Schofield in Minneapolis. He thought of the house with the six boys as he had last seen it – now it seemed to bear scars of them, like the traces that pictures leave on a wall that they have long protected from the mark of time. Since he did not know what had become of Schofield's sons, he refrained from referring to their conversation of ten years before until he knew whether it was dangerous ground. He was glad of his reticence later in the evening when Schofield spoke of his elder son, Wister.

'Wister never seems to have found himself – and he was such a high-spirited kid! He was the leader of every group he went into; he could always make things go. When he was young, our houses in town and at the lake were always packed with young people. But after he left Yale, he lost interest in things – got sort of scornful about everything. I thought for a while that it was because he drank too much, but he married a nice girl and she took that in hand. Still, he hasn't any ambition – he talked about country life, so I bought him a silver-fox farm, but that didn't go; and I sent him to Florida during the boom, but that wasn't any better. Now he has an interest in a dude-ranch in Montana; but since the depression—'

Barnes saw his opportunity and asked:

'What became of those friends of your sons' that I met one day?'

'Let's see – I wonder who you mean. There was Kavenaugh – you know, the flour people – he was here a lot. Let's see – he eloped with an eastern girl, and for a few years he and his wife were the leaders of the gay crowd here – they did a lot of drinking and not much else. It seems to me I heard the other day that Howard's getting a divorce. Then there was the younger brother – he never could get into college. Finally he married a manicurist, and they live here rather quietly. We don't hear much about them.'

They had had a glamour about them, Barnes remembered; they had been so sure of themselves, individually, as a group; so high-spirited, a frieze of Greek youths, graceful of body, ready for life.

'Then Larry Patt, you might have met him here. A great golfer. He couldn't stay in college – there didn't seem to be enough fresh air there for Larry.' And he added defensively: 'But he capitalized what he could do – he opened a sporting-goods store and made a good thing of it, I understand. He has a string of three or four.'

'I seem to remember an exceptionally handsome one.'

'Oh – Beau Lebaume. He was in that mess at New Haven too. After that he went to pieces – drink and what-not. His father's tried everything, and now he won't have anything more to do with him.' Schofield's face warmed suddenly; his eyes glowed. 'But let tell you, I've got a boy – my Charley! I wouldn't trade him for the lot of them – he's coming over presently, and you'll see. He had a bad start, got into trouble at Hotchkiss – but did he quit? Never. He went back and made a fine record at New Haven, senior society and all that. Then he and some other boys took a trip around the world, and then he came back here and said: "All right, Father, I'm ready – when do I start?" I don't know what I'd do without Charley. He got married a few months back, a young widow he'd always been in love with; and his mother and I are still missing him, though they come over often—'

Barnes was glad about this, and suddenly he was reconciled at not having any sons in the flesh – one out of two made good, and sometimes better, and sometimes nothing; but just going along getting old by yourself when you'd counted on so much from sons—

'Charley runs the business,' continued Schofield. 'That is, he and a young man named Winfield that Wister got me to take on five or six years ago. Wister felt responsible about him, felt he'd got him into this trouble at New Haven – and this boy had no family. He's done well here.'

Another one of Barnes' six accounted for! He felt a surge of triumph, but he saw he must keep it to himself; a little later when Schofield asked him if he'd carried out his intention of putting some boys through college, he avoided answering. After all, any given moment has its value; it can be questioned in the light of after-events, but the moment remains. The young princes in velvet gathered in lovely domesticity around the queen amid the hush of rich draperies may presently grow up to be Pedro the Cruel or Charles the Mad, but the moment of beauty was there. Back there ten years, Schofield had seen his sons and their friends as samurai, as something shining and glorious and young, perhaps as something he had missed from his own youth. There was later a price to be paid by those boys, all too fulfilled, with the whole balance of their life pulled forward into their youth so that everything afterwards would inevitably be anticlimax; these boys brought up as princes with none of the responsibilities of princes! Barnes didn't know how much their mothers might have had to do with it, what their mothers may have lacked.

But he was glad that his friend Schofield had one true son.

His own experiment – he didn't regret it, but he wouldn't have done it again. Probably it proved something, but he wasn't quite sure what. Perhaps that life is constantly renewed, and glamour and beauty make way for it; and he was glad that he was able to feel that the republic could survive the mistakes of a whole generation, pushing the waste aside, sending ahead the vital and the strong. Only it was too bad and very American that there should be all that waste at the top; and he felt that he would not live long enough to see it end, to see great seriousness in the same skin with great opportunity – to see the race achieve itself at last.

A FREEZE-OUT

Saturday Evening Post, 19 December 1931

'A Freeze-Out' was probably the last story Fitzgerald wrote in Switzerland before sailing home with his family in September 1931. The Post *paid $4000.*

In this story Fitzgerald found an American subject and avoided the Depression, returning to St Paul for his setting. 'A Freeze-Out' is a reversion to the confident spirit of his earlier stories, showing none of the troubles or troublesome people who appear in some of the other stories written in this period. In 'A Freeze-Out' the problems are solved by good sense and right instincts. The depiction of old Mrs Winslow is noteworthy, showing Fitzgerald's lifelong respect for solid characters – representatives of old American standards – who do their duty.

Here and there in a sunless corner skulked a little snow under a veil of coal specks, but the men taking down storm windows were labouring in shirt sleeves and the turf was becoming firm underfoot.

In the streets, dresses dyed after fruit, leaf and flower emerged from beneath the shed sombre skins of animals; now only a few old men wore mousy caps pulled down over their ears. That was the day Forrest Winslow forgot the long fret of the past winter as one forgets inevitable afflictions, sickness and war, and turned with blind confidence towards the summer, thinking he already recognized in it all the summers of the past – the golfing, sailing, swimming summers.

For eight years Forrest had gone East to school and then to college; now he worked for his father in a large Minnesota city. He was handsome, popular and rather spoiled in a conservative way, and so the past year had been a comedown. The discrimination that had picked Scroll and Key at New Haven was applied to sorting furs; the hand that had signed the junior prom expense cheques had since rocked in a sling for two months with mild dermatitis venenata. After work, Forrest found no surcease in the girls with whom he had grown up. On the contrary, the news of a stranger within the tribe stimulated him and during the transit of a popular visitor he displayed a convulsive activity. So far, nothing had happened; but here was summer.

On the day spring broke through and summer broke through – it is much the same thing in Minnesota – Forrest stopped his coupé in front of a music store and took his pleasant vanity inside. As he said to the clerk, 'I want some records,' a little bomb of excitement exploded in his larynx, causing an unfamiliar and almost painful vacuum in his upper diaphragm. The unexpected detonation was caused by the sight of a corn-coloured girl who was being waited on across the counter.

She was a stalk of ripe corn, but bound not as cereals are but as a rare first edition, with all the binder's art. She was lovely and expensive, and about nineteen, and he had never seen her before. She looked at him for just an unnecessary moment too long, with so much self-confidence that he felt his own rush out and away to join hers – '. . . from him that hath not shall be taken away even that which he hath'. Then her head swayed forward and she resumed her inspection of a catalogue.

Forrest looked at the list a friend had sent him from New York. Unfortunately, the first title was 'When Voo-do-o-do Meets Boop-boop-a-doop, There'll Soon be a Hot-Cha-Cha'. Forrest read it with horror. He could scarcely believe a title could be so repulsive.

Meanwhile the girl was asking: 'Isn't there a record of Prokofiev's "Fils Prodigue?"'

'I'll see, madam.' The saleswoman turned to Forrest.

' "When Voo—"' Forrest began, and then repeated, ' "When Voo—"' There was no use; he couldn't say it in front of that nymph of the harvest across the table.

'Never mind that one,' he said quickly. 'Give me "Huggable—"' Again he broke off.

' "Huggable, Kissable You"?' suggested the clerk helpfully, and her assurance that it was very nice suggested a humiliating community of taste.

'I want Stravinsky's "Fire Bird",' said the other customer, 'and this album of Chopin waltzes.'

Forrest ran his eye hastily down the rest of his list: 'Digga Diggity', 'Ever So Goosy', 'Bunkey Doodle I do'.

'Anybody would take me for a moron,' he thought. He crumpled up the list and fought for air – his own kind of air, the air of casual superiority.

'I'd like,' he said coldly, 'Beethoven's Moonlight Sonata.'

There was a record of it at home, but it didn't matter. It gave him the right to glance at the girl again and again. Life became interesting; she was the loveliest concoction; it would be easy to trace her. With the Moonlight Sonata wrapped face to face with 'Huggable, Kissable You', Forrest quitted the shop.

There was a new book store down the street, and here also he entered, as if books and records could fill the vacuum that spring was making in his heart. As he looked among the lifeless words of many titles together, he was wondering how soon he could find her, and what then.

'I'd like a hard-boiled detective story,' he said.

A weary young man shook his head with patient reproof; simultaneously, a spring draft from the door blew in with it the familiar glow of cereal hair.

'We don't carry detective stories or stuff like that,' said the young man in an unnecessarily loud voice. 'I imagine you'll find it at a department store.'

'I thought you carried books,' said Forrest feebly.

'Books, yes, but not that kind.' The young man turned to wait on his other customer.

As Forrest stalked out, passing within the radius of the girl's perfume, he heard her ask:

'Have you got anything of Louis Arragon's, either in French or in translation?'

'She's just showing off,' he thought angrily. 'They skip right from Peter Rabbit to Marcel Proust these days.'

Outside, parked just behind his own adequate coupé, he found an enormous silver-coloured roadster of English make and custom design. Disturbed, even upset, he drove homeward through the moist, golden afternoon.

The Winslows lived in an old, wide-verandaed house on Crest Avenue – Forrest's father and mother, his great-grandmother and his sister Eleanor. They were solid people as that phrase goes since the war. Old Mrs Forrest was entirely solid; with convictions based on a way of life that had worked for eighty-four years. She was a character in the city; she remembered the Sioux war and she had been in Stillwater the day the James brothers shot up the main street.

Her own children were dead and she looked on these remoter descendants from a distance, oblivious of the forces that had formed them. She understood that the Civil War and the opening up of the West were forces, while the free-silver movement and the World War had reached her only as news. But she knew that her father, killed at Cold Harbor, and her husband, the merchant, were larger in scale than her son or her grandson. People who tried to explain contemporary phenomena to her seemed, to her, to be talking against the evidence of their own senses. Yet she was not atrophied; last summer she had travelled over half of Europe with only a maid.

Forrest's father and mother were something else again. They had been in the susceptible middle thirties when the cocktail party and its concomitants arrived in 1921. They were divided people, leaning forward and backward. Issues that presented no difficulty to Mrs Forrest caused them painful heat and agitation. Such an issue arose before they had been five minutes at table that night.

'Do you know the Rikkers are coming back?' said Mrs Winslow. 'They've taken the Warner house.' She was a woman with many uncertainties, which she concealed from herself by expressing her opinions very slowly and thoughtfully, to convince her own ears. 'It's a wonder Dan Warner would rent them his house. I suppose Cathy thinks everybody will fall all over themselves.'

'What Cathy?' asked old Mrs Forrest.

'She was Cathy Chase. Her father was Reynold Chase. She and her husband are coming back here.'

'Oh, yes.'

'I scarcely knew her,' continued Mrs Winslow, 'but I know that when they were in Washington they were pointedly rude to everyone from Minnesota – went out of their way. Mary Cowan was spending a winter there, and she invited Cathy to lunch or tea at least half a dozen times. Cathy never appeared.'

'I could beat that record,' said Pierce Winslow. 'Mary Cowan could invite me a hundred times and I wouldn't go.'

'Anyhow,' pursued his wife slowly, 'in view of all the scandal, it's just asking for the cold shoulder to come out here.'

'They're asking for it, all right,' said Winslow. He was a southerner, well liked in the city, where he had lived for thirty years. 'Walter Hannan came in my office this morning and wanted me to second Rikker for the Kennemore Club. I said: "Walter, I'd rather second Al Capone." What's more, Rikker'll get into the Kennemore Club over my dead body.'

'Walter had his nerve. What's Chauncey Rikker to you? It'll be hard to get anyone to second him.'

'Who are they?' Eleanor asked. 'Somebody awful?'

She was eighteen and a débutante. Her current appearances at home were so rare and brief that she viewed such table topics with as much detachment as her great-grandmother.

'Cathy was a girl here; she was younger than I was, but I remember that she was always considered fast. Her husband, Chauncey Rikker, came from some little town upstate.'

'What did they do that was so awful?'

'Rikker went bankrupt and left town,' said her father. 'There were a lot of ugly stories. Then he went to Washington and got mixed up in the alien-property scandal; and then he got in trouble in New York – he was in the bucket-shop business – but he skipped out to Europe. After a few years the chief Government witness died and he came back to America. They got him for a few months for contempt of court.' He expanded into eloquent irony: 'And now, with true patriotism, he comes back to his beautiful Minnesota, a product of its lovely woods, its rolling wheat fields—'

Forrest called him impatiently: 'Where do you get that, father? When did two Kentuckians ever win Nobel prizes in the same year? And how about an upstate boy named Lind—'

'Have the Rikkers any children?' Eleanor asked.

'I think Cathy has a daughter about your age, and a boy about sixteen.'

Forrest uttered a small, unnoticed exclamation. Was it possible? French books and Russian music – that girl this afternoon had lived abroad. And with the probability his resentment deepened – the daughter of a crook putting on all that dog! He sympathized passionately with his father's refusal to second Rikker for the Kennemore Club.

'Are they rich?' old Mrs Forrest suddenly demanded.

'They must be well off if they took Dan Warner's house.'

'Then they'll get in all right.'

'They won't get into the Kennemore Club,' said Pierce Winslow. 'I happen to come from a state with certain traditions.'

'I've seen the bottom rail get to be the top rail many times in this town,' said the old lady blandly.

'But this man's a criminal, Grandma,' explained Forrest. 'Can't you see the difference? It isn't a social question. We used to argue at New Haven whether we'd shake hands with Al Capone if we met him—'

'Who is Al Capone?' asked Mrs Forrest.

'He's another criminal, in Chicago.'

'Does he want to join the Kennemore Club too?'

They laughed, but Forrest had decided that if Rikker came up for the Kennemore Club, his father's would not be the only black ball in the box.

Abruptly it became full summer. After the last April storm someone came along the street one night, blew up the trees like balloons, scattered bulbs and shrubs like confetti, opened a cage full of robins and, after a quick look around, signalled up the curtain upon a new backdrop of summer sky.

Tossing back a strayed baseball to some kids in a vacant lot, Forrest's fingers, on the stitched seams of the stained leather cover, sent a wave of ecstatic memories to his brain. One must hurry and get there – 'there' was now the fairway of the golf course, but his feeling was the same. Only when he teed off at the eighteenth that afternoon did he realize that it wasn't the same, that it would never be enough any more. The evening stretched large and empty before him, save for the set pieces of a dinner party and bed.

While he waited with his partner for a match to play off, Forrest glanced at the tenth tee, exactly opposite and two hundred yards away.

One of the two figures on the ladies' tee was addressing her ball; as he watched, she swung up confidently and cracked a long drive down the fairway.

'Must be Mrs Horrick,' said his friend. 'No other woman can drive like that.'

At that moment the sun glittered on the girl's hair and Forrest knew who it was; simultaneously, he remembered what he must do this afternoon. That night Chauncey Rikker's name was to come up before the membership committee on which his father sat, and before going home, Forrest was going to pass the clubhouse and leave a certain black slip in a little box. He had carefully considered all that; he loved the city where his people had lived honourable lives for five generations. His grandfather had been a founder of this club in the nineties when it went in for sailboat racing instead of golf, and when it took a fast horse three hours to trot out here from town. He agreed with his father that certain people were without the pale. Tightening his face, he drove his ball two hundred yards down the fairway, where it curved gently into the rough.

The eighteenth and tenth holes were parallel and faced in opposite directions. Between tees they were separated by a belt of trees forty feet wide. Though Forrest did not know it, Miss Rikker's hostess, Helen Hannan, had dubbed into this same obscurity, and as he went in search of his ball he heard female voices twenty feet away.

'You'll be a member after tonight,' he heard Helen Hannan say, 'and then you can get some real competition from Stella Horrick.'

'Maybe I won't be a member,' said a quick, clear voice. 'Then you'll have to come and play with me on the public links.'

'Alida, don't be absurd.'

'Why? I played on the public links in Buffalo all last spring. For the moment there wasn't anywhere else. It's like playing on some courses in Scotland.'

'But I'd feel so silly . . . Oh, gosh, let's let the ball go.'

'There's nobody behind us. As to feeling silly – if I cared about public opinion any more, I'd spend my time in my bedroom.' She laughed scornfully. 'A tabloid published a picture of me going to see Father in prison. And I've seen people change their tables away from us on steamers, and once I was cut by all the American girls in a French school . . . Here's your ball.'

'Thanks . . . Oh, Alida, it seems terrible.'

'All the terrible part is over. I just said that so you wouldn't be too sorry for us if people didn't want us in this club. I wouldn't care; I've got a life of my own and my own standard of what trouble is. It wouldn't touch me at all.'

They passed out of the clearing and their voices disappeared into the open sky on the other side. Forrest abandoned the search for his lost ball and walked towards the caddie house.

'What a hell of a note,' he thought. 'To take it out on a girl that had nothing to do with it' – which was what he was doing this minute as he went up towards the club. 'No,' he said to himself abruptly, 'I can't do it. Whatever her father may have done, she happens to be a lady. Father can do what he feels he has to do, but I'm out.'

After lunch the next day, his father said rather diffidently: 'I see you didn't do anything about the Rikkers and the Kennemore Club.'

'No.'

'It's just as well,' said his father. 'As a matter of fact, they got by. The club has got rather mixed anyhow in the last five years – a good many queer people in it. And, after all, in a club you don't have to know anybody you don't want to. The other people on the committee felt the same way.'

'I see,' said Forrest dryly. 'Then you didn't argue against the Rikkers?'

'Well, no. The thing is I do a lot of business with Walter Hannan, and it happened yesterday I was obliged to ask him rather a difficult favour.'

'So you traded with him.' To both father and son, the word 'traded' sounded like traitor.

'Not exactly. The matter wasn't mentioned.'

'I understand,' Forrest said. But he did not understand, and some old childhood faith in his father died at that moment.

II

To snub anyone effectively one must have him within range. The admission of Chauncey Rikker to the Kennemore Club and, later, to the Downtown Club was followed by angry talk and threats of resignation that simulated the sound of conflict, but there was no indication of a will underneath. On the other hand, unpleasantness in crowds is easy, and Chauncey Rikker was a facile object for personal dislike; moreover, a recurrent echo of the bucket-shop scandal sounded from New York, and the matter was reviewed in the local newspapers, in case anyone had missed it. Only the liberal Hannan family stood by the Rikkers, and their attitude aroused considerable resentment, and their attempt to launch them with a series of small parties proved a failure. Had the Rikkers attempted to 'bring Alida out', it would have been for the inspection of a motley crowd indeed, but they didn't.

When occasionally during the summer, Forrest encountered Alida Rikker, they crossed eyes in the curious way of children who don't know each other. For a while he was haunted by her curly yellow head, by the golden-brown defiance of her eyes; then he became interested in another girl. He wasn't in love with Jane Drake, though he thought he might marry her. She was 'the girl across the street"; he knew her qualities, good and bad, so that they didn't matter. She had an essential reality underneath, like a relative. It would please their families. Once, after several highballs and some casual necking, he almost answered seriously when she provoked him with, 'But you don't really care about me'; but he sat tight and next morning was relieved that he had. Perhaps in the full days after Christmas—Meanwhile, at the Christmas dances among the Christmas girls he might find the ecstasy and misery, the infatuation that he wanted. By autumn he felt that his predestined girl was already packing her trunk in some eastern or southern city.

It was in his more restless mood that one November Sunday he went to a small tea. Even as he spoke to his hostess he felt Alida Rikker across the firelit room; her glowing beauty and her unexplored novelty pressed up against him, and there was a relief in being presented to her at last. He bowed and passed on, but there had been some sort of communication. Her look said that she knew the stand that his family had taken, that she didn't mind, and was even sorry to see him in such a silly position, for she knew that he admired her. His look said: 'Naturally, I'm sensitive to your beauty, but you see how it is; we've had to draw the line at the fact that your father is a dirty dog, and I can't withdraw from my present position.'

Suddenly in a silence, she was talking, and his ears swayed away from his own conversation.

'... Helen had this odd pain for over a year and, of course, they suspected cancer. She went to have an X-ray; she undressed behind a screen, and the doctor looked at her through the machine, and then he said, "But I told you to take off all your clothes," and Helen said, "I have." The doctor looked again, and said, "Listen, my dear, I brought you into the world, so there's no use being modest with me. Take off everything." So Helen said, "I've got every stitch off; I swear." But the doctor said, "You have not. The X-ray shows me a safety pin in your brassiere." Well, they finally found out that she'd been suspected of swallowing a safety pin when she was two years old.'

The story, floating in her clear, crisp voice upon the intimate air, disarmed Forrest. It had nothing to do with what had taken place in Washington or New York ten years before. Suddenly he wanted to go and sit near her, because she was the tongue of flame that made the firelight vivid. Leaving, he walked for an hour through feathery snow, wondering again why he couldn't know her, why it was his business to represent a standard.

'Well, maybe I'll have a lot of fun some day doing what I ought to do,' he thought ironically – 'when I'm fifty.'

The first Christmas dance was the charity ball at the armoury. It was a large, public affair; the rich sat in boxes. Everyone came who felt he belonged, and many out of curiosity, so the atmosphere was tense with a strange haughtiness and aloofness.

The Rikkers had a box. Forrest, coming in with Jane Drake, glanced at the man of evil reputation and at the beaten woman frozen with jewels who sat beside him. They were the city's villains, gaped at by the people of reserved and timid lives. Oblivious of the staring eyes, Alida and Helen Hannan held court for several young men from out of town. Without question, Alida was incomparably the most beautiful girl in the room.

Several people told Forrest the news – the Rikkers were giving a big dance after New Year's. There were written invitations, but these were being supplemented by oral ones. Rumour had it that one had merely to be presented to any Rikker in order to be bidden to the dance.

As Forrest passed through the hall, two friends stopped him and with a certain hilarity introduced him to a youth of seventeen, Mr Teddy Rikker.

'We're giving a dance,' said the young man immediately. 'January third. Be very happy if you could come.'

Forrest was afraid he had an engagement.

'Well, come if you change your mind.'

'Horrible kid, but shrewd,' said one of his friends later. 'We were feeding him people, and when we brought up a couple of saps, he looked at them and didn't say a word. Some refuse and a few accept and most of them stall, but he goes right on; he's got his father's crust.'

Into the highways and byways. Why didn't the girl stop it? He was sorry for her when he found Jane in a group of young women revelling in the story.

'I hear they asked Bodman, the undertaker, by mistake, and then took it back.'

'Mrs Carleton pretended she was deaf.'

'There's going to be a carload of champagne from Canada.'

'Of course, I won't go, but I'd love to, just to see what happens. There'll be a hundred men to every girl – and that'll be meat for her.'

The accumulated malice repelled him and he was angry at Jane for being part of it. Turning away, his eyes fell on Alida's proud form swaying along a wall, watched the devotion of her partners with an unpleasant resentment. He did not know that he had been a little in love with her for many months. Just as two children can fall in love during a physical struggle over a ball, so their awareness of each other had grown to surprising proportions.

'She's pretty,' said Jane. 'She's not exactly overdressed, but considering everything, she dresses too elaborately.'

'I suppose she ought to wear sackcloth and ashes or half-mourning.'

'I was honoured with a written invitation, but, of course, I'm not going.'

'Why not?'

Jane looked at him in surprise. 'You're not going.'

'That's different. I would if I were you. You see, you don't care what her father did.'

'Of course, I care.'

'No, you don't. And all this small meanness just debases the whole thing. Why don't they let her alone? She's young and pretty and she's done nothing wrong.'

Later in the week he saw Alida at the Hannans' dance and noticed that many men danced with her. He saw her lips moving, heard her laughter, caught a word or so of what she said; irresistibly he found himself guiding partners around in her wake. He envied visitors to the city who didn't know who she was.

The night of the Rikkers' dance he went to a small dinner; before they sat down at table he realized that the others were all going on to the Rikkers'. They talked of it as a sort of comic adventure; insisted that he come too.

'Even if you weren't invited, it's all right,' they assured him. 'We were told we could bring anyone. It's just a free-for-all; it doesn't put you under any obligations. Norma Nash is going and she didn't invite Alida Rikker to her party. Besides, she's really very nice. My brother's quite crazy about her. Mother is worried sick, because he says he wants to marry her.'

Clasping his hand about a new highball, Forrest knew that if he drank it he would probably go. All his reasons for not going seemed old and tired, and, fatally, he had begun to seem absurd to himself. In vain he tried to remember the purpose he was serving, and found none. His father had weakened on the matter of the Kennemore Club. And now suddenly he found reasons for going – men could go where their women could not.

'All right,' he said.

The Rikkers' dance was in the ballroom of the Minnekada Hotel. The Rikkers' gold, ill-gotten, tainted, had taken the form of a forest of palms, vines and flowers. The two orchestras moaned in pergolas lit with fireflies, and many-coloured spotlights swept the floor, touching a buffet where dark bottles gleamed. The receiving line was still in action when Forrest's party came in, and Forrest grinned ironically at the prospect of taking Chauncey Rikker by the hand. But at the sight of Alida, her look that at last fell frankly on him, he forgot everything else.

'Your brother was kind enough to invite me,' he said.

'Oh, yes,' she was polite, but vague; not at all overwhelmed by his presence. As he waited to speak to her parents, he started, seeing his sister in a group of dancers. Then, one after another, he identified people he knew: it might have been any one of the Christmas dances; all the younger crowd were there. He discovered abruptly that he and Alida were alone; the receiving line had broken up. Alida glanced at him questioningly and with a certain amusement.

So he danced out on the floor with her, his head high, but slightly spinning. Of all things in the world, he had least expected to lead off the Chauncey Rikkers' ball.

Next morning his first realization was that he had kissed her; his second was a feeling of profound shame for his conduct of the evening. Lord help him, he had been the life of the party; he had helped to run the cotillion. From the moment when he danced out on the floor, coolly meeting the surprised and interested glances of his friends, a mood of desperation had come over him. He rushed Alida Rikker, until a friend asked him what Jane was going to say. 'What business is it of Jane's?' he demanded impatiently. 'We're not engaged.' But he was impelled to approach his sister and ask her if he looked all right.

'Apparently,' Eleanor answered, 'but when in doubt, don't take any more.'

So he hadn't. Exteriorly he remained correct, but his libido was in a state of wild extraversion. He sat with Alida Rikker and told her he had loved her for months.

'Every night I thought of you just before you went to sleep,' his voice trembled with insincerity, 'I was afraid to meet you or speak to you. Sometimes I'd see you in the distance moving along like a golden chariot, and the world would be good to live in.'

After twenty minutes of this eloquence, Alida began to feel exceedingly attractive. She was tired and rather happy, and eventually she said:

'All right, you can kiss me if you want to, but it won't mean anything. I'm just not in that mood.'

But Forrest had moods enough for both; he kissed her as if they stood together at the altar. A little later he had thanked Mrs Rikker with deep emotion for the best time he had ever had in his life.

It was noon, and as he groped his way upright in bed, Eleanor came in in her dressing gown.

'How are you?' she asked.

'Awful.'

'How about what you told me coming back in the car? Do you actually want to marry Alida Rikker?'

'Not this morning.'

'That's all right then. Now, look: the family are furious.'

'Why?' he asked with some redundancy.

'Both you and I being there. Father heard that you led the cotillion. My explanation was that my dinner party went, and so I had to go; but then you went too!'

Forrest dressed and went down to Sunday dinner. Over the table hovered an atmosphere of patient, puzzled, unworldly disappointment. Finally Forrest launched into it:

'Well, we went to Al Capone's party and had a fine time.'

'So I've heard,' said Pierce Winslow dryly. Mrs Winslow said nothing.

'Everybody was there – the Kayes, the Schwanes, the Martins and the Blacks. From now on, the Rikkers are pillars of society. Every house is open to them.'

'Not this house,' said his mother. 'They won't come into this house.' And after a moment: 'Aren't you going to eat anything, Forrest?'

'No, thanks. I mean, yes, I am eating.' He looked cautiously at his plate. 'The girl is very nice. There isn't a girl in town with better manners or more stuff. If things were like they were before the war, I'd say—'

He couldn't think exactly what it was he would have said; all he knew was that he was now on an entirely different road from his parents.

'This city was scarcely more than a village before the war,' said old Mrs Forrest.

'Forrest means the World War, Granny,' said Eleanor.

'Some things don't change,' said Pierce Winslow. Both he and Forrest thought of the Kennemore Club matter and, feeling guilty, the older man lost his temper:

'When people start going to parties given by a convicted criminal, there's something serious the matter with them.'

'We won't discuss it any more at table,' said Mrs Winslow hastily.

About four, Forrest called a number on the telephone in his room. He had known for some time that he was going to call a number.

'Is Miss Rikker at home? . . . Oh, hello. This is Forrest Winslow.'

'How are you?'

'Terrible. It was a good party.'

'Wasn't it?'

'Too good. What are you doing?'

'Entertaining two awful hangovers.'

'Will you entertain me too?'

'I certainly will. Come on over.'

The two young men could only groan and play sentimental music on the phonograph, but presently they departed; the fire leaped up, day went out behind the windows, and Forrest had rum in his tea.

'So we met at last,' he said.

'The delay was all yours.'

'Damn prejudice,' he said. 'This is a conservative city, and your father being in this trouble—'

'I can't discuss my father with you.'

'Excuse me. I only wanted to say that I've felt like a fool lately for not knowing you. For cheating myself out of the pleasure of knowing you for a silly prejudice,' he blundered on. 'So I decided to follow my own instincts.'

She stood up suddenly. 'Good-bye, Mr Winslow.'

'What? Why?'

'Because it's absurd for you to come here as if you were doing me a favour. And after accepting our hospitality, to remind me of my father's troubles is simply bad manners.'

He was on his feet, terribly upset. 'That isn't what I meant. I said I had felt that way, and I despised myself for it. Please don't be sore.'

'Then don't be condescending.' She sat back in her chair. Her mother came in, stayed only a moment, and threw Forrest a glance of resentment and suspicion as she left. But her passage through had brought them together, and they talked frankly for a long time.

'I ought to be upstairs dressing.'

'I ought to have gone an hour ago, and I can't.'

'Neither can I.'

With the admission they had travelled far. At the door he kissed her unreluctant lips and walked home, throwing futile buckets of reason on the wild fire.

Less than two weeks later it happened. In a car parked in a blizzard he poured out his worship, and she lay on his chest, sighing, 'Oh, me too – me too.'

Already Forrest's family knew where he went in the evenings; there was a frightened coolness, and one morning his mother said:

'Son, you don't want to throw yourself away on some girl that isn't up to you. I thought you were interested in Jane Drake.'

'Don't bring that up. I'm not going to talk about it.'

But it was only a postponement. Meanwhile the days of this February were white and magical, the nights were starry and crystalline. The town lay under a cold glory; the smell of her furs was incense, her bright cheeks were flames upon a northern altar. An ecstatic pantheism for his land and its weather welled up in him. She had brought him finally back to it; he would live here always.

'I want you so much that nothing can stand in the way of that,' he said to Alida. 'But I owe my parents a debt that I can't explain to you. They did more than spend money on me; they tried to give me something more intangible – something that their parents had given them and that they thought was worth handing on. Evidently it didn't take with me, but I've got to make this as easy as possible for them.' He saw by her face that he had hurt her. 'Darling—'

'Oh, it frightens me when you talk like that,' she said. 'Are you going to reproach me later? It would be awful. You'll have to get it out of your head that you're doing anything wrong. My standards are as high as yours, and I can't start out with my father's sins on my shoulders.' She thought for a moment. 'You'll never be able to reconcile it all like a children's story. You've got to choose. Probably you'll have to hurt either your family or hurt me.'

A fortnight later the storm broke at the Winslow house. Pierce Winslow came home in a quiet rage and had a session behind closed doors with his wife. Afterwards she knocked at Forrest's door.

'Your father had a very embarrassing experience today. Chauncey Rikker came up to him in the Downtown Club and began talking about you as if you were on terms of some understanding with his daughter. Your father walked away, but we've got to know. Are you serious about Miss Rikker?'

'I want to marry her,' he said.

'Oh, Forrest!'

She talked for a long time, recapitulating, as if it were a matter of centuries, the eighty years that his family had been identified with the city; when she passed from this to the story of his father's health, Forrest interrupted:

'That's all so irrelevant, mother. If there was anything against Alida personally, what you say would have some weight, but there isn't.'

'She's overdressed; she runs around with everybody—'

'She isn't a bit different from Eleanor. She's absolutely a lady in every sense. I feel like a fool even discussing her like this. You're just afraid it'll connect you in some way with the Rikkers.'

'I'm not afraid of that,' said his mother, annoyed. 'Nothing would ever do that. But I'm afraid that it'll separate you from everything worth while, everybody that loves you. It isn't fair for you to upset our lives, let us in for disgraceful gossip—'

'I'm to give up the girl I love because you're afraid of a little gossip.'

The controversy was resumed next day, with Pierce Winslow debating. His argument was that he was born in old Kentucky, that he had always felt uneasy at having begotten a son upon a pioneer Minnesota family, and that this was what he might have expected. Forrest felt that his parents' attitude was trivial and disingenuous. Only when he was out of the house, acting against their wishes, did he feel any compunction. But always he felt that something precious was being frayed away – his youthful companionship with his father and his love and trust for his mother. Hour by hour he saw the past being irreparably spoiled, and save when he was with Alida, he was deeply unhappy.

One spring day when the situation had become unendurable, with half the family meals taken in silence, Forrest's great-grandmother stopped him on the stair landing and put her hand on his arm.

'Has this girl really a good character?' she asked, her fine, clear, old eyes resting on his.

'Of course she has, Gramma.'

'Then marry her.'

'Why do you say that?' Forrest asked curiously.

'It would stop all this nonsense and we could have some peace. And I've been thinking I'd like to be a great-great-grandmother before I die.'

Her frank selfishness appealed to him more than the righteousness of the others. That night he and Alida decided to be married the first of June, and telephoned the announcement to the papers.

Now the storm broke in earnest. Crest Avenue rang with gossip – how Mrs Rikker had called on Mrs Winslow, who was not at home. How Forrest had gone to live in the University Club. How Chauncey Rikker and Pierce Winslow had had words in the Downtown Club.

It was true that Forrest had gone to the University Club. On a May night, with summer sounds already gathered on the window screens, he packed his trunk and his suitcases in the room where he had lived as a boy. His throat contracted and he smeared his face with his dusty hand as he took a row of golf cups off the mantelpiece, and he choked to himself: 'If they won't take Alida, then they're not my family any more.'

As he finished packing, his mother came in.

'You're not really leaving.' Her voice was stricken.

'I'm moving to the University Club.'

'That's so unnecessary. No one bothers you here. You do what you want.'

'I can't bring Alida here.'

'Father—'

'Hell with Father!' he said wildly.

She sat down on the bed beside him. 'Stay here, Forrest. I promise not to argue with you any more. But stay here.'

'I can't.'

'I can't have you go!' she wailed. 'It seems as if we're driving you out, and we're not!'

'You mean it looks as though you were driving me out.'

'I don't mean that.'

'Yes, you do. And I want to say that I don't think you and father really care a hang about Chauncey Rikker's moral character.'

'That's not true, Forrest. I hate people that behave badly and break the laws. My own father would never have let Chauncey Rikker—'

'I'm not talking about your father. But neither you nor my father care a bit what Chauncey Rikker did. I bet you don't even know what it was.'

'Of course I know. He stole some money and went abroad, and when he came back they put him in prison.'

'They put him in prison for contempt of court.'

'Now you're defending him, Forrest.'

'I'm not! I hate his guts; undoubtedly he's a crook. But I tell you it was a shock to me to find that Father didn't have any principles. He and his friends sit around the Downtown Club and pan Chauncey Rikker, but when it comes to keeping him out of a club, they develop weak spines.'

'That was a small thing.'

'No, it wasn't. None of the men of Father's age have any principles. I don't know why. I'm willing to make an allowance for an honest conviction, but I'm not going to be booed by somebody that hasn't got any principles and simply pretends to have.'

His mother sat helplessly, knowing that what he said was true. She and her husband and all their friends had no principles. They were good or bad according to their natures; often they struck attitudes remembered from the past, but they were never sure as her father or her grandfather had been sure. Confusedly she supposed it was something about religion. But how could you get principles just by wishing for them?

The maid announced the arrival of a taxi.

'Send up Olsen for my baggage,' said Forrest; then to his mother, 'I'm not taking the coupé; I left the keys. I'm just taking my clothes. I suppose Father will let me keep my job down town.'

'Forrest, don't talk that way. Do you think your father would take your living away from you, no matter what you did?'

'Such things have happened.'

'You're hard and difficult,' she wept. 'Please stay here a little longer, and perhaps things will be better and Father will get a little more reconciled. Oh, stay, stay! I'll talk to Father again. I'll do my best to fix things.'

'Will you let me bring Alida here?'

'Not now. Don't ask me that. I couldn't bear—'

'All right,' he said grimly.

Olsen came in for the bags. Crying and holding on to his coat sleeve, his mother went with him to the front door.

'Won't you say good-bye to Father?'

'Why? I'll see him tomorrow in the office.'

'Forrest, I was thinking, why don't you go to a hotel instead of the University Club?'

'Why, I thought I'd be more comfortable—' Suddenly he realized that his presence would be less conspicuous at a hotel. Shutting up his bitterness inside him, he kissed his mother roughly and went to the cab.

Unexpectedly, it stopped by the corner lamp-post at a hail from the sidewalk, and the May twilight yielded up Alida, miserable and pale.

'What is it?' he demanded.

'I had to come,' she said. 'Stop the car. I've been thinking of you leaving your house on account of me, and how you loved your family – the way I'd like to love mine – and I thought how terrible it was to spoil all that. Listen, Forrest! Wait! I want you to go back. Yes, I do. We can wait. We haven't any right to cause all this pain. We're young. I'll go away for a while, and then we'll see.'

He pulled her towards him by her shoulders.

'You've got more principles than the whole bunch of them,' he said. 'Oh, my girl, you love me and, gosh, it's good that you do!'

IV

It was to be a house wedding, Forrest and Alida having vetoed the Rikkers' idea that it was to be a sort of public revenge. Only a few intimate friends were invited.

During the week before the wedding, Forrest deduced from a series of irresolute and ambiguous telephone calls that his mother wanted to attend the ceremony, if possible. Sometimes he hoped passionately she would; at others it seemed unimportant.

The wedding was to be at seven. At five o'clock Pierce Winslow was walking up and down the two interconnecting sitting-rooms of his house.

'This evening,' he murmured, 'my only son is being married to the daughter of a swindler.'

He spoke aloud so that he could listen to the words, but they had been evoked so often in the past few months that their strength was gone and they died thinly upon the air.

He went to the foot of the stairs and called: 'Charlotte!' No answer. He called again, and then went into the dining room, where the maid was setting the table.

'Is Mrs Winslow out?'

'I haven't seen her come in, Mr Winslow.'

Back in the sitting-room he resumed his walking; unconsciously he was walking like his father, the judge, dead thirty years ago; he was parading his dead father up and down the room.

'You can't bring that woman into this house to meet your mother. Bad blood is bad blood.'

The house seemed unusually quiet. He went upstairs and looked into his wife's room, but she was not there; old Mrs Forrest was slightly indisposed; Eleanor, he knew, was at the wedding.

He felt genuinely sorry for himself as he went downstairs again. He knew his role – the usual evening routine carried out in complete obliviousness of the wedding – but he needed support, people begging him to relent, or else deferring to his wounded sensibilities. This isolation was different; it was almost the first isolation he had ever felt, and like all men fundamentally of the group, of the herd, he was incapable of taking a strong stand with the inevitable loneliness that it implied. He could only gravitate towards those who did.

'What have I done to deserve this?' he demanded of the standing ash tray. 'What have I failed to do for my son that lay within my power?'

The maid came in. 'Mrs Winslow told Hilda she wouldn't be here for dinner, and Hilda didn't tell me.'

The shameful business was complete. His wife had weakened, leaving him absolutely alone. For a moment he expected to be furiously angry with her, but he wasn't; he had used up his anger exhibiting it to others. Nor did it make him feel more obstinate, more determined; it merely made him feel silly.

'That's it. I'll be the goat. Forrest will always hold it against me, and Chauncey Rikker will be laughing up his sleeve.'

He walked up and down furiously.

'So I'm left holding the bag. They'll say I'm an old grouch and drop me out of the picture entirely. They've licked me. I suppose I might as well be graceful about it.' He looked down in horror at the hat he held in his hand.

'I can't – I can't bring myself to do it, but I must. After all, he's my only son. I couldn't bear that he should hate me. He's determined to marry her, so I might as well put a good face on the matter.'

In sudden alarm he looked at his watch, but there was still time. After all, it was a large gesture he was making, sacrificing his principles in this manner. People would never know what it cost him.

An hour later, old Mrs Forrest woke up from her doze and rang for her maid.

'Where's Mrs Winslow?'

'She's not in for dinner. Everybody's out.'

The old lady remembered.

'Oh, yes, they've gone over to get married. Give me my glasses and the telephone book . . . Now, I wonder how you spell Capone.'

'Rikker, Mrs Forrest.'

In a few minutes she had the number. 'This is Mrs Hugh Forrest,' she said firmly. 'I want to speak to young Mrs Forrest Winslow . . . No, not to Miss Rikker; to Mrs Forrest Winslow.' As there was as yet no such person, this was impossible. 'Then I will call after the ceremony,' said the old lady.

When she called again, in an hour, the bride came to the phone.

'This is Forrest's great-grandmother. I called up to wish you every happiness and to ask you to come and see me when you get back from your trip if I'm still alive.'

'You're very sweet to call, Mrs Forrest.'

'Take good care of Forrest, and don't let him get to be a ninny like his father and mother. God bless you.'

'Thank you.'

'All right. Good-bye, Miss Capo— Good-bye, my dear.'

Having done her whole duty, Mrs Forrest hung up the receiver.

Herbert R. Lottman
Albert Camus: A Biography £3.95

Since the tragic death in a car crash in 1960 of Albert Camus, author, philosopher of the Absurd and comrade of Jean-Paul Sartre, the legends surrounding his brief but remarkable life have obscured the facts. Here is the first full-scale biography of Camus; a portrait not only of the man, but of the times that made him.

'A portrait of the artist, the outsider, the humanist and sceptic, simultaneously sensuous and austere, righteous and guilty, that breaks the heart' JOHN LEONARD, NEW YORK TIMES

Germaine Greer
The Obstacle Race £5.95
The fortunes of women painters and their work

In her first book since the pioneering and bestselling *The Female Eunuch*, Germaine Greer considers the fascinating question of why there have been so few women painters of the first rank. Ms Greer demonstrates brilliantly that the answer is not hard to find: 'you cannot make great artists out of egos that have been damaged, with wills that are defective, with libidos that have been driven out of reach and energy diverted into certain neurotic channels'.

'Instils respect, asks bold questions, does not make wildly exaggerated claims' MARGARET DRABBLE, LISTENER

'Passionate yet lucid . . . a book that explains . . . the psychological, economic and even aesthetic reasons for the virtually unchallenged patriarchalism of all our artistic establishments' ERICA JONG

Picador

☐ The Beckett Trilogy	Samuel Beckett	£1.95p
☐ Willard and His Bowling Trophies	Richard Brautigan	£1.25p
☐ Bury My Heart at Wounded Knee	Dee Brown	£2.75p
☐ Our Ancestors	Italo Calvino	£2.95p
☐ Auto Da Fé	Elias Canetti	£1.75p
☐ Hidden Faces	Salvador Dali	£1.95p
☐ Nothing, Doting, Blindness	Henry Green	£2.95p
☐ Household Tales	Brothers Grimm	£1.50p
☐ Meetings with Remarkable Men	Gurdjieff	£1.50p
☐ Bound for Glory	Woody Guthrie	75p
☐ Roots	Alex Haley	£2.50p
☐ Growth of the Soil	Knut Hamsun	£2.95p
☐ Meanwhile	Max Handley	£1.50p
☐ When the Tree Sings	Stratis Haviaras	£1.95p
☐ Dispatches	Michael Herr	£1.75p
☐ Earth Magic	Francis Hitching	£1.00p
☐ Kleinzeit	Russell Hoban	£1.00p
☐ The Greenpeace Chronicle	Robert Hunter	£2.50p
☐ Three Trapped Tigers	G. Cabrera Infante	£2.95p
☐ Man and His Symbols	Carl Jung	£2.50p
☐ The Other Persuasion	edited by Seymour Kleinberg	£1.75p
☐ The Act of Creation		£1.95p
☐ The Case of the Midwife Toad		£1.25p
☐ The Ghost in the Machine	Arthur Koestler	£1.75p
☐ Janus		£2.25p
☐ The Roots of Coincidence		£1.00p
☐ The Thirteenth Tribe		£1.50p
☐ The Memoirs of a Survivor	Doris Lessing	£1.50p
☐ The Road to Xanadu	John Livingston Lowes	£1.95p
☐ The Snow Leopard	Peter Mattiessen	£1.95p
☐ The Man Without Qualities, Vol. 1		£1.95p
☐ The Man Without Qualities, Vol. 2	Robert Musil	£1.75p
☐ The Man Without Qualities, Vol. 3		£1.75p
☐ Great Works of Jewish Fantasy	Joachim Neugroschel	£1.95p
☐ Wagner Nights	Ernest Newman	£2.50p

☐ The Best of Myles			£1.50p
☐ The Dalkey Archive			£1.50p
☐ The Hard Life	Flann O'Brien		80p
☐ The Poor Mouth			90p
☐ After My Fashion			£2.50p
☐ A Glastonbury Romance			£2.95p
☐ Owen Glendower	John Cowper Powys		£2.50p
☐ Weymouth Sands			£2.95p
☐ The Crying of Lot 49	Thomas Pynchon		£1.50p
☐ Hadrian the Seventh	Fr. Rolfe (Baron Corvo)		£1.25p
☐ On Broadway	Damon Runyon		£1.95p
☐ Snowblind	Robert Sabbag		£1.25p
☐ The Best of Saki	Saki		95p
☐ Sanatorium under the Sign of the Hourglass	Bruno Schulz		£1.50p
☐ Miss Silver's Past	Josef Skvorecky		£1.95p
☐ The Bad Sister	Emma Tennant		£1.50p
☐ The Great Shark Hunt	Hunter S. Thompson		£2.95p
☐ The Forest People	Colin Turnbull		£1.50p
☐ The New Tolkien Companion	J. E. A. Tyler		£2.95p
☐ From A to B and Back Again	Andy Warhol		£1.25p
☐ Female Friends	Fay Weldon		£1.50p
☐ The Outsider	Colin Wilson		£1.75p
☐ Fairy and Folk Tales of Ireland	edited by W. B. Yeats		£1.95p

All these books are available at your local bookshop or newsagent, or can be ordered direct from the publisher. Indicate the number of copies required and fill in the form below

Name _____
(block letters please)
Address _____

_____

Send to Pan Books (CS Department), Cavaye Place, London SW10 9PG
Please enclose remittance to the value of the cover price plus:

25p for the first book plus 10p per copy for each additional book ordered to a maximum charge of £1.05 to cover postage and packing
Applicable only in the UK

While every effort is made to keep prices low, it is sometimes necessary to increase prices at short notice. Pan Books reserve the right to show on covers and charge new retail prices which may differ from those advertised in the text or elsewhere